A novel based on the life
of Ella Wheeler Wilcox

Ella Moon

For Paula —
many thanks for taking such good care
of me!! All my good wishes,
Ed Ifkovic
10/10/06

Ed Ifkovic

wp

Waubesa Press
The quality fiction imprint
of Badger Books Inc.

Printed by McNaughton & Gunn of Saline, Mich.
Edited by Pat Reardon

First Edition

Hardcover: ISBN 1-878569-72-4
Softcover: ISBN 1-878569-73-2

Badger Books Inc.
P.O. Box 192
Oregon, WI 53575
Toll-free phone: (800) 928-2372
Web site: http://www.badgerbooks.com
E-mail: books@badgerbooks.com

This book is in memory of Carol

Author's Note

Ella Wheeler Wilcox (1850-1919) was, in the words of her only biographer, "not a minor poet, but a bad major one." In her lifetime her name was a household word. A contemporary magazine reported: "More copies of Wilcox's work have been sold" in her lifetime than Coleridge, Wordsworth, Shelley, and Keats sold together in theirs. One says "Wilcox" "just as one says 'Shakespeare.'" Another reviewer: "A man who has his Wilcox needs no Shakespeare." She was called a genius, but the highbrows mocked her and soon forgot her.

But early in the twenty-first century, her name is oddly still a commonplace on the Internet, where Home Pages quote favorite Wilcox lines. Book collectors scramble for her out-of-print volumes. Richard A. Edwards of Evergreen State College has created a web site devoted entirely to her life and work. His devotion and scholarship have been inspirational to all of us who still remember Wilcox.

For this fictionalized version of her life, I have relied on her own autobiography (*The Worlds and I*, 1919), her earlier magazine pieces on her childhood, and the published accounts by her friends. The one biography is Jenny Ballou's *Period Piece* (1940), an impressionistic, romantic work. I also read many of her letters, some of which I own, but especially those in the rare book rooms at Columbia University and Harvard University. As well, decades ago, living just miles from her Bungalow in Branford, Connecticut, I talked with some old-timers who were children when EWW was queen of the seashore. I still recall their awe of the woman.

Ella Moon is, of course, a fiction. I have altered dates, locations, facts in the name of the larger truth of fiction. For example, Robert uses a Kodak camera a few years before it appeared on the market. But he did use one later. This is not literary biography: it is how I imagine her. Fancied dialogues are interspersed with lines from her own work. In an attempt to be true to some essence of the woman I myself imagine, I have sometimes turned history upside down. In the process I wanted to find a different EWW, the one who existed outside her verse — the one I carry in my mind.

- Ed Ifkovic

A Solar Eclipse

In that great journey of the stars through space
    About the mighty, all-directing Sun,
    The pallid, faithful Moon, has been the one
Companion of the Earth. Her tender face,
Pale with the swift, keen purposes of that race,
    Which at Time's natal hour was first begun,

Shines ever on her lover as they run
    And lights his orbit with her silvery smile.

Sometimes such passionate love doth in her rise,
    Down from her beaten path she softly slips,
And with her mantle veils the Sun's bold eyes,
    Then in the gloaming finds her lover's lips.
While far and near the men our world call wise
    See only that the Sun is in eclipse.

—Ella Wheeler Wilcox

Warning

High in the heavens I saw the moon this morning,
    Albeit the sun shone bright;
Unto my soul it spoke, in voice of warning,
    "Remember Night!"

—Ella Wheeler Wilcox

    The wan moon is sinking
    under the white wave and
    time is sinking with me, O!
        —Robert Burns

When the moon was at the full, I found the place.
        —Ella Wheeler Wilcox

Prologue

1895
New York

Marcus is writing a poem in his head. Sitting in the lobby of the Everett Hotel, located just on Union Square, he's waiting impatiently for his celebrated sister to return from an afternoon literary reception. He is sequestered in an overstuffed green velvet chair, drawn up to the front window, overlooking the scurrying passersby, but Marcus barely acknowledges the bustle of the icy-cold winter street. He is creating a short lyric, an elegy really, about a bitter Wisconsin winter he recalls from two decades ago.

But the poem refuses to come. Frowning, he takes his sister's letter from a breast pocket, unfolds it, then re-reads it. His lips move with the hasty, flamboyant scrawl. "I know you're headed through New York on your way back home. Please stop at the Everett Hotel, where we're staying. We are there part of this winter season." No signature, but the melodramatic penmanship — all swoops and twists — is recognizable. She had that same eccentric style when she was still a young girl.

My own poem, he thinks, trying to return to his own creation. That winter, he says to himself, almost out loud, there was so much ice the cows became disoriented, like light-starved moths. They actually pushed against the rickety barn siding, tottering like drunken city boys. A poem, he thinks.

He hears a noise — a sudden hum of voices — and then he sees her approaching. Such a small woman, like a young girl, but she is very grand in an ostrich-plumed hat and thick purple boa. She is taking her time, stopping to smile at a little child, scribbling her signature on an offered card. Marcus hears her giggle. She takes a slender volume from a young girl and writes a sentiment on the flyleaf, her arm moving almost automatically. She never stops smiling. People flutter around her, like sunmad flies. She smiles. She bows, deliberate. She is, after all, Ella Wheeler Wilcox.

The Poetess of Passion.

She spots him, waiting by the window, watching, and at that moment the body freezes. She frowns, her lips pulling together like a seam. For a second it gives him pause: why always this reaction? The whole world gets unyielding, canyon-wide smiles, but not Marcus Wheeler, the older brother. Himself a poet, though as yet unpublished.

Wildly he thinks: I am not jealous of her success. I'm not. She is having her moment — admittedly already a decade long, and worldwide, that literary reputation — but fate turns, seasons shift, new stars appear in the sky. The plow upturns shiny flint each spring.

She is, after all, immensely famous. "I have a responsibility," she wrote to him, some time back. "The lovers of poetry — the lost souls in love — demand my heart wails, my words of comfort." It was a line he'd heard (and read) many times, almost a chiseled verbatim line, rehearsed, as though she were talking not to a brother who tended to her as a bawling, colicky baby but, rather, an East Coast press corps. "My name is treasured throughout the world." She always emphasized the last word. It always annoyed the hell out of him.

Now, still staring at him, she breaks away from a persistent fan, a pocked-faced girl in braids, who seems determined to recite her own inspired verses to his sister, and she leans into him. "Marcus," she says, smiling, "how wonderful."

They kiss briefly, like old friends. His hand touches her shoulder. He finds himself irritated with her powerful scent: a heady Persian lilac, he thinks, which reminds him immediately of the old farmhouse, the muddy spring-time back in Wisconsin, the sagging of the barn beams. The lowing of the cattle, the whisper of the cricket. The acres to be plowed. Ella nods, glances over her shoulder at a watching waiter, and Marcus stands. They are escorted into the breakfast room, and at once there is a sudden hum in the room: guests buzz, smile, glance, wave. Ella herself does the same, but adds bowing. It's actually some sort of little-girl curtsy. When they are seated, tea is poured by a nervous red-faced boy in a tight white jacket with brass buttons. He doesn't take his eyes off Ella. Marcus fidgets, a little nervous now and angry at himself for being so, and then he realizes that she is staring at his clothing. He is wearing a new formal suit, bought at a men's shop in Milwaukee just before he traveled East, and until this moment he's been proud of it, gloriously so, a dark thick garbardine, the color of old musty charcoal. But he has seen no one in New York with any such suit, he suddenly realizes. So he's made another mistake. He bites his lip, loses his composure. The country bumpkin come East. The carnival attraction.

His sister's eyes reveal it all: not just quick disapproval, but some kind of horror.

Suddenly, it makes him smile. What the hell! he thinks. There is no way I can win. He relaxes, sitting back in the chair.

"So," he says, smiling.

"So?" she asks, her voice high.

He just watches.

"So."

He knows they will argue in a few minutes. They always do. After the hasty exchange about family and the old farm, they will tumble into battle. This time, feeling crazy with pleasure, he deliberately starts it. Slowly he withdraws a folded article cut from *Demorest's* magazine, spreads it open sloppily, and drums his thick finger on the Contributor's Page ("About the Author"). His nail is broken, cracked. "Ella," he says, looking up, "I read again the awful words. You, a writer, should write to them. Tell them November 3, 1850. Four years after your brother Ed was born. Don't you speak for truth? You, the artist?" He goes on and on, barreling ahead, refusing her space for comment. She's familiar with his argument. Over and over the literary commentators, the interviewers—in publications like the *New York World* and the *Ladies' Home Journal* — record her birth as 1855.

The redundant error has driven Marcus mad. He has written her many times, admonishing her to correct the error, documenting the abuse, underlining, circling the mistake. Marcus has neat, schoolmarmish penmanship that always annoys her. She once told him it reminded her of the rigid line of fence posts bordering the farm. An awful regularity. A devil's symmetry. Unrelenting exclamation points. He didn't find the remark amusing.

"For land's sake, Marcus," she interrupts. "Not that again."

"Well, Ella—"

Glancing around, she tries to change the subject. "I do have to get home to the farm," she begins, but she stops, realizing Marcus will resent the remark: after all, she escaped the bleak, thirsty farmland of Westport, Wisconsin—all that dim slate-gray sky and unloved bone-dried soil—for the busy East Coast world of rotogravure publication, Sunday musicales, select literary salons, dances on Newport summer lawns, and the fawning attention of William Randolph Hearst.

Marcus won't let it rest. He nibbles the corner of a piece of toast, gulps lukewarm coffee, swallows, and, like a melodramatic trial lawyer, reaches into his breast pocket again, and extracts another document. "Here," he says, loud enough for some heads to turn. She finds herself staring at a yellowing, frayed birth certificate.

His fingers punctuate the air. "I found this where you hid it," he says. "Under the floorboards in the front parlor."

"I did not —"

"Sure, sure. Let me tell you, Ella, Anglo-Saxon civilization demands the authority of recorded birth."

The line makes her smile. "Really, Marcus."

She looks at him as if he's gone stark mad. There is spittle accumulating at the corners of his mouth, mixed with crumbs from the piece of toast he's chewed on.

"Ella, I'm an historian."

"No, Marcus, you're a — farmer." But that last word falters, as though she regrets the cruel barb.

"As are you," he says.

She winces. "Marcus, does it really matter?"

"Of course, it does."

"But why does it bother you? I just don't know how it happened — the mistake —"

"You told them yourself."

She is quiet.

"You were born on a cold day, Ella, with the bite of frost on the land, and the winter of your unrobust health upon us all."

"Are you writing a poem now, Marcus?" she asks, biting.

He ignores the sarcasm. "Another child was born in the same county that same horrible day, Ella, another girl child, named Mary Eloise Randall, who," he adds gleefully, "happily acknowledges her birth in 1850."

"Marcus —" She lifts up her head.

"She was born on the same south crossroad, but just over in Bradford."

"For God's sake, Marcus, this is not of any real importance —"

"Then tell the truth. Mama feels the same way. You know that. I was there when she told you." Pausing, they both clearly remember the old woman, now bitter as late-winter cider, mumbling: "I wouldn't truck any nine years

passing between the births of my children. You and Ed.
Such spacing is unhealthy for a delicate woman."

"You're forty-five, not forty," he says.

Ella winces. She doesn't like this reminder. She shoots
back, "And you have only this story like a burr in your
leggings."

Suddenly, a young woman approaches the table tentatively, mumbling an apology, but asking for an autograph.
Her face is crimson, blotchy, and her voice breaks. "I buy
all your books of poetry," she says, stuttering. "You are
the world's greatest poet." Ella turns, an automatic smile
on her face, the eyes wide and twinkling, and she becomes the famous poetess of passion the world knows
her as. She throws back her head, gives a faint laugh,
invites the young girl closer and whispers her humility.
"Oh, my, no, no." Marcus, listening, fumes. When Ella
begins to scribble a few lines of verse on a napkin—

> *Laugh and the world laughs with you*
> *Weep and you weep alone.*
> *This sad old earth must borrow its mirth,*
> *But has sadness enough of its own.*
>
> *— Love, Ella Wheeler Wilcox*

Marcus stands, noisily pushing back his chair.

"Marcus," she begins, alarmed.

But he is leaving. "Your public will never know the sad
little girl you still are, Ella."

"Marcus," she whispers, "sit down."

"You'll always be that fitful child you always were,"
he says. "You were only happy when the world took note
of you."

Shrine

1850/1862

Dear Reader:

Musing over tea yesterday afternoon, waiting for my husband to finish necessary business, I found myself misty-eyed and nostalgic: watching some untidy immigrant family pass by in the street, all disheveled and ill-kept, I recalled the pure joys of family and childhood. For a moment, I forgot the struggles, the want, the cruelties, and allowed God to fill me with one sensation—love. My mother is reading poetry to me, her voice soft as a lady's whisper; my father, fresh from the fields, smiles with approval; and my brothers and sister, blessed children all, rosy cheeked and tough from the sun, nod in unison as I, the baby, their favorite, try to speak my first words. So I say to all of you naysayers, those who mock the Christian household and the unadulterated joys of the hearth, listen to me, your poetess. I contain the only answer that matters....

— Ella Wheeler Wilcox, "My Days and Yours,"
Demorest Magazine, November, 1895

There are six of us in the family now. I am the baby. Marcus, the eldest, is sullen but talkative, a boy always at your elbow, leaning in, grabbing at you. Ed is fickle and moody, sometimes tossing me into the air, whooping and laughing, other times ignoring me. And my sister Sarah is pretty and energetic, all ribbons and bows and gap-toothed smile. She's a popular young girl, already an eye catcher. She blinks her eyes a lot. I listen to every conversation, and Sarah's prettiness is a familiar topic. My parents are worried. They prefer children less talked of. "Thank God," my father says once, "our little Ella looks to be a plain woman someday." He nods at me, as though I've been tossed a compliment. It hurts me, although I'm confused. I'm five years old now, smart as a whip, everyone's shadow, a storyteller morning till night, but the cracked mirror in the hallway, when I stand on a chair to look into it, tells me I'm gangly and awkward, plain as dust. "For heaven's sake, Ella, get away from the mirror," Mama says over and over. Yet, desperate, I spend hours searching for beauty in this mirror. I'm waiting for my hair to turn golden, my eyes the color of a June sky. It doesn't happen. At night my mother reads out loud to us the romantic stories of fiery heroines out of Mrs. E.D.E.N. Southworth, and it seems to me Sarah is such a born beauty, all sunshine blond and carefree frills and pressed crinoline. I'm, well, old bleached burlap, freshly ironed. Pretty enough, I guess.

I am sitting in the large kitchen with Mama, surrounded by late autumn smells: a vase of shock-yellow chrysanthemums, overripe apples, pulped blood-red tomatoes ready for canning. "Mama, I have a new story for you." I share all my stories with her, and she is always asking for a new one. She stops her work to listen. "This one came to me last night."

It had come to me in a flash. After the supper dishes were scrubbed and stacked, I stood outside the kitchen door, looking over to the barn where the unmoving cows, being herded in by Papa, eyed me suspiciously, and I screamed my new wild fiction to the soft night wind: my nursery rhyme is about the frantic bumblebee who couldn't find flowers to love. I thought I was alone, tucked into the twilight shadows, but halfway through my recitation—I like the sound of my voice in the outdoors, the wind shifting through the thick Lombardy poplars and the stars blinking behind clouds—Ed and Marcus jumped out of hiding, startling me, and then falling to the ground, their cheeks streaked with tears, their sides splitting. I ran inside. I can still hear their prankish buzzing bee sounds, making fun of me. Bzzz bzzz bzzz bzzz. Then the high, stupid laughter of crude farm boys.

Now I am sitting with my mother, and she stops her work, touching her palms together, sits back and says, "Tell me the story." She's smiling.

Mama is always my audience.

I do, my voice loud and sure. When I am through, I stare up at Mama, and there is a slight, melancholy smile on her face, and her intense violet eyes, always so startling in their deep rich color, absolutely shine.

"Before you were born, Ella, I knew that you, my last-born child, would do the things I could never do. "

"Like what, Mama?"

"Well, for one, I knew you'd be a writer."

Her words thrill me, sweep me up to the ceiling. They're the ones I expect now. I suddenly have to move, rushing around the kitchen, bumping into the cabinets, banging off the walls. There's not enough space for me to fly.

"Mama, Mama," I yell.

"That's why I always read to you, even when you were inside my body."

"What?" I ask. I stop near her. She has started beating eggs for a pumpkin pie. Her hands are stained dusky orange from the lumpy pulverized pulp. I stand on a chair, lean over the table. I smell fresh churned butter, warm yeast and ripe smoky molasses.

"You were a writer in my body."

"How, Mama, how?" I ask.

"Prenatal influences." Mama looks at me and smiles. She whispers: "I planned it all. Before birth. That's what prenatal means."

"How, Mama?"

Mama sighs, licks beaten egg off a stained thumb. "I always thought I would be a poet myself, you know, worshiper that I always was at the shrine of literature."

"Shrine?" I've never heard the word before. This is a new word she is adding to our ritual.

"A place of worship," she says in a singsong voice.
"Shrine," I say, loving the word. "Shrine."
Yes, shrine.

"Before you were born, coming up in my body like a sunrise, I read all I could of Shakespeare. Let me tell you—I even memorized cantos of Byron and Scott. I read novels that uplifted. Like the wonderful *The Gates Ajar.*"

"Thank you, Mama." I am out of breath. I climb down from the chair, twirl in circles. I am five, my head not yet level with the kitchen table.

"I would stand right in my old kitchen, not this one, but in Johnstown"—and Mama now points to a spot on the hard-swept floor, just by the cluttered mud room, as though this is that very spot, sacred and inviolable—"before I got to cooking, and I'd touch your body in mine, feel the movement, and the language was there, I swear, the sonnets, the words jittery on my fingertips going into you." She stops. It's a familiar speech, at least a good part of it, the cadences practiced and sure. My mother's jaw nods up and down, in rhythm. I can repeat it back to her.

"Thank you, Mama."

She smiles. "When you were just a year or so old, just starting to talk, in fact — already a talker, I must say, hard to believe — you began creating these stories. You'd stand up and talk of this or that, things imagined or real, no matter. You were a wonder." She laughs. "We — and the neighbors — thought you were, well, blessed."

"I remember that," I say. Really I don't. But I've heard the story so many times that I've come to believe I do, indeed, remember it. What I do recall is my father teaching me the alphabet from the covers of an old tattered almanac, methodically pointing the letters out and me mimicking his perfect Vermont diction. I don't remember how old I was then, maybe just under a year, but I do recall standing outside by the barn and screaming out this new knowledge, a gibberish of chaotic letters. At night, in winter, Mama sat by the fire with me on her lap,

and she read to me, sentimental stories of romantic dying love, of Christian sacrifice, of lost causes and noble
mission, of beautiful women helplessly in love. I remember that I understood so little of its meaning, but I also
remember that my mother's emotion was contagious: we
both wept. The tears ran down her cheeks. Sometimes
she held me so tight it hurt me, but I was afraid to say
anything. She looked so sad.

"I remember."

"You were a child of my ripened age, my last. I told
your grandmother — my child, this child, you, will be a
girl, and she will be a writer."

"A writer," I echo.

Mama is looking over my shoulder. "She'll begin young
and travel all her life. She'll live the life I never had."

"Thank you, Mama." It's like being in church, her
words. I went once or twice with my grandmother, never
with my own parents, who chose not to give much weight
to the Scriptures. But I am getting nervous now: when
my mother says these last words, her face tightens, becomes rigid. Her eyes seem blank, cold. The blood drains
from her thin lips. These talks we have sometimes go on
too long, I know now, and I see her become unhappy,
her head tilted at angles. Sometimes she looks like she
will snap in two, like a weathered twig. There is too much
hollow space between her words.

Mama is a wiry, jittery woman, with a thin, bony frame,
a tired face freckled from the sun, her brown wispy hair
always breaking free of the deliberate bun she creates each
morning. I like to help her, holding her combs, brushes,
her ribbons. When, before bed, Mama combs her hair, I
love to sit and watch it fall across her back and shoulders, hair without sheen, speckled with gray and white,
and Mama always looks waif-like these times, but a little
menacing. The static from her comb makes her hair fly
away wildly. She becomes the witch in some fairy tale. I
hate this idea: after all, I love my mother. I like her better
early in the morning, before dawn, when the salt-pork

biscuits and new apple butter smell up the kitchen, Mama leaning over the wood stove to retrieve a pan of smothering gravy, and humming a dance song from her childhood. That's the only time I can catch Mama happy. Mornings, I guess, promise her something. As the day goes on, she gets more frantic, more harried, the rich violet of her large eyes, set deep into a high cheeked face, becoming murky and thick, like storm sky. "I am a caged animal," she sometimes says to me, confiding in a whisper, "driven to numbing farm work by duty." By late afternoon she is fatigued, irritable, silent. By nightfall, Mama's eyes follow one of the children around — choose one, anyone — but rarely me — or worse, my father, fresh from the fields, scrubbed at the well for dinner — and the deep-muttered barbs begin, the cruel words low and breathy, otherworldly.

Papa fights back, ready to do battle. Their voices rise to the rafters.

I hate it when they fight like that. Their voices fill up all the rooms of the house. Then there is nowhere to run to.

One time I begged them to stop, and they both stared, confused, as though they had no idea what I was talking about.

Marcus chided me afterwards. "They got to enjoy doing it," he said.

"Why?" I said, baffled.

"I dunno. But they must — they do it all the time." He laughed then, and it made me smile, but I wasn't happy.

Lately, these battles make me hide in the room I share with Sarah, hugging my kitten, a squawking brown ball of fur. Mama doesn't like cats, but her protests have stopped: I am allowed to keep my kitten in my room, out of sight. I hate dolls, except for the makeshift ones I fashion, like the crooked-neck summer squash I once dressed in old yellow lace, a doll I named Mary. It was lovely until it became rotten, began to smell like the barn, and fell apart in my hands, all sticky and foul. But cats are warm, unassuming, and cling to me. They seek me out. In winter when ice settles into the cracks of the clapboards, I hide under pillows. Or I wander outside, especially if it is spring or summer. If the clamor in the downstairs parlor gets too crazy and angry, I disappear into the dark landscape of the surrounding fields. There, my arms wrapped around me as I sway in the night breezes, with my body rocking back and forth, as though hypnotized by the night wind and the *cheep cheep cheep* of the wood crickets, I always start to cry. I point wildly into the nighttime sky, lit bright with faraway stars and drifting moon shadows. I am pointing to Milwaukee, but I don't really know where it is. But I know it's out there somewhere, near enough so that my father and brothers can travel there by wagon in a long day, returning just after dark. It's a growing city, I know. A city. People: stores: buildings: noise: music. I stretch out a thin, bony arm. There. Milwaukee.

One time Ed fights with me, shoves me, and then announces, "We fight like them, you and me." He spits out the words. Then he leans into me, maliciously. "Someday there will be murder on the farm."

"No," I scream, and run away.

I hear his laughter trailing me. I hide in the barn.

"I hate Ed," I tell the cow, who ignores me.

The battle rages in the long winter night. Inside, exhausted from her sarcasm, the kitchen clean and ready now for breakfast, the wood stove stoked, my mother retreats to a pine-backed chair in a corner and dips her face into Mary Jane Holmes' *Lena Rivers*. In the dim light of the kerosene lamp, she holds her face inches from the pages. Outside, I stand on the south hill, snow covering my ankles, cold seeping into my pores, wind against my cheeks.

"Ella," my father calls from inside the farmhouse. I wander towards him. "Ella," he yells. "Don't you just cap the climax." He steps out of the doorway, coming close, and touches me on the shoulder. I look into his leathery, wrinkled face, a face that always reminds me of tanned hides hung on the barn rafters. "You'll catch your death. Don't forget cousin Arlo."

I start to grin as I take his hand: Cousin Arlo. Cousin Arlo took a nighttime stroll after supper, in the deep of a brutal winter of ice and Arctic temperature, caught a bone-marrow chill, fell into frightful pneumonia, and died a grievous death. I always smile because Arlo was nearly a hundred when he took sick. He had lived, decades before, in old Vermont, where I've never been, on a farm so cold the water, so says family lore, had ice in it ten months out of twelve.

Today I turn seven. I hide in the cold lean-to out back, sitting on a wood pile and surrounded by oak buckets filled with late-summer grain, gazing out through cracks in the boards at sunlit flower beds. I'm scribbling my new romance: the thrilling episode of Mr. Larkspur's love for Miss Hollyhock. A passing honey bee, peevish and ornery, becomes jealous of the beautiful flower lovers, and the eternal triangle, played out in my fanciful summer garden, erupts. Flowers bend to the sun for support— the honey bee buzzes and frets and annoys. My own words exhilarate me, make me get up and walk in circles, as though dizzy with heady pollen and fragrance. I do nothing else for days. I ignore chores, avoid my brothers, and skirt my father. Everyone stares when I walk by. I don't care. The family is readying for winter, but I'm still back in the summer garden that has long since fallen to autumn's frost.

I write every day, ignoring the frowns I get.

Tonight the supper is barely underway when the subject is brought up.

"I know I spoil you," my father says, shaking his head. There had been a little conversation about the crops, then a long silence. Then Papa cleared his throat. "I know I spoil you." The first words he says. There's been prompting, I know, from my brothers. I've been told this before.

I spoon potatoes into my mouth and stare at Marcus and Ed.

"Lazy wandering," says Ed, his mouth full of food. "The whole family has to struggle—"

"Wait," my mother says, interrupting sharply. "Ed, swallow your food before—"

"I know," Ed says.

"Obviously, you don't."

Purposely he gulps.

I know I'm at fault—farm girls help their mothers in the kitchen, help with yard chores. I'm old enough to shoulder the care of chickens now, the carrying of the water from the well, weeding the vegetable patch near the house. I do a little of my chores, then stop. Most days I roam the yard, shooing lazy chickens and squatting ducks from my path, flapping my arms at them. I sing at the top of my voice.

"I spoil you," my father says again, but he's staring at the boys, who sit there, moody and grim.

"Yes," my mother says, looking up from her dish. I notice she has only picked at her food tonight, barely sampling the stew she's labored over. "It may be as it has to be." The odd, scary words hang in the air, like a storm cloud. We turn and stare, all of us: a wisp of iron-gray hair has broken free of her tight bun, and hangs, limp, over her forehead. I think that bothers all of us, but I don't know why.

Sarah giggles, but stops when my father clears his throat.

"What the hell does that mean?" he asks, staring back into his own plate of food.

There is awful silence at the table. My mother winces and bites her lip. Both of my brothers smirk and elbow each other, and Sister Sarah covers her mouth, gasping. We know where the conversation is going now. "Now, Marcus," my mother says, slowly, "we've discussed the use of profanity in the household—" But then she stops, looks down into her plate. She seems to forget what she is talking about.

My father simply shrugs and runs his tongue over his upper lip, an action that always infuriates Mama, I know.

We are not a religious family, but cursing has a way of eating into Mama's quiet nights. "It's a debasement of the spirit," she mumbles now, almost to herself. She has told me, more than once, that my father and the two boys — who mimic his casual *hells* and *damns,* as they hurl themselves into their farm chores, like shoveling chicken manure into buckets — purposely mock her careful rules on family etiquette and conduct.

"It makes us lesser people," she says, looking into his face. "It takes the God out of us."

I nod, obedient. God: in me. Yes: I like this notion.

"You've acquired rougher ways," Mama says. She stands up, signaling that supper is over. I've been told by my mother, over and over in a singsong litany, that Papa's painful removal from staid old Vermont to the wasteland of the new and desperate Wisconsin territory ruined him. "He was a different man there. He was." He was a gentle man, cultured, almost refined, she told me. He loved the violin and the quiet, harmonious evening. Life was niggardly, but whole. Solid. Life was tough there, and poor. A seeker after happiness and prosperity, running away from poverty, he was part of the great migration west, with visions of the breathtaking lush farm in the clovered dale, some earthly paradise, but he somehow tossed it all away. He didn't have a clue, Mama said. "Your father is a delicate man" — in Vermont he had done little manual labor — "nary the picking up of a fallen wood chip," she told me — until he came to the Wisconsin wilderness. "Not true," he always says, because she says this when he is nearby, listening: "I knew my way with hammer and saw."

But what I do know is we have failed here. Whatever he touches turns to dust and stale air, the rich, fertile land itself turning against itself, refusing his hesitant and clumsy touch, crops drying out under the August sun, the yearly wheat harvest paltry, the spring wind furious against the tender shoots, ice hanging on the eaves of the decaying, rotting house, the paint finally peeling off his soul. We live, I know, a nightmare. We talk of it every day and night. It's our only folk tale.

So after supper he sits in the parlor, nursing cold chicory coffee and chomping on hard crackers, next to the fire that he has allowed to run down so that the wind insinuates itself through the old wooden clapboards, and he is playing his violin. Alone — Mama sits sewing in the kitchen — he plays *Barbara Allen* and other old songs over and over. Mournful, wonderful old ballads that I love, sitting as I am on the staircase and watching his rough callused farm hands gripping the bow. I watch the exaggerated violent shadow his thrusting arm makes against the back wall, lit by a smoky kerosene lamp. In Vermont he taught violin and dance and deportment to the farm youth whose families had ambition and hope. But that is long ago now, a world I can't imagine. So they moved to Johnstown, Wisconsin, my family, where I was born, then a year later we moved to Westport, near Madison, on the north side of Lake Mendota. There they built this farmhouse, and settled in. We are here forever. We'll end our days here. Everyone likes him, I know, but no one listens to his rambling and dire weather and harvest predictions. Papa is not a man who knows his way around a farm field.

When I walk into the kitchen for milk, my mother stops her work. "I worship at the shrine of literature," she says. Her voice is laced with venom and exhaustion. "Not him. Music for him is learning the alphabet. I genuflect at the shrine. For me literature is the soul." Her eyes are glazed over with fatigue.

It will be one of those nights, I know. When Mama talks like that, her lines sounding lifted from romantic magazines, I know she is somewhere else. She's unhappy. She hates Wisconsin, the farm, the deep cold. She's lost.

"Paradise," she says, and I think of the old red stained

chest upstairs, pushed back against the cedar closet, where I hide my copies of *Arabian Nights Entertainment, Gulliver's Travels,* and *John Gilpin's Ride.*

Papa's music stops suddenly, and he shuffles into the kitchen. He opens a cabinet, fumbles around, withdraws nothing, but stands there, thinking. He ignores Mama and me. Outside it is a cold December, bone raw, with wind rising. Mama looks up from the antimacassar she is embroidering — it contains a verse from Phoebe Cary's "The Heart Knoweth the Answer"— and speaks to the faded whitewashed wall. But her one word is mumbled. I watch my father close his eyes, the shoulders stiffen, the muscles at the corners of his mouth tremble. "Ethan Allen," he mumbles.

Mama makes an indignant sound, a sharp clicking noise, and the silence is heavy as fire wood.

So it begins, I think. All my father needs to do — the surest route to bring Mama to the edge of desperate abandon — is the simple mention of the Green Mountain boy himself, that legendary Revolutionary War hero from his home state. Papa is, as he has long since proclaimed to every living soul he meets, a direct descendant on his maternal side. This is sacred American lineage here. His grandmother, he always adds, was the first white child born in New Hampshire. Pioneers, brave men and women. Ethan Allen. American hero.

Silence in the kitchen: ice.

The name hangs in the air like a summer dust cloud: it blinds, frustrates, paralyzes the moment. You can't hide from it, I know. But tonight Papa wants war, not the gnawing silence Mama seems to love. So he begins: "The implications are obvious." He waits, watching, his fingers nervous on the cabinet door. He has a way of speaking in stilted, formal language — Mama once called it pretentious — but I always notice it gets exaggerated when he's angry or tense. The Norwegian day-laborers or kitchen-helpers he hires at canning or harvest time — in the rare good season — stand there, baffled, at his orders to do something. "When perhaps you can manage the opportunity." What word is *opportunity?* And *manage.* Mama translates, matter-of-factly, laughing. It is our only family joke, I think. Even Papa can laugh at it.

My mother waits now, and I see her rehearsing her words in her head. She is of less noble Revolutionary stock — although a grandfather Billy Pratt did fight in the war, but never became part of the national folklore — she is descended from Pratts who go back to early tall ships and deadly Massachusetts and Connecticut winters. "Pocahontas," she says.

I am listening and I mouth the delicious syllables: *Pocahontas.* I love the word.

Papa scoffs. "No, not that Indian girl again."

"Her blood is in my family."

"But how?"

"Through marriage."

"Rumor. You have none of her blood. It's an old wives' tale, full of dumb hope."

"I have Indian lineage. And royal."

"Mythology."

"Fact."

"No."

"Yes."

"Foolish."

"Blind."

Each monosyllable is louder and louder, like summer thunder building to crescendo.

"Liar."

"Fool."

"Spoiler."

Of course, I've heard it all before, all of us have, over and over, but I still find it thrilling. I don't mean the chilly battle, but our family tree. My brothers and sister don't care, I know. When I bring it up—I want to be Pocahontas—they laugh at me. They don't believe Mama or Papa. But I understand that mine is a treasured past, somewhere away from this lonely, meager Wisconsin

present. Mama insists that I see myself — the future writer
— as that exotic red heroine. The taboo romance of that
beautiful Indian maiden, the mythic moment when she
saves the head of that ne'er-do-well braggart John Smith,
her mysterious and dark marriage to settler John Rolfe
and her sudden sad removal to England—that wilderness and pagan blood — as savage as a meat ax, as my
grandfather once termed it — that blood, if in my
mother's body, is also in mine. A woman from the dark
woods, now legend. Red skin. I, Ella Wheeler, Indian
maiden. My Aunt Abigail, red-brown as an Indian, barefoot all summer, with long, straight, glistening black hair,
with the pronounced nose of the warrior, with nut-brown
steely eyes, always reminds me of a squaw from a cheap
dime novel. To me it's proof enough.

So for the next hour they argue, carrying the battle back
into the parlor where they can be comfortable, sitting on
opposing chairs, their palms resting on inherited, leatherbound family Bibles that do not unite them in this marriage, tossing names and lineage back and forth, circling
familiar territories, their voices overlapping.

My mother screams the names of French, Spanish, and
Irish forebears, local heroes of long-ago wars, of frontier
settlement, of Boston harbor, and Revolutionary stock-
ade.

My father talks of himself as an elegant gentleman—as
respected teacher of violin, deportment, dance. In
Thetford, Vermont, in the old homestead, there was a
huge ballroom on the second floor. There the town swells
congregated on Saturday nights, and, on the back wall
of the large boxlike room, under massive patriotic bunting
and an original thirteen-star flag, a framed, oversized
lithograph of Ethan Allen hung center stage, a founding
father who blessed the farm boys dancing the fox trot.
"It was always embarrassing," Mama says, "the way you
insisted strangers get a close-up view."

He reminds her: "Sarah, you left your home in Bradford
to live with me in Thetford."

Mama gets sarcastic: "That's as bad a definition of marriage as I've heard."

"It's Christian duty."

"As well I know. I am a dutiful Christian woman."

"But bitter."

"Bitterness is not a sin. It's a cross to bear."

"And I gave you that cross?"

A few minutes of silence, heavy as lead, then more spitfire words.

The clock on the fireplace mantel ticks away the night, but then slowly begins to run down. I am sitting at the top of the stairwell, knees drawn up to my chest, and I hear the sudden dragging of the mechanism. Someone has not wound it this morning. Ed's chore: he's the keeper of the clock. I close my eyes, frightened. It's what I most dread, in fact, this constant running down of the clock, and the failure of the family to rewind it immediately. It is, to me, like the stopping of time, some loss of precious minutes. Gone now, irretrievable. Time is altered, twisted, finished. My family plays fast and loose with everyone's minutes: they believe in long, drowsy farm seasons, but not the simple hours of a day. When I'm grown, I'll have clocks everywhere, and servants to wind them. The chiming of the hour will seem a thunderstorm. So now, all of a sudden, I cannot focus on my parents' pitched battle because I have to give all my attention to the faltering clock. I have no choice. Panicked, I wait for the *tick tock* to end.

Finally, running more from the end of time than from the war between the Wheelers, I slip from the stairwell and into the kitchen, pull on heavy galoshes and the thick wool coat and scarf, and flee into the back yard, welcoming the cold night air. Animals in the barn hear me, and they rustle and sway. The cow moans. I sense the flutter of cooped animals. Leaning against weathered railings where the pigs grunt, I stare back at the house, lost now in shadows, tucked under a cobalt blue night sky. My breath puffs out before me, and my eyes tear.

I am lonely. I can't make any sense out of the hollow feeling in my chest, the echoey, fluttering sensation. Far away, in Milwaukee where I've never been, there are different people, I know. There are other, happier worlds. There have to be. I've read about that world in the newspapers Papa brings back home. Not people like me, seven-year-old girls in ringlets and cotton-sack dresses, hands red and swollen from boiling the laundry once a month, but dark-swept raven beauties with pearls and gilt mirrors. Girls I read about in the pages of romances by Ouida. I imagine them standing in place, like statues, unmoving, waiting, waiting. For what? I don't know — I don't even understand. I have no idea. But I know about them through the poems I read, the romances taken from my mother's shelves. The paper-backed romances on my grandmother's night stand. My mind is cluttered with words and phrases that mean little: drawing room, salon, theater box, calling card, vis-a-vis carriages. This is the exquisite vocabulary of a city I've yet to visit.

But another word always intrudes: the dreaded "bottom." This is Mama's warning to me, always—you must run from the commonplace, avoid the bottom. Oh, the awful bottom. The bottom is empty and dirty and starved and bleak. "We are so close to it," she whispers in my ear, over and over. "Look around." She directs my gaze to the rough-hewn puncheon floor boards, the splintery lumber of log cabins. "The bottom."

"The bottom." I echo her. This is my new nightmare.

Looking around now, I stare back at the ramshackle farmhouse, blunt and square and ugly, with its leaking roof, its one dreaded window with the spider's web crack. The beams sag under the attic roof where I sleep, so that I always feel the possibility of collapse and death. So I stare at it now, a hunger for words rising within me, a mishmash of romantic phrases I've memorized from Mrs. Southworth. Yet I find no words for it: Mrs. Southworth only describes mansions and villas and elegant appointments. Lush grape arbors cascading over Mediterranean villas. Newport in the summer, New York in the winter. Paris. *That* world, not this. Even out here, in the dark yard, I can still hear the spiteful prattle of my parents — strings of dead names, hurled out like thunderous begets from the Holy Bible, drift to me, but I close my eyes, hoping the night wind will protect me.

How many nights will I cry myself to sleep? How many nights, my face buried in the pillow so Sister Sarah won't hear? I fight it — this feeling — because I have to. But last night I scribbled in my notebook: "I know wonderful things will happen to me." When I wrote it, it seemed so — *true*. From my bedroom window to the north, stretching up the road lined by Lombardy poplars, I stared into the night sky. Most nights I only know the pain of longing — nights when I pin the curtains down to keep out the soft, inviting moon's rays. On those nights, in bed under the sloping eaves, blankets over my head, I think: "Another beautiful night of youth wasted and lost."

Frankly, I am a heroine out of a romance.

It's the only life I want.

Riches can end loneliness. Ball gowns mask sadness. Tiaras take away tears.

So now, standing alone in the dark, I invent myself again: I am little Edna Earle, or some precocious child from *The Wide Wide World* or from *The Gates Ajar*, some bookish little heroine, all smart aleck mouth and pretty blonde demeanor, abandoned at birth, or born to a hateful family, now getting ready to leave the unfeeling, insufferable homestead, heading out to a life of fame and fortune as a poetess or romancer. Little Miss Ouida. The princess hidden under the dirt-stained guttersnipe's facade. Clocks strike the hour forever in that lovely world: there is no break in time. No clocks wind down, stop. I feel it in my gut the way I identify with orphaned and abused girl heroines. But then I stop, out of breath, elated, filled with wonder at the frosty night, standing on the hill just south of the house, and I point. I point to Milwaukee, out there somewhere.

I say out loud: "Before this night is over something beautiful will happen to change everything."

Suddenly, happy, I can go back into the house.

On the night of my ninth birthday, a November day without cake or notice, I begin my novel, sneaking into the cold shut-up kitchen after the family is in bed, slipping behind the wood stove and fingering a small slip of loose wallpaper from the wall. The backside of the sheet is clean and smooth, though speckled with dried glue. By candlelight I slip sheets of paper from the parlor table drawer, and the next morning I begin the first confident pages of *Minnie the Tightwad and Mrs. Dunley. A True Story* by Ella Wheeler, author. In twelve small chapters, bound by the decorated wallpaper cover, I tell the simple story, even composing the verse mottos that introduce each segment of the plot:

> *A head covered with pretty curls;*
> *A face white as the snow,*
> *Her teeth are like handsome pearls;*
> *She's tall and stately too.*

The villain is the indomitable Mrs. Grant, "neither handsome nor pretty, but always fretty." It's a line I like.

Cleaning wood scraps behind the stove, Ed discovers the wallpaper crime after I've written four chapters, and deliberately brings up the thievery at supper. I haven't thought a bit about it: after all, it's behind the stove. I didn't think anyone would notice.

"Not only can't she retrieve fresh eggs from the coop without being reminded time and again, and she's always daydreaming while churning butter, and ruining it," he begins, "but now little Ella's ripping up the kitchen." Ed pauses, dramatically, and the family gapes, uncomprehending. "It comes of being spoiled," he adds.

"Now don't start that," Mama said.

"Am not starting anything," he says.

I stare.

"Ed, what are you talking about?" From Papa.

"Am only trying to point things out."

"What things, Ed?" From Papa, impatient.

"Am only trying to point it out," Ed says, louder this time.

"Use subjects in your sentences, Ed," Mama says.

"And?" Papa begins, waiting. Ed sits there, smug as a preacher, proud of this moment.

"Look behind the stove." Then he grins. *"You* look behind the stove. Subject verb."

"Don't be smart, young man," my father says.

I don't open my mouth.

All eyes turn, as though a field mouse has scurried across the floor, and Papa gets up to investigate.

Quietly, nervous, I say: "I needed covers for my novel."

My brother Marcus shakes his head, nodding at Ed with approval.

"We do have writing paper," Mama says.

"You only have to ask," Papa says, gently.

"It's precious," I say. And that is true. I've heard the late-night conversations about money, the chronic lack of dollars, the failure of field crops, season after season, the few pennies for this, pennies for that. The overdue account at the general store. The roof leaking. The well drying out. Late at night the plastered crumbling walls echo with recrimination and accusation. Sometimes, when I read Mama's family Bible, fingers tracing the *begets* as though deciphering code, I think: because they have no God in them, they have only a grubbing life. They are Godless. This is God's handy work, this decay.

Quaking and nervous, running up to my room and rushing back, I produce the slender pages of the novel, with the big black-ink printing, and Mama surveys them carefully. Parts are read out loud by my mother, in a voice that grows louder and more triumphant, as though she herself has discovered something rare and special in the basement of the heart.

The family listens, but bodies move, arms twist, impatient.

My words sound odd now: somebody else's.

"Where did you get these little verses?" Marcus says, leaning over, drumming his finger on my little lines of poetry that introduce each chapter, sentimental lines that summarize the action to follow. I admit writing them myself, but I'm amazed when Marcus laughs at me, his chuckling so loud and false that my cat moves out of its corner by the stove and gets lost in the wood box. "Don't you know anything, Ella," he says. "Novelists use other poets' words for that. They use Shelley or Wordsworth or Shakespeare or something. They don't write their own. Goes to show you know nothing of writing." Marcus's eyes hold mine, unblinking, angry.

I understand he is being purposely hostile, his usual faultfinding self, but I'm still shocked: why hasn't anyone told me? It seems a serious blunder. There is so much I have yet to learn about literature, I think. So much. Writing is a secret kingdom, with clues and padlocks and passwords. And literature is to be my life. Someday soon, in Milwaukee. I know that.

"There will be no more taking paper off the wall," my father announces. "Your mother will give you writing paper."

I turn to my brothers, with a smug look, my eyes wide with glee. I can't help but gloat now. I can't help it. Ed frowns and mumbles one word: "Pampered." Papa shoots him a harsh look, and my brother is silenced. For the moment. I catch him looking at Mama. Nothing is ever finished in this family.

Days later, I finish the small novel, but I've lost interest in it after that family squabble. Once my secret was out, I feel the story line slipping away from me, sullied by my mocking brothers who mumble my own words back at me as they go about the farm chores. "Minnie Tightheart," Ed says, grinning. "Minnie Trite Tart." Marcus nudges me: "Mincemeat While Hot." "Dudley the Dunkerhead."

None of it is funny to me. In my room I cry for hours.

Late at night, hidden under covers in my drafty bed-room, I'm unable to breathe. I know it has nothing to do with the thick coverlet or the closed room, the stifling bedtime air, or even the low-pitched rafter beams just above my head: no, it's something else. It's happened before. The terrifying sensation comes upon me when I least expect it, mostly when I lie in bed, but not always. When I go about my kitchen chores during the bright daylight, paring the juicy apples for the deep dish pie, gathering frosted huckleberries or Juneberries for pie, the quick, choking feeling slaps me like a smothering ghost, holds me momentarily to the spot, strangles me. "What's the matter, Ella?" my mother asks. "You look like you just saw a ghost."

I have, I think, but I never admit it. If you can't put your finger on it, then it must be a ghost. I feel waves rocking me. My head spins. If I can, I stagger outdoors. Outside, gulping drafts of fresh farm air, I regain my bal-ance. In the yard or in the barn, among the milling ani-mals, I stare at the silent creatures the farm depends on. My mind a blur, my vision tunneled, they look demonic to me, misshapen breathing forces from some sinister nether world, panting creatures with vacant, dreadful eyes. The cow is gargantuan, the horse a Lucifer, the chick-ens clucking across the yard in their coop are fallen an-gels come to suck my breath away.

These times I am quiet for days.

I know I am on the edge of eternity, these moments.

I expect one of these times I will die.

When I am twelve, my only friend is Emma. She's my first real friend. Emma's a romantic dreamer like myself, but not poetic. A thin little girl, a year older than me, she's all jutting bone and neatly cropped puritan hair, her mother's severe creation. Together we laugh and mock and roll across the prairie fields. She's my first real friend — I've always been alone. The other girls avoid me — think I'm odd. Neighboring children — though far removed — always run from me, spooked.

Emma and I try to see each other every day. In spring, with winter's chill still on the thawing ground, we seek the fragile pasque flower that sometimes pops up through the late snow. To me, such a flower is a paradox, dangerous, out of its element, a flower rushing the season's change. So it's the flower I most covet. It looks so special there, with delicate petal against melting ice. Some days we chase strutting pheasants into huckleberry thickets. We watch baby rabbits hopping behind their mother. We hide in a grove of beech trees by the pond on Emma's land and recite poetry learned in school. Some days we make garlands of wild orchids and violets and wear them under the noontime sun. I can't express how good it is to have a friend. I never thought it would happen.

Lying on moss-smooth tree mounds, staring into cloudless skies, we invent lives for ourselves: I am a princess in a British court. I am a lady of fashion in a New York salon. Emma is a Romanov lady-in-waiting.

Bored, we spend long hours after school spying on a mad young boy, who is given to rambling fits of howling across the land, or sitting in the dirt road so carts risk turning over as they careen by him, a boy with madness so deep in the eye corners that German Catholic immigrants from one town over, crossing his path, bless themselves, and sometimes kneel. He is called Crazy John.

He's become our obsession. He's all we talk of.

We're convinced he holds the answers to inviolate mysteries: madmen always talk of God and holes in the universe. Pathways to heaven and hell. I tell Emma that such men step out from one plane into another. They fall through the cracks in the sky. They chatter with angels, who listen.

"And answer back," Emma says, agreeing.

He scares us.

"Has he killed?" I ask.

A pause. "Probably."

We both scream like wild Indians.

Each day, after leaving school, we hope to see him scampering far off at the horizon. To me he is a nonsensical fool out of Shakespeare, dropped onto Wisconsin fields. Emma and I have created a life for him. Blighted in loved, he went mad.

In school Miss Smith, a young intense woman, mentions him, and tells us to be kind. "I've heard some of you are less than kind to him," she says, and I blush a deep red. But it can't be me and Emma she means: we watch from afar. I listen because I admire Miss Smith. She teaches me to bath in ice-cold water — "Every day, mind you, not the once-a-month bathing we know" — to rub the skin furiously in a cold room, and to care for my teeth and to keep the body clean. Clean clothing every day. She calls it life's regimen, and I, ever devoted to the woman who has praised my verse, understand how important it is. Some locals consider Miss Smith eccentric and radical, grousing about her. "Ain't she supposed to be parsing sentences?" But I embrace her teaching with a passion: the naked body in the ice-cold morning tub is a habit I know I'll never relinquish: it jolts me into the day. It thrills me.

Miss Smith also allows special rewards to the good students, one of which is to retrieve water for the classroom from a bubbling spring on nearby farm land owned by an irascible English settler, Mrs. Elliot. Here the wild peppermint grows in abundance, the aromas intoxicating, the cold water clear as window glass. It is an oasis of emerald green and ice-cold amid small rock and barren scrub grass. I love being selected — and I am, often, since I'm a teacher's pet — because I can lie in the grass, covering myself with the perfume of wild mint, delaying my return, and I always bring bouquets back to the classroom, bunches of peppermint the other children crave. In the afternoon the classroom smells like a spring field.

But one day, sitting in the peppermint, the pail unfilled

at my side, my eyes riveted to a sunny blue sky and my head filled with lines of verse, I hear an eerie chirping. When I sit up, startled and frightened, there is Crazy John, cooing at me. I know he is Mrs. Elliot's son, but I've never seen him close up. I am used to seeing him far away, walking in circles and talking to himself, his laughter echoing off the horizon. Now, closer, he chirps at me like a baby robin in a spring nest. He is just a few feet from me. I can *smell* him: a baby's colicky breath, sweet and sour. But now, suddenly, tentatively, almost gently, he reaches out and touches me on the shoulder, his fingertips tapping me, and I freeze. I look around: there's no one near. A raspy sound escapes his throat. But he doesn't run away. Instead he laughs, staring right into my face, his laugh a gurgle deep in his throat, and at that moment I know he's looking deep in me. His eyes, unblinking, hold mine. He's seeing something there, and I want to ask him. What? What is it you want? What? I get really still. So does he: we hold eye contact. His eyes are so wild with heat I know I can be seared. But I can't open my mouth, no words form, and the only name for him I can recall is Crazy. That isn't a name, is it? I panic. Do you call someone who's crazy *Crazy*? What kind of name is that?

Help me.

He says something incoherent, drool at the corners of his mouth, pointing at me and still smiling, but his words release me: I stand, grab the empty pail and run back to class. Sweat pours off me. I trip into class, hair disheveled, and out of breath. "My, my," says Miss Smith, rushing to me, "you look mighty peaked." I let the class believe I've been frightened by a copperhead that slithered across my feet. Miss Smith allows me to lie in the cloakroom for the afternoon. I cry softly, my fingers cold and clammy.

"He knows something," Emma says, when I tell her the story.

I sigh. "It was like he knew me." I point to my chest.

"In here."

"Heaven's whisper," Emma says.

"Deep in the soul," I add.

"How wonderful," Emma says. "Pa says he's brilliant. He's sure of it. Crazy John lost his mind because of it. You can, you know, be too smart for your britches, Pa says. I told Pa it was because of love, but he—" She stops.

I am frowning. I suddenly remember his face — those bright, mooncalf eyes and that mobile mouth. A puppeteer's head. So close to me. I shiver. "I don't want to talk about it," I say. Suddenly I am crying.

At night, sleeping, I dream of Crazy John. His voice: the weird chirping from a dying animal. Startled awake, I remember his face out of my nightmare. He is pointing at me, one bony dirty finger, and laughing out of control. The head rolls from side to side, like a doll's head broken from its socket. I am being mocked. I lie in my bed, covered with sweat and panic. My cat lies next to me, and idly I stroke its fur so it will be still. But I can't escape Crazy John. Somewhere out there, in a house of madness, he knows me.

What does it mean?

Help me.

As for Crazy John, he disappears. There are rumors of his being taken to the state asylum. I didn't know we even had one, but the idea fills me with dread. It's one more future I fear. Will I go crazy? Locked up: alone. I avoid the spring and peppermint beds. I hear the area is overgrown now with weeds and scrub oak. Snakes nestle there. Night owls weep in the maples. There is another rumor: that he has run out West, looking for gold. But I don't believe it. I know, in my heart, he's locked away.

"Milwaukee," I say to Emma one day. "It's over there." We are standing on the hill behind my home.

Emma is a better, all-round student. I shine on Composition Day, my essays lively and praised. But Emma embraces geography like a map to some pirate's secret trea-

sure: rivers and mountains and state capitals are the stuff
not so much of escape but of total wonder. She can spell
Monongahela. She knows the Okefenokee. She talks of
the source of the Nile. She can list the seven wonders of
the world. She knows about Etna and the power of cascading lava. She can recite all the state capitals. "No,"
Emma says, with some pontificating, "it has to be over
there." She points east. "That's Milwaukee."

I follow Emma's outstretched little hand, the fingertips grubby with farm labor, a thin line of black dirt under each broken nail. It doesn't matter to me the accu-
racy of geography: what matters is that it's out there. Over
there. Within reach. A day's journey. It lies like an oasis
beyond Madison, the new state university town. Better,
it lies in the direction of New York. Doesn't Emma understand that? It is somewhere beyond acres of towering
pig corn and spring lettuce and snake-filled wood scrub
and glowing winter wheat.

Out there: destiny.

Help me.

Breathless, I understand that, at the whim of anonymous fate, I can have untold wealth, as sudden as a spring
shower. I can have fame. I look around: the buttercups
and daisies are now lush hothouse orchids and feathery
tea roses. Milwaukee is, after all, a state of mind.

Back inside the house, at supper time, remembering
Emma's dirty nails, I take a longer bath than usual, scrub-
bing myself furiously with porous stone, pails of hot,
boiled water hurled over my thin shoulders, then pow-
dering my body with store-bought talcum as I know refined ladies of leisure do in Milwaukee salons. In the hot,
foamy water, I close my eyes. I am far away.

Arabia.

Milwaukee.

Heart

1864

Dear Reader,

I am asked often about fame and how to achieve it. You acquired it so early, I am told, that it must seem habit now, a routine. I have only one answer to these q u e - ries, innocent though they be. Yes, fame came early to me, but to the child prodigy — as commentators were wont to immodestly describe me — fame and talent are the speech of God who, in His wisdom, sprinkles otherworldly dust on the tender-eyed child. So we are, of necessity, to speak only of Goodness and Truth; to profane our talent is to slap at God's intention. And only certain children are chosen, special ones, deep romantic souls. . . .

— Ella Wheeler Wilcox, "My Days and Yours," *Demorest's*, December 1897

"Ella," Emma says, breathless, "you're famous." I smile. "Oh, don't say that."

"Why not? It's true. You're just fourteen, and famous."

"Maybe. A little." I'm a little out of breath.

"And in New York, for lord's sake."

My body suddenly shakes. "Yes," I say. "In New York. A little. I am, well, famous."

I stare into her wide, expansive face, all smiles now. Famous.

Maybe I'm exaggerating, I tell myself: I am just now beginning the journey of the famous. This is just the beginning.

At long last, I'm finally published. My childhood dream — my inevitable career — has happened. I've hungered for it — hungered. I'm fourteen years old, my hair still in ribboned ringlets. All the planning, dreaming, scribbling has finally paid off. For years I've devoured Ouida, Mary Jane Holmes, and Mrs. E.D.E.N. Southworth. I've memorized poetry by the Cary sisters. I've read the narrow, eye-straining columns of the *New York Mercury*, the *Ledger*, the *Waverley*, following the serial novels or the epic verse narratives of errant or undying love. I've lived in their worlds, my hands black with smudged newsprint, my heart on fire with the easy rhymed couplets. Isolated, five miles from a post office, where the call of a neighbor at the farm is an event, our small village receives mail only three times a week. But suddenly the post office has become my lifeblood conduit to the East Coast editors. Out there, beyond Milwaukee. New York. In the morning, three times a week, I leave home in a lumber wagon or the old runabout, headed for the post office. It's my journey to Camelot.

I am famous. Sort of.

Well, sort of.

A beginning.

At fourteen I have two short romantic essays published in the *New York Mercury*. I've read this newspaper for years, old copies handed on to me by Aunt Abigail, living down in nearby Janesville, but they stopped coming when the subscription lapsed and wasn't renewed. I was devastated. I was right in the middle of a gripping serial by Rose Terry. And there is no money for subscriptions, my father announces, when I plead my case. Of course, my family knows nothing about my carefully-penned submissions. Through an older friend, a freshman at the new university at Madison, I send the two essays on to New York. Two months pass, and one day my friend writes me, saying she's seen my work published under my chosen pen name Eloine. At first I'm overjoyed, but then I become furious. Why the silence? I've heard nothing from the newspaper. I'm published — but unaware. So, indignant, I write a sharp letter to the editor, using my most grown-up penmanship, demanding money or gifts. "Something," I say, heatedly. "Some token. After all, you did *choose* to publish my work. Send something. Or even the paper itself, at least, as pay for my work." I scribble two pages of rambling diatribe. The editor, obviously amused — "You seem a tad wrought" — sends a stack of back issues, as well as a piece of porcelain bric-a-brac, the ungainly package arriving at the local post office and causing a stir.

Word spreads from farm to farm. Farmers pause in their fields, wave.

Famous all over town: people point to me. "Our Elly. A child."

Our family parlor displays the newfound treasure, a figurine of a shepherdess, placed in the center of a stained table. Newspapers containing my words are stacked around the object. "Lovely," my mother says. "They think we're sheepherders out West."

I frown.

My father warns me. "Don't get crazy on this writing, Ella," he says. But I don't care.

Tonight I write in my school notebook: *The music begins.*

Then suddenly it stops.

For some reason — it actually keeps me awake at night — the *New York Mercury* refuses my poetry. Every day I scribble verses. The rhythms and rhymes come easily, the words falling onto the pages effortlessly, and they are what I want to see in print. I don't really care for my throwaway tepid essays on blighted love. My poetry! That's where my soul quakes, where my heart bleeds. As Eloine, I have written high-charged love lyrics, which I submit to their "Ladies' Promenade" column. My verse is rejected. Worse — and this is what destroys me — the newspaper even quotes two lines of my precious unpublished verse in a editor's column, without my name, of course — but using my own words as a cautionary tale of what a poet should never do.

She flew to her room, locked and bolted the door,
And in anguish and grief threw herself on the floor.

I stare at my own lines — my first East Coast poem, my first poetic publication — and it's quoted only to be mocked. The simple couplet the editor quotes is one I cherish: its rhythm exhilarated me when I wrote it, late one Sunday morning after gathering the eggs from the coop and getting pecked by the ornery rooster.

In his column the editor advises me, nameless though I am — and others reading his column who are planning such puerile verse — to avoid the mock medieval scenarios, the damsels in turrets, the wildly distant British posturing, the Sir Walter Scott thievery. "Harried virgins in towers is a theme perhaps overused," he suggests. Write prose, the editor says glibly — "never again attempt poetical expression." Fighting back tears, I tuck the newspaper in a drawer — I will ignore it. For a second I consider flying to my room, locking and bolting the door, and hurling myself on the floor. But I don't. I don't like it when life imitates art.

I don't care. I don't believe him. I continue to send out elaborate narrative poems, medieval in setting, located in Scotland or ancient Britain, canto after canto of jousting and jesting in mead halls and fanciful fortresses. They are scrupulously copied and recopied in my neat, severe penmanship, deliberately firm so that they think I am much older than fourteen. They're all returned. I send them out again — immediately. Again and again. I'm unrelenting. I live at the post office. Finally, one editor writes, pleading — "Send heart wails." And: "Give me simple love lyrics, minus the medieval tapestries." Love songs.

"Give me heart wails."

America wants heart wails, he says.

I dip into my little-girl soul: Unrequited love? Broken hearts? Separation and tears? A first kiss? Coquettes and rogues? War triumphs? A mother's loss, a baby's dying? An old woman recollecting happiness?

All right, I'll write heart wails.

I can describe love in any costume.

The drama of history, well, people can read that thrilling, abundant story in school books. Or take Walter Scott or Leigh Hunt from the bookshelf. But the heart is a territory we all inhabit now. Right now. Here. All of us. I know heartache. I'm fourteen now, fresh from an infatuation with a local general-store clerk I discovered is engaged to be married to a woman I consider plain stupid and dull. I know flirtation. On weekends Miller's Hall is a glitter dome of kerosene lamp light and inviting shadow, as well as banjo and fiddle music. The dances held there are legend — on Saturday night the strummed music wafts far and wide across the quiet fields and desolate roads — and I make certain I understand the intricacies of the latest dance movements. I have learned that dancing, my obsession now, is a good way of being looked at. My body is becoming a woman's. A farm boy, strolling by me on the dance floor, makes me oddly dizzy.

Mama doesn't understand and refuses to attend the dances, staying home with her sewing and grumbling. Convinced that dancing is suspect, with all that swooping and touching and twirling, she claims that all unnecessary movement in public is folly. "Why make a public spectacle of yourself?" she says, a favorite line. She prefers a quiet rocker on a porch. The book of Mrs. Hemans' verse, read by firelight. One night as I get ready, tying elaborate bows in my hair, humming a tune, she comes into my room and stands there, staring. "People *look* at you," she says to me.

"I know," I say.

"Don't smile about it, Ella."

"I dance like a goddess."

She makes a *humph* sound. Then: "I just don't understand it."

"It's like art," I say, a little arch.

"No, Michelangelo is like art."

"But it's all grace and angle and—"

I stop. Suddenly I'm afraid I might be forbidden to go. "Dancing is part of the family," I say, defensively.

My mother frowns. "It's your father's only real talent. He likes to keep his feet well off the ground. That way he doesn't have to step in it."

"In what?"

A long pause. "The debris he leaves behind."

"What else is there to do around here?"

"Don't become a woman too fast, Elly. I warn you." She stares at my body and shakes her head.

I know my father is in the parlor downstairs, reading a newspaper. Waiting for me and Sarah to get ready, he's probably heard every word. I know he loves these evenings as much as I do. They take him away from the farm, too. He gets lost in fiddle music.

We go off to the dance in the farm wagon, leaving Mama in the kitchen with a neighbor, Brazier Ellis, who, with his wife Olyette, has a habit of dropping in for blackberry pie and hot coffee and Sister Sarah's melodious voice at the piano. As we leave, I look back. Papa is silent — I think he doesn't care for these neighbors who visit too often. But it is Mama who catches my eye. Her face is ablaze with energy, the lips trembling, and the eyes fiery. There is a reddish hue on her cheeks, and the hands never stop moving. I understand at once the kind of evening I'm leaving behind. Brazier likes to bait Mama into fierce debates on the folly of mankind. He always starts it, recollecting some news item that has alarmed him in the newspapers. He does it purposely, I know. Mama insists that mankind is doomed to chaos and despair. Life is a black cloud waiting to rain. "Most men are but animals in store-bought duds," she has said. Brazier likes a rosier

complexion to the world. "God lets man bungle and falter, but human beings are known to shine."

The evenings always end with Mama calling Brazier a
simplistic fool. His wife sits there agreeing with both of
them.

I go off to dance.

At these dances I fall in love. I know infatuation, and I
know love. I also know a loneliness that eats at me late at
night, stuck in this house of fighting and isolation. It's
the battlefield of love.

All right, then.

Heart wails. Give me heart wails.

All right then: I will. Heart wails it will be.

Words just come, flood over me, drown me. Revive me.
Words come unheralded: washing tomatoes and cucumbers, sweeping the yard, boiling the laundry. I write at
least two finished poems a day — if I don't, I consider
that day is a failure.

In my notebook I scribble: *Hosts of rare souls are approaching. Splendid banquets are in preparation for me.*

Within months, I have found my voice.

My first published poem, in the *Waverley*, brings ten
dollars:

> *An infant lies in her cradle bed;*
> *The hands of sleep on her eyelids fall,*
> *The moments pass with a noiseless tread,*
> *And the clock on the mantel counts them all.*
> *The infant wakes with a wailing cry,*
> *And she does not heed how her life drifts by.*
>
> *A child is sporting in careless play;*
> *She rivals the birds with her mellow song.*
> *The clock unheeded ticks away,*
> *And she counts the moments that drift along.*
> *And she does not heed how her life drifts by.*
> *But the child is chasing the butterfly.*

A maiden stands at her lover's side
In the tender light of the setting sun.
Onward and onward the moments glide.
And the old clock counts them one by one.
But the maiden's bridal is drawing nigh,
And she does not heed how her life drifts by.

A song of her youth the matron sings,
And dreameth a dream; and her eye is wet.
And backward and forward the pendulum swings
In the clock that never has rested yet.
And the matron smothers a half-drawn sigh
As she thinks how her life is drifting by.

An old crone sits in her easy chair;
Her head is dropped on her aged breast.
The clock on the mantel ticketh there,
The clock that is longing now for rest.
And the old crone smiles as the moments fly
And thinks how her life is drifting by.

A shrouded form in a coffin-bed,
A waiting grave in the fallow ground;
The moments pass with their noiseless tread,
But the clock on the mantel makes no sound.
The lives of the two have gone for aye
And they do not heed how the time drifts by.

At night I read my own words. The only sound in the house is the clock downstairs. The ticking soothes me, lulls me, warms me. Later, waking, I hear silence: again the clock downstairs has stopped, unwound or broken. Only if the clock keeps moving can I escape this farm. Clocks take you into the future. Let my poetry take me away from here. That sure, hypnotic cadence is all my future. Time will move me into fame and fortune.

It's just a matter of — time.

That first check for ten dollars comes as a surprise. It is a shocking amount of money for a single poem, and the family looks in awe at the careful black ink lettering made out to Miss Ella Wheeler. While the family deliberates — this is a farmhand's monthly salary, Papa says, in awe — the very next morning I ride in a lumber wagon the twelve miles to the nearest bookstore — Ed is carrying wheat to market — and I methodically jot down the editorial addresses of every New York periodical on the meager shelves. Then, energized, I bombard them with my wares. I beg for money for postage from Papa. The poems go out, meticulously copied. Most editors decline my sentimental heart wails, some ungraciously. *Miss Wheeler, such writing is perhaps not salutary.* The poems sail to New York, sometimes to fifteen different editors, back and forth, until one finally finds a home in the poetry columns of *Harper's* or *Demorest's* or *Scribner's*. Or *Century*. *The Saturday Evening Post* sends me the complete edition of Dickens, leatherbound. Ten dollars from *Frank Leslie's*. Fifteen from *Harper's*. Dog-eared, stained, my work is recopied only when the ink fails. I keep a log book, a page for each magazine, and slowly the acceptances grow. Sometimes they send advice — *less mechanical rhythm, Miss Wheeler* — but I ignore it. I know what I am doing. If no money is sent, then prizes and gifts — tiny crystal vases, leatherbound and lavender vellumbound books, silverware, decorative knickknacks, arabesque picture frames in filigreed silver, brass candlesticks. When a new post office opens only three miles away instead of five, with daily delivery, with the coming of the extended railroad line out of Madison, I delight in retrieving—or having my brothers or sister retrieve—the splendid New York parcels and checks. And, of course, the dreaded rejections.

One afternoon a check for forty dollars arrives from *Frank Leslie's*. The sum is staggering. The household is paralyzed the whole day. Forty dollars: a fortune. This is, at last, real money.

The check sits, untouched, on a parlor table, almost as though there's something horrible or taboo about it. Everyone comes to look at it, their faces creased with awe. Neighbors drop in. This is a season's wages, a farmer's dreamed fortune. It sits there like a flame that draws—entices—the moth closer. I grow weak contemplating it, circling around it, heart beating. Papa looks ashen and lost, Mama all jittery and nerves. She sips a Dr. Favor's Indian Elixir and Tonic for her nerves and sleeps the afternoon away.

We know, without saying it, that our lives have changed forever.

By summer's end the old homestead assumes a new look. The parlor is resplendent — and cluttered — with my accumulation of decorative objects. The once bare, starved rooms, dreadful in their plainness, now sparkle with gilt and polished silver. If editors give no money, then I request the gifts usually given to those who round up new subscribers. "Give them to me," I write to them. The mails increase. There is no room in the parlor for more decoration.

"Anything in the mails, Ella?" Papa asks each afternoon. The room reminds Papa of a warehouse.

"A poem taken by *Home*. A refusal from *Atlantic Monthly*."

"Fools."

I smile. "Somebody will buy it."

"I know."

"But the one in *Home* was refused by ten—"

"Any money?"

"No money today."

For a moment he looks angry. "Ask for money instead of prizes, Ella."

"I can't ask always ask them, Papa. They—"

"Money is better."

"I know."

"Money."

I nod.

"The place looks like a damned museum already."

I nod.

"Too much clutter. I like things simple — clean."

One dozen silverplate forks arrive, in payment for a verse about springtime love. I polish each one long and hard, replace each one carefully in the velvet-lined box. They have the gleam of royalty and the aura of magic.

Neighbors, I've heard, gossip that I now support the desperate Wilcox family. The young girl child, they say, is the breadwinner. People say it when Papa is in earshot, or when I'm standing at the general store. Their voices creak with envy. Visitors spread stories of gold and silver doodads in every corner: the Wheelers have a few sawbucks to throw around now, or so they say at the Grange meetings. Even Brazier Ellis, visiting on a Saturday night to hear Sarah play waltzes on the piano, has something to say: "Things are looking up a bit, wouldn't you say?" Am I imagining it or does his voice also reveal a trace of envy? For years we have been pitied — we are the ones who cannot succeed in the new wilderness. Everyone knows that the Wheelers are not cut out to be farmers. Neighbors' farms flourish, even the new immigrants' farms, the German and the Norwegian farms multiplying like locusts, but ours falls further into ruin and debt. We lack the touch, others say boldly. But now— now! I am the only topic in town: Ella is the Wheelers' Godsend, they say. They point me out, and for once the attention I crave rankles.

I crank out four or five poems a day, now and then eight. I force myself, driven. Often they are about death and dying. Funeral processions are big this year. The magazine readers want funereal lyrics — all that dark bunting and heavy floral wreath. So many poems are about children dying, all wailing and tears and fainting and unrealized promise — sometimes I weep myself to sleep. I find myself moping around, teary under my own solemn words. A day without a poem is a shudder, a loss, a fallen tear.

But now I do understand the awful truth: I am indeed carrying the family on my fragile back. I am turning fifteen and I am paying bills, depositing the money in the bank, paying off the pesky creditors who hound us. Feed bills, long unpaid. Seed for planting. A new cow.

Marcus calls the new cow Ella Junior. I fume.

I can deal with all this, I suppose. What I have trouble with is the change in the household. It's as though everyone has lost energy, stopping in place. The farmhouse is a quiet shrine now, all gleaming silver and sunlit crystal — and silence. I scribble poems constantly, furiously, in between baking and cleaning and washing — a virtual dynamo of activity — and all the life of the homestead revolves around me. A part of this exhilarates me — makes me proud — this is what I want, being the center — but whole days I'm scared. I keep thinking of Mama's perpetual fear: the bottom. When will we ever get far enough away from the bottom so I can breathe easily? When? Something has happened here that isn't good. My father and brothers go through the motions of the farm, but they seem now in slow motion, dreamlike figures against a static landscape, and I notice my father sits more these days. Farm chores are done haphazardly, often after Mama's cutting barbs goad the men out of the house. Afternoons, Papa drops himself into the shaky Windsor chair by the fireplace, his spectacles off his nose, and he stares. He no longer reads. He drums his fingers on the wooden armrests. He never touches the violin now, and it gathers dust in a corner. Early one morning Ed announces — we are all lumbering out of bed — that the roof of the barn has caved in during a night storm. We already know that the roof of the house leaks. When it rains, water drips from the kitchen ceiling into an oaken bucket once used for the cow. Sometimes I wake to the smell of rotting wood. Insects burrow into roof beams. A bat flutters a wing against the window, and the whole house seems to shudder.

Or am I imagining so much of this?

"Money today, Ella?"

I'm walking to the stairs, my arms filled with letters.

"No, Papa."

"Ask for money, Ella."

"Yes, Papa."

"Money fixes things. Buys food for the table."

"Yes, Papa."

"Your words look mighty lovely in print, Ella."

"Yes, Papa."

"Amazing. Such dollars for words."

"Yes, Papa."

"Who would've thought it?"

Outside the south field lies unplowed, unseeded. The spring rains are over. Giant red ants travel in regimented lines across the window sills, looking for food.

I have nightmares that I lose my talent, my voice, and nothing comes from me. The family disappears into the starved, caked dirt.

I have the house painted a dull chalky white, the roof shorn up with oak planks, the nagging leaks fixed with pitch tar, but the sagging house seems a sponge: dollars for this lead to dollars for that. The paint on the house disappears into the porous wood, the new coat doing nothing. Wind and rain strip the boards. Shingles slip off the roof, crushing the geraniums in the flower beds. At night the sound of sliding shingles wakes me: I wait for the thud as the wood hits the earth.

Will there be more money? Please. God.

On weekend nights, riding with my brothers and sister in the new top-buggy to Good Templars' Lodge meetings, or to singing class with Mr. Padley who makes me a first soprano, I am singled out. "There's Ella Wheeler," I hear a farmer say, loudly. "The poetess."

At home I write late into the night.

During a sharp blast of cold air one late October, part of the parlor wall buckles, and a gaping hole looks out on the dying pasture. Wind howls through the rooms, up the stairs, waking us, coming at us like an unwelcome intruder, and for a moment it seems the whole house will topple down around us, smother us, crush us. Pulling our night clothes around us, shivering in stockinged feet, we stand on splintered boards and shards of glass, staring at a pink and lavender dawn rising over the pasture. The high morning sky is pale blue and smoky white. And the family turns to me, still drowsy with sleep.

"Ella," my father said, shaking his head. "You have more poems inside you, no?"

"Yes, Papa."

"You're sixteen now," he says. "You've just begun."

I don't like being here, most of the time. Not these days. Everything seems off balance, askew, unturned. Overturned. I am a part of the family, but oddly distant—they treat me so gingerly sometimes I think of myself as a fresh egg, held carefully in an open palm, seconds from falling and splattering. Everything is unnatural. Is this supposed to be love?

Because I also know one other thing now, and it shows most with Ed and Marcus. Their sense of joy and wonder at my fame — their thrill of common pocket change and pretty girls flirting with them at the lodge dances — doesn't mask the edge, the resentment — yes, even the wariness — they reveal when we're together. I've become a hothouse plant. How many seasons will it flower?

They watch me from the corners of their eyes.

Ed and Marcus try to bite their tongues, even when I irritate or abuse them — annoy them with my posturing, my lordliness, my self-congratulation. After all, I'm sixteen now, and romantic and moody. I know I can be obnoxious, swelling with myself. How can I avoid it? I'm famous all over town. All right, it's true — I can get dreadfully superior at times. I scream at nothing. My nerves on fire. They step around me gingerly, a delicate vase of fragile flowers, afraid of kicking up dust. Soon the supper conversations are familiar: What is best for Ella? How can we help Ella grow? Find time to write? Be happy?

Help her.

They talk as if I'm not there — like assessing the potential of this bank account or that profit from the sale of winter wheat. Oddly, I am a neighborhood cynosure who has become invisible at the supper table.

Hello! I want to scream. Look at me. I'm here. I'm not that check lying on the table in the parlor.

And their solutions for me are suddenly alarming. They decide on financial sacrifice, sending me to the new state university in nearby Madison. Education, they tell me, is something I can use. Successful poetess I may be, and published, with money, but a college degree is entry into — what?

"What?" I ask at supper, angry.

Mama answers: "Salons."

"What?"

"You have to be able to hold your own in literary salons. I've read that."

"But I'm published—"

Mama smiles. "I always told you that you would be the writer, didn't I? I knew it all along. Trust me, Ella."

"But college?"

"You need some refinement."

"I am refined."

Papa interrupts. "You need validation."

My brother Ed adds, "You only have a country education."

I get angry. "It's not a curse."

Marcus smiles, "How do you know?"

"Please, Ella." From Mama, her eyes narrowing. "Your future as a famous poet."

Papa: "University education will polish you. Make you comfortable with rich folks."

"I don't want to be comfortable with rich folks."

Mama: "You'll have no choice." Flat out, direct.

Ed: "You have to carry yourself like a lady."

I bite my tongue. I want to scream: I am a lady.

Frankly, I'm terrified of the university. I don't want to leave my little vacuum, my little world where I'm famous. I'll be off center there.

I'm getting ready for Milwaukee — and New York. Not books and teachers and blackboards.

I give in finally, weary of their sacrifices for me. I dread studying again. It's a step backward. I always hated grammar school — I always faltered there. English and writing I mastered, of course — excelled at. But arithmetic destroyed me. Geography leveled me. Science bored. Latin put me into a coma. But Mama says: "Back East they judge you by your education." It is, truth to tell, something I hadn't even thought about. Suddenly I force myself to listen. Until now, I considered the fledgling University of Wisconsin as a place where the bookish unmarried men and women go, the young women seeking Normal School training to become teachers in the country schools, the young men training for agricultural wisdom and the intricacies of animal husbandry. I am, of course, a poet, self learned. Published. Paid. Patronized. So far beyond this. But dutifully I go to Madison to the university. I am just seventeen, still a child of the household. I'm holding up the walls of the farmhouse.

This can't work, this new world of studying.

So I write home. "I hate it here."

So they write back. "Give it time."

No: I hate it. I write: "There is nothing here for me."

I despise my fall semester there, hiding in the corners of the classroom, the anonymous student in the back row by the door. I find myself unknown among brash, citified students, whose verbal dexterity in classes alarms me. Everyone seems witty and friendly. They have so much to say. They all seem to know one another. I seem backward, in my mannerisms, my simple homespun dress, my flat-out nasal speech. This is not the world I imagined or want. So I am quiet for days, a frightened field mouse, tucked into corners of reading rooms away from other students, waiting for time to pass so I can escape. I can't open my textbooks because the paragraphs mean nothing: gibberish phrases, nightmarish syntax. Herodotus insisted, I read in an assigned passage, that the language used by the Pelasgi could be ascertained only by conjecture. What? God help me. I read the words again. And again. What does this mean? I sink into oblivion and sleep.

I miss the Lombardy poplars of the yard back home.

I miss Emma, now making apple pies and readying for winter.

Nor can I write poetry. No one cares that I am a poetess, published by East Coast journals. No one acknowledges me.

I assumed someone would notice my genius.

In Freshman Writing, a required class I balk at taking, my professor Miss Ware — a severe youngish woman with a *pince nez*, a careless hairdo, and an unfeminine mole hair on her cheek — announces that while I have some obvious native talent — I have told her about (and showed her) some of my published poems—my writings are effusions, given to overwrought sentimentality and not a little melodrama. I sit there cringing, and she seems to be enjoying the task of outright humiliation. My submitted love story is greeted with derision by the class. I stare, stunned: that same story is now actively circulating in New York editorial offices as we sit here. Amused, Miss Ware tells me, "Miss Wheeler, stop reading the *New York Ledger*." She snickers. I can't believe it, looking from the smug teacher to the amused class, all of them nodding. It looks almost calculated, this battalion of censure. Wildly I think: they hate New York. That's it. They resent my life elsewhere. This is rank provincialism, writ large. "Such reading thins the blood of literature," Miss Ware declares finally. The class laughs too long, too hard. I want to scream out, to shriek—after all, I am making money from my pen, I am holding up a sinking farm, I bought the new cow with a lyric about summer rain on roses—but there is really nothing left to say: within minutes, alone, I stagger out of the classroom, weighed down by sadness, and spill my books onto a lawn. I never want to touch them again.

"You need Art," Professor writes on a paper. "What you give is Heart." Miss Ware likes to use capital letters, I have discovered.

Art and Heart. So that is the fearsome equation, I think, bitterly. Once stated that way, turned into an either/or dichotomy, some dialectic out of the Logic class I know I'm failing, an idea digested late at night in the rooming house bedroom, I understand what is happening: this is no territory for me. They have nothing to teach me here. This is the sanctified province of discipline and classical wisdom — proscribed Art, mannered and stilted. Highfalutin' phrases and philosophies. What they don't understand is that I am a rightful worshiper of the Heart — I listen to a different beat now, one from deep within me, a pounding breathless sensation that makes my heart wails touch nameless women's souls throughout the vast Republic. I am priestess of that shrine. From — what? — the first years of my life! What prosody talks of that? What manual of meter and rhyme scheme addresses that? What law of Poetics covers that? Now I understand my calling:

> *Though critics may bow to art, and I am*
> *   its own true lover,*
> *It is not art, but* heart, *which wins*
> *   the wide world over.*
>
> *Though smooth be the heartless prayer,*
> *   no ear in Heaven will mind it.*
> *And the finest phrase falls dead,*
> *   if there is no feeling behind it.*
>
> *Though perfect the player's touch,*

little if any he sways us,
Unless we feel his heart throb
Through the music he plays us.

Though the poet may spend his life
skillfully rounding a measure,
Unless he writes from a full warm heart,
he gives us little pleasure.

And therefore I say again,
though I am art's own true lover,
That it is not art, but heart,
which wins the wide world over.

This is no place for me. I plead with my parents — I am a little girl again, all helpless and fretting — to return home, pleading in a letter so frantic Mama insists the blurred ink of the sprawling signature is the result of copious tears.

"All right, Ella," she writes. "Come home."

I go home, happy now for the first time in months. When my trunk is delivered from the train depot, I go through it, discarding class notes, materials, papers, course schedules. I burn them all. I discard anything with the logos of the University of Wisconsin. That was yesterday. Suddenly I feel purged of folly.

The first evening home, after supper, I drift into the yard, at candlelight, standing in the cool shadow of the barn, near the towering naked boughs of the lone sugar maple. I get frightened standing there: I've been gone a scant couple of months, but I feel a stranger here. Nothing has changed, to be sure. Winter just makes everything starker, bolder. Everything is black and white. But it all is strange. As though I've been cut and pasted onto a dark tintype. Where do I belong? Not here, not this homestead. That I know deep in my soul. This is sordid, what with the sagging beams and the stench wafting from the nearby barn. No, not here. I am freezing now, shaking, but I have no desire to go back inside.

I have nowhere to run to.

So I'm in tears when Papa calls me. Just as when I was a little girl, he used to find me in the dark yard. "Ella," he says, quietly.

"I'm here." I step out from the shadows.

"Ella, what's the matter?" He is alarmed, coming near.

I look at him, and I know the light from inside the house catches my tear-stained face.

"I don't know," I say. "I honestly don't."

"You want to go back to the university?"

I shiver. Not that. Oh, no. I shake my head.

"Then what?"

"I don't know."

"Is it being back here?"

I don't answer.

"Your poetry has put you in your own world, Ella."

I don't say anything.

"It has to. All those magazines coming with your name and poetry in them. Your world is somewhere out there."

"I don't know." My voice is wispy, mosquito thin.

"You still have your poetry," he says.

"I don't know." I haven't written in months. I'm afraid I never will again. The university has strangled me.

"You can't lose that, Ella. It's in you."

"I don't know. I'm afraid."

"Of what?"

"I don't know. I don't."

"I don't understand what is good for you, Ella," he says.

I don't answer.

I don't understand myself. Wildly I point out into space, into the starless cold night sky, and Papa tries to follow the direction of my hand. I am speechless.

He smiles. "Ella Moon," he says, grinning.

I find my voice. "What?"

"Even when you were a little girl we'd see you standing in the yard, over by the south hill, just standing, your hand pointing to the moon." We both look up at the clear sky, at the dim pale wafer of a waning moon, and I am surprised to see it there. "You know that was the first word you ever spoke," he says. "Moon. You stretched it out —long and long. Mooooon. Like that. How we enjoyed that, your mother and I. And then you'd be out there in the yard at night, five or six years old, your hand stretched to the moon. Like now."

I pause, look at my own outstretched hand, seeing it as though for the first time, an addition to my body that has nothing to do with me.

"Ella Moon," he says.

"What?" I say, confused.

"Your mother and I secretly called you Ella Moon," he says. "Sarah was sun, Marcus a star, and Ed earth. It's because you wanted to reach it."

He describes all those years when I strolled at night to the south hill, stood there dreaming. My parents watched me silhouetted against the moonlit sky.

I start to say something but I can feel laughter starting to rise within me. "Ella Moon," I mumble, low and breathy. "No."

Then I am suddenly furious with my father. I want to run away, filled as I am with the feeling that I have never been a part of this family — that I'm a lost child, a bundle of someone else's love dropped into a rundown dooryard.

"Like now," he says, "your hand against the sky."

I suddenly hate him. I can't help it. I want to scream out loud. My life, I feel, has been made a cipher, my days blotted out, reduced to nothing.

"No," I say, but my voice is gargled.

"Ella Moon," he says again, chuckling, enjoying his own joke.

"No," I say, turning away.

I look away from him, afraid to face him. My face is tight, set.

Doesn't he know that I was pointing to Milwaukee?

Climb

1872

*. . . Your letter thanks me for my romantic words, and
you particularly mention your naming your newborn girl
child by the name of my new heroine. How grand! How
glorious! Your words are testament to the power of my
written verse to inspire. That is my destiny, my gift from
God. I have no other purpose than to uplift, to lead one
from despair to optimism, from sadness to glee. Your daughter—the inheritor of my literary heroine's name—will be
a good Christian woman. As I am a good Christian daughter of a loving mother and household, so, too, do you set
such an example. . .*

> — Ella Wheeler Wilcox, "Advice to Young
> Women" *New York Ledger*, 1889

I travel back and forth between Milwaukee and the
farm, the poetess on the move. Yet the farm remains
my home year after year: I write, sell poems, stay here,
visit friends in Milwaukee, return home, listen to the family squabbles, I write, I write, I write. In the spring the
choking, fetid smell of cow manure, spread on the fields,
makes me dizzy. I don't write on those days. I'm sick to
my stomach. I visit Madison and people bow to me. I
return home to chickens dying from the heat of a long
summer.

I am praised for my simple love lyrics, but they are
immediately forgotten — sometimes even I confuse one
with another. I think I'm rewriting the same poem over

and over. The sameness of my success alarms me. Sadly, I can compose them in seconds. I'm weary of it, frankly. I'm so busy these days — I've been declared the "Poetess of Wisconsin" by Governor Lucius Fairchild — I run around the state writing and reading commemorative poems for Civil War memorial celebrations — and I am sometimes too tired to sleep. There are so many civic functions for my celebratory verse.

My life has become routine.

I am asked to edit the literary page of a struggling trade journal in Milwaukee. Of course, the idea has little appeal — me an editor? — but, after all, it is Milwaukee and not the farm. Though my brothers and father are fearful — Milwaukee is a growing boom town and steady rumors of flagrant immorality have surfaced, what with those beer-swilling Germans—it is Mama who rallies to my cause. At night, alone with her in the kitchen, she whispers, "Go." Just one word, but it is enough.

My father talks of drunkenness in rum-halls, of farm girls tempted with lace and operettas.

"Go," my mother whispers.

I listen.

In the three short months I live there — the ill-born trade journal falls apart in so short a time because the owner has no idea what he is doing, and advertisers flee the columns — Milwaukee exhilarates me, suppers and operas and well-dressed folks and Sunday teas and formal visits, the embossed calling cards stack up neatly on my night stand. Friends host dinner parties for others to meet me. There are salons to visit, breakfasts in flower-filled rooms, dinners in candlelit restaurants. Wonderful women, with lily-white hands that never knew farm labor, wear gowns that have been shipped from the East Coast. And one, I learn, from Paris.

Back and forth. The farm.

I detest the job: the boring routine sitting at a desk, the numbness of editing text, the punctuality of an organized office. All that for forty-five dollars a month. I can make that amount with one or two poems in one good morning. But when I go back home by train, visiting the family, picked up at the depot by Marcus, I always find myself hungry to return to the city.

But it isn't long before I realize Milwaukee is a kind of limbo I've created for myself: a static state between escape from the dreary farm and some elusive romantic vision of a future elsewhere. Milwaukee satisfies, but my last days there make me feel nervous and edgy, as though I've had too little sleep.

Milwaukee fails me, but when it does, it no longer matters. Sometimes, writing in my journal, I wonder whether this will be the pattern of my life: a keen hunger for something, raw as wild game, only to discover that it pales next to my daytime dreaming. Ever since that night when I returned from the university in Madison and had the brief, unsettling moment with my father, I find it difficult to remain on the farm. But I have little choice. Where can an unmarried young woman go alone? What choice do I have?

What does make it all bearable is the attention. Letters arrive daily, a flood of fan mail addressed to me, letters from devoted, lonely farm girls who read my uplifting verses, who weep at my words, who find solace in my musings.

I'm all contradiction, I know. I rattle from one pole to another.

Sometimes, alone in the house when the family is away visiting, I love the solitude, relish it. Then, other times, I feel as though they have nailed me into a coffin. I desperately want noise, but then there is too much noise. The house is always noisy now, my brother Ed married and living there with a talkative, intruding wife named Delphia. Little babies cling to me, vomiting on my chest, gurgle through chaotic suppers.

Leaving the homestead for Milwaukee was not a problem, but I knew the farm was still my home: the rooms all lie under my touch now, the muslin curtains and oak-framed Currier and Ives portraits and hand-painted bric-a-brac are mine. Each new treasure is not stored away, of course, but displayed. I don't believe in secreting objects from sight: these goods are true signs of my success. The walls creak under the weight of wall hangings. Tables sag from silverplate. There is no room to put down a cup of tea. No one else has a say. Frankly, I don't know why I've become so imperious, but I need to surround myself with all this—stuff. After protesting that excess is a trait of the common—a remark that makes me furious for days—my mother has become quiet about the furnishings.

I'm all edge and nerve.

Mama encourages me to leave the farm, to accept any invitation, but she can't contain her own mixed feelings. She tells me I will be the world's most famous poet, but in a split second she mocks me, unable to resist sarcasm. It's as though she hates a whole part of me. A split seam in a dress that I wear home from a triumphant visit to Milwaukee ignites her venom. "We Pratt women are known for our slender bodies," she notes.

"I'm a Wheeler, then," I respond, angry. "We look into the heart where the violins are playing."

"I'm not saying anything," she says.

"Yes, you are."

"You're mighty touchy. Those Milwaukee airs."

"The air there is the same as here, except there I don't have to watch over my shoulder."

"There's no need for nastiness."

"There's every need, Mama. Can't you let me have my happiness?"

"There's no need to take it away from others, Ella."

"I don't know why you say these things, Mama." I am livid now, shrill.

Silence.

Then: "Mama, I have shared my good fortune."

Quiet, quiet.

My mother sighs. "Yes, you have. Indeed. That's the

price we've paid, I guess."

Silence and turning away throughout the evening: by morning she offers fresh hot butter biscuits as a peace offering. I smile and chat about the weather and the flower beds that need pruning. I hand her money for household goods from the general store. Quietly, her lips pursed, she tucks the dollar bills into the large pockets of her apron. I try not to notice that the apron has faded flowers on it, withered reflections of what was once new two or three years back. There is no need for her to wear old clothing.

My dollar bills pepper the landscape.

I act like a little girl again. I often do when I sit in the kitchen with her. In Milwaukee people stop me on the street. Strangers smile. I form the OBJ Club. The Oh, Be Joyful Club. To be sure, Milwaukee has many clubs: The Wonderful Life Club, The Bookman's Club, the Theorem Painting Club, on and on. But the OBJ Club is the most talked about club in Milwaukee. During our meetings there is lots of hilarity, contagious in fact, with animated story telling and lively anecdote, but it is always followed by sober reflection on the need to be constantly joyful and joyous and in joy. We are all proper young men and women. Christian youth. I insist on that. But when I return home to the farm, I feel that joy leaking out of me, seeping out of my blood pores into the infertile soil of the farm.

What does bother me about Milwaukee is the overwhelming presence of foreign residents. I can't explain my resentment. The city is filled with Germans, Scandinavians, Russians, Hungarians, Slavonians, Bohemians, all a babel of odd tongue and peculiar dress and, worse, smell. That's what first makes me notice them — lighting from a carriage, I skirt past a staggering old man, whiskered and disheveled, and the reek of beer comes off him. I feel faint. My family is anti-drink. Back home beer is death. Forbidden. Once noticed, I realize beer is everywhere in Milwaukee — the aromas seem to waft from doorways, from the gin-mill taverns and beer halls and breweries. The beer stein is raised throughout the city. Milwaukee is, well — beer.

During my three-month stint there, I become obsessed with temperance, and my pen moves furiously. My anti-drink lyrics come easily to me, two or three at a clip, and each one burns with a fire that takes my breath away. I reread *Ten Nights in a Barroom*. I ask for, but never locate, Walt Whitman's *Franklin Evans*. The manuscript sheets pile up on my dresser, a fearsome diatribe against the bottle of demon rum. Finally, assembled, my own collection of simple but passionate temperance poems is called *Drops of Water*, and I am overjoyed when a national Temperance Society agrees to issue the volume. I like my own title: water, I think, is salvation, but drops of water, I've read, can be Chinese torture.

Weeks later, when I hold the slender compact volume in my hands, opening the package fresh from the post office, I stare at the name in gold gilt on the chocolate-brown cover: Ella Wheeler. I run my fingers across the embossed letters, feeling the rise and fall of the script. A fearful balance, I think — the double e and the double l, all the e's and l's. The tongue plays with it, and enjoys such a name. It's a melodic name for a poet or novelist, I know. The l's roll like liquor, I imagine — like a word slurred by a drunkard. I blush: and this is a volume of anti-drink poetry? My heart beats, because at this moment, alone in the parlor, I understand that I can become the household word I so want to be. Not through the love wails I toss out so glibly now — "Send more love poems," the editors beg — but through the nobility of purpose. Temperance is my door to recognition. *Have you met Ella Wheeler, the young poet who helped close down the rum-holes of Manhattan?* I will be like Harriet Beecher Stowe, a changer of history. Alone in the house, with the family in the fields and my mother in the barn among eggs and feed, I hold the slender volume before me, threw back my head, and scream to the rafters:

> *Don't drink, boys.* Don't!
> *If the loafers and idlers scoff, never heed:*
> *True men and true women will wish you "God-speed."*
> *There is nothing of purity, pleasure, or cheer*
> *To be gotten from whiskey, wine, brandy, or beer.*
> *Don't drink, boys.* Don't!

The cat, startled, flees the room.

But there is no national outpouring of attention, no state proclamation or invitation to the White House, and in some quarters my verse is mocked and parodied. I am interviewed by a Chicago paper, and in a booknote the commentator remarks that such wholesale platitudes can only be excused coming from the mouth of an untutored child. One such poem is bearable, he says, but a whole volume taxes the senses. Luckily, the reviewer adds, Ella Wheeler, "a country girl," is just nearly eighteen. This "is the product of an imaginative church girl still in her teens."

I shake my head, reading those words.

For I told the interviewer, when probed, that I have always wanted to have my first volume of poetry published when I was a mere girl, still in my teens, a child prodigy really.

I didn't mention that I was already twenty-two.

But one night I dream a girl's name, and I know I've found the heroine for my new poem. I get out of bed, stare out the window at the dark night, and mouth the delicious word. The lovely name. My head is buzzing. I smile. "All right," I say out loud. "Yes. This is it." For a week I've been struggling with a book-length poem, or at least the idea of it. A novel in verse, with all the lofty sweep of romantic, dramatic fiction, the thrill of story-telling, but with glorious iambic cadence. Utter uplifting drama. I now want to tackle the monumental romance.

I walk around the bedroom, unable to sleep. Temperance promised me fame, but it didn't happen. I plodded on. But now I believe I have it — the illustrious girl's name that will make me famous. A heroine's spectacular name. I hear humming from somewhere in the house, an insect maybe, a lone wasp caught in the eaves, frantic to get away. I walk in circles, wrapping my arms around my chest, panting. I have the name of my new sweet heroine: this, I know, will be the poem that will take me East.

New York.

Last week, having butter cake with Emma in her mother's kitchen — Emma, I noticed, now has the settled look of an unmarried relation, the prudent young spinster, reconciling herself to a life lived under her younger married brother's skittish shadow, old age insinuating into her pores even though she's still a young woman — she smiled and said, "Go for sensation, Ella." Her eyes were cloudy brown, like winter molasses.

I laughed. "I always do, no?"

"Don't you think people are just sick and tired of politics. All this business of Reconstruction. Ever since the war. All this talk of carpetbaggers and all that. It's disgusting—"

"I don't pay attention to politics," I say.

"It's mud." A flat-out voice.

"I write about love."

Emma laughed: "And demon rum."

I looked to see whether she was mocking me. "I'm a Christian girl."

"Well, then," she said, "write the great love poem. An epic."

We talked about it all afternoon, but nothing came to me. Am I doomed to pen the obligatory, slight one-page poems that profit me ten dollars, twelve, twenty, a silver candlebox, a candle snuffer, a bound copy of the Cary sisters' collected verse? "I need something more," I said.

"Then do it."

"I think that the farm stifles my art. What can grow out here?"

"These are excuses," Emma said, staring into my face. "The farm has made you a coward." I frowned, and thought: how like Emma to try to hurt me.

But at night, after supper dishes and an hour of desultory reading, I began scribbling ideas for the grand poem. Suddenly, oddly, there was tingling in my fingertips, a moment of utter alarm as a plot seized hold of me. Tears came into my eyes. My lips trembled.

This is, then, my fame.

I envision a woman in absolute control, a woman of exquisite measure, the sharp-eyed, poised maiden, the resolute and brilliant — and stunningly beautiful — artist. This dynamic heroine, driven by ambition but also by nobility of spirit, this new American girl writ large, this Elizabeth Barrett Browning of the vast Midwest, travels abroad where she finds acclaim for her New World paintings. She returns to America to find the love she has earned. In my journal I write: *She is America showing the world.*

But I couldn't make the long poem happen. I needed a name. *Her* name.

And tonight I dream her name.

Now, thrilled with this name, I feel close in the bedroom, so I wander down into the parlor. The family is sleeping: the *creak creak creak* of my bare feet on the uneven steps is too loud now, too deafening. I want to scream out: I have found the name!

I want my noble heroine to be singular and memorable, with a name that catches the eye.

Reading bits of Nora Perry's little verse *Norine* did it. So I have it: Maurine. The feminine equivalent of Maurice. It has never been used before. I've never read it anywhere, but it's a natural name—and beautiful. That much I know: I've never heard it before. It's rare. Suddenly my flamboyant, hearty heroine has a name. My creation, this name. Mine alone. My invention from the Courts of Love.

Maurine.

My Maurine.

In white heat, forgetting my quiet routine of two maybe four poems a day, I write throughout the day. Sometimes through the night. I need to pen at least ten good lines a day, I tell myself, revising and revising, while still writing the prose pieces I can sell for quick cash. Discarded lines on crumpled paper clutter the floor and my table. I am driven by fire: I'm afraid if I stop I'll lose it all, the verse and rhythm dissipated. Here, I remind myself, every moment that I'm at it, tapping the manuscript and dipping the pen into dark India ink that glistens before it dries, *here:* so long as man can read. . . . This will be remembered. I know it. *I am writing a masterpiece.* Then I close my eyes against the thought: *I am being silly.*

But am I?

I don't know what to think.

Every night I sleep, worn out, as though from too much pleasure.

I have trouble getting up in the morning.

"Ella," Mama yells from the kitchen, "the potatoes need peeling."

I turn my body to the wall.

"Ella." My mother's voice sounds weary.

It is a warm, idyllic summer, these days with the beautiful Maurine. She becomes a real person to me, a friend to turn to, to confide in. Friends visit and listen to Maurine's story, and they give me praise.

I ask Mama to read the manuscript, and then ignore all the comments. I'm hungry for praise. "Ella," she says to me, "the woman is too daring." I frown. "Not enough, Mama. Not enough." No, I know, this is all right as it lies on the page.

Maurine is the bold and forthright American maiden in Europe.

When it is done and recopied, the sheets lined up evenly and packed into a carton, I send the book to Chicago, to the distinguished publishers Jansen & McClurg, who immediately decline it. Maybe my accompanying letter to them was a little presumptuous: "I am Ella Wheeler," I began. I explained the conditions for their publishing my masterpiece: the layout, the marbled boards, the illustrations. But they wrote back: "Pardon us, my dear Madame, but we do not know the name."

I tear up the letter, furious.

I've been published over and over in *The Waverley* and *Demorest's*. How can they not *know* me? So the book travels the circuit of the other Midwest publishers, all declining it. They quibble, it is such a long poem, and not even published first in a magazine. I refuse to get discouraged. So I carry it by hand to Milwaukee, meet face to face with publishers, and Cramer, Aikens, and Cramer finally issue the volume, but with no requisite fanfare. Mr. Aikens is honored to publish Miss Wheeler, he tells me, patronizingly, but womanhood had better be careful here, because, quite frankly, Maurine — he does love the name, the sheer novelty of it — while laudable in morality, is a little questionable in her overweening ambition. Women may get the wrong idea, he says. He stands over me when he speaks, a heavyset man with jowls and spittle, and I cringe.

I fume: I am an ambitious woman, I think. But I say nothing.

They expect only modest sales.

They are happy my inventive name propels sales.

It sells less than modestly, the first few months, but it does continue to sell. Against all odds. Word of mouth makes women seek it out—order it from local booksellers. They pass it on to friends. The reviewers like it. There are commentaries in the press. The novelty of the name Maurine excites them — even if the poem doesn't. Even that venerable Chicago house, Jansen & McClurg, recants, offering in a conciliatory letter to republish it under their own imprint, with the addition of other poems. *Maurine and Other Poems*. I agree, incurring the displeasure of my initial publishers. Then the first letters from the readers arrive, all in praise. A trickle becomes a flood.

I now understand that my dream is coming true: Maurine is becoming known throughout the land.

Strangely, though I've sensed it before, I now understand my curious power to talk to women. I haven't fully realized it till now. Avidly I read the letters that pour in, the simple ungrammatical declarations on torn shelf paper, from shop girls in Lawrence, Massachusetts, from Buffalo, from Newark, from Roanoke. I always read my mail eagerly. They all say the same thing: *What you say, I feel in my heart.* Or: *Your poem on young mothers touched me. I, too* — So I understand this curious strength of mine, but now, with the publication of my first noteworthy book, the one that embraces ideas like women's sacrifice, pure love, and selfless duty, I am smacked in the face with the idea, a blast of cold awareness: I am now speaking for millions of women.

This is to be my destiny.

The revelation comes in one letter, from a housewife in Rhinebeck, New York: *You are all womenkind's sister, those words you use.* Staring at the words, transfixed, I know, then. For whatever reason — and I know there is a reason, just as I know that God indeed spoke through Harriet Beecher Stowe to write her beloved anti-slavery tract — that the same watching and loving God has chosen me to be the voice of the lonely woman, the sad woman, the deserted mother and wife, the lovesick girl child, the fallen woman, the coquette, the dying matriarch, the spinster at the winter hearth.

Miss Ella Wheeler, myself surprised, quite simply, has her calling.

The letters arrive, pile up at the post office. Soon I call them the "Maurine" letters. "You may find this strange, but I read your wonderful poetry and I just gave birth and so named my daughter Maurine." "My next daughter will be Maurine, named after your brave heroine." "I want my daughter to be like her. Successful. Artistic, a woman with a purpose." "My new daughter,

Maurine. . . ." "I love that name Maurine."

In my journal I quote one letter: *You will give the world in every corner of America Maurines, so long as the earth shall last.*

In Chicago, I learn, there is talk of starting a Maurine Club.

In Boston three women, giving birth the same day, all name their daughters Maurine. It makes the news.

So long lives this and this gives life....

Grainy daguerreotypes inserted in letters show surprised, Sunday-dressed girls: *my daughter Maurine....*

The truth frightens me. Was God really at the end of my fingertips?

Suddenly everyone wants me. Editors announce they discovered me. New editors plead for submissions. Old editors regret their cavalier refusals. *Send more.* Genteel ladies of fashion from Chicago and Milwaukee and Madison remember advising me on my career, on my unrefined manners. *She was first at my Sunday musicale.* Social climbers seek me out, begging for a visit. I pooh-pooh it all, but paste the clippings in a scrapbook, my mother and I — and always Emma — first rereading each, frowning or smiling. My mother is bothered by the falsehoods, the biographical errors, especially the birth date. 1855? Not quite, she says, sarcastic. Nothing is true in print, I realize. It's so easy to fabricate. To tell the truth is to be misquoted. My interviews, no matter how truthful I am, are transmogrified into pithy quotations I never uttered. They talk of my poverty in ways that make the farm a dark-laced gnawing life, some primitive hovel in a forgotten corner of God's kingdom. I know I never described it that way because I don't want anyone to know. I may believe it myself, but I want it a secret from the world. My mother winces at the unflattering description: "We are above that, Ella. Tell them. Tell them."

"I try to."

She looks at me, distrustful. I turn away. I do try. No

one listens. I have become good press.

Then a crude line drawing of our homestead appears in a Chicago newspaper, a grainy rendering that makes the block-like house, with its clumsy trim and its vagrant off-center front window, look like a derelict barn. It's a dreary hovel. Seeing it, I burst into tears. It looks so — poor. Some illustrator has secretly sketched our home, all of us unaware. I don't live in *that* house, I tell myself. But I do. And standing outside I realize how poor I look to the world out there. We are poor — still, after all my years of writing. The structure soaks up money like parched earth sucks up rare August rain. I hand bunches of money to Papa, wads of cash bound by twine, and he hires men to add this, repair that, to paint this. But the end result is that the rotting beams sag further, the heat of summer fades and flakes the fresh paint, and the brutal cold of winter cracks the window panes. Dry winds haunt the house. I've come to believe my father built it on cursed land.

After the drawing appears, stupidly I nurse wild river vines up the twisted clapboard sides, so that leafy greens cover the facade. I transplant wild cucumber from the woods, twisting abundant plants with sweet white blossoms, but I soon learn that garden snakes love the wild plant too, drawn, I suppose, by the pungent, cloying smell. This explains the increase of underfoot snakes resting in the sun outside our door, the ones that surprise and alarm me. So the cucumbers disappear, and, instead, the blue morning glory flourishes.

The snakes, doubtless confused, slither elsewhere.

I escape to Milwaukee and Madison for longer and longer visits, hiding out in the drawing rooms of my circle of friends in these towns, friends like Judge and Abigail Braley, friends from my days back when I edited that journal. But there are new invitations now: Milwaukee has a number of privileged salons. I've *heard* about them, places of music and readings and chatter. Places of utter refinement. Now they bid me welcome. All they ask for is my high-pitched laughter and my droll conversation. And my name. *Maurine* sits on endless parlor tables. All I require from them is escape.

I am famous all over town.

And another wonderful event waits for me, I believe. I am talking about romance: a large-scale Shakespearean romance, a literary wedding of giant proportion. Dare I say mythic?

This is what I mean:

For over a year now I've been corresponding with one of America's most celebrated poets, James Whitcomb Riley, the Hoosier Bard, whose gentle country evocations of old boyhood swimming holes, autumn chill on the frosty pumpkin, and brisk winter sleigh or hay rides to welcome hearths have so endeared him to readers across the land. America, I know, calls him Sunny Jim, takes him into its heart. He's our most revered domestic bard.

He wrote me first, inspired by one of my little verses that began:

They met each other in the glade—
She lifted up her eyes;
Alack the day, alack the maid!
She blushed in swift surprise.
Alas, alas, the woe that comes from lifting up the eyes!

He said he saw it as a simple love story.

His letter — the first one from such a noted writer — took my breath away.

"For years," he wrote, "I have been wanting to find you that I might tell you how much I like your writings — both prose and verse."

I wrote back, thanking him, flattering him.

So the letters went back and forth. "It's delightful that we have so much to say to each other," I wrote him.

"Of course," he responded. "Two like-minded souls — two poets."

The yearlong correspondence is amusing, lively, filled with idle verse bits, and eventually it gets a little flirtatious. "My poetess," he wrote, "is a coquette at heart."
And I answered: "And you the cavalier flatterer."
His letters make me giddy.
We send each other books and talk of meeting for dinner. I follow his activities in the magazines: his traveling, his hunting expeditions, his interviews. I am immensely flattered by the letters, and one night I dream of him as a long-awaited lover, riding towards me in silver armor. I get crazy with the notion. Lovesick and breathless, I sit up in bed, perspiring. Oh my Lord! Is it possible? After all, Riley is a major-league American writer, the equal of Longfellow and Whittier, who has sought *me* out. He's as famous as I want to be. He sends me a humorous parody of the poem he loves, anticipating a visit to my home:

He sat beside her in her home;
   He let her call him "Jim."
She let him hold her hand in his,
   Which was great fun for him.
Alas, alas, the woe that comes from calling fellows "Jim."

I see the piece as a revelation of love. Whenever I read it, it thrills me. He is worldly, debonair, established — and a famous bachelor. His name is commonplace in New York magazines and newspapers. President Garfield mentioned him, I've been told. I wait for his letters. This is a long-distance courtship that intoxicates us both. Inevitably, we talk of each other to friends, and word gets out. Already there is mention in the Chicago press of Riley's praise of me, and I of him, and I've mentioned our letter writing in the popular press. Perhaps we've said too much. Rumors are afoot. The Hoosier and the Badger poets, I'm the up-and-comer, to be sure, and he the popular versifier. Emma, when I visit her, always begins by asking to read Jim's latest letter, but these days

I show her only a few. This is getting awkward. Some I consider too personal — too touching, too moving. He ends one letter by saying: "Heaven sent for you, Ella. Heaven sent." His schedule, he says, is grueling: he has little time for friends, and he has trouble sleeping. I tell him he is just too busy: "You are like a violin with all the strings let down; the strings must be drawn up slowly or they will snap." Relax, I advise. Relax. In my journal I write: *Sooner or later we shall meet in person. I trust.*

I reveal my own views on my talent to him: "If I have any talent, I am chosen of the gods, even as you are, and we go with them — you and I — up into the mountain tops and down into the deep valleys. I thank heaven every time I suffer and I bow my head with reverence every time I am joyous, because I know what it all means." I know he understands the awful vocation of the poet.

"My verse," he informs me, "manly in its emotion, with its memory of boyhood, is in need of its feminine counterpart. *Maurine* tells me — I feel it to my soul — that perhaps you are the woman's voice I need."

I send him a poem in thanks.

"It has to happen," I tell Emma. "We have to meet."

Months pass.

"But you're both delaying. Why?"

"We're not. He's busy —"

"Really, Ella. Think about it. It's not like you live in China."

"We will."

"When?"

"We will."

Finally we plan to meet in Milwaukee. He is headed off on a hunting excursion with the Reverend Myron Reed, but will stay later in the city just for my sake. "It is *time* to meet," he says in a letter. I wonder why he has underlined the word *time*. He makes a point of saying the delay is *for me*. The rendezvous has to be led up to — made monumental. He makes reference to Dido and Aeneas, to Cleopatra and Antony. But I shudder: those romances were ill-fated.

Funeral pyres and deadly asps.

I stand as he emerges from a doorway in the Baldwin Hotel, one of my hands clutching fresh-picked violets, the other the back of a chair. I am a little dizzy because this is, I know, the awesome moment I've anticipated. Not only is this *the* James Whitcomb Riley, the frost-on-the-pumpkin poet whose words thrill me — and all America — but this is perhaps love. At last. I extend my hand and smile broadly.

"I —" I stop, confused.

There is a deep frown on his face, and for a second his tongue slides across his lower lip. Wildly, I think of a field snake apprehending a mouse.

"Mr. Riley?"

"Miss Wheeler." Not a question but a simple declaration. "We meet at last."

The voice bothers me: a little effete, squeaky at the edges.

I had expected a tall man, a towering man. Launcelot, with rhythm.

I am waiting for him to suggest tea and biscuits in the hotel restaurant, as we planned, but he stands there, staring, his eyes wide as shelled eggs. And beady: a forest animal's marbled eyes, small and glossy. He looks uncomfortable and I don't know what to do. Dressed in a charcoal frock coat over wide galluses holding up neat-pressed trousers, he looks, to me, well, like a Sunday-pressed itinerant preacher. I am not impressed. We face each other. He just stares.

Silence.

I begin to tremble. "What is it?" I know my voice is too loud.

"Nothing," he says.

"But you're staring at me."

"I'm sorry. I'm rude—"

"Well, yes, you are."

"I'm sorry."

"Stop saying that, please."

He waits a second. "Why are you dressed like that?" Again the movement of the tongue on the lower lip. A snake slithering through the wild cucumber vine.

Now I stare, dumbfounded. I've spent considerable time on my appearance, anticipating this romantic visit. Everything has to be perfect for Sunny Jim. I've been to a lawn party earlier this afternoon — which I planned on telling him, hoping he'd be impressed—and I bought this special gown. In fact, I used all the money from the sale of three poems to *Frank Leslie's*. It is the first real fancy gown I've allowed myself to buy — midnight black with little ornate piping of pale blue beads, cascading down from the throat, modish, fashionable. Very European, I believe. Heads turned when I walked into the hotel earlier. Emma gasped when I showed it to her. "You take my very breath away," she said. "And, I expect, Sunny Jim's too."

He is shaking his head. He still hasn't shifted his rigid position, facing me like a teacher staring down an errant student. "Your hair," he says.

"What?"

"I'm sorry, I —"

"Mr. Riley, you confuse me." My hand flutters to my temple, then drops back down to my side. I don't know what to do.

This morning, before leaving, I bobbed my bangs over my forehead, in the current French style, teasing them so they spread like a wide-toothed comb. I know I look vaguely Parisian, as I've seen sketches in *Godey's Ladies' Magazine*.

"Mr. Riley —"

He thunders. "Do you think Elizabeth Barrett Browning would wear such a dress?"

"What?"

He waves his hand. "These frills, these — adornments."

"In Paris —"

"No genius would dress like this — like a dance hall girl."

"I have been at a lawn party," I say, defending myself, sputtering.

"Even worse."

I try to impress. "There was dancing."

He throws his hands in the air. "Dances are idiots with brains in their feet."

"Dancing is an art — poetry, music, song — all —"

"Dancing is frivolous."

"I don't agree. Mr. Riley, dancing is joyous."

"You should be above it."

"Why?"

"You're a poet."

"Look, Mr. Riley — I was with cultured people."

"You were with bores if you were at a lawn party."

"Don't you think you're just a little too hard?" My knees knock, ready to give way. I need to sit.

"Your letters never gave me a clue—"

Anger now: "To what?" I say.

"To this —" He waves his hand. I notice his hand is pale, freckled, the fingers long and narrow. "Gaudiness," he says.

"Gaudiness," I repeat, flabbergasted.

"For heaven's sake, Miss Wheeler —"

"I don't know what to say." I'm stunned, dizzy.

"My dear Miss Wheeler —" He bites his lip.

We stand here, the two of us, opponents now, Riley a little out of control.

He starts turning sideways, a quick jerking of his shoulder, as though looking for escape. My grip on the chair tightens, and when I look down, I realize I've dropped the violets into the folds of my dress. The hand that held them flutters in front of me. I sense the hum of voices around us, idle strollers through the lobby, and I panic: this will be reported, I think. This will be nasty gossip in the Chicago papers. Somehow a reporter is listening to this. Wildly I think: American literature is not served by such unfortunate display. But I can't move. He stands in front of me like a blockade, all steel and stone. I can't move.

But neither does he, although his eyes rivet into me.

Finally, breathing hard: "Mr. Riley, if you do not understand the fashions of the day —" Oddly, I feel naked in front of him.

"Fashions," he says, grumpily. "I thought you were a poet."

"Sir —"

"A genuine poet."

I'm furious now. "I *am* a poet."

"I'm sorry. I just I don't like your frivolous appearance. I don't like any frivolous appearance." He waves his hand in the air.

"This is hardly — frivolous."

"And foolish. You look foolish. I expected, well, a poet."

I add, curtly, "I *am* the poet. But did you expect me in a cotton shift, my hair in a farmer's wife's bun, my feet in barn shoes? For goodness sake, we are in Milwaukee. Look around you."

He actually swivels his head, but then looks back at me.

"A girl with a milk pail would be preferable to a girl with hair struck by lightning."

"How dare you."

"Miss Wheeler —"

"You're mistaken, Mr. Riley."

"That may be, but —"

"A hick," I say.

"Excuse me?"

"A hick." I enjoy the word. "You're a hick." I emphasize the word.

But I don't know what to do. Standing there, I realize I find him incredibly ugly. Never attracted to blond men, to begin with, I realize Mr. Riley is totally blond — the wispy pale hair like tapioca, the pale freckled skin that reminds me of parchment, the washed out eyes, the slight, unmanly frame. He is all whitewash. This is no knight in silver. He is all white light, blinding sunlight. He is a piece of sun-bleached straw wheat, this sad excuse for a man. Frankly he is the ugliest man I've ever met. He's a gnome. Worse, his voice is hollow, too high-pitched, a drumming rat-tat-tat of nasty words.

I want to get away.

"Perhaps this is the wrong time —" I begin, hoping.

But the poet seems in a fury, sputtering now about how that "God-woman Mrs. Browning" — he actually uses these words — would look in a fashionable gown and lacquered bang. "Mrs. Browning," he says, "a womanly woman, but brilliant."

I interrupt, finding my voice. "Sir, have you seen pictures of Mrs. Browning? Let me tell you something. I suggest she replace those little-girl corkscrew curls and village bonnet with something to suggest a trace of femininity. She looks like a simpering cow maid."

"Femininity?" He has trouble saying the word.

Suddenly, deep inside, I sense that I am stronger than he is: while I cower, shaken to the core, I now know that I overwhelm him. Blood rushes to my head. He strikes me as fey, ethereal, ghostlike, a frail man. A feeble attacker. Worse, he is a man unsteady and unsure. All swagger and bluster, all desperate posing, like so many country bumpkins I've known from my youth. I may be all frills and golden hair and bauble, but now I am a battalion of a woman.

He wants to get away.

We scarcely nod good-bye. He rushes off. I sit in the lobby, not trembling as I expect, but calm. But inside I rage.

Later in my journal I write: *It was like a cat and dog coming at each other. All scratching meow and male growling.*

He writes me a bitter, nasty note, almost immediately, which I answer. But when he returns from hunting, he calls unannounced at my door, asking for a brief interview. He knows I'm staying a month in Milwaukee. I am on my way out — I am really on my way out, to dinner, a show — but I give him five minutes. "That's all," I say, backing into the room. He apologizes, and says we should remain friends. "I was less than a gentleman, and you were certainly a lady," he adds.

Fair enough, I think. Well, maybe —

I nod, and he leaves. I feel empty inside, used up, washed away. Adrift.

But his next letter is, I believe, snippy and peevish. He whines about my delay in writing back. He is now an irritant, a country boy out of his league among gentle folk. A thistle against the skin. My next letter is cavalier and distant. Purposely: two can play these sickly games. He writes to me immediately, noting "the waning strength of your regard." He adds, "How sad, and after I humbled myself with apologies."

Well, I think, at least he can read between the lines.

I write back — two poets should never marry, I add. "The union will always be unhappy. They will destroy each other — iambic crashing against trochaic." I think I am being immensely clever, but I regret the letter, once sent. I sit there, bitterness in my throat.

He writes back, "I am resolved to die unmarried, unwept and unsung."

To Emma, I say, amused, "Good choices on his part."

Weeks later, after silence, I scribble one last time, asking for the return of my many letters to him. I fear their intimacy. "I don't want posterity to know how foolish my time was spent writing you." I like writing that line. I actually giggle when I write it down. We send bundles of bound letters packages back and forth, although I insist he holds back letters. He denies it. In my journal are the dates of letters sent, and some are missing.

Unwittingly, he speaks ill of me to a reporter, taking pleasure in his own sarcasm, and his nasty uncivil remarks — "Poetess of the beaded French gown, poetess of yellow ribbons" — are widely quoted. Apologetically, he writes to warn me of the upcoming interview, but I write back saying that gentlemen are discreet in all conversations, regardless of the press being there or not. I think very little of his lack of gentlemanly manners. "You're a foolish man," I add. It doesn't matter: the various letters and exchanged poetry are duly destroyed.

I write in my journal. *The loss of that correspondence deprived American letters of a fascinating exchange of intelligence and humor.* It has, I insist, been a spirited and sparkling series of letters, a rival to the Brownings' own letters. Robert penning his love to that cork-screwed ill-coiffed sonneteer.

One magazine gleefully notes the end of the marriage engagement of Ella Wheeler and James Whitcomb Riley. Somehow I am blamed. I steam. One more untruth in the press.

I turn my back on the matter: he is yesterday. I have enough to deal with the voluminous letters from fans throughout the country. How many copies of *Maurine* have I inscribed? So many times I'm stopped on Milwaukee or Madison or Chicago streets: "Please, Miss Wheeler —" I have my responsibilities: I am now called the most famous practitioner of the Milwaukee School of Poetry. Whatever that is, I have to ask. But I know that the future of American literature is in the Midwest. We hear the hum all around us, we writers out here. A buzz in the air: zephyrs through the pine trees. All over, the daughters and sons of farmers are picking up pens and writing. This is the new pulse of American literature: the prairies, the rolling hills, the bustling cities of Milwaukee and Chicago. And they single out Ella Wheeler as the chief luminary. Me: leader. I am pioneer, I am poet laureate of the young state of Wisconsin. My work is everywhere. I am, as everyone now knows, the mother of Maurine, the American girl who has taken Europe by storm. My name is everywhere.

Take that, Mr. James Whitcomb Riley.

Take that.

Passion

1883

To be misunderstood is a door that, once opened, may lead to a multitude of sadnesses. One must always be well-intended, to be sure, but the world sometimes misinterprets the good, righteous gesture. Some find sensation where what was intended was simply illumination. Some find scandal where what was intended was simply idle suggestion. Is the world so maddened with boredom that innocence is metamorphosed into ribald experience? Sometimes the gentle writer — especially the quiet woman writer — is more sinned against than sinning.

— Ella Wheeler, "A Response to the Rev. Simpson's Letter to the *Tribune*," 1883

I'm ready for passion. I'm not sure what I mean by the thrilling word — not exactly — but I know it speaks to the rush of blood through my veins. In my hot summer bedroom, under wooden rafters close to my head, I dream of it: it takes the form of ripping night wind, a fierce Midwestern storm that tears off roofs and leaves bare the strained heart. My newest verses record this nighttime wonder, my wide-awake quaking, all the screaming of the tornado wind and the lonely crying of a bird flying in the dark. I am ready, I know, for passion. No, I'm not talking here about schoolgirl infatuation. No, I'm certainly not thinking of romance here — nothing erotic, surely — although men find in my innocent verses some

dark and stark reflection of their own unexamined desires, men who write and pursue me: *I think if you meet
me, you will understand that I am a hard-working man who
loves* — but rather, I am dreaming of a passion that sweeps
me into the faraway heavens, hurls me like a sandstorm
above the clouds, a passion that allows me to shut out
the bone-bare farm around me. I'm talking about a passion that uplifts.

In my dreams of passion I am always alone.

Saying this, I realize I don't know what I mean at all.

In my mind, though I write of earnest lovers and unrequited love and profoundly broken hearts and the death
of lovely coquettes, sometimes weeping at the words I
use, I see myself as a mere slip of a girl. I'm just a servant
in the Courts of Love. My ideal visions of romance are
rooted in Byron or Scott or Mrs. Hemans or Aphra Behn.
I describe romance — pure and true.

No, this is a passion that is as raw as longing. It's a
quaking inside me.

What I do know is the loneliness of the isolated farmhouse. "All the wasted nights of passion." Over and over,
the same line. From girlhood to womanhood, a line
scribbled in my journal. "Another night of youth wasted."

The line undercuts my days.

So I write about it. I turn such sadness into rhyme and
meter. During a cold February journey to visit the Judge
and Abigail in Madison, I find myself sitting alongside a
young woman dressed in deep mourning black, her
muffled sobs wracking her slender body. I recognize her
as a young widow, of only a week, a local beauty who
only last year found a happy marriage. A rheum cough
has taken the young husband. I scarcely knew them. I
board the train in Windsor for the ten-mile trek to Madison, and the whole while she is crying into her shoulder.
Sitting here, uncomfortable, I can't say anything, but the
young woman's grief overwhelms me, freezes me, makes
tears come into my own eyes. I want to reach out, but
how can I? Such grief is a barrier. The young woman's

body is turned to the window.

As I am met and escorted to Judge Braley's home, I think of nothing else: the awful sorrow of that beautiful woman in dark satin funeral weeds. At night, surrounded by my dear friends, laughing at the elaborate plans Abigail Braley has orchestrated for my visit, momentarily I forget the young woman, exhilarated as I am by my own anticipated pleasure. Life is good for me. On Saturday I'm attending the Inaugural Ball of the Governor. I have bought a new white gown, trimmed with swansdown, and it has cost me the profit of four poems. It's the important event of the season. After a long evening of laughter and story-telling, I stand smiling in my bedroom, before a mirror, remembering the pleasure of my friends, but then I start to tremble, and I grip my throat. The smile disappears, replaced in the mirror by a sober pale face that reflects the melancholy I now feel. Then I remember the sad young woman, hidden somewhere now in a Madison home, but sheltered among friends who cannot get her to laugh. Oddly, I'm one with her. Then, sitting down, still shaking, I experience a wave of nausea and depression: images of my home flash to me, coming at me like rifle fire, the simple clapboard structure removed from civilization. No, not just civilization: from people. It is an unlovely world, I sense, one filled with bitters and acid. So much bile. I reach for pen and paper, and furiously scribble:

> *Laugh and the world laughs with you,*
> *Weep, and you weep alone;*
> *For this sad old earth must borrow its mirth,*
> *But has trouble enough of its own.*

I stare at the lines: I know this is my beautiful fame here, pure and true. I know it to my very marrow. I pace the room. The lines ring in my ears, echo through my skull, dance off the shadowy mirror before me. Mouthing them silently, I watch my lips move in the reflection.

Closing my eyes, I feel the words illuminated in the darkness. I can scarcely sleep. It's as though someone else has spoken the words to me, a recitation from beyond. It comes to me whole, entire, complete, nor will I consider revising a word of it.

I know there are souls in the spirit world who use the living as vessels. Have I been touched?

In the morning, weary eyed and haggard, I tell the Braleys about the power of the grieving widow and my own happiness visiting my good friends, and then, quietly, without preamble, I recite the quatrain. The Judge and his wife applaud me. Judge Braley, himself well versed in Shakespeare and always proud of it, announces, "Ella, if you keep the remainder of the poem up to that epigrammatic standard, you will have a literary gem." I am speechless.

Abigail touches my hand. She smiles.

But his words scare me — these first four lines came out of nowhere, and they seemed so perfect at the instant. How can I follow them? Is my spectral soulmate — that otherworldly voice — still with me? Whenever I see the Judge throughout the day, he seems to have an expectant look on his face, and it annoys me: why doesn't anyone understand the peculiar wellsprings of my creativity?

But two nights later, after returning from a whirlwind of dinner and theater — I have not stopped the partying since that breakfast reading — I excuse myself from the revelers, secreting myself in my upstairs room to finish the poem. I know it has to be done before I return to the farm, else the moment will be lost.

I sit at the desk in the room, but the pad lies in my lap, my fingers tapping the blank page.

I hear laughter downstairs, and music. Someone is playing a waltz on the piano.

In the morning I find the Judge alone in his library, smoking his morning cigar, idly thumbing through a collected Milton. He smiles: "I'm thinking of rereading

Paradise Regained." He smiles as though he's made a joke. I don't understand it, but I say nothing. There is so much I haven't read—understood. I've never read a word of Milton. I simply say, "I have called it 'Solitude.'" I wave a sheet at him. The Judge calls in Abigail from the kitchen. And I clear my throat.

> Laugh, and the world laughs with you;
> > Weep, and you weep alone;
> For the sad old earth must borrow its mirth,
> > But has trouble enough of its own.
> Sing, and the hills will answer;
> > Sigh, it is lost on the air;
> The echoes bound to a joyful sound,
> > But shrink from voicing care.
>
> Rejoice, and men will seek you;
> > Grieve, and they turn and go;
> They want full measure of all your pleasure,
> > But they do not need your woe.
> Be glad, and your friends are many;
> > Be sad, and you lose them all—
> There are none to decline your nectared wine,
> > But alone you must drink life's gall.
>
> Feast, and your halls are crowded;
> > Fast, and the world goes by.
> Succeed and give, and it helps you live,
> > But no man can help you die.
> There is room in the halls of pleasure
> > For a large and lordly train,
> But one by one we must all file on
> > Through the narrow aisles of pain.

I stop, watching the faces of my two friends: "I'm afraid it isn't quite up to the mark."

"Ella," Abigail says, quietly, "it's fine. Indeed."

The Judge claps his hands. "Ella, it's the stuff of literature that will last."

"Beautiful," Abigail echoes.

Tears collect in my eyes.

The Judge is a tall man, over six feet, and broodishly handsome. He stands now, towering over us both, as he goes to light his cigar again, and he rocks back and forth, bending his trick knee as he speaks. It is a habit he has when he's nervous or excited. "Ella, that is one of the biggest things you ever did. It is all good and up to the mark."

Abigail grins. "And this from a Shakespearean scholar."

I burst out crying.

Later in the afternoon, my trunk packed, readying to return to the farm, I hand a carefully-penned copy to the Judge and his wife. "Your convivial companionship," I write on it, "has given me Solitude."

The poem is published in the *New York Sun* on February 21, 1883, and I pocket a check for a mere five dollars. It seems so trivial payment for such a heartfelt piece. But I know in my bones that the life of the poem — and mine, attached to it like a clinging vine — has just begun. Within the week there are letters of praise. In short order it is reprinted, often without my permission, often without my name, throughout America, and I hear it has been put to music for the dance halls. When I mention that I'd written it to some strangers on a train, they don't believe me. They've seen it published without an author's name. So be it. It is, I discover, the most popular poem in America. Children memorize it in school. Grandmothers embroider it on samplers.

It is passion, I know — that poem. It has come from the depth of the heart.

Some say I am fast becoming America's most popular poet — its first real treasure since the Civil War. I've actually read these words here and there, and they make me blush. And also thrill me. I'm afraid to believe them. Whitman is in his decline, the *Roanoke Journal* writes, and I am heir apparent. I tremble at the prospect.

Is this a gift I will lose? How do I hold onto it?

I stare at my bedroom wall. The bottom, I think. The awful bottom. My mother's voice haunts me. I shut her out—for the moment.

I use the five dollars to replace the decaying wooden steps.

So much for passion.

At night I survey my manuscript book, reading an occasional poem, musing on a line or two, and I begin to assemble a new volume of poems I omitted from *Maurine and Other Poems*. I've written so much that is melancholic and tragic, so many sad dreamlike love lyrics — that peculiar passion of the soul — and now I want to publish them as a book. My ever popular love songs, those love wails — letters arrive daily requesting copies of all my published verse — have appeared in the best East Coast journals. My tender love lyrics, sentimental and touching, vie for attention with my slightly *outré* verses about coy coquettes and husbands whose eyes wander at the opera. So I innocently conceive of a volume to be called *Poems of Passion*. A lovely title, I think — alliterative and eye-catching.

Shuffling the poems, I begin with "Love's Language," of course, because I speak that language, and I end with the "Farewell of Clarimonde," with its wonderful line: "I knew all arts of love." I package the volume — bound in blue twine — and send it off to my Chicago publishers Jansen & McClurg, the very ones who had reissued *Maurine and Other Poems* after first refusing it, and then begged for reprint rights.

I tell Emma, who is visiting: "This is the stuff of my arrival." Then suddenly I realize I have made similar grand comments for *Maurine*. Even for my temperance poems *Drops of Water*. So be it. Emma just smiles. But the idea suddenly makes me laugh out loud. "Am I taking myself too seriously?" I ask. It all comes over me like a wave of water. I stop laughing, a little panicky now. But

I relax and grin. "Immortality is just an iamb away," I joke. But I am scared now, afraid of something I can't put my finger on.

That night, in bed, I can't breathe, gasping for air in the tight room. What's wrong with me?

I'm at home when the letter arrives, delivered in a bundle of acceptances and fan mail by my brother Ed, who has stopped at the post office after going to a feed store. He unloads the overstuffed bag at my feet, without comment. He makes a sound that suggests physical exhaustion. I am working on an essay about a mother's love for a sinful daughter, and I put my work aside. I will never finish it.

The letter begins: *Dear Miss Wheeler,* and it is, I'm startled to notice, a rejection of my book. At first the words make no sense: how can this be possible? My manuscript is being returned under separate cover. I can't believe it. I reread the letter. But what stuns is the tone of the refusal — a blatant admonishment that my work is, indeed, immoral. The publishers are horrified that they've *handled* such a torrid volume. My scarlet themes suggest a woman of questionable reputation, I'm told. "You deal with passions and emotions best left undisclosed by womankind." That's one insulting line. Another: "We question your deliberate need to explore the seamier side of life, the uncontrolled and unbridled illicit romance of the young." Whatever does this mean? "The musings of scarlet women are best left to Europeans, like the French." And last: "America is the land of proper gentility, of men and women robust in work and family, not in boudoirs and perfumed affairs." I sit here, stunned, reading and rereading the short accusatory letter. My face burns. They can't be talking about my poems, can they?

My mother walks into the parlor.

"What is it, Ella?" she asks. "You look like you've seen the end of the world."

I have. I can barely find words. "Mama, I'm called immoral." My voice is scratchy, almost inaudible.

Her face closes in, the mouth tight. "Ella, is it dangerous?"

"Dangerous?"

"Will there be scandal?"

I smile. "I doubt if there will be publication."

"I don't understand what you're saying."

"I'm saying that my publishers think I am — well, a loose woman."

She breathes in quietly. "Oh, Ella, I've warned you of the world."

"Mama, my lines of love —"

"But what did you write?" she interrupts.

"I wrote about love — ideal love."

"Carnality?"

"Mama, for heaven's sake."

"I need to ask. You spend so much time in Milwaukee that we scarcely know you any more."

"Milwaukee has nothing to do with this."

"Maybe you've lost perspective."

"I just write of simple fantasy —"

"Gaslight throws an erotic reflection —"

"Mama, please."

"But girls go there from the farm."

"I'm not a farm girl."

"Ella —"

"I'm God fearing, Mama."

"I assume that," she says. "But what?"

"I feel helpless."

I turn back to the letter. I notice my hands are trembling.

My mother is sighing. "It's one more curse of women," she says.

I've stopped talking, but she rambles on and on, deliberating the fate of the good but misguided woman in our time. It is, oddly, a theme I've often explored in my verse. But now I believe it has nothing to do with me.

When she pauses, out of breath, I say, "Don't tell Papa."

My mother laughs. "He's on your side, Ella. You're his daughter."

"I know, but —"

"All right," she says. "All right." She seems annoyed.

"What?" I say.

"Nothing." But she frowns.

Days later, visiting in Milwaukee, I carry the dreadful, crumpled letter with me, as well as the dog-eared manuscript of the poems, returned to me in the same blue twine. I've memorized the accusatory words, but each time I read them, tears well in my eyes. I am confused: I'm a Christian girl, I am. A virtuous child, God's child. A good country girl. But I need confirmation from my close friends, I need to get a clear eye: what has gone wrong here? I fold and unfold the letter, spreading it out, examining it.

I know my friends will be my devoted advocates, of course, these true-blue friends. But the letter is passed around my circle, returning to me stained and even more wrinkled, but the effect is the same. Everyone is horrified at my treatment by my publishers. How uncivil to treat a modest, unassuming woman of my gentility with such accusation in as advanced a year as 1882. This is insult and ignominy. There should be lawsuit. One man suggests fisticuffs. I smile at that. No matter: I can still hold my head high. I've done nothing wrong. They tell me so, over and over, as they watch me dissolve yet again into tears. We're all confused.

For some reason, their words do little to comfort me. I don't know how to read the moment. I feel as though my career is stymied — that somehow I've missed a beat, that some secret God-given power I obviously have — I am, after all, so young and so easily famous — is now taken from me. Will I ever be published again? This shakes me — this thought. I'm frightened. To me publication is everything — not only the incredible financial rewards, but the constant acclaim. All that glory for the taking. So easily had, at so young an age. My name is

writ large in printer's ink: this narcotic is hard to shake.
I *need* the fame. It's all I have.

"May I show this letter to someone?" one of my woman
friends asks. "He's a lover of your work."

I don't ask who, but give my permission.

Within days the sensational morning newspaper he is
affiliated with features the story, on the first page, under
a gaudy and catching headline:

TOO LOUD FOR CHICAGO.
THE SCARLET CITY BY THE LAKE SHOCKED
BY A BADGER GIRL, WHOSE VERSES
OUT-SWINBURNE SWINBURNE AND
OUT-WHITMAN WHITMAN.

The bottom of my world drops out.

All is black.

Neighbors knock on my door, some with faces set in a
stern unyielding line, others just curious. Puritans rapping at the door. Cotton Mather bearing a peach pie.
Relatives stop visiting, nervous. Some friends are horrified, my parents indignant, my brother Ed fumes and
threatens violent reprisals. Sitting all day in the kitchen
with a cup of cold chicory coffee before me, I say nothing. I wear a simple cotton frock, and refuse to move.
People circle me like hungry, ripping sparrows. The article details my questionable poetry, defending me with
emphatic declaration, but the newspaper clearly savors
the sensational aspects of the story. I am suddenly news
— and not good news. Front page, no less. Running my
fingers over the words, as though a beginning reader, I
reread the lines. My name looks important here. It looks,
well, elegant. I can't help it: I get a thrill out of it. When I
look up, in answer to my father's harsh question about
my behavior — why is everyone finding fault with me?
— I find myself smiling. Glowing, happy. Just smiling. I
can't help it. Swinburne. Whitman. Two of the greats.
Two of the immortals. And I am outdoing both. To outdo,
to go one better. To surpass. I can't help but smile.

"You don't want notoriety, Ella," Ed says, drumming

his fingers on the table. "Do you know the difference?"

My eyes flash. "I'm the writer here, Ed. Not you. I know the meaning of words."

He leaves the room. I hear a door slam. The cat screeches.

I sit there, quiet, quiet.

I hear Mama talking to my father. "Will they destroy us, Marcus?"

Silence.

Within the week it is apparent that the tantalizing story has been picked up throughout America, as every newspaper leaps on it, relishing it, and the re-tellings become more and more sensational and exaggerated. The innuendo of erotic *sub rosa* verse whets some jaundiced American appetite, I fear. My name, it seems, is everywhere. "Is there nothing else happening in the country?" my father asks, looking at the clippings.

Ed smirks. "That's what happens when we're between wars."

"How cynical," my mother says. "Is that how I raised you?"

"Well, yes."

"Ed," my father says, "be thankful for peace."

"I did fight in the Civil War," Ed says. "Everyone seems to forget that."

"And bravely," Mama says.

I watch him. He had not come near battle, I know.

"Is the only alternative to war in America a heavy dose of scandal?" she adds.

Ed frowns. "More like a heavy dose of sugar."

I keep my mouth closed.

The next mails bring negative letters, harsh admonishing, insane accusations. Every lunatic in America, I believe, has picked up pen and paper. "What kind of farm girl are you?" one asks. Another: "This is the result of a falling away from God." And this: "You sinful harlot." My God! They baffle me, but don't alarm. It is as though they are talking about a different Ella Wheeler, some other unknown poet. Someone out there — not here. I am not this hideous woman the letter writers imagine, all scarlet and licentious, erotic words dripping from my lips like honey from a comb. In my life I've read a smattering of Swinburne, a little of Gautier, a lot of Ouida, some accessible Byron, and can still recall my mother's singsong intonation of Shakespeare. Romeo and Juliet, dark swept lovers. Troilus and Cressida. Other figures from the old story books. Heloise and Abelard lost at the Court of Love, Rebecca and Ivanhoe in an isolated medieval tower. The most questionable: Hester Prynne in Hawthorne's dark moralistic romance. My life is hopelessly parochial. I know Milwaukee, Madison, Chicago, and the small pitiful farm towns where no one reads. I read. This is what I do. I read. What is my own experience with love? What? Nothing. Absolutely nothing. A young man touching my arm at the Oh, Be Joyful sleigh ride or the candy pull?

I am, well, a hometown girl.

But I find myself smiling — thrilled.

In my journal I write: *At breakfast in thousands of American households my name is spoken of.* I smile, and say out loud, "I am Ella Wheeler."

I sit quietly in the parlor. I am famous. Again. Or, maybe, truly for the first time.

I feared the end of my life as a poet, but my career, I now realize, does not end here. Rather, it begins. My spreading notoriety — the volume of mail gets larger and larger, the postmaster groaning under the weight that awaits me in bulky burlap bags—leads another distinguished Chicago publisher to offer a lucrative contract. I more or less knew that someone would — I am learning something about the new industrialized and citified American life, all that craving for titillation and glitter — but I am surprised by the name of the publisher. I expected a more sensational press, something pitched a notch above the grotesque paper-backed dime novels, a yellow-backed Beadle piece of pulp, but W.B. Conkey has

a distinguished name I've heard of. I sign at once.
Poems of Passion is published in 1883.

The next week, all across America, I am famous. I don't know this with any certainly for weeks to come, but I know it deep in my bones. Holding the red-covered volume, tidy and compact, heavy and rich looking, with my facsimile signature in gold on the cover, it falls naturally to "Solitude." Yes: I know what it means to weep alone. Now more than ever these lovely words written in Madison ring true. I stay in Milwaukee this week, and the attention ricochets between kind and ferocious. I expect it now. In some way I savor the unpredictable reactions. The reviewers are merciless — they run with the easy denunciation of gross morality, especially coming as it does from such a young unmarried woman, and from the Midwest no less, not from the noxious cesspools of the Northeast. It is almost too much to be borne, they say. Page after page of cloying French perfume and suspect harlot's lace. No one really reads the poems, I believe — readers probably hurry to the few infamous ones quoted in the press.

I am famous — at last. I've gotten what I want — but at what price? Alone, one night, wandering in the summer garden of a friend's home, lost among the Juneberry bushes and the scent of sweet Persian lilac, I tell myself I have nothing to worry about. I am a moral, upright Christian woman, decent as dust, and this is the attention I crave, attention that will eventually lead to respect — and honor. Getting known is the first step — virtue and esteem follow.

A local reviewer: "Wisconsin's first important literary figure is, alas, its first embarrassment."

I write a letter giving him a piece of my mind.

An old acquaintance from the university, someone I haven't seen in years, writes me: "Shouldn't you have waited for marriage or death before allowing such public display throughout your poems?"

Angry, I scribble in my journal. *I can only wonder at the*

frailty of friendship. Why do I need a husband or a tombstone to protect me from the assaults of a misguided public?

The book, my publishers write, is popular throughout the country. They predict sixty thousand by year's end: a runaway best-seller. People are also asking for *Maurine* again, and that volume is reissued. *Poems of Passion* is in demand everywhere, the distributors report, its *sub rosa* reputation making it the topic of conversation in households throughout the country. I've heard that some ministers denounce it from their pulpits. One supposedly fell into a fit on the pulpit, all red and paralysis and blubbering. So be it. Amen, I think. But I also realize a legitimate audience is out there. They will find me now. Many women are lingering over the beautiful love lyrics, the wholesome avowals of wedded bliss, memorizing them, and telling friends. I get letters: *I copied your verses into my diary.* This is the audience I crave. *I am newly married, and your verse touched me.*

Meanwhile the tempest rages. "A Protest against Ella Wheeler." Another headline that chronicles my careless wrongdoing. I am dispensing "poisoned candy." Mine is the path of scarlet wickedness. "The Scarlet Letters." "Poems of the boudoir." "The awful stench of France on the Midwest prairie." Another: "America's Sappho."

I paste them all in my scrapbook. I'm famous all over town. A big town, this time.

Even the venerable Richard Dana, writing in the *New York Sun* where I first placed the much heralded "Solitude," decides he can't weep alone on the subject, and devotes a good part of a column to an hysterical diatribe against my excessive use of the sexually provoking word "kiss" which, he noted, is highly immoral. To make his point he quotes the offending stanza. He uses the word over and over, drunk with its power. The word "kiss" speckles his angry paragraphs like hailstones against a roof.

When scores of letters reach me requesting where the volume can be had — and note their thrill of reading the titillating stanza in the stern Mr. Dana's column — I take pen to paper again. "Dear Mr. Dana, what a clever helpful device for advertising my slender volume. You are responsible for making it known and sold. Yours, Ella Wheeler, Poetess of, excuse me, Passion."

I hear later that his large, expansive face turned tomato red above a tight starched collar.

A Chicago news article, sent to me by my publisher, announces smugly that Ella Wheeler thinks she has discovered sin. "Civilized man is well aware of the underlying sin that accompanies some questionable love. Must Miss Wheeler dwell on the perverse, the sinister hand of Satan afoot in her prosody?" Another clipping: "This reviewer once lauded Miss Wheeler's galvanizing *Maurine,* a beautiful narrative poem of selflessness and ambition. We touted her as the leader of the popular Milwaukee School of Literature. That judgment may need revision now: Miss Wheeler now is the questionable leader of the Erotic School of Poetry."

The Erotic School of Poetry, indeed. Into the scrapbook goes the clipping.

By now I know exactly what passages so horrify a sober nation.

It is, I know, chiefly the word *passion* alone that does it. And Love:

> *How Does Love Speak?*
> *In the wild words that uttered seem so weak*
> *They shrink ashamed to silence; in the fire*
> *Glance strikes with glance, swift flashing high and higher,*
> *Like lightning that precedes the mighty storm;*
> *In the deep, soulful stillness; in the warm*
> *Impassioned tide that sweeps through throbbing veins*
> *Between the shores of keen delights and pains;*
> *In the embrace where madness melts in bliss,*
> *And in the convulsive rapture of a kiss—*
> > *Thus doth Love speak.*

And this from "Delilah":

She touches my cheek, and I quiver—
It trembles with exquisite pains;
She sighs—like an overcharged river
My blood rushes on through my veins;
She smiles—and in mad-tiger fashion,
As a she-tiger fondles her own.
I clasp her with fierceness and passion,
And kiss her with shudder and groan.

O ghost of dead sin unrelenting,
Go back to the dust, and the sod!
Too dear and too sweet for repenting,
Ye stand between me and my God.
If I, by the Throne, should behold you,
Smiling up with those eyes loved so well,
Close, close in my arms I would fold you,
And drop with you down to sweet Hell!

One minister constructs an entire sermon based on that last line: "And drop with you down to sweet Hell." And this:

Whosoever was begotten by pure love,
And came desired and welcomed into life,
is of immaculate conception.

And one of Richard Dana's most dreaded poems, "Ad Finem":

On the white throat of the useless passion
That scorched my soul with its burning breath,
I clutched my fingers in murderous fashion,
And gathered them close in grip of death;
For why should I fan, or feed with fuel,
A love that showed me but blank despair?
So my hold was firm, and my grasp was cruel—

I meant to strangle it then and there!

I thought it was dead. But with no warning,
        It rose from its grave last night, and came
And stood by my bed till the early morning.
        And over and over it spoke your name.
Its throat was red where my hands had held it
        It burned my brow with its scorching breath
And I said, the moment my eyes beheld it,
        "A love like this can know no death."

For just one kiss that your lips have given
        In the lost and beautiful past to me,
I would gladly barter my hopes of Heaven
        And all the bliss of Eternity.
For never a joy are the angels keeping
        To lay at my feet in Paradise,
Like that of into your strong arms creeping
        And looking into your love-lit eyes.

I know, in the way that sins are reckoned,
        This though is a sin of the deepest dye
But I know, too, if an angel beckoned,
        Standing close by the Throne on High,
And you, down by the gates infernal,
        Should open your loving arms and smile,
I would turn my back on things supernal,
        To lie on your breast a little while.

To know for an hour you were mine completely—
        Mine in body and soul, my own—
I would bear unending tortures sweetly,
        With not a murmur and not a moan.
A lighter sin or a lesser error
        Might change through hope or fear divine
But there is no fear, and hell has no terror
        To change or alter a love like mine.

These are the infamous passages that can make youth reckless and virgins falter. Factory girls — farm girls — abandon virtue for gaslight and perfumed lace.

The pulpits and decent folk term it The Red Book. The Scarlet Book.

My close friends are fearful that I am in danger of being crushed under the weight of public outcry. To them, I seem too calm, too accepting. They watch me from across rooms, over dinner tables, in drawing rooms. I just sit there. That's what they don't understand: I am always so animated, so vocal about everything. I swirl around at social functions, the center. Now I just watch. I say so little. They're afraid I'm inwardly seething. I'm really not. Not at all.

"Everything is all right," I say, when pushed.

They don't have to worry: I am under control, balanced. This is some floating, euphoric dream state that I occupy but am strangely aloof from: some other Ella in some other drifting flow that I can gaze on, can be baffled by, can sympathize with, can smile at. I'm not unhappy although everyone tells me I should be.

"You've acquired a taste for sensation," the Judge says, perhaps understanding, but smiling. He finds the whole brouhaha amusing, remarking that these days people have too much time to enter another's life and condemn.

Famous all over town. I am.

Battered from without, the scapegoat of the sneering moralistic, I discover that my home state draws rank around me. The more the East Coast attacks me — and even upstart Chicago, where the poems were published — the more my insular world of Wisconsin protects me. I'm one of their own, of course. There is even a testimonial for me in Milwaukee, an evening of inflated speech and fruit-punch celebration attended by over five-hundred stalwart Milwaukee citizens, all dedicated to affirming their faith in the moral little country girl — our "talented, hard-working, cheery little songbird" — who made it big. They cheer — some stand on chairs — when I enter. Mr. E. E. Chapin, an acquaintance who organizes the event and declares himself one of my discoverers — I wince at that — begins by saying I am "a representative of the genius of poetry and song, of democracy and progress, of the young America motto on our State coat of arms." Me, as Goddess of Liberty. I make a vow to look at Wisconsin's state coat of arms: what exactly is on it that I now represent?

Wisconsin, one speaker says, is the new Athens. We are the new heartland of American civilization. "Ella is now no longer an unknown girl, a soldier on the frontier, but a literary general, whose words receive attention. Wisconsin is proud of Ella Wheeler."

Out-Swinburne Swinburne indeed! I am the poetess of the prairie. Of the lumber camps.

I stand, bow demurely. I know my face is scarlet. The applause is deafening.

They present me with a purse of five hundred dollars, an astounding collection of money, raised by the proud local citizens, and my hand shakes as I receive it. I am used to five dollar checks, the occasional ten or fifteen dollar check from an Eastern editor who likes this poem or that. But this — this is, well, a king's ransom.

This is the stuff of lost cities of gold.

Days later, still basking in the glory, I receive a brief letter from Ed back home, posted two days after my great evening. The whole family has read with enthusiasm the account of my success. Proud of me, thrilled, they will be sending on the clippings to Sister Sarah, now trying to create a life in Illinois with her husband and children.

"But, Ella," Ed ends the letter, "we read of your account as we dash around the kitchen. Outside there is a fearsome rain, the worst in years, they say, and the kitchen is filled with stove pans and cow pails to catch the falling rain leaking through the old roof. It would be comic were it not so sad."

He apologizes for bringing up the real world.

Sitting in Milwaukee, lingering over steaming coffee and buttery poppy-seed rolls in a breakfast room where servants quietly ask me if I am content, I reread these lines. For a moment I close my eyes: lightning flashes, blue-black sparks, yellow light flashes. No, I think, no. There is always the dark strain, I tell myself. In the very midst of my success — my antidote to the ugliness of accusations of sin and immorality, my glory moment — I am reminded of a life I can never leave behind. I am jotting notes for a poem, idly playing with some fanciful light verse about morning and summer calm and the end of spring, but now I write lines I'll later transfer to my journal. *This is a testing. I am chosen for something larger than this.* As I write the line, I lift my hand, stretch it out before me. Pointing. But because I am in Milwaukee, I am now the epicenter of this city, its literature, so I point to the sky somewhere above this bright and sunny morning room. Somehow it makes me feel good.

I use the five hundred dollars to rebuild the roof on the old homestead. This makes Ed happy. At last the oaken buckets can be moved back to the barn. There is also an addition built, but that is my idea. What money remains — what I intended for new ball gowns and dinner dresses, for finery like silk gloves and high-button carriage boots — goes for the needs of the growing number of nieces and nephews who now live in the homestead. My brother is a failed farmer, and the children need clothing, books, playthings. When it is all spent, I have nothing left for myself. I stare at the debit ledger. Five hundred dollars, a gracious gift — to me, for me. In my journal: *What about me?* But, I tell myself, there now is silence at home.

For now.

But then, as the weeks go on, I find myself spending more and more time at home, away from the city. I purposely choose to stay home. The mails are filled with invitations. Too many, in fact. They overwhelm — keep me from writing. Telegrams, in fact, arrive, delivered by a young man who stares at me as though I am a freak of nature. Sign this, sign this. Everyone wants at me. And it isn't as though the homestead offers solace and comfort: it is a bloody battlefield these days with my mother striking out at her daughter-in-law, Ed's annoying wife. The two women are at cross purposes constantly, firing salvos and then nursing wounds. Mama lashes out, then broods, sullen. Ed's wife Delphia whines and then weeps, runs from supper tables in frenzies. I sit, watching it all. At least they leave me alone now, most of the time. I hide in my room.

Some days I walk away from the farm, through the fields, hiding in groves of thick sugar maples that ring the land, reading and composing. Everything seems too quick a pace — the life too frantic in the city — and while I crave it, I know something is slipping away from me, some momentum. Everything whirls about me. *Swept away,* I write in my journal. *I am swept away. I do not want to disappear.* Am I a genius? Should I believe my friends? I am, frankly, fearful that I may lose the mysterious genius of creation. What is happening to me? Everything seems tenuous now — as frail as a spider's web on an evergreen bush. My routine of two poems a day — sometimes as many as five or six — sometimes falters in the big city. One distraction leads to another. The city scares me. All the parties. And stores. And stares. In my journal: *Why do I miss the pleasure of despair? Must I write from brooding?*

"Go home," a friend says, when I stay too long in the city. "You look unhappy here."

But once home my father asks, "When are you going back?" He doesn't mean it as it sounds, I know — he simply is surprised that I am home at all.

But I stay, a ghostlike presence much of the time, skirting the domestic skirmishes of the kitchen and hearth, avoiding the grabbing children I love but find bothersome and sometimes anonymous, barely talking to my father who is drifting into permanent melancholia. Some days, disoriented, he talks to walls. My mother just shakes her head. She, too, always looks unhappy.

I walk the fields. The poetess in the pasture, in farm boots caked with cow manure. How romantic.

At night, unable to sleep in the dark, close room, I stare wide-awake at the dark ceiling. The rafters are just above my head. Across the hall one of the children is groaning in her sleep, the three year old named Ella after me, the cute one who clings to me, drools on me, bats her eyelids like a vixen.

I rise, throw a light blanket over my shoulders, tuck it in, and slip out of the house. It's a dark night and the faraway horizon is shades of indigo and coal black, with a pale summer moon making the landscape shadowy and dim. Clutching the blanket around me, I wander, avoiding the barn — I don't want a clamoring from the animals that will raise the family — but I wander in my bare feet along the dirt path that leads to the spring well. It has been years since I have felt the cool, packed soil under my bare feet. It is quiet, quiet. Suddenly, involuntarily, I gasp: a rush of emotion sweeps through me, and I begin to cry. I jam my fists into my eyes.

The ground is cold beneath my feet. The bottom, I think — and cringe.

This morning I received a letter from a publisher in London where *Poems of Passion* has just been published: it is immediate success, even more so than in the States, he says, with British readers embracing my lines. There is a request that I visit England as soon as possible. There is talk of a royal audience. Someone in the royal family loves one of the poems. "Solitude" is sung in the dance halls. *Maurine* is now in a third printing there. Already the ripple effect suggests a Wheeler mania, a flourish of excitement. "England is your next conquest," the letter ends.

I don't understand any of this.

England: I've never been there, of course, yet I conquered it. The paradox shakes me.

In the darkness I flush, a little embarrassed. And then, biting my lower lip, closing my eyes, I start to sway, twirling around, dragging the loose blanket like a misshapen cape. For the first time the impact truly hits me, overwhelms. I am famous. What I always expected — yet feared might not happen — has indeed happened. I am famous — will be famous — in England. Throughout the world. I'll travel to unknown lands, I know — just as I always dreamed. Just as my mother always wanted for herself but now wishes for her daughter. The Orient. Will they read my verse in Japan? In China? The north of Africa? In the Spanish speaking countries? In translation? French — I need to study French. I make a mental note: learn French.

My body trembles, and I think I might fall.

My heart races wildly. I recite a poem from *Poems of Passion* to the wind, mumbling the words:

In the still jungle of the senses lay
A tiger soundly sleeping, till one day
A bold young hunter chanced to come that way.

"How calm," he said, "that splendid creature lies,
I long to rouse him into swift surprise!"
A well aimed arrow, shot from amorous eyes,

And lo! the tiger rouses up and turns,
A coal of fire his glowing eyeball burns,
His mighty frame with savage hunger yearns.

He crouches for a spring; his eyes dilate—
Alas! bold hunter, what shall be thy fate?
Thou canst not fly, it is too late, too late.

Once having tasted human flesh, ah! then,
Woe, woe unto the whole rash world of men,
The awakened tiger will not sleep again.

I scream into the night, still twirling, but weak now. The awakened tiger will not sleep again.

I hear movement in the house, see the flicker of a kerosene lamp, and I duck into the shadows. I watch as my mother plods to the necessary out back, her body all angles and purpose. My mother: my mother praises me without a smile, bids me travel without any blessing. Watches me without softness in her face. All her kindnesses are like orders or dismissals. She lacks the gentle edge, I know. Forgive her. It isn't her fault: some bitter vein has been tapped deep in her blighted, unrealized soul — made worse by the absence of God — and what results is a tide of despair and bile.

I shudder. This is my mother. She's in me.

I refuse the thought, hungering for the sensation I just experienced — the goddess screaming in the jungle against a deep-black night sky.

No, I think, not this time. Let me stand here in the pitch of night, swirling among mild breezes under an apricot moon, let me twirl around and around, a little girl again, barefoot girl with dreams of the moon, because I am famous. Yes, I am famous.

Without thinking I scream into the night air: "Yes!"

Startled, I listen to see if my mother, far away from me now, hidden behind an outhouse door, hears me. But there is silence in the yard. It seems I am just talking to the moon.

Lover

1884

Courtship and marriage are religious events because they succeed only in the blessed realm of spirituality. Issues of carnality, of conventional romance, of legal documentation, are trivial: what matters is the voice of God through the touch of hands and the brush of lips. That is the ideality of Love. There is no other Love. If you listen to the voice of Eros, turn aside: lies, disharmony, fear. I will never marry if I cannot marry Spirit. There is no other spouse worthy of the name.

— Ella Wheeler, "Advice to Young Maidens on Marriage" *Good Housekeeping,* 1880

"**R**obert who?" Abigail asks, confused. I smile. Indeed, I do have a secret. I've had it for almost a year. There is actually someone in my life. At last.

In fact, I become engaged the week *Poems of Passion* is issued. In secret. I've told no one about him — not even my closest friends. I don't want his name in the press, especially now that my name is bandied about so frequently in the news columns. It's the secret love I won't — can't, really — write about. Romance, on the page, is simple: you love, you lose, you fall again, you marry sometimes, you bloom, you die, you grieve. The stations of love, a *bas relief* of the powerful heart. But I wasn't ready for the confusions brought on by the attentions of a flesh-and-blood man, one who is stolid and earthbound. Quite frankly, I wasn't ready to be so out of control.

I have enough to keep my life in balance as the *Poems of Passion* controversy swirls around me.

Robert and I met just when I became part of the Milwaukee social scene, in the rosy, glowing years after *Maurine*. In those rhapsodic days I was so intoxicated with my own celebrity that I scarcely had time to notice the world around me, so certainly I had little time for the vainglorious attentions of the scattered, flattering men I met through my burgeoning social circle. Instead I smiled and nodded through the attentions of so many hangers on.

I didn't realize I was waiting for Robert.

But I didn't expect him to be a mundane, heavy-breathing sales representative for a silverplate company in Connecticut, this very large man, wide as a door frame. The only thing he brandished was that tremendous — but fashionable — walrus mustache, something that covers his upper lip with the emphasis of a summer storm thunderbolt. You just can't take your eyes off it. I quite like it. Within months my little aside at a party — *Kissing a man without a mustache is like eating an egg without salt* — becomes the witticism of the hour. Well, at least in Milwaukee.

I almost missed him, but that, I know, was Fate testing me. I am in town for a round of social visits, a madcap spree of activity, much of it centered on myself, visiting at the home of Colonel and Mrs. Benjamin on Prospect Avenue. One Friday afternoon I go shopping, leisurely picking up gloves and ribbons for a dinner party. Late in the afternoon, suddenly conscious of my total absorption in the millinery shop I've lingered in, I rush out, stop on the sidewalk, glance at the sun in the sky, and realize the hour is late. I know the Colonel is a stickler for punctuality. I want no more sharp glances from him as I scurry in, out of breath, packages flying. I lack a watch.

So, hurriedly, I step into Nelson Jewelry, an establishment long familiar to me. I've bought baubles from him from time to time, especially the emerald brooch I no longer wear.

I am harried. "Mr. Nelson," I say, leaning around some woman idling over a necklace. I do manage to glance at it: a thin sliver of silver filigree with a cluster of garnets. It is so undramatic and predictable. I wonder why some craftsman bothered to finish it. But no matter. I would never wear such a plain trifle. My jewelry flashes like winter lightning.

"Miss Wheeler," the man says. "A pleasure." He half bows.

Apologizing for interrupting, I ask for the time, he gives it — I have more time than I anticipated, but not that much more — and we exchange a few pleasantries. I rush out of the store, a little more relaxed now, and head back to the grand house two streets over. Of course, I thought nothing of the event, nor had I been conscious of anyone in the shop except for myself, the frumpy woman considering the necklace, and the sprightly Mr. Nelson, always a cheerful man, famous for his recitations at the pianoforte.

To be honest, I hadn't noticed the large gentleman standing nearby, rifling through his display carryall, sorting and unsorting silverplate samples. He tells me months later that he looked up as I strode in, and he stood there, mesmerized, as I demanded the time. His eyes followed me. Such a bold, determined woman, he later says, smiling. All purpose and beauty.

"Who was that, if I might ask?" he asked Mr. Nelson.

Mr. Nelson smiled. "Mr. Wilcox, that is our dear Miss Wheeler, a poetess of some reputation."

Robert Wilcox has never heard of me — of *Maurine*, and certainly not my temperance diatribes *Drops of Water*. What he did notice were my eyes: they held him. Brown as sun-baked coffee beans, he tells me later, with a luster and flash that suggest a worldliness and a passion.

"Would it be untoward to ask her address?" he asked

Mr. Nelson.

The older man smiled. "I'll obtain it for you."

"If it would be no trouble."

"Not at all." Mr. Nelson grinned. "She's a favorite of mine."

When Robert's first letter arrives a week or so later, it takes me by surprise. I am used to the overstuffed bags of mail — entreaties for poems, for autographs, for money, for favors, for marriage, even pleas that I straighten out my errant life — so the long blue envelope stands out, with its thick clean creamy crispiness, its robin's egg blue tint, its very soberness. He's written my name — *Miss Ella Wheeler* — with a precision that catches my eye. He identifies himself, stating he is writing from the state of Georgia on a rainy Sunday afternoon, and saying: "I know this is questionable, such direct writing to you, and I wish to remain a gentleman in the service and honor of a lady as yourself." He describes a lazy afternoon in his hotel room, the rain beating against the window, the day boring and long. He mentions friends in common, which relaxes me — I happen to like these people a lot — but the letter is just too unseemly. Who is this man? What does he look like? And yet the letter oddly attracts. Not because of the gentle platitudes or the easy gentility, but the casual, worldly charm of his phrases. There is humor: "I was the largest man in the shop but obviously did not occupy your eye corner." I smile at that. I have no idea who he is. And: how fat is he? No, he says large — muscular? Bulky? Bulk, I think. Bulk.

But he doesn't ask for an autograph or a book of poems, and what finally intrigues me is that he never mentions my being a poetess. Ordinarily that would pique me — how I thrive on such facile compliments, I admit it, even as I dismiss them — but this time the omission plainly titillates. Who exactly is this Robert?

May he, he begs, arrange a meeting through a mutual friend?

Of course not.

May we perhaps have an evening of theater, with friends of my choosing?

Of course not.

But I like the way he fashions his letters: an elegant, nobly-styled penmanship, a rarity, I tell myself — a man who takes time with his lettering.

In my leisurely reply I write that any further correspondence is out of the question, unseemly — "I am, after all, a Christian woman" — but at the last moment, pausing — this is one letter I do not dash off, as I usually do with my voluminous correspondence — I leave an opening. "Whatever prompted you to be so forward?" I ask. I smile: when a lady asks a question, a gentleman needs to answer. I love the quandary I place him in — do not write further, but, well, please answer my question.

In his letter he names a day he will be in Milwaukee, but I reply that I will be back home at the farm, which I call "the country place." I wince at that. The country place. My estate.

Good God!

I'm not surprised when he tries again, another letter in the same creamy blue stationery, with that same manicured penmanship. He mentions he was an orphan at seven, raised first by a grandmother and then by his beloved Aunt Hattie after the grandmother died. Briefly, he mentions traveling throughout exotic lands like tsarist Russia and the Bavarian Black Forest. Lord, I think, a far cry from Madison, Wisconsin. Again, I write I cannot meet him. He sends me Thomas a Kempis's *Imitation of Christ*, then *Cross of Burney*, then Theophile Gautier. I keep the books in a special pile, with his letters underneath. I spend long hours with the books, but I realize the words mean nothing: when I scan the words, I find myself trying to construct a picture of how Robert looks. I drift off into romantic reverie, and struggle with the image of an aggressive man.

I was the largest man in the shop.

Then another blue envelope arrives, and this time in-

side is a gift: a slender Oriental paper knife, an exotic bit
of sandalwood and copper, carved with simple designs.
It is a small piece, but beautiful. Looking at it, I tremble.
I stare long and hard at it, biting my lower lip, and the
delicate knife is heavy in my small palm.

I am sitting in my bedroom, my mail strewn around
my feet.

"Enough of this talk behind my back," my father is saying in the family parlor. His voice is loud and strained,
drifting upstairs, and I feel my chest tighten: I know he
is alone in that room. He is speaking to the wall.

My mother, shucking peas in the kitchen, clicks her
tongue loud enough for me to hear. I can hear the banging of a pail against the floor, the slamming of a cup-
board door, the dropping of a dish. My mother, arming
for battle at supper time.

But my mother's skirmishes are not with my father
these days, slowly slipping as he is into a world of his
own, his conversations built on injustices decades gone,
mainly in Vermont, his grasp on the here and now as
unsteady as his hand on a glass of water. No: these days
my mother's battles are pitted against Delphia, Ed's wife,
a scatterbrained woman she considers arrogant and unworthy, an interloper in the household, and each night
there is new altercation and fire. Years back, Marcus left
the farm, taking his wife and two sons to the Dakotas to
run a ranch, but that is, I know, a pioneering move much
like my father's desperate move from Vermont to Wisconsin. Dead end and bleak: hopeless hope. We Wheelers love to choose the darker trail and call it light. My
sister lives in Illinois now, a teacher, the wife of a doctor.
Ed and his wife chose to stay on the farm to conduct personal war with my parents. The children are born with a
regularity that I compare, unhappily, to the springtime
birthing of farm animals.

Later the terrible words are predicable.

"I have a say," Delphia announces, and the words are
somehow a slap in the face of my mother: there can only

be room for one redoubtable Mrs. Wheeler in the dilapidated farmhouse.

"To have a say is to assume some intelligence," my mother says.

"What are you saying?"

My mother addresses the wall. "Another proof of what I'm saying. She doesn't understand plain English."

"I understand that I'm overworked here. You grumble and yell, and Papa needs to be led around. I do it."

"You are not overworked here, Missy."

"My name is Delphia."

"I'm aware of that."

"The long hours serving this —"

"What are you saying?"

"I have children —"

Sarcastic: "And a fit mother truly."

"What does that mean?"

My mother points to a crying child, sitting in a corner, her nose running and her face grimy. "Look at her."

"What are you saying?"

"I'm saying, you are — spent."

"Because children did me in, what with the other things I have to do."

"Like what?"

Delphia waves her hand around. "Keep this place up."

My mother frowns. "Children should be a blessing, not a curse. It's your own doing."

"I do my best."

"Meaning?"

"Meaning I do my best."

Mama gives a fake laugh. "This house is never quiet. I will be an old woman before my time here." Her voice rises. "I am ruined in my own home."

"And me? And Ed? He works like a dog for the crumbs off the table."

"Ella keeps this house afloat," my mother says. "Not Ed."

"Ed is the backbone —"

"Ella's gifts, her money, her —"

On and on. It never stops, replayed, rephrased, morning to night. Sarah Wheeler and Delphia Wheeler only have each other now. Papa is mostly silent, and Ed flees to the barn and the fields.

Upstairs, I hold the paper knife in my hand, and I shake. I hold it in front of me. It glows in the dim light of the room. It's warm to the touch. My fingers trace the circular indentations. A talisman of utter worth and power. I think of distant lands, Arabia, China, sampans, incense, bolts of shimmering silk the color of water, lands out of Ouida and Arabian Nights. "There is no money," Papa says to the wall.

"Look at him," Delphia says. "He's talking to the wall."

My mother shoots back, "So am I."

I travel to Chicago to visit my publisher, and on the day I leave the farm I receive another letter from Robert. He will be in Chicago the very day I arrive. Once there, almost on a whim, with the lingering aura of the scented sandalwood paper knife drifting about me, I send a note to the Grand Pacific Hotel, stating I will be at the Palmer House and he can visit for a half hour. When the messenger leaves with the note, I stop myself: Am I being unwise? But it's too late to call back the note.

We meet in the hotel reception area of the Palmer. I've asked my friend Irma Tallman to pass through, to monitor the brief meeting, to watch for signals. "Help me escape." I am trying to be melodramatic. "If necessary." But somehow I know I won't have to: this, I sense, is a gentleman.

"What if he's mad?" Irma asks, nervous.

"Madness I can deal with," I say. "I just fear dullness."

He is dressed in a severe businessman's suit, charcoal gray, with a simple gold watch fob, and I would think him hopelessly conventional, though smart — he has the air of a man given to authority in the workplace — except for the two rings he wears: filigreed silver, with curious hieroglyphic carvings. Staring at his fingers, I think of vagabondia, of bohemian heroes from faraway romances.

"I didn't think you'd see me," he says, just after sitting across from me. He has a deep voice, an echoey bass, probably the deepest voice I've ever heard. I immediately like his voice — it reminds me of sonorous church bells, deep and round.

"I didn't plan to." I have trouble focusing: thoughts of the penury at home, the fights, come to me. I have left behind a new crisis on the farm: Delphia has broken one of Mama's favorite water pitchers, one carried from Vermont supposedly used during the Revolution.

"Then thank you."

I falter. "I had to be here anyway —"

"Well, thank you." He smiles.

"No, no, I didn't mean it so — glibly. I'm sorry."

"Don't apologize."

"It's just that I didn't plan on seeing you."

He is staring at me. "But your letters are so charming."

"It is one thing to write letters, another thing to have conversation across from a gentleman you don't know." Idly I think of dreadful James Whitcomb Riley and the aborted hotel rendezvous. How different that was! For a second I blush, remembering.

He laughs. "My clumsy prose."

"Not at all," I insist. "You actually do have a flare —"

"You are kind."

"— For words."

"I try."

"You are too modest."

He bows. "Words from a poetess are validation for my inferior pen."

"Not at all."

We smile, then both turn away. I feel stupid. What in the world are we talking about?

We sip lukewarm tea, but I stop after I realize his eyes stare, transfixed, on the raising of my arm to my mouth.

The cups sit there, untouched, on the rosewood inlaid table.

A moment of silence. Then, nervous, I begin again: "You've traveled —"

"— All over," he says, finishing my sentence.

In his letters he mentions he has been to Paris, to London, to the Italian Alps, to Russia, to Vienna. I've memorized the list, drawing mental lines between cities, tracing his itineraries. "I love traveling," he says.

"I haven't," I say.

"Traveled?"

"No."

"But you will."

I smile. "I mean, I've been to Madison, of course, and Milwaukee and — here —"

"You will."

"As I want to. I *plan* to."

I suddenly feel drained. This is just too much work. What can I say to this cosmopolite? In his eyes I'm a small-town hick girl, untutored, with my sentimental verses and my bunch of dried pink roses stuck to a fashionable hat. Here he is, a man of the world, a calm and easy man, a successful mover in the growing American Republic, some new-breed businessman, roaming the country by train, deep into the heartland, with his bag of silverplate. This is America on the move. I have absolutely nothing left to say.

"Are you planning on going to Europe soon?"

I shake my head, unable to speak. Whatever for?

He smiles. "Someday."

"Yes," I say, softly. "Someday."

Then slowly, the deep voice almost a whisper, he talks about his business world but I have trouble following it. International Silver in Connecticut, in a town called Wallingford, is famous for silver and silverplate — exquisite flatware, tea sets, jewelry, silverplate for the common man. A new democracy in the dining room: everyone can afford to be elegant. I stare. But I can't understand his relationship to the firm. He seems to be more than a typical traveling salesman, which at first I think he is. He isn't like the drummers in rumpled suits with battered suitcases I see getting off the trains in Milwaukee. No itinerant peddler, he represents silver *objects d'art*, I realize. He exports culture to the provinces. Not only this, I sense he has his own money — and the leisure time to travel. His attire, I notice, is meticulous and costly.

"I crave an occupation on the road," he says, summing up.

"You've been, well, everywhere."

Suddenly, out of the blue, he announces: "I have family to support."

I gasp, draw my head back. I imagine a dutiful wife and babies settled back in some East Coast city, sheltered under rose arbors, lawn tennis in the afternoon. Here is this roving *roué*, debonair and coy, playing havoc with a simple Midwestern girl. My eyes get wide with alarm. I look for my friend Irma: escape.

"You're married." I can barely say the words.

His eyes get wide now, but filled with laughter. He bursts out laughing, tears forming in the corners of his eyes. A heavy man, he rolls from side to side. "Oh, heaven's no. I don't mean that."

I don't feel like laughing.

He explains. "I only meant I have relatives — aunts and nieces and others — who depend on me. That kind of family. Oh, my. I didn't mean the other." He is in his late thirties, he says, never married. "I swear," he says.

Now I laugh. "I'm sorry. I assume the worst."

"I would never do that to you."

"Of course."

He clears his throat. "I don't ever plan on marrying," he says.

The words hang in the air like a thick curtain. I don't know what to say. I stare past his shoulder: one of the waiters is flirting with a young serving woman, circling her, grinning. They are trying to avoid looking at each other. All right, I think. There really is nothing to say: Robert is purposely telling me something. But why? Why this meeting at all? Why the charming letters, arriving at my home with such regularity, a gentle warm wind against my daily routine?

I think of the oriental paper knife, which I carry in my purse.

I start to say something that comes out a garbled "Me neither," but the words get lost somewhere. Because I know I don't mean them. I want marriage, I know: it has to happen. Of course, I want marriage. If not marriage, then what? An unmarried woman, like Aunt Abigail, barefoot and moody in the farm fields? I don't want to be Emma, serving at her brother's table, waiting for the crumbs to fall. Already I am past thirty, an idea I seldom entertain.

So I just nod.

Then, almost as though we now have nothing to lose, we relax into each other. He sits back, crosses his legs, and the eyes get small and lazy, almost amused. The wide, florid face softens. I settle into the chair, realizing how tense my body has been. My arms and shoulders ache. I begin talking about Milwaukee friends, and my poetry, and *Maurine* — the letters from women naming their daughters after my heroine still arrive daily — and I find myself regaling him with frivolous tales out of society, curious and amusing *faux pas* witnessed from the narrow social world I travel in. Story after story spills out of me — funny, energetic stories — and he leans into me, savoring each anecdote. I feel as though I've known him for the longest time, and I even stare into his face: I like what I see — large, expansive, a dark brooding glance in the eye, a sliver of gold in the walnut brown eyes, the full head of neat and brushed hair, and the whole body leaning forward, towards me, expectant. I can reach out and touch his face. I roll on, and he laughs easily, genuinely.

"Ella, Ella," he says, almost in punctuation to my

ramble, and it is a chuckle, a goading, an affirmation.

I like the way he says my familiar name: he makes it warm and melodic.

I see my friend Irma passing by, looking for a furtive signal — she looks suspicious, her body stiff and obvious — but a casual wave — I hope — of my hand tells her to leave. This is good — all good.

The tea cups sit, untouched, on the table.

We talk throughout the long afternoon.

Finally he pauses. "My dear Miss Wheeler, Ella, I'm keeping you. You promised me a half hour."

I look across the room at the grandfather clock. Vaguely I noted the quarterly ringing of the Westminster chimes, but it hasn't mattered. Afternoon shadows have fallen in the lovely room. Evening shadows creep up the curtains. Now I smile. We've been talking for over three hours. Time now is rich and completely mine, to savor and control. Time is an ally now, a partner.

"It's been a pleasure," I say to Robert, leaning forward. "It was all mine."

We bow to each other, for a moment back to being stiff and uncomfortable, that vast tract of easy familiarity disappearing for a second. Then we both smile.

Something has happened to me this afternoon. Deep inside me something has shifted, turned. My body hums. I know it with the force of a poem that comes to me in the night.

Alone on the train, returning home, I can feel the depression building, like awful flood tide, sweeping over and into me, crushing, smothering. Back at the farm, I am morose: I walk in circles, distracted, unable to settle down. Later, tucked into my cold, tight room, the sandalwood paper knife on the night stand, where I can grasp it — my dark, powerful talisman — I am happy the house is unusually quiet, with all the family in bed. Quiet, quiet, with only the night wind seeping into the old woodwork. Wide awake, tense, I am incredibly lonely. I am stranded here, marooned. Out there — in what hotel? On what train headed East? — is a handsome, breezy man with a voice so deep it vibrates. I've never met a man with a voice so low, so resonant. Now, recalling it, I imagine thunder, catastrophe, distant suns exploding. I twist in the narrow bed, my arms folded around my chest.

Is this desire?

I'm unable to sleep. This will be a sleepless night, all nerves and jitters. At my desk, sitting in my flannel nightgown in the early morning, I leaf through my published volumes, fingering the gold-gilt spines. In the past just holding them made me whole. Now, turning to my poetry for solace, rereading verses I love — I can remember when every line was written — they seem empty, devoid of any real emotion. Meter without substance: the poetry of dead souls.

In the quiet of the night I hear my father's labored snoring, one of the children sighing in his sleep, the faint nightmare meow of a cat. I imagine I hear shingles falling from the roof, the *creak creak creak* of house mice.

I'm the daughter of the black-dirt plowed field, the profane lumber camp, the brilliant harvest moon, the square-dance at roughneck Miller's Hall. He is Paris avenues and gaslight and tropical sun. A bulky Ulysses, sailing into strange, uncharted horizons.

But I am determined. I once wrote — and still believe:

> *One ship drives east and another drives west*
> *With the selfsame winds that flow*
> *'Tis the set of sails and not the gales*
> *Which tells us the way to go.*

This has always been my philosophy — *is* my philosophy. My own driven life.

I hear gasping sounds from across the hall. My father is talking in his sleep, mumbling something about the wind that rips out the heart of the night. He fears weather now. Listening, I think I hear my mother sigh in the darkness. I close my eyes, but all I see are quick, breathless lightning flashes, darts of rainbow light blazing through the black ink of my mind. The earth holds us, the dark earth holds us on the jagged rocks and the dried clumps of frozen grass and winter ice.

A few days later, in the morning's mail, there is the familiar blue envelope, the same thick creamy linen. For a second, holding it, I believe I will faint: I grab the table end. Carefully I open it. Inside is the letter I dread. "Dear Ella, I know how horribly disappointed you were after seeing my ugly phiz. I saw your disgust in your eyes, but you might, at least, drop a fellow gently and not with a sickening thud. You might, at least, write and tell me if you received the book I sent just before we met." He mentions the innumerable good dinners that have added weight "that is neither becoming or comfortable." He is, he knows, a tremendously large man, someone who occupies every corner of a chair — or room. "My life is a failure. I have burned the candle of life at both ends — most recklessly." But I — I, the "charming authoress" — is star shine, a jewel herself — "you sow the warm earth, with gems of flowers, and stimulate them with bright sunshine, and kiss so gladly those that bud and bloom." I read and reread the letter, holding it so tight I actually tear off a corner. I am stunned by his modesty. At night in my journal: *He doesn't understand his true beauty, his power. He is all the tiger of the blood.*

I have no choice now. I write back. So we begin a quaint epistolary romance of sorts, removed and genteel, so much left unsaid, but a submerged romance nevertheless. I'm afraid to have him read my published verse, fearful of what it will tell him about me. But he asks for my books. I send my *Maurine* to him. He loves it. Or says he does.

I consult a psychic in Milwaukee, a skittish woman named Mrs. Porter. I've seen other card readers, but they know me. So I disguise myself in a garish red wig, and

Mrs. Porter talks of carnivals and stage revues and bearded ladies. I bristle. Then she stops, startled by her own words. She actually giggles. She says: "Love the size of a mountain is waiting."

That one line is somehow salvation for me.

Another friend reads my palm: "Love is coming with spring rain."

In April he makes a sudden return to Milwaukee, staying at the Plankinton House. I send a note, telling him where I will be staying in the city. He sends a basket of yellow tulips, with a plea for a brief visit. I consent, reluctantly. When he arrives early, I meet him in a simple borrowed housedress — my trunk has not yet arrived from the depot — and he lingers throughout the afternoon. In my ill-fitting housedress, without powder or finery, I relax. We could be old friends meeting for lunch. I look like a woman ready to scour dishes or knead dough for bread. But near the end of the visit, Robert reaches out and picks up a teacup. I am talking, but suddenly the quick movement stops me. I find myself staring at his fingers, and my words hang in the air. I am mesmerized. The long, thick fingers, with the hairy knuckles and the stubby tops, all hard angle and bone, a large man's bulky, ungraceful fingers — I am totally enthralled by them. I think: if these fingers could touch my face, my neck, I would surely faint.

The next day he writes his first overt love letter.

I tremble when I hold it: after all, I know, deep in my heart, that I am hopelessly in love myself.

Eventually the time arrives for his visit to the farm. I've delayed long enough, ignoring the subtle hints in his letters.

But the dreaded visit gives me nightmares. My old restlessness returns, that same sensation of being smothered under the rafters of the roof. He is to come at the end of spring, the worst time so far as I'm concerned, although, truth to tell, any season is the wrong season. Spring at the farm is thick, sloppy mud, the bittersweet odor of rutting animals, the spreading of manure on freshly sowed fields, the upturning of rotten leaves. The most I can hope for is that the green of spring — the budding sugar maples, the boughs of fragrant lilac, the wild flowers in the hills, all those banks of violets and buttercups — will soften the stark landscape.

Anticipating the visit I hire contractors to build an addition to the house, a pleasant room where guests can be entertained. But problems immediately arise. A war between my father and the builders erupts. Standing in their way, he argues constantly with them, arms folded over his chest, hiding their tools, sabotaging their work. Everything has to be done by Robert's visit. This is my intent. But my father delays it all, setting back the work for days. Lumber mysteriously disappears, later discovered hidden in the barn. Saws and hammers have to be kept under lock and key. Boxes of nails are found under the milk pails.

"Shoddy," he screams at Ole Swensen.

Swenson simply stares, lays down his hammer, starts to walk away.

"I beg you," I plead, stepping in, rushing from the parlor. And Ole agrees to resume the hammering.

I am frazzled, irritable, always on the edge of tears. "I'll whip their weight in wildcats," my father declares, shaking his fist. I supervise the construction but nothing works: I take the buggy for a brief visit to Emma's house and when I return I find the builders pouting and red-faced, my father flaying his arms, as though to ward off incredible demons. No work has been done. The addition remains a sagging skeleton of empty window frame and piled lumber.

"See what has happened," my mother says of Papa. "We have one more child in the house — to join — those." And she points with horrid accusation at the gabbing, fidgeting grandchildren. Her daughter-in-law, to be sure, is nearby, listening, and that battle begins.

The supper table is stone silence.

Finally the farm is in order — the addition sparkling and clean, the last sawdust swept up hours before the visit. Rich red damask draperies soften the boxlike feeling. But I know the house looks like it has grown an unneeded appendage, a dead tree stump with a tender shaft of new green. Nothing can alter that: so be it, I think.

I buy a new hat for Papa, a trim neat derby, but he refuses to wear it. "I plan to die in my familiar one," he says. Angry, I burn his old one. It's a rash, stupid gesture. And he is filled with rage. I turn away from my family's accusing eyes. Mama mumbles, "You've done a cruel thing, Ella." I don't care. I will feel guilt later — that I know. For now, I don't care.

Robert is on his way.

Robert is the conscious gentleman. He carries gifts of monogrammed silver for my parents, windup wooden toys for the children, he smiles constantly, he bows, he compliments, he fawns. Everything is lovely, and each thing is lovelier than the last. Every moment is worthy of a sudden, deeper intake of breath. Seemingly dazzled by the Lombardy poplars on the walk, he stares as though looking at trees for the first time. My mother serves fresh egg nog, and he declares it the world's smoothest, creamiest. The slight hint of grated nutmeg is inspired. Oddly, I think, it doesn't come off as phony or even unctuous. He makes it seem natural and matter-of-fact. Suddenly I believe this is not an act: this is some sort of reverence.

I find myself gawking at him, as at a circus. Words — truth to be told — fail me.

"Mrs. Wheeler, I see where Ella gets her looks." It is a difficult line to say, I realize, for Mama bears little resemblance to me. My mother is shriveled now, a small bony woman, with a tight humorless face, all wrinkles and anger. But even in this withered face there is no memory of my own small-boned face with its round edges. I missed the violet shade of her eyes — which makes her face so memorable. My eyes, at best, are the hue of summer mud. Robert's careful gallantry pays off because Mama beams for the first time in months. It sickens me a bit: Are we all that desperate? Are we all so transparent — so easy?

Do I act this way?

But any attempted conversation with Papa comes to nothing. "How are you, Mr. Wheeler?" Robert extends his hand.

Nothing. My father glares.

"It's an honor, sir."

Silence.

Then: "My hat," he says.

"Excuse me, sir?"

"My hat."

"It's all right," I interrupt.

"My hat."

He has told me he won't speak a word to Robert until his hat — the real hat, not the dandyish confection I gave him this morning — is placed on his shiny balding head. "Naked without it, Ella," he says, almost in tears.

Robert doesn't mind the silence, smiling through it all. I prepared him for my seventy-year-old father's rapid slipping into dotage. I know I talked too much about it, boring him. Pleading somehow. He understands, he tells me, because he's seen a beloved grandmother take that same sad route. "An awful journey," he says. In her last days she remembered being with Jesus at the well, and He had told her everything she'd ever done. That was her last and constant memory. Nothing else remained.

Now Robert shakes the old man's hand, reaching out for it, though Papa tries to pull back, as though contaminated by something foul.

Robert smiles.

"The new room is lovely," Robert says. He is standing in the square, church-like room.

"Lovely," my mother echoes. "It's what Ella wanted.

It's her money that keeps us."

"Mama, please."

"It's true, sad to tell. Upturn the normal order of things."

"It's lovely. Plain lovely."

"Nothing plain about it," she says. "It's Queen Victoria's throne room."

Robert changes the subject. "Planting time, Mr. Wheeler?"

No answer.

Ed's children get underfoot, peevish and annoying. This morning, imploring, I asked Delphia to please keep the children out of sight. Delphia, always helpless, now watches them tumble in from the kitchen. The noise in the room is deafening. One stumbles into Robert, dirties a pants cuff. The giggling children run around the large man as though he is a harvest maypole. "Ella's fella. Ella's fella," they chant. I freeze. I know Ed's been mouthing this puerile phrase behind my back, mockingly, and obviously his children have appropriated it. Wonderful timing, to be sure. But Robert laughs. "I'm a toy," he says, looking as though he enjoys this. One of the children hiccoughs.

My mother smiles. I can't. Her head follows the wild children's antics.

Later, strolling alone with him across the green pasture, I begin to relax. We are away from the house. My dull headache is easing. Grimly I think: perhaps I can survive this horrific day. I wanted the day seamless, but over — Robert safely on the train.

"I wanted to come here," Robert says. "To see where you were raised."

"It's dreadful," I say, flatly.

"Oh, it isn't," he says.

"I am sorry."

"No, don't," he says. "It's not. It's just what they have to do with their lives."

"It's so — ordinary."

"It's not ordinary — it's just a family trying to survive."

"Everything is so — empty."

"But it isn't really."

"Look, Robert."

"But I have." He smiles.

"What must you think?" I look at him.

"Why does it matter?"

"It does."

"You don't have to impress me, Ella. You should know that by now."

"I know, I know. But I wanted everything so right for you."

"This is just the way things are — here. It *is* right. Come on. Look."

"I know, but they drive me mad sometimes."

Robert laughs. "Your family is like every other family — sometimes a pain. Every family drives everybody crazy. That's what families do."

"Robert—"

"But you're the worst off here." His voices lowers.

"What?"

"It's in your face. Your anger at them."

"I can't help it."

"Of course you can. It's tearing you apart."

"I can't help it."

"Of course you can. Listen to yourself. You're the one around here with the imagination."

"Robert—"

"They made you the famous poet you are," he says, interrupting. He waves his hand back to the farmhouse, and I turn, following his fingers. I see what I always see: decay and poverty and ugliness. I can't help it. There is nothing beautiful here. I don't even have to look at it: it's locked in my eyesight like a familiar picture. Unchanging. Robert is grinning. "This is where you come from, Ella. This is your corner of America."

"It's just so pinched."

"They are good people," he says, simply.

I feel I'm going to cry.

"I know," I say, slowly. "I do love them."

"Of course you do."

"I worry about them. But they tax me."

"You're going to have a life rich and different from them. Keep that in mind. You already do. If you hold something against them, if you resent them, you'll stay here with them, no matter how far you go away from here. Fame won't take away the bile. You'll stay locked in this house, a prison."

I look at him, and I'm flushed with joy. Here he is, understanding me, this big overflowing man, meticulous in a travel suit, beads of sweat on his brow, this big man, understanding me.

Behind him is farm land, awakening with spring, with tender shoots speckling the black soil. He stands against a backdrop of pale blue sky. This is, I know, a picture.

"Out here I sometimes feel in touch with God," I say. "When I'm walking in these fields. This is God's good work here—this view."

"A spring day," he says. He looks into the sky.

I smile. "All the dead must wish to come back in spring. When the plants grow."

"God's season," he says, and I look to see if he's being sarcastic, cynical. No: there is something reverential about him now. He pauses. "Sometimes, on days like this, I believe the spirits of my dead loved ones are with me."

I tremble. "You believe in the psychic world?" I wait.

"Everything is possible in God's kingdom."

His words thrill me.

He smiles. "I have a confession. A spiritualist in Baltimore — the wife of a friend — read my cards."

"And?"

"And she talked of me looking westward every chance I get."

I grin.

I draw in my breath. Can this man be real? So different — so perfect. He is the poem I wrote before I ever met him.

She had looked for his coming as warriors come,
With the clash of arms and the bugle's call;
But he came instead with a stealthy tread,
Which she did not hear at all.

She had thought how his armor would blaze in the sun,
As he rode like a prince to claim his bride;
In the sweet dim light of the falling night
She found him at her side.

She had dreamed how the gaze of his strange, bold eye
Would wake her heart to a sudden glow;
She found in his face the familiar grace
Of a friend she used to know.

She had dreamed how his coming would stir her soul,
As the ocean is stirred by the wild storm's strife;
He brought her the balm of a heavenly calm,
And a peace which crowned her life.

"Show me your favorite childhood spots," he says.

Laughing, I take him to the little ridge where as a child I used to stand and point to Milwaukee. Robert takes my hand and moves it, as though I'm still a child. "Relax your arm," Robert says. He begins to move my arm, as though he's a puppeteer. "There," he says, "That's Chicago. And there's — that's New York. I live just north of New York over there." He is moving my arm around at will. "Heaven," he says, laughing, extending my arm to the sky's zenith.

"France," I request, and he raises my arm to the horizon, past imaginary seas and distant ports.

He rotates my arm. "And the world. The North Pole."

"Cold," I say.

I am so comfortable with him. It's the only word I can use. He makes me feel natural with myself. Here I am, in the middle of a visit I most dreaded, most feared — and he makes me so relaxed. We're playing childhood games here. He makes me ashamed that I feel ashamed. To Robert, it is all a world of ebb and flow, a flux that takes us along for the ride. Here's a man comfortable with himself, I think. It reminds me of how uncomfortable I am with myself — so often. So awkward, so afraid of the censorious glance of the stranger.

Behind me cows groan, a goat brays, and one of the children is bawling in the house. We have to return there, for a small lunch Ed's wife has supervised. I don't expect much. I know that Robert will praise burnt wood, if served, and, oddly, even enjoy it.

The day now has a serenity about it.

I tell him about my parents believing I was pointing to the moon. "I'd stand right here and point." I dig a toe into the soil. I say how they secretly called me — affectionately — Ella Moon.

"You were pointing to the moon," he said.

"No," I laugh, "I told you. Milwaukee."

"No," he says again, shaking his head with emphasis. "A girl like you, the little child who dreams and imagines and composes poetry about worlds she's never met, that child is pointing at the moon."

There is nothing I can say.

"I'm going to call you Ella Moon," he says.

"Oh, please, no," I say, quickly. "It reminds me too much of this place."

"That's why I'm going to do it."

"But Robert—"

He winks. "But like your parents I'll only do it in private. I promise."

We marry a year later, on May 2, 1884. Our ceremony is purposely a small one, a quiet one, held with just a few friends in attendance, in Milwaukee. Colonel and Mrs. Benjamin offer their home. I surprise my friends who think I'd crave celebration, newspaper reporters, fanfare, trumpets, tintype. The reason is simple: Robert says no. This has nothing to do with my poetry. In response to a friend, I say, "I will not read poetry that day." Then I smile. "I might, however, write one."

The local press does get wind of it, which is not surprising: one guest is a local newspaper editor, the same one who broke the story of the *Poems of Passion* scandal a year before. The published news account talks of my wearing a handsome traveling costume, very smart, and Robert "being about forty years of age, tall, dark and handsome, a gentleman in every sense of the word." It is society page hyperbole, but it is on the front page. Famous all over town.

No one questions why my parents and my brothers and sister are not here. Not one blood relative comes. I know my father has grown to like Robert—has, like a country philosopher, termed him a huckleberry above a persimmon, a back country expression of real praise, I know. But I do not invite them. I know it sounds harsh, terrible. But there have been too many hints that I not do so. "Out of place" — from Delphia. "If we have to, I suppose" — from Mama. So it isn't done. Mama never travels with my father anymore because she fears his conduct in public. My brothers are tight-lipped about the whole thing.

"Are you sure?" Robert asks.

"Oh, I'm sure," I say.

Robert wants them at the ceremony.

I do, but I don't. They don't come.

On our honeymoon night, tucked into a top-floor suite at the hotel, I lie awake long after Robert falls into a tremendous, snoring sleep. For a while I am unable to concentrate, so conscious am I of the presence of a man in my own room, and so large a man, whose echoey night noises fill the very corners. I am happy, but I will go mad, I think, and then I realize I am in love. I mouth the words in the dark. They are true. The idea tempers my annoyance. I watch Robert sleeping: a peaceful sleep, totally content, the blankets rising like wind rippling the summer wheat.

I'm thirty-four. Robert is forty. We're no longer children.

Lying in bed, waiting for sleep, dreamy with the day's bliss and congratulation, with the early evening passion, I think I will be able to sleep now. I'm happy. But for a second I am overwhelmed with the sounds made by a contented man, sounds which push me into the corners of the room, and experience that same smothering feeling I've had so often since childhood. It makes me furious, the return of that dark sensation — held to the earth, a pillow to the face, the eyes closed against terror, the lungs gasping for breath. Smothered: lost in a cavern. *I can't breathe.* No, I think, not now. No, no. Now I am free of it. *I don't want that now.*

And then, as when I was a child, I escape such darkness by dreaming of my poetry, the gentle easy rhymes that come so quickly and happily to me. Even without words, the rhythm of poetry clicks in my head. The East: fame. I'm going East—like Twain, Howells, Bret Harte, homespun Western girl going East, too. Celebration: publication: sales. These rhymes save me — will bring me fame and money and glory.

My body starts to relax. I am headed East, land of Longfellow and Emerson and Whitman. I sense sleep start to fall on me, and my sighing begins. Famous, I think. I shall be even more famous. Anonymity is a pit you can't get out of. A corner in a dark room. The sense of myself fills the room now, and the heavy sighing of Robert disappears. There is only a poetess in the grand bedroom. I fall asleep to iambic tetrameter. ABBA. No words yet, just meter and rhyme, clicking in my head like the *chug chug chug* of a train. Robert my new husband is also somewhere in the room, sleeping. But it doesn't matter: the intimacy of my own iambs lulls me into dreams.

Winifred
1885

I can name only one word in all the English language that is fraught with such power and spirit that there can be no close second. And the word is Mother. It must be said as a prayer — breathless, trembling, with awe. I shudder when I consider the wayward mother, the sinful mother, the neglectful mother, and the ice-cold mother. These species are oxymoronic — after all, mother is another face of God. . .
— Ella Wheeler, "Letter to a Newly-Wed Woman," *Frank Leslie's Weekly*, 1881

We spend our first summer at a small beach cottage Robert owns on Thimble Island off Stony Creek, in Branford, off the coast of Connecticut. For me, it's an experience I've only dreamed of, this world of beach sand and sea spray. I become intoxicated with the sun-drenched ocean — I've hungered for waves and tides and sunsets, I tell him, all those landlocked years in Wisconsin. How many poems of mine talked of oceans I'd never seen? I promised myself — and my mother — that someday we'd see tides rising, watch squawking seagulls soaring, watch the moon reflecting on the water like a field buttercup under her chin. Robert and I plan to spend only a week here — Robert dislikes the cottage — but the twilight drag of the water and the simmering heave of the horizon makes us linger, the visit growing longer and longer.

This is, of course, a honeymoon.

I take up swimming. Daily, before dawn sometimes, I hurl myself into crashing waves, and let the sun lull me into dreams. In the hot August afternoon, I lie on the burning sand, drunk with heat and the lapping sounds of the waves at my toes. Swimming, I insist, is the perfect exercise because it takes you away from land. The shore holds you with its mundane and pesky problems. The sea doesn't care. The ocean is constant movement, renewal. Endless space. "My mother would not approve," I tell Robert, because she insists only women careless with their reputations swim. I don't care. I stare out over Long Island Sound, where the slate-gray sky hits the water and the fog settles in. *I was born in the wrong land,* I write in my journal. *I am not clay, but salt water. I am island, not acre. I am seagull, not wren.* This is where I belong. This is where I want to die.

But not yet.

In October, with the first chilly autumn wind and the turning of the leaves into kaleidoscopic color, we settle into a rented house on Colony Street in Meriden, a modest industrial city up the river from New Haven. Robert's connection with International Silver, housed in the area, demands his residence here. We arrive at night, without our trunks, and the city streets seem vacant and deadly to me. One carriage moves slowly by us, the driver swearing at and whipping his frantic horses. I cringe: I despise any cruelty to animals. This is not a good omen, I know.

I panic. Meriden seems too isolated, coming as it does after the fearful but lovely isolation of the small cottage at Thimble Island. There, at least, the ocean went on forever. Worse, Meriden doesn't have the academic feel of New Haven with its gothic ivy, nor does it have the literary leanings and robust theater life of New York. It just seems to be — well, nowhere. It's just — here. It's a city that no one seems to move to. Like Westport, back home, it's a place you dream of leaving. To top it all off, across the street is the notorious Connecticut State School for

Boys, and from my front porch, each long day, I can see the regimented incorrigible lads being disciplined, marching military fashion to their chores. They seem so horribly Prussian, uniformed and terribly thin, their singsong yelled responses to commands wafting onto my quiet porch. They seem a regiment from a boy's war.

One night I dream America is at war.

"There are good people here," Robert says, watching my face during my first days in the rambling house. I nod, obedient. The air is different here: still, acrid, faintly smoky, far from the briny wind of the seashore.

I watch the days go by slowly, battling waves of depression. I am becoming frightened: what has happened? Robert himself seems different now, less flowing, less jovial, less confiding. At times he seems too quiet, almost moody. He sits in his den, smoke circling his head, and the account books pile up in front of him. I can see the top of his head — and all that cigar smoke.

I worry about money. But my pen is idle.

One night, coming to bed, Robert speaks of a vision he has had: an old woman in a rumpled gray Shaker bonnet and long gray gown passes through the upper hall. She appears for a second, taking him by surprise, and then disappears into the walls. Robert doesn't want to discuss it. At various times in his life he has seen spirits, starting back when he was a child. I get chilled. There is no good that comes of this house, I think. This is a house lost in space, its moorings unhinged. In my journal: *A house is always the soul of the dead who build it. Good souls leave good houses. The bad —*

Everything seems so far from Wisconsin. A different planet, as it were. It's an elegant house, an ornate gingerbread construction with complicated alcoves and velvet-covered window seats, with floor-to-ceiling windows and wraparound porches, with stained and leaded glass windows — I am starting to understand that Robert is a man comfortable with wealth — and Robert immediately fills the rooms with lovely furniture, the plush overstuffed sofas I love, the frilly ottomans, the Turkish Victorian chair with rich brocade, the burgundy velour draperies, the platitude-laced samplers cluttering every wall, none spouting my own versified wisdom, I must add. I don't want my own words looking back at me. Not here, at least.

I empty my trunks for treasures: all the objects I've gotten for my verses are placed in the rooms. I become a little more comfortable with my own objects around me. Yet for a moment I long for the farmhouse back home.

Robert, of course, finds my tendency to clutter amusing. "You're afraid of empty space," he tells me.

"Ridiculous."

"No, it's true. Space makes you nervous. Like empty time."

"No," I say, feebly.

"Don't be afraid of anyone, Ella."

And I suppose Robert is right: there has always been too much space in my life. All those rolling vacant acres back home and those empty quiet rooms of childhood. That is poverty to me. Space, and endless, unmoving time. And that frightens me. I can't help it. So in the downstairs parlor I cover the elaborate Italian black-and-rose marble fireplace with fire screens in the shape of Oriental dragons, with gargoyle andirons guarding the hearth. On the mantel are vellum-bond volumes of other poets: inspirational verses, as well as vases of dried flowers and candlesticks and filigreed silver frames filled with redundant tintypes of Sunday-posed relatives from the Midwest.

Only in rooms where there is no room to move can I breathe freely.

I don't like it here — the house, Meriden, the East — but I try not to let Robert know it. I smile a lot. Actually I smile too much. I know this because at night my jaw aches for the effort. I write a little for publication, but none of it is poetry. Somehow the idea of poetry seems anathema to Meriden. I watch the manic delinquent boys across the street, all bluster and sinew and red-faced energy. They always seem on the verge of breaking free of their enforced stride, rushing into the streets, upturning lives in their paths. A poem? I can't see how. So I sit in the parlor, and wait. This is really all I do these first few months because almost immediately Robert has to travel extensively for business. Unanticipated, he is off to Pennsylvania and then Ohio. Then to Delaware. Then to Alabama. It makes me long for Wisconsin, for friends in Madison or Milwaukee. I miss my close friends deeply. Whenever I receive letters from Abigail and Emma, I start to cry before I even open the flaps. When Robert returns, he is over-attentive, apologetic: at night we wander through City Park, off Benker and Park Avenues, long strolls before bedtime. Sometimes, alone, happy for change, I take the river boat out of Hartford, via Old Saybrook, into New York. With Robert I visit nearby New Britain, and dine at Cooke's Tavern. With Robert, I go to the Delevan Opera House to watch *The Count of Monte Cristo*. By myself I shop at Ives Upham and Rand's Store, the city's signature store, I'm told. I return with bundles of clothing I will never wear. Robert disappears many nights into the Home Club on Byxbee, for card playing, for cigar smoking, for the male camaraderie he so craves. At night, in the few balmy days of Indian Summer, listless and melancholy, I sit on the front porch of the home on Colony, a porch already packed up for impending winter, the rockers and tables stowed under wraps, and I watch the winding street before me. The ne'er-do-well boys rush in that straight Prussian line to fields beyond my view. Sometimes they strike me as so beautiful, these errant boys taken from freedom. Sometimes I believe I'm one of them, the last in line, unseen. I run with them, in step, towards the horizon. Running away.

This is New England. Hurrah! Frankly, I expected adulation, wonder, and sensation. I am, after all, Ella Wheeler — now Ella Wheeler Wilcox. Poetess of Passion. The notorious Mrs. Wilcox, who described kissing so unabashedly. The lingering aura of *Poems of Passion* still rocks the press, but obviously not in Meriden. Stopping for a long stay with friends in New York, I am the darling of the modish literary set: wherever I stroll in Manhattan I am pointed at. I see my books *Maurine* and *Poems of Passion* in the booksellers' windows. This is the stuff I dreamed of, those long nights back on the farm. This is the East. Mark Twain is in Connecticut. Harriet Beecher Stowe. Rose Terry Cooke, up in Hartford. Ik Marvel, over in New Haven. FitzGreene Halleck's shadow lingers over Guilford. This is what I think of when I think of Connecticut. Charles Dudley Warner. *The Gilded Age.* Refined life. Literary occasions to which I'm invited.

But I discover that Connecticut is not Meriden, which largely ignores literature. Worse, Meriden seems not to have heard of me. This isn't true, of course, because there are women who know my *Maurine* and who mumble their love of "Solitude." Some actually knock on my door for autographs. There is a brief, carping interview buried deep in the local newspaper, but the reporter talks about me as though I'm just passing through the city. There is a lot made of Robert's being an important local businessman. I am the wife who scribbles questionable verse.

There is a one-paragraph notice in the papers, copied from a New York daily, that my novel *Mal Moulee* is being read by six publishers. Each want it. There is said to be fierce competition. It isn't true — I've no idea how that story got started — but it certainly is a tantalizing rumor. I wait for comment from my neighbors. My Lord, I have a novel coming out. All the major New York publishers want it. Silence. Then one comment: the craggy postman—I've never seen the old man smile—asks, after dropping off bags of mail, what does that mean in God's good American English? Dryly, I remark, "Badly Molded." He still looks confused as he walks away.

In my journal: *Obviously the title should have been saved for a history of Meriden.*

The days drag. I sit alone in my little white Josephine house gown, waiting.

"Give them time," Robert tells me. "New Englanders are reserved people."

I'm difficult: "They are cold, impassive, laconic, bent inward. They are rocks in their own glacial soil."

Robert laughs. "Ella, a little over the top, no?"

I frown. "Understatement at best."

"You'll see."

"I doubt it."

"I'm a New Englander."

"You're, well, different."

"No, I'm not."

"Thank God you are."

And then, one miserable night, Robert just returned from an excessively long sojourn, we have our first big quarrel. We've had our share of little squabbles, to be sure — many over the notoriety of *Poems of Passion*, when Robert insisted I craved sensation and he feared for my Christian soul — but during our first year of marriage we approached each other like genteel companions, nodding and smiling.

After dinner, with Robert in his favorite chair, a cigar in his mouth. "You seem out of sorts, Ella," he begins.

We've barely spoken since he's arrived back home. He's been organizing his papers.

"I hate Meriden." Flat out.

"We've been through this —"

Suddenly the words rush from my mouth. "And you, Robert — you're different here. You're so — quiet."

He closes his eyes for a moment.

"Ella, please."

I fall apart. "You shouldn't have done this to me, Robert. "

His voice is clipped. "Done what?"

"Take me away from my world back home."

"Give it time."

I scream, putting my hands to my ears. "Stop it, just stop it. Give *what* time? I'm like a prisoner here. I'm like those boys across the street, locked in at night. For me it's day and night."

A long silence: "I'm uncomfortable with outbursts."

"What?"

"You're screaming at me."

I am, I know. I don't care. "You're on the road, seeing people. Having a good time."

"You think my life is all play? Out there?" Color rises in his face, the eyes narrow.

"Well, it's better than this."

"So I've enslaved you."

I wait, then: "Yes."

"For God's sake, a little extreme, no?"

"Don't patronize me."

"I don't want this conversation," he says.

"Well, we have to have it."

"No, we don't." He turned to look at papers in his lap.

I scream again. "Yes, we do. I think I'm going out of my mind. I look in the mirror and see my father's madness creeping up into me."

"Shall I lock you up, Ella?" There is such anger in his words.

"You already have."

He leaves the room, and the rest of the night he hides away, moody. I avoid him.

I'm ashamed of my tantrum, my screaming, but I'm still angry with him. I can't help it.

We pass each other in the hallway, and look away.

In the morning there is silence.

In the afternoon we pass, and Robert stops me, touches the side of my face with his big palm. I smile, and he grins.

"I thought the hurricane season had passed," he says.

I lean into him. I relax. Then I think: we needed this quarrel, Robert and I. Now we can relax with each other.

All the polite months, the circumspect phrases, the restrained love — all that baggage has been curiously removed. For the first time I believe we are — what? — an average husband and wife. I need him. Without him I am chaos.

We smile at each other.

"Coffee?" he says.

"Of course."

He is my refuge in this barren town.

In winter I see the effects of cold on the already isolated heart. The citizens of Meriden do not greet me the way neighbors back home do — there is no open, hearty backslapping here, no bonhomie. Instead, people rock on porches in good seasons, nod to passersby, and hide by hearths in bad weather, their yards surrounded by tight white picket fences. I am never so lonely as the days when Robert leaves by train for New Haven — and then off to the rest of America. I want *that* America too. He leaves me behind with people as stone-cold as the dirt they build their houses on.

When Robert returns from his trips, I find it impossible to stay away from him, trailing him through the hallways, like a hungry puppy, my arms cradling poems and books and letters — and sometimes flowers. I want him to see everything. I can't stop the insane chatter because I have to tell him everything. I follow so closely I sometimes collide with his massive back when he stops short. Robert watches me from across the room, across the supper table. Sometimes I spot apology on his face, and it hurts me. What can he do? Nervous, he invites friends — his and mine — for long weekends, people I like from Manhattan, even some local women I mention offhandedly as either bright or pretty or friendly. Whenever he leaves for trips, he tells me to invite New York friends to stay. Or go to New York for a while. Slowly I begin to relax, but just a little. Robert hides out in the local clubs, playing whist, bridge, auction. He is a fierce poker player, cigar in mouth and silver coins piling up near him. He has a reputation for loud laughter, generosity, and a quick anger at any ribald or questionable story.

What I do enjoy — it's the only thing I can, in fact, enjoy—are the times we visit his large family in nearby New Britain. His mother's sister, his Aunt Hattie Booth, lives with Uncle Lester and their five daughters in the growing industrial city, and frankly I don't know what to make of this brood. Robert was raised in that homestead after his grandmother died. There's always so much noise there, but good noise certainly: these are people genuinely fond of one another, who banter and giggle and hug and thrill to one another's company. For me, it's baffling, their clutching fondness for one another. It's like falling into a warm spring: the body suddenly relaxes, the eyes close, the fingertips tingle. They accept me into their lives without missing a beat, especially Aunt Hattie, an overflowing earth mother, all grin and grit, who frowns on despair and silence. "No room in God's kingdom for a frown," she announces. She demands that you move with her happy Christian rhythms. She won't abide moodiness. She shakes you into happiness, like a picker jiggling the bough of an apple tree for that resistant piece of fruit.

It startles me, all this Christian uplift. When I think of my own dedicated Christian sermonizing — so prevalent in my verse — I wonder if I appear so — intense.

I celebrate my first real Thanksgiving at Aunt Hattie's. I ride the new horse-drawn streetcar through the autumn streets. I call it an omnibus, to Robert's amusement, and think civilization may, after all, be coming East.

"But twenty-one people," I tell Robert. I haven't met most of them.

He laughs. "That's my family."

"But twenty-one."

"Twenty-two with you now."

"Where do you put them?"

"There's always room."

"What will I talk about?"

"Don't worry. No one shuts up."

"But they will talk to me, no?"

"You'll be the center of attention."

"That's what I fear."

"Ella, you love the sunlight on you."

I frown. "Only from a distance. Close up, people see my flaws."

"You have none."

I laugh. "Don't get too close."

"I'm your husband."

"Even more reason to keep you distant."

It seems too much a crowd, all these kissing, embracing relatives in one sprawling place. Back home Thanksgiving, for the Wheelers, is a meager quiet affair — a little extra food perhaps, lingering a little longer at the table because the farm duties are suspended — but it is hardly a celebration, especially in recent years with my father chewing and spitting and belching — with my mother's steely eyes angry, her lips bitten till a thin line of dried red blood shows. And the distance makes travel difficult — my grandparents' home is fifty miles away. No: that is Thanksgiving at the old homestead. It ends with my mother, swaying in the Boston rocker I bought, saying, "Plum tuckered out, I am. Just that — tuckered out."

Hattie covers the table with platters of steaming roasted turkey, mounds of chestnut stuffing, baskets of steaming hot rolls, oysters on half-shells, creamy potatoes and turnips, cranberry relish, olives, pickled celery and nutmeg radish, onions floating in milk-cream, giblet gravy. So much food I just stare, unable to eat. I have never seen anything like this. I feel like weeping: there is so much laughter and food here, everything in abundance, everything filling the corners of the room. "Eat," Aunt Hattie implores, pushing mincemeat pie at me, a huge ungainly piece covered with peach ice cream. "Eat." She pours hot, heady coffee. I close my eyes: I don't know these people, and they say they love me.

"Eat, darling. You need some fat on them bones."

I watch how two of the five daughters — plagued with scarlet fever as toddlers, and unable to move easily — are treated as though nothing is wrong. It amazes me. Uncle Lester, Hattie's husband, is given to bouts of depression, I am told by Robert. He gets morose and mopes in a corner, smoking a pipe, eyeing his family with some confusion and distrust. No one understands what brings these rare fits about, but they frighten everyone. Robert says Lester can't abide so much unrelenting good humor — it isn't natural, such constant good cheer — but I notice Robert smiles when he says this. Only Aunt Hattie can deal with Lester's "fits," as she calls them—smiling and cajoling and pampering until, in surrender, Uncle Lester, his eyes weepy with some internal demon just defeated, looks up at her and gives her a thin, undemanding smile. The family relaxes. Hattie folds her arms around her chest: another crisis surmounted.

"You are now part of the family," Aunt Hattie says, hugging me.

"Aunt Ella," they call me. "Miss Ella." One of the small children: "The lady with the hair like buttermilk."

I don't know whether I want to be part of such an assembly, but by the time Thanksgiving night is over, I find myself relaxing. This will be fine, I think. I see a wholeness here, a completed circle. These are decent Christian people, well evolved. I believe people enter the world at different levels of evolution, based on previous lives. Robert and I, I do believe, are highly evolved, the result of successful previous lives. I know it's snobbery of sorts, and a little arrogant, but what can I say? How else to explain the good and bad people of the world?

Hattie and her crew are deeply evolved. There is so much love in them. They understand Robert's love for me. For Aunt Hattie says in her Thanksgiving blessing that they are thankful for me. For me! "Our dear Robert had no intention of taking a bride," she announces, "because he has so much family to love. But God chose to send him Ella."

My heart leaps in gratitude. I smile and thank them.

I discover that the family is part of the distinguished Connecticut Bulkeleys, a venerable old Calvinist family, known in politics and business. Even in art. They are governors, they are clergy, they are intrepid leaders of industry. But, more importantly, Robert, I learn, is a direct descendant of Ralph Waldo Emerson. The venerable Bard of Concord. He never mentioned it to me. I've gone on about Ethan Allen and Pocahantas, and he never said a word. I'm speechless. When Hattie tells me this, across the table, Robert frowns, but the rest of the family nods, triumphant.

"Impressive, no?" Hattie says, grinning.

"Certainly."

Robert says, "I don't seem to have inherited his way with words."

"But you have," I interject. I look at Hattie. "He has." I want to mention the eloquence of his love letters, but of course I don't.

"Now, Ella, flattery, flattery." But he looks pleased.

Suddenly I'm a little intoxicated with the possibilities here. I feel so beautifully *American*. It's all coming together. When we have a child, that child will have the Indian royal blood of Pocahontas, the fiery soul of Ethan Allen, and the Transcendental spirit of Emerson. And the blood of the new American poetess of passion, Ella Wheeler Wilcox, freshly come from the Midwest territory. I'm truly giddy in the moment. This is gorgeous genealogy, I know. This is the geography of greatness.

Ella Wheeler Wilcox. My married name now seems somehow dark with power. It's how I now sign my new work, liking again the tongue-teasing alliteration, the continuation of the l's and the w's. My husband's surname is just the next poetic stanza to an already melodious name. Women writers with three names, I believe, are forces to be reckoned with. Ella Wheeler Wilcox. And now Emerson, part of the awesome lineage. That brave child will be America. In the next wonderful twentieth century. Greatness. Awesome.

"Stay with me," Aunt Hattie repeatedly says when Robert leaves for longer and longer trips.

"Stay with Hattie," Robert says.

Sometimes I do. Meriden is cold and distant, but New Britain has loaves of warm thick bread, fragrant cinnamon apple pies, creamy Indian pudding, hot buttered corn, succotash, chokecherry jam, homemade vanilla ice cream with apricots or raisins. My face grows chubby. My morning gowns strain at the seams. My days and nights with Hattie leave me with a glow. I love her, of course, even though Hattie confides she's never read a line of my verse. "No time," she says. I smile.

"No matter," I say, and mean it.

"I'm having a child," I say to Robert first, and then to Hattie, using the same words with both.

Aunt Hattie squeezes me, and then weeps. And her first comment: "More children for Thanksgiving."

Robert, I know, wants his own children. We both do. While we seldom speak of such things — I am often amazed at our reticence and shyness about such personal matters — Robert's few comments include a namesake son. Once he startled me by quoting by heart the opening stanza of one of my more popular poems:

Have you heard of the Valley of Babyland,
The realm where the dear little darlings stay,
Till the kind storks go, as all men know,
And oh! so tenderly bring them away?
The paths are winding and past all finding,
By all save the storks who understand,
The gates and the highways and the intricate byways
That lead to Babyland.

Robert wants a son. A namesake.

Of course he does: he is surrounded by nieces, every one a darling, I know, but nieces. All his life he's been surrounded by girls — after all, he was the only boy. He wants Robert Wilcox Jr. Of course. As for me, I want Emerson for the new century, some robust lad who, like the heroic boys out of the pages of Horatio Alger tales, will come of age in the new and exciting twentieth century. This child will move mountains, will become a power in the world, will be a poet, will be President.

Aunt Hattie whispers that we are wrong: it will be a girl. She has watched my movements, the slight twisting of my body, the shadowy look in my eyes, the incline of my gait. A girl: she knows, she says — after all, she's had five lovely daughters. You carry a girl differently: closer to the bottom of the heart. I find that amusing, if touching. I write to Robert, then in Florida for two weeks, telling him that Robert Wilcox, Jr. will have to wait. In the basement of the heart is a girl.

We call the unborn girl Winifred. It's a name I remember from a poem I read as a child, and I love the sound of it — the alliteration of it: Winifred Wilcox. She'll be another poetess, or an actress perhaps, a woman of society. She'll be a woman to be reckoned with. Winifred Wheeler Wilcox: powerhouse. The name has energy and force. No one will trifle with a girl so named.

On his return home from the road, watching my body slowly change and knowing the birth is soon and palpable, Robert lies in bed with me, fantasizing the life of little Winifred. We talk back and forth through the night, adding to her young biography. She is all of the new century in America, all its wonder and sensation. She'll be beautiful of course, and talented. Descendant of Pocahontas, a dark mysterious beauty, and Emerson, an intellectual and obviously transcendental one.

She is, I realize, Maurine.

I created her years ago.

Winifred becomes a real presence for us both, someone

we refer to on a daily basis, someone we actually talk to. "Good morning, Winifred," Robert says first thing, leaning over to kiss me. "Tell Winifred that she'd better wait until I return from Trenton," he says, laughing.

"Women have minds of their own. They wait for no man."

"Winifred," Robert says, touching my stomach. "You're setting the rules already."

"As well she should."

"I am fated to be a man surrounded by women."

I grin. "Be thankful the gods have smiled on you."

Robert subscribes to *St. Nicholas,* which amuses me. The magazine for children — admittedly for children older than newborn — delights us both. Soon copies litter tables and bureaus. Robert reads nursery rhymes out loud. I plan to send the editor some of my verse from *The Beautiful Land of Nod.* Children love that book.

But Robert is away from home fully half the carrying time, and more so near the delivery time, so I rely on Aunt Hattie, who hovers and smothers and assumes. Meriden may be dark and lonely, but New Britain sometimes becomes too cozy and warm. One place has too much silence, the other too much talk. Voices swirl around me. Everybody hugs me. Alone, against advice, I catch the 7:52 express train which arrives at Grand Central at 11:05. Friends are waiting. I spend a peaceful weekend in the New York streets, walking, my footfall heavy on the city sidewalks. I am mellow: I smile at the passing crowds of strange, immigrant faces. Buildings throw shadows on me, so I cross the street for sunshine. I love everyone.

My friend Anna Robertson Noxon, a sometime poet from down South, sends her lines of cheer, called "Winifred":

> *Winifred, when bees are humming*
> *We shall listen for your coming.*

I copy the lines into my journal, adding: *Winifred is already part of the foundation of my new home. She is the stone on which I build my future poetry — and marriage.*

Winifred, already the glue of my days.

When Robert is away in the West, he writes me in New York, where I am staying for a two-week period: "I am so glad you have Winifred with you, in all your happiness in New York. Though she is very young to go into society, I feel she is very safe, snuggled up so closely to your warm heart; and the little confidences that she receives from its whispered pulsings must be delightful to her. I should think you would be talking to her all the time. A kiss to her."

I read Winifred the letter. I feel the child move in my womb.

Your father loves you, I whisper.

In May, a rainy day of early spring that washes away a scant morning frost, I give birth to my child, and not to Winifred, the expected, but to a son. A boy, yammering as furiously as a puppy runt I recall from Wisconsin. Robert Wilcox Jr. himself. Staring at the wizened red bundle, so small and feeble, hiccoughing and slobbering, eyes closed tight, I panic: a son of mine. I don't know who this child is. Because I know Winifred so well, have lived with a daughter all these nine expectant months, I think of the baby I hold as a stranger's. Winifred is already in the family, a caretaker, a dutiful daughter. I feel as though I've missed a beat. No matter: the struggling baby boy tucks its pale red body into mine, and my heart swells.

Hattie wires Robert, then in Tennessee.

But as the day goes on — the rain is furious, beating in relentless sheets against the window panes — the faces in the household get longer and longer, more stricken, and I lie in my sheltered room, unvisited. The baby lies in the nursery across the hall. A doctor tends me first, then the boy. "What?" I keep asking, when someone brings refreshment. "What?" No one answers. Something is wrong, I sense this. The faces get longer. "What?" I beg. "What?" Heads turn away. Medicated, I am still in pain from the difficult birth. The doctor gives me an elixir, a syrupy opiate that makes me boozy and light headed, drugged. I can't focus on anything. "What?" I beg. No one will answer me.

In late afternoon, Aunt Hattie, in tears, her body rocking back and forth, tells me that my baby boy has died, after struggling for twelve hours on this earth, gasping and begging for life that wouldn't come to him. A half a day of a lifetime. That's all. "God took him home," she says, holding my hand. Shattered, I weep out of control, and the doctor prescribes more medicine. I go into a deep troubled drug-morphine sleep, all nightmare vision and jerky lightning flashes and wild demonic screaming. I can't wake up, can't calm myself down — so strong is the power of the drug. I wake periodically, choke on my own pain, feel my eyes go puffy from crying, and drift back into my stupor. Night and day become one: I sleep, but only fitfully. The doctor keeps me barely conscious, and at one point I mumble, "No, no," wanting to be awake now, desperate to be in control, wanting to understand what has happened. No one listens to me. When people enter the room, I imagine I am waving wildly at them, but I know I scarcely move: my arms lie inert at my side.

Hattie holds back Robert's telegram, sent before he learns of the dying. "Who is this Robert M. Wilcox weighing ten pounds? What is his hurry? Where is Winifred? Is it the first instance on record when a Wilcox stepped in so impolitely before a lady? Yet he and his mother have made me the proudest man that walks the earth tonight." Hattie carries it in her apron pocket, and every so often she runs her fingers over it, as though hoping it will disappear. She just doesn't know what to do with it.

When he returns a few days later, rushing to my side, his hair uncombed and his suit wrinkled from travel, he

finds me insensible, confused, my hair unwashed and
stringy, my eyes vacant with a dull panic, an invalid
huddled in a chair. I move my head slowly when he calls
my name, but trancelike, asleep. I am trying to shake off
the drug. I am all flesh now, no bone, a woman dissolv-
ing at the touch. He holds me, fearful that I too am dying. "Winifred is dead," I whisper.

Robert starts. He takes my face between my palms.
"No," he says. "Robert."

I stare into his face. "You're Robert."

Because, he knows, Robert the dead baby is not real to
me: he is someone who came by chance, by error, a
strangely quiet baby I held for a moment, an unmoving
doll, wrinkled and red as sunset. He was just something
to confuse my days — to take away a future.

"Oh, my Ella," he says, and then he cries.

Robert is shattered. Back in the house in Meriden, we
both move like ghosts through the vast, empty rooms,
avoiding each other, mumbling like strangers, I give in
to sudden bursts of ragged crying, Robert to teary eyed
reflection, his grief bubbling at the corners of his mouth
without warning. When we mention the baby, the name
we use is Winifred, not Robert. Somehow this is safer. It
is almost as though we have, indeed, lost a child we have
lived with for nine glorious, happy months. Winifred is
very real to us, a part of the family. She has slept among
the family, like an invited cousin who always amuses but
is very little bother. She has a name, an emphatic personality, a planned future. We have slept with her for months.
We've known her.

One night, coming to bed, Robert says he has just seen
a fleeting vision of his boy child: a dying baby tucked in
blankets in the corner of the room, a boy with hollow
eyes and no hair. Robert is pale with the image. He tells
me: "He will now wait for us in the other world." And
that night I can't sleep until early morning. Later that
day, at my desk, I write:

Twice I have seen God's full reflected grace.
Once, when the wailing of a child at birth
Proclaimed another soul had come to earth.
That look shone on and through the mother's face.

And once, when silence, absolute and vast,
Followed the final indrawn breath,
Sudden upon the countenance of death
That supreme glory of God's grace was cast.

When summer arrives, we flee Meriden. I want to leave for good. This place stuns me into depression. Meriden pales: the sight of the chanting, delinquent boys across the street, boys running in line, their robust voices pitched high against the trees and sky, makes me weep out of control.

We rent a small cottage on Shelter Island, off the coast of Branford. Here, secluded, we hold onto each other. We avoid visitors, even family. I sit on the sandy beach, the water lapping my feet. I sit here all day, basking in the hot sun. I refuse to move. Afternoon drops like a mourning veil on my day.

Swimming is no release: my arms feel leaden in the salt water. So I refuse to enter the water.

And Winifred is always with us. We point out beautiful young girls walking with their parents on the street. "There," I say, "there's a Winifred." And Robert: "Look at that young one over there," he says, pointing to a giggling, happy child. "That's Winifred." Winifreds populate our horizons.

By summer's end Robert has to return to the road, and I don't want to return alone to Meriden. I want to live somewhere else now, somewhere where Robert and I — and Winifred — can be happy together. Winifred will stay with us because she is a real memory now, a fixture in the life of each day, that haunting, longed for voice. She is the cement that holds us together. Without her, I feel, there is void and darkness. Sometimes I think I'll go insane: all around me children — chubby, healthy — are being born. I write:

> *The bird flies home to its young;*
> *The flower folds its leaves about an opening bud;*
> *And in my neighbor's house there is the cry of a child;*
> *I close my window that I need not hear.*

At night the sea calls me, its whispered cadences are little girl voices reassuring, soothing. I believe in an afterlife, where Winifred now waits for us. Robert talks of it all the time, that astral world just a moment away. It's just a question of time. Winifred is an angel preparing for salvation. Robert insists spirits circle us, hovering, waiting. Yet sometimes, lost in that melancholy thought, I panic: how prepare for heaven, when she never was? Then: but she *was*. She was in our hearts.

As for Robert Jr., he is someone I know, though dimly. And sadly: all that pain and wailing. All that gasping and struggle for life. Of course, he is here too: I held the frail boy in my arms. He is the beloved son. But I can scarcely mention him without tears. He is just too real to imagine. He will always be my son. Our son. He is also in heaven, readying. Will I know him in heaven?

But at night, alone and drowsy, I still talk to Winifred.

Salon

1887

One must look at the woman in society — High Society — with suspect and askance eyes: after all, this creature, while often noble in charity and in maintaining the appointment of her businessman husband's home, nevertheless, is by definition an artificial creature. By that I mean, of course, she is decidedly removed from the fabric of everyday life. The woman in her country kitchen, the farm wife making her biscuits, the shop girl at her factory bench — these woman can never understand a woman who has given up everything save the superficialities of being in Society. Such a woman must, perforce, make any woman nervous: who created this being?

> — Ella Wheeler Wilcox, "The Pitfalls of Society Women," *Farm Journal*, 1885

I can't sleep nights. My mornings are blurry with stale coffee and unread mail. "Ella, lie down," Robert says, as he prepares for his morning walk.

I stare. "For what?"

"Then come with me for a walk?"

"Why?"

He watches me all the time.

Then, one morning, Robert announces. "We need to be around people."

I frown. "Not yet."

Robert nods. Then he smiles, "We need New York."

I know he is right.

We decide to spend our winters in Manhattan, where

so many of our friends now live. Robert's silver company is actually headquartered there, in Union Square, so he can work out of that office. In the blink of an eye Meriden is packed up, discarded, and sifted through — the bundles of tied-up *St. Nicholas* magazines are sent across the street to the Boys' Reformatory — and then we are living where I always thought I might someday live: enticing Gotham, that territory of grand opera and writers and artists and supper clubs and street magic. All the successful people live there — or stop there. In New York I'm constantly feted. New York is energy and possibility.

The hurt of my baby's death is still raw. "I'll forget in the city," I write to Emma. But I don't believe that. So I add: "No, I don't want to forget my baby. I just want to sleep throughout the night without nightmares."

"Oh, Ella, " Emma writes back. "Your poet's heart suffers so much."

When I read her letter, I cry. My days are all of one piece: no peace.

New York is noise.

Lots of noise.

Robert, in a panic himself, it seems, rushes me around: roller skating — until I balk — it makes me dizzy and I feel childish. Theater — *A Trip to Chinatown* at the Madison Square Garden. I think it puerile, although I do find myself smiling in places. We learn the two-step and follow the manic dance crowds. Robert announces, "I move like a giant redwood." Everyone laughs. Robert snaps my picture in Central Park with his little new Kodak. "Snapshots," he calls them. He's into newfangled machinery.

I'm miserable.

I choose our first apartment, and it's a tiny, cramped place on East 19th Street, but to me it's elegant, the rooms sunny and high ceilinged, the kitchen decorated with a tin-plate panels, the front windows looking out on a small, leafy park where evening strollers promenade and servants rock babies. I choose everything—because Robert has to leave town unexpectedly. Alone, a little unsure, I rent the place, feeling tremendously important, and then methodically I shop for furnishings, choosing overstuffed sofas and polished chestnut tables that are too big for such tiny rooms. I don't care: everything is beautiful. I learn to shop for food — oddly I've never done this in my whole life, an observation I stupidly share with anyone who'll listen — and I interview and hire a sixteen-year-old girl named Louisa as my day maid. I wanted an Irish girl because of the English language, but settle on a German girl whose English is stilted but understandable. Louisa is bashful and takes up little room: she is a small girl, and painfully skinny, which allows her to maneuver quietly through the cluttered rooms. I would like a live-in maid but there simply isn't room. The first week, exhausted, I sit in a thick brocaded rocker, my legs up on a bulky ottoman, alone, after dismissing Louisa for the day, and I sigh: this is my creation, all of it, my own. I smile at it all, as though I've just finished appointing a palace. Robert will be startled—but pleased. Well, I hope he will be.

The small urn containing our baby's ashes sits, quietly, on the corner of the fireplace mantel.

When Robert sees the apartment, he bursts out laughing, and for a moment I am on the verge of tears.

"What?" I ask, my lips trembling.

"No, no," he says, taking my hand. "It's beautiful but it's so — small." He stands there, a man already larger than he was on his wedding day, and looks like he can extend his arms to the side walls.

"I didn't want to spend your money."

"We have money."

"But Robert, you earn the money."

"It's our money," he says. "Yours and mine."

Because I still don't accept that he is indeed very comfortable. We rarely talk about money. Like some emotions and all hygienics, such conversation is risky.

"I like it," he says. "We will be happy here. It's a robin's nest apartment, for two love birds. You and me. Next spring, if we need more space, we'll move to a larger place."

"Are you sure?"

"Ella, this has your touch here. It's wonderful."

He touches the back of a chair.

"I bought that chair for you."

He smiles. "Heavy duty. Good."

"I didn't intend that," I say, a little angry.

"It's wonderful."

I nod. I stare around the room, cramped with overstuffed furniture: it doesn't seem so grand now, so splendid. My eyes take in the ornate plush sofas, with the brocatelle covering, all tassel and velvet fringe. It seems a storeroom, some closet-sized hall where the large Shakespearean etchings in heavy black walnut frames seem to overpower the tiny space. No, I think: this is our first real home. It is a place we'll come to love.

"We will be happy here," Robert says.

And I finish the thought: *at last*. At last we will be happy and carefree. At last.

Robert sinks into his new chair and looks like he's been sitting there forever.

I become one of Mrs. Frank Leslie's lionized darlings. This tremendous monument of a woman, this no-nonsense blunt woman, all force and deliverance, had assumed the reins of her dead husband's vast publishing empire. Some of my first poems appeared in *Frank Leslie's Weekly* back when I was fourteen. She is now a major force for entertainment and society in New York. In a city where fashionable — and not so fashionable — salons begin and finish with the flick of an eyelid — where there are careful lists of acceptable people, and most not, hers is envied, though only in certain quarters. Her judgment and word break or create struggling careers: her acerbic tongue is widely quoted in a trashy scandal-mongering sheet called *Talk of the Town*. She doesn't care: she savors her *outré* reputation. It doesn't matter to her. She cultivates it, to be sure. If the upper crust or even the *nouveau-riche* ignore her — the famous Ward McAllister 400 — the rarefied world of the Astors and the Vanderbilts — it doesn't matter. She has found her exquisite level. Her stratum holds the Nelly Blys, the nascent yellow journalists, the second-string opera divas, the energetic vaudevillians, and, at last, me: Ella Wheeler Wilcox. Poetess from the West.

In this city of celebrated at-homes and literary and cultural salons, where the advent of the fall social season is cause for nervous excitement, hers is one of the most coveted invitations because it is, frankly, lively and talked about. Her mix of guests — seemingly chosen at random, but, I've come to believe, calculated with much aforethought — always come together in an evening of spirit and fun and spitfire talk. People rush to get there. In some way she is a citified Aunt Hattie, a woman who refuses to let you be unhappy in her house.

My move to this city has been much heralded in the press, and I am immediately all the rage at so many functions. Of course, it intoxicates. But why not? It's easy to become immodest here — the invitations do pile up, topple over on the hall stand — so I try not to let it go to my head. Robert always maintains I am too easily taken in by flattery. It's our one recurring squabble. What he means, I think, is that I crave flattery too desperately. But the mail excites me: invitations arrive, and I tremble. My celebrity from *Poems of Passion* — the Badger State's scarlet girl come East — makes me desired and quoted, and I discover — pleasantly — I am not a leper or immoral pariah here, but instead trend-setter, pioneer for women's expression of sexuality, for the cause of the New Woman. People have a lot to say about me here. They speak *for* me, maintaining that I am *this* or *that* — some rebel for a chosen cause. Of course, much of the time I have no idea what they are talking about. I am called the New Woman.

But I balk: I am just a decent Christian woman. It doesn't matter: I am out of the apartment all the time. The newspapers, even the august *New York Times*, comment on my goings, and, like Mrs. Leslie, I thrive on it. Robert often stays home with a cigar and a book — or heads to the card players at the Century Club. My costume becomes more and more expensive and eccentric, of necessity — the ostrich plumes more lavish, the dyed peacock feathers flying, the grand bonnets topping my head precariously. My neck aches from the weight of hats laden with plaster fruits and silver baubles. I know I amuse — and annoy — people with my elaborate dress. She is a slight little thing, says one gossip columnist, but her hat is analogous to the world Atlas was compelled to shoulder. I smile at that, clip the item to show Robert when he returns from a business trip. But novelist Gertrude Atherton, whose novels I find impossible to read, snippily remarks in print that I am a mousy little woman who has to use gaudy excess to be noticed.

"She doesn't understand your soul," Robert says, thumbing the article.

I look in a mirror: I am not a mouse. And then I think: I will never be that cruel to another woman.

I first meet Mrs. Frank Leslie at a musicale, a week after the move to New York. "My dear," Mrs. Leslie says, drawing me aside, "your infamy precedes you." She whispers the line, her eyes twinkling, and I smile foolishly. Miriam Leslie immediately wants me at her side. Ella this, Ella that. Have you met my Ella?

"Do you know, darling," Mrs. Leslie says, "when you first sent your verses to my husband, all those many moons ago, we assumed someone else wrote them. Your penmanship was so — childlike — but the lines were so mature. We discussed you endlessly."

"You read them?"

"Dear, I was your advocate."

"I wrote your husband my age." I pause, suddenly

wondering just what age I'd actually told Frank Leslie.
"Ella, dear, in New York we all lie about our age."
"I try never to do that."
Miriam Leslie raises her eyebrows. "All women do. We
have no choice."
"I try not to."
"What? Lie?" The woman shakes her head.
I look away, embarrassed.
"Really, Ella, dear. You're lying now."

I admit I'm often ill at ease with Miriam Leslie, although
we've become best of friends: confidantes, the two of us.
We meet for luncheon, for opera, for poetry recitals. I
know I'm eager for friendship this first year in New York,
yet I always feel I don't understand everything that happens. Sometimes she talks above me, making me feel like
a hayseed. She talks over my swallowed words, a habit
that bothers me. Worse, Miriam loves the *double entendre*,
most of which I rarely catch, and she likes the secret wink:
a gesture that always suggests more than what is apparent to me. A country bumpkin — that's how I often feel
in her presence, some provincial off a rickety farm wagon,
all trussed in homespun and Midwestern twang. She has
the brisk, unrelenting speech of the New Yorker, all locomotive and drive. When I'm with her, my voice gets even
lazier, sleepy almost.
    "I don't like her," Robert announces, returning from a
rare visit to the woman's salon. He went in order to hear
the words of her guest, an East Indian monk named
Swami Vivekananda, a preacher of uplifting thought and
inner spiritual peace. His theme is the harmony possible
and necessary between the world of modern business and
that of the soul. Given his belief in other spiritual worlds,
Robert is fascinated by such practical mysticism. He talks
of befriending the Swami — "a man of truth and spirit"
— but our conversation sadly turns to Miriam Leslie.
    "She's just a woman who likes to be talked about," I
admit.

"This can be bad, Ella."

"It can, but she's all noise."

"She's in the gossip columns every day."

"It's — game-playing. She's a woman in a man's world of power. She's, well, blustery."

"Yes, that's true. She salvaged her dead husband's faltering empire, turning it into a success. But at what price, Ella?"

We are dining alone in the restaurant of the Carlton Hotel, off Union Square, a small dining room with more staff than patrons. Robert leans into me.

"Ella, you like everybody too much. Think about it — and I mean this kindly. Because someone has talent doesn't make that person good."

"Robert, we've had this talk before."

"And I've yet to convince you."

I laugh loudly. "Perhaps it's because I'm right."

He frowns. "Or stubborn."

"No, Robert," I add, grinning. "You know I'm not stubborn. I just always need to be right."

But Robert becomes angry. "For God's sake, Ella, listen to yourself. A reputation lost is gone forever. We call ill afford—"

"I am a Christian woman!"

"— Who has a scarlet reputation because of her poetry."

I falter. "But you know me—"

"Yes, *I* know you as a good woman."

"But—"

"But others will see you as a hypocrite — all moral talk and licentious scribbling."

I purse my lips. "I don't scribble."

"I mean —"

I stand and walk away, furious.

I don't believe it, Robert's cynical view that an artist can be evil. I don't want to believe it. God would not make someone hauntingly talented — that lofty singing voice, that deft way of acting, the clever turn of phrase, the art of being hostess of a stimulating salon, the Rockefeller touch in business — and also make that person mean-spirited, narrow, immoral, suspect. No, I insist. Beauty equals Goodness equals Truth. A balanced philosophic trinity. Transcendental. That's my equation. There has to be a harmony in the universe, I feel: to believe otherwise is to invite chaos in. A sinking into the void.

Robert believes otherwise.

Yet Mrs. Leslie, over and over, is my staunchest advocate. At a social function in Manhattan, a woman cruelly remarks, in my earshot, that Julia Ward Howe announced that while I am a talented poet I need discipline. My work is slipshod, overly sentimental. Of course, I remember the published remark all too well. Even my editors copied it for me in a letter. Howe said, "Miss Wheeler does show some talent and, with study and hard work, she might become a real poet." Her words especially rankle. People love to quote them to me. Like a shot from a gun. Enemies, all. Now, sitting at the party among society women — we are having coffee after having Otto Bahn performing at the pianoforte — I hear the story again. The teller affects concern for me, but I am stunned. I don't know the woman speaking, other than as the wife of a histrionic and failing Broadway actor. For some reason — have I said anything to her? — I am under attack. The woman glances in my direction. Miriam Leslie comes to my defense.

"My dear Ella," she says, "Miss Howe hardly understands the beat of the woman's heart. Your passionate writing scares that sterile frump of a harridan."

Some women frown, annoyed, a little angry — after all, Mrs. Howe is the august Battle Hymn of the Republic, those venerable grapes of wrath and all that — but others nod, sympathetic. They are protective of me. "That battleship of the repulsive," one rakish wit mumbles. Miriam comes to my side, touches my hand protectively, and smiles. I feel a rush of gratitude.

Yet, though I hate to admit it, I'm not always charitable towards Miriam Leslie myself. An easy woman to make fun of, she is enormously difficult to be with: irritable, intrusive, and sometimes just annoying. I'm not allowed my privacies. I find myself slighting her appearance, trying to make Robert laugh. I become a horrid gossip, I'm afraid. And a little bit of a hypocrite. Really, I don't like mocking my friends.

"She's a woman whose beauty is exaggerated, and thus imperfect," I say one night. "Her Roman nose, so emphatic, throws her face magnificently out of focus, but her alabaster skin, as shiny and shadowy as mother-of-pearl seashells, seems lit from within." Her pale blue eyes, overlarge, like bluebonnet flowers, diminish a tiny pouting mouth, with those thin lips. She effects an hourglass Lillian Russell figure, pulled dangerously into form by breathless corsets. Frankly, I tell Robert, "I am always stunned by her feet — baby's feet, a child's feet, clad in miniature doll shoes. She looks like she might topple over any minute. They remind me of the bound feet of Chinese women."

Robert always laughs at my overwrought (his word) — and often unfair (my word) — descriptions. I suppose I do it because I know he frowns on the friendship. He'd rather I not see her. It's a way of containing the friendship perhaps, but allowing it as well. "Ella, you are malicious," he says, grinning.

"Only when the spirit moves me," I say.

I notice the next time he is near her — we meet at the opera — his eyes helplessly drift down at her tiny feet, and, when I catch his look, he winks, mysteriously. I blush, I swear, to the roots of my dyed yellow hair.

What he doesn't find amusing is the lingering taint of scandal always surrounding the woman. After her full-scale assumption of her dead husband's affairs, organizing his business ventures and strengthening the magazine production (she tells me, "My husband preferred twenty magazines with one thousand circulation each, to one magazine with twenty thousand"), she seems to attract a host of hanger-on men, flash-in-the-pan young dandies who are drawn to her celebrity and her considerable fortune. She is a dynamic, uncanny businesswoman who, oddly, can't resist the idle flatterer. Her talent, she discovered, is the world of business, not that of the boudoir. But she refuses to believe it.

"For a woman with so much power, so much hunger for money and position," Robert notes, "she can't spot a crook when he's eye to eye with her."

"Women are always off-balance with men," I say. "We wait for their nod."

"Meaning?"

"Meaning we are like children. We're forced to be —"

"But she doesn't need a man's nod."

"Every woman does, Robert."

"But these men are questionable choices."

"But available," I say.

"I can't follow you," he says, exasperated.

"All I'm saying is, even with all her power and money, she's still playing by man's wishes."

"Really, Ella. You make us seem so autocratic."

"Well—"

The slick men with the pompadour hair and the narrow, cynical eyes are everywhere in New York. They wear high-button patent leather shoes from Paris — all glossy and sleek — and display fresh cut flowers in their lapels, even in the dead of winter.

Miriam has romanced a series of such fleeting Romeos, all interchangeable, all charming and glib and debonair. They come and go like seasons. She has been married before. There is an undiscussed first marriage, I hear whispered about in gossipy circles, then a second forgotten marriage to a man named Squires, also rarely mentioned. Then Frank Leslie divorced his wife and convinced Miriam to do the same with Squires, so they could wed each other. It was, Miriam told me, true love, and she had no choice. Of course, it was the delicious scandal for that long New York season. Currently she is madly in love with the ubiquitous Marquis de Leuville, an oily confection of a man who has the nasty habit of slinking around people at social affairs, sliding in and out of conversations, one minute up against you, the next minute insinuating himself with some dowager across the room. He reminds me of a sneaky cat, one shoulder always higher than the other, the body at angles. I don't like him.

"He's a fraud," Robert says, after one meeting.

"Now, Robert. He's a dreadful man, I admit, but he may be royalty."

"I've traveled Europe," he tells me. "I've met royalty. Real royalty. He's not royalty."

"But he says —"

"Ella, Ella," he says, in the patronizing, older brother tone he sometimes assumes with me. "He's a fraud."

"Wouldn't someone know?" I ask.

"Not necessarily."

"But, Robert, people know these things. It gets around."

"Maybe no one wants to know."

"I just think he's pathetic."

"That's not the word I'd use."

"Miriam is just so trusting."

"That's not the word I'd use."

"Robert, really."

We stare at each other. Robert looks at my face, grins, and we burst out laughing.

Miriam Leslie adores the Marquis, head over heels in love. She intrudes his name into every conversation. The Marquis is admittedly melodramatic and handsome, with long flowing hair, a wiry pencil-thin mustache, and a slight rockaway walk because of his dangerous high-heel boots. Glib, savvy, smooth-talking, he flatters and cajoles the older women, many of whom — not all, I happily note — titter and swoon. Miriam Leslie appropriates him. Years older than the young man, she is smitten, this hard-boiled New York journalist-publisher. I've noticed the color rising in her cheeks when he enters a room. She allows no one to speak ill of him, so I don't dare bring him up in conversation.

"Isn't he wonderful?" Miriam coos at me.

I simply nod.

Months go by.

"Isn't he wonderful?"

There are, of course, the rumors which Robert insists are based on truth—that the young Marquis is really a clever, enterprising son of a Minnesota barber, a smooth-talking young man who earlier worked his charms in Chicago society, then slipped unexpectedly into New York to worm his way into that society. That is, moneyed circles. He understands the heartbeat of the rich, older woman, Robert says. He also says such men won't dare show their faces at the men's clubs he frequents. "We men don't tolerate the bogus dandy," he says. I make him laugh when I say: "But you men do tolerate the genuine dandy?" Miriam Leslie is this fellow's greatest achievement, a stunning catch, to be sure. He wishes to marry, I have been told, but not by Miriam Leslie herself. Whenever she speaks of the young man, she becomes rhapsodic. She has, quite simply, only one story.

Robert views everything with a jaundiced eye. He wants me to be a part of the literati—he knows it makes me happy — so I have to attend the fashionable salons, but Robert is around so seldom, his business taking him out into America. He fears my slipping into vainglorious ideas. The power of the fatuous suggestion. The cloying perfume of the drawing room. The salons are breeding grounds for casual, cosmopolitan affairs — so many young men believe they can acquire their newest and sweetest mistress among the poetic and artistic — and often moneyed — women who attend the at-homes. Sometimes Robert worries. He trusts me, obviously, knowing I am a devout Christian woman above all, a woman totally faithful to her husband: he simply fears the contagion of lecherous men around me. He hates the idea of it. *Talk of the Town* once commented on a function I attended: "Ladies of leisure looked lewdly on lovers." I fumed: such a travesty of alliteration. Robert happened to read the notice.

"Be careful, Ella. A reputation lost is —"

"The end of life. I know, I know. We've covered this ground before."

"I meant it." He is shaking his head.

"Don't be foolish," I tell him.

"I don't believe Mrs. Leslie is a proper model."

I frown. "Robert, I'm too old for models. I haven't had a model since I was eight."

"Probably not even then," he says, grinning.

The grin surprises me. Usually his attack on Miriam leads to a quarrel.

"I always knew my own mind."

"Yes, you, the child prodigy."

I laugh. "I still am that child prodigy."

"Please, I'll be arrested on charges."

"Robert!"

He laughs. "Well, perhaps I don't mean she's a real model — "

I cut him off. "All right, then, Miriam Leslie is a vain, foolish woman. Happy now?"

Robert gets serious. "But she's your friend."

I pause: this is true, and a problem. "Yes," I say, quietly, "she is."

I have an unsettling conversation with Miriam — it leaves me so weak I take to my bed, a hot cloth on my head. We are sipping tea at the Everett when a young woman passes our table, glowing with expectant motherhood, with a rosiness about her petite frame, ethereal, sprite-like.

I smile, nod towards the woman. Melancholy flows over me: I choke. I'm afraid I will cry.

I think of Robert Junior, dust in the Egyptian urn on my mantel. Winifred, in my soul.

"Ella, my dear," Miriam says, following my gaze, "children are horrible. Quite."

I literally freeze: my Winifred is everything to my imagination. My Robert, Junior.

"My husband and I—" I begin, feebly.

"They make a woman destroy her figure, her complexion, and no doubt a husband's love for this sacrifice. They drain the face of beauty. I would as soon touch a worm as a newborn baby."

I falter. "You're joking, no?" My voice is a whisper.

"Of course not. For heaven's sake, Ella. Any husband's eye will wander."

"But —"

"No, no, don't give me rosy claptrap, Ella Wheeler Wilcox. Babies are not a boon."

"But Mrs. Leslie —"

"Call me Miriam, please."

"Miriam," I start, unable to find the words I want, "babies are — well, everything." To me, to me.

Miriam Leslie actually shudders.

"To me," I say.

She stares at me. "For heaven's sake, Ella. Children are the death of femininity. You mustn't sentimentalize. You—"

I rush away, waiting until I am back home before I burst into tears.

Suddenly I realize — why hadn't I seen this before? — that no one ever mentions my dead child — my Winifred, my Robert Jr. It's a forbidden topic in this sinful city. For the people I meet, my only children are my books. Everything else is taboo. All those afternoon soirees, all those musicales — it's a world without children, Without family. Moneyed society ladies with carefree figures and expensive opera glasses. It's a world, well — removed. I'm in the middle of it.

The next afternoon, spotting Miriam Leslie at a charity ball, smiling, I leave within minutes. I don't want to be in the same room.

The old feeling of feeling suffocated returns suddenly, and I gasp for breath. Will I die in the street?

Watching me struggle with the Miriam Question, as he terms it, capitalized, a little too facilely, Robert suggests I create my own salon. It surprises me because he has such antipathy towards them. "Why?"

"It will be a moral center," he says. "You avoid all hint of scandal — avoid all the rogues."

"A moral center," I echo.

"Show them you can be artist — and a good person. An afternoon without suggestion or scandal."

"Do you think it's possible?"

"Certainly it is. Do it."

"Robert, really?"

"Ella," he says, sharply, "you've been waiting for me to give you my blessing."

I laugh. "Robert, am I that transparent?"

He doesn't answer.

Of course, Robert knows my mind. I've already played with this idea for a while — already created such a wonderful salon in my mind. It's inevitable that I will host a gathering of artists, and so I quietly institute my own salon for Sunday afternoons. It's an immediate success, my afternoons attracting New York's popular literati and theater folk, not the deadly serious Henry James ilk, to be sure, the William Dean Howells realists, but the vanguard of popular journalists and romancers — those writers with three names, like Kate Douglas Wiggin and Francis Marion Crawford (visiting from Rome) and Louise Imogene Guiney. Frances Hodgson Burnett. *Little Lord Fauntleroy.* Those in the public journalistic eye: the ones who keep *Century* and *Demorest's* magazines afloat. The pioneering Nelly Bly. And painters and sculptors. Musicians and actors, from Broadway to vaudeville. Julie Opp — that young ingenue, recently from a convent school, now treading the Broadway boards, is my stalwart companion these days. Jenny June, the ardent feminist, shows up with pamphlets and allies for the cause of suffrage.

Poems of Passion still has currency. And now *Poems of Pleasure,* a collection of magazine poems I've just published, cements my fate. Window shops showcase the new volume, along with a photograph of me, standing before massive Greek columns, an ostrich fan under my chin.

Miriam Leslie attends my Sundays — I have to invite her, of course, we are friends — arriving late, and she acts as though the salon is her idea. The first Sunday, dressed in black satin with the most outrageous beaverskin hat, she confides to anyone who'll listen. "How perfect this is. How perfect. Just as I told her to do it."

Listening, I fume.

Our names are invariably linked together in the yellow press, week after week. She drops in unannounced, moves about freely in my apartment, and generally proclaims that she brought the famed Poetess of Passion into New York's cultural whirlwind. Now, at my own salon, Miriam Leslie announces that she is the impetus behind it. I am speechless.

My salon becomes one of the most talked about that winter season.

It makes me dizzy.

But after the busy winter season, with the coming of summer and the removal of anybody who is anybody to seashore resorts on Long Island or in Connecticut or Rhode Island, I have to admit that my own salon is a pale reflection of Mrs. Leslie's more abundantly luminous one. It is, I suppose, the high moral tone I purposely effect: no roués or slatterns need apply. I don't care. Be that as it may. As it is, I can't always escape the dilettantes, those dandified young men and sloe-eyed ambitious young women, in the latest cut of Parisian fashion, who worm their way in on the arm of some society dame or crusty doting gentleman. From my position on the settee by the fireplace — a centrally placed piece of furniture, designed to give all focus to me, a settee covered with a musty brown and orange velvet fabric that always manages to match with my chosen salon gown — I monitor the movement of my guests. I bow through the afternoons. I prefer to dress in yellow, always. These days brilliant yellow is also the color of my dyed hair. Yellow is everywhere in the apartment: I live in the center of the light. And I surround the settee with floor urns of flowers, golden or rust-colored chrysanthemums in fall, white hothouse roses in winter, and daffodils in spring. In the summer I am off at a resort, of course. Sitting on the settee, among my flowers, drunk with the perfume of a hundred blooms, I feel as if I'm the sun in the sky, all dazzle and brilliance and heat.

Ella Sunshine.

Some snide writer in the *Talk of the Town:* "Ella Wheeler Wilcox, at home, looks like fiercest noontime. The viewer begs for a total eclipse of the sun."

Such popularity, to be sure, always is accompanied by a host of shrill detractors.

I have my resolute enemies — that much I know. I still cannot get used to it. Why enemies? I ask myself, over and over. I'm just a poet. Now with my new *Poems of Problems* in the bookstores, the venom increases mercilessly. I am constantly maligned in the press as a frivolous poetaster. A writer of sentimental claptrap. In my journal: *The highbrows never have any use for me.* I hate it. I respond to one New York critic who dislikes a particular poem, stupidly remarking: "The rhythm of the last two lines in each stanza is entirely my own creation, and was never used before by any poet." This, I think, shall stop the philistine in his tracks. Instead, he quotes me word for word, then makes light of me. I shudder. They mock my work. They especially mock me for taking it seriously, announcing to the world that I have found the Heart — if not the Art — of mankind. What's wrong with that? I ask.

I find myself thinking of my days on the desolate farm. Help me.

I feel my throat tighten. I suck on air, as though drowning.

I'm just a poet.

Why, then, my vast and passionate readership?

Then, while I'm still smarting from the vile reviews of my newest book, the nagging specter of an old, long-standing ugly battle resurfaces, as I know it will till the day I die. John Joyce is planning — again — to sue me. My hated nemesis: that wastrel John Joyce.

Just after the publication of "Solitude" in 1883 when the "Laugh and the world laughs with you" refrain was hungrily crocheted into grandmothers' Christmas parlor samplers, this destructive Mr. Joyce publicly announced that he had written those timeless words—and that a brazen, upstart Ella Wheeler had stolen them from him. Robert eventually hired New York detectives to debunk Joyce's dumb claim. It seems Joyce, indeed, published a volume called *A Checkered Life* in 1883, the same year of the poem, but his version wasn't in it. He claimed to have written it in 1861 on the head of a whiskey barrel in the wine room of the Galt House in Louisville, Kentucky, scribbling the lines on a sheet of paper borrowed from the barkeep. In his volume he recounted the story of his life, confessing that he'd been in a mental asylum for a few months. He seemed to find his mental illness some sort of validation for his claim, because, in fact, Joyce quoted his own medical records ("form of mania, perpetual motion"). In fact, he claimed he wrote many of his verses while in prison on whiskey fraud. A later edition included my poem, with the same copyright, thus giving it greater focus. He's a convict, a drunkard, a lifelong ne'er-do-well—three terms I rehearse and present to the world. And I am told by all who love me — Robert most emphatic of them all — to not let it bother me. I can't help it: I stay awake nights, fuming, weeping. After all, these are my most famous lines.

Since coming East, there has been silence. I assumed the matter is dead. But no such luck, I'm afraid.

Now a noisome lawsuit. I counter: I offer five thousand dollars (as a donation to charity) if someone can locate the Joyce publication *before* my own publication. Meanwhile Joyce reiterates his story across the country, traveling the lecture circuit, mouthing my famous lines over and over. He announces he bought a headstone for his eventual grave: the lines of verse are carved into its facade. Photographs of the monument appear in the press.

Bitter, I wish he were buried beneath it.

My New York enemies — those excluded from my salon, those who feel slighted by my words — revel in the spice of the renewed controversy. More than once I hear a jealous upstart whisper as I pass: "Laugh and the world laughs at you." Worse, from the *Talk of the Town*: "Laugh and the world laughs with Joyce." "Weep, and you fall into the deep alone." I never find any of this amusing. The more press I get in New York, the more this controversy arises. Mr. Joyce will not go away. Once, at a party, I foolishly call him a "filthy drunk," but the stares I get teach me to be more cautious.

In my journal I write: *For the greatest pleasure there is always an underpinning of bleakness to remind us that we are not gods.*

I ready for my bed, depressed. I have just read my precious words quoted under Joyce's surly name. In, of all places, *The Review of Reviews*. They know better. Why? Why won't they believe me? I am here alone. And miserable: lonely, empty. Robert is at the Lotus Club, smoking his cigar and playing whist. Suddenly, for no reason I can understand, I recall the words of Swami V from his talk at a salon yesterday. "All we have is the essential self and its rainbow prism of power light." It baffles me, this notion that I contain all in one—myself. All the world's light is filtered through me. I dress for bed but can't sleep. Me: Joyce: laugh and the world laughs with you. At you. At me. I am that light: me. Suddenly I sit up, take pen, and begin to write. The room is dark and the pen flows across the page in the dim light from another room. I write blindly, passionately. The black ink spills onto the page. Within seconds, the work was done. I have written "Illusion":

> God and I in space alone
> And nobody else in view.
> "And where are the people, O Lord," I said,
> "The earth below, and the sky o'er head
>   And the dead whom once I knew?"
>
> "That was a dream," God smiled and said,
>   "A dream that seemed to be true.
> There were no people, living or dead,
> There was no earth, and no sky o'er head
>   There was only myself—in you."
>
> "Why do I feel no fear," I asked,
>   "Meeting you here this way,
> For I have sinned I know full well,
> And is there heaven, and is there hell,
>   And is this the judgment day?"
>
> "Nay, those were but dreams," the Great God said,
>   "Dreams, that have ceased to be.
> There are no such things as fear or sin,
> There is no you — you never have been —
>   There is nothing at all but ME."

When Robert returns from his club, he finds me sitting in a corner, chilled, staring into space.

"Ella," he says. "What is it?"

"Robert." I turn to him. "Have I been dreaming?"

"Why?"

I hand him the paper.

He reads it, shakes his head. "A spirit has moved through you."

Each season the hold of Miriam Leslie gets tighter and tighter, but each new autumn — and the return of everyone to the city and the onset of salons—gives me more power, more independence. I am not in such awe of the woman. People look to me for leadership, something I discover I enjoy. Crave — perhaps a better word. What is there about my photograph in the rotogravure? Why does that thrill still move up my spine when I hear my name in public? I *need* it.

But I spend less and less time with Miriam now, purposely so. She has the unending power to grate on my nerves, her own frantic love affair with the Marquis — yes, he lingers on the social scene like malicious gossip itself — spilling like waste water into every conversation. I turn away from it because it leaves an awful stench.

I especially resent her ignoring Robert, her purposeful dismissal of him as important in my life. In *any* life. To her he is invisible. He is simply the large man who sits morosely in the corner of the Sunday salon room, cigar in mouth, eyes narrowed against the inanities he sometimes witnesses. I always compel him into conversations, draw him out, then force people to turn his way. Nervous and excited, I'm always afraid he isn't having fun. He looks unhappy. "Have you met my husband Robert?" I ask.

"Yes, we have."

"Oh, I keep forgetting who has met whom."

When I prattle on and on about Robert's often undiscovered charms and powers, interjecting my euphoric words into any conversation, Miriam warns me about my excessive attention and love for him. This stuns me. What's wrong with loving your husband? One afternoon, to my horror, I overhear a catty comment about me from one of Miriam's friends: "She really bores me. You talk to her for ten minutes and she bumps you up against a huge overweight husband."

"I love my husband," I say, over and over, whenever

the opportunity presents itself. I do it naively at first, then purposely, aggressively. The idea of it: a modern New York woman professing love for her husband with such simplistic, bald sentiment. This is, of course, the end of the nineteenth century, the *fin de siècle* of *The Yellow Book*. It's almost 1900, they tell me. The age of the New Woman, capitalized. Cigarette smoking, bicycle riding. Well, I wrote the Red Book, didn't I? Of course, women love their husbands, I'm told, but to dote on them?

"Men," Miriam Leslie tells me at luncheon, "must be treated like slaves." Which is how she treats the young men who fawn around her, including the young Marquis.

"No," I say. "I can never do that."

Miriam Leslie is dipping her spoon into raspberry sherbet. She holds the spoon in the air, deliberately. "Don't tell your husband you love him. Keep him in doubt."

"No, Miriam," I say. "Really."

The sherbet slips off the spoon and onto the table. A young waiter, poised nearby, rushes over and cleans it up. She smiles. "See what I mean, Ella?"

"You're paying him."

"It doesn't matter. They serve. Oddly, they *want* to."

"Women have no power —"

"Because they refuse to take it. Men keep offering it, knowing we won't take it."

"I believe men and women balance out each other —"

"Ella, you're not writing a column now."

"That's unfair, Miriam," I say.

"Let's be realistic."

"You're not realistic."

"I am. Look around you. Men want us."

"God intended—"

"Oh, please. Leave Him out of it."

"Miriam!"

"I'm jesting."

"My husband Robert —"

"Don't bring him into the conversation either, Ella. Two

men who have too much power. God and Robert. Let me just say this: affairs keep the emotions flowing."

"No," I say. "I could never have an affair."

"How sad!"

"You're just playing with me now."

"But darling," Miriam says, "Those lines you wrote." She refers to the current scandal in the newspapers, especially the *Talk of the Town*, which relishes the oft-quoted lines from my new book *Three Women,* in which the hero:

> *Drew her face up to his, on her frightened lips pressed*
> *Wild caresses of passion that startled and shocked,*
> *While his iron arms welded her bosom to his. . .*
> *Well, that bruise on your lips tells the story!*

People are talking, clergymen condemning. "But," I say, "that's romance."

"Enough," Miriam says. "Let's talk about something you know about."

I read, in the columns of that trashy weekly *Talk of the Town* — why is it none of us can put down this hateful paper? — that Miriam and the Marquis are the subject of unpleasant talk circulating both in America and England, the stories particularly lurid. Nothing specific, to be sure, but the malicious innuendo and eye-wink suggestion are now, pardon the expression, the talk of the town. Miriam has just returned from a long sojourn in Europe, leaving behind anger and disgust. The dust still hasn't settled. Whatever did she do there?

We meet for breakfast at a hotel in Manhattan, seated at a reserved corner table, while frantic waiters attend to us both, pouring steaming coffee and ladling eggs on platters. Instinctively, we lean into each other, smiling. Miriam has been away for months, traveling the continent, and I have missed her. I really have. We can chat idly for hours. I expect her to be filled with the latest news of England, of mutual friends living there, the new fashions from the Continent, the doings of royalty, but I fear she'll drift into whatever scandal precipitated the remarks in the press. I really don't want to know.

I notice the eyes of the other dining guests on us. I was stopped for an autograph on the way in. And I am oddly pleased — I'm embarrassed to say — that I am better dressed than Miriam, who is sporting an eccentric dress the color of burnt umber. Then, suddenly, I worry that such a dress may be in fashion in Paris at this very moment. And no one has told me. I've worn a new day gown, all brilliant daffodil and sunset pink, with dyed pheasant plums that seem to emerge from my scalp. I'm a sight, I know.

"I'm getting married," Miriam says, confidentially, after just a few minutes of small talk. "I wanted you to know."

Without thinking, I blurt out, "To whom?"

Miriam frowns. "To the Marquis, of course." She says the last word too loudly, with an edge, and a waiter looks over, as though she has called him.

"Why, Miriam?"

Testy: "Why ask why? Why not say, best wishes?"

"Of course, I want you to have happiness."

"But?"

Now I lean in. "Are you sure you want to do this?"

Miriam looks surprised. "Whatever are you talking about?"

I hesitate. "Marriage is so — risky—"

Miriam clicks her tongue. "You didn't seem to think so."

"But divorce is so commonplace in the nineties."

She smiles. "As I, of all people, know. Is that what you're saying to me?"

"That's not what I meant."

"Then what do you mean?"

I'm becoming nervous: this is not the conversation I planned. I sigh. I plunge in, foolishly. "Robert was saying that you were being discussed at his Lotus Club, you know, some scandal in Europe—"

"I am always being discussed. Any woman worth her salt is the topic of talk, much of it worthless and definitely questionable."

I am fidgeting with my fork, shifting the eggs from one corner of the plate to another.

"But you must know that the Marquis is being questioned as to his — origins."

I stop. The look on Miriam's face is horrible: the corners of her mouth twist in, the small, pouty mouth shrinks, then the lips bulge out. I am reminded of exotic fish in resort ponds.

Then, breathing in audibly, expelling a grunt, she looks as though she has been slapped. "What?" It comes out like a long screech, someone pushed from the tower.

I falter, losing my breath. "Didn't you? For years — I mean, years ago, when he first appeared — I —" I stop. "You must have heard?"

"I don't listen to common gossip."

"Didn't you ever ask him?"

"I trust him."

"But your comments on the — unfaithfulness of all men — on marriage — on babies—" I'm rambling, insensible. I think, wildly: has she ever listened to her own diatribes against men?

"He is different?"

Boldly: "How?"

"He's a Marquis, for one thing."

"And that proves what?"

"Lineage."

"Miriam, really." I noticed her grip on the cup tightens.

"I thought that rumor died years ago. It's just a rumor fanned by envy."

"Did you check?"

"What? Hire Pinkertons?"

"No, I mean—"

"I trust my lovers, Ella."

"Of course, but—"

"But what?"

"You have a reputation to uphold."

She laughs. "I ignore the idea of reputation."

"But you can't."

Surprise: "And why not?"

I wave my hand. "Well, social circles."

"The Marquis is a loving man. I trust him. You talk like love is a business deal."

For a second I think: for the Marquis it certainly is. It's common knowledge. Miriam's money — we all talk about it. But I say, "Just be careful."

"Just what are you saying?"

"You know I'm your friend."

She makes a gagging sound, the mouth again twisting into that odd pout.

Suddenly I want to be away from the table, away from the unblinking stares of the other guests. Miriam's loud scream and her facial contortions have drawn attention to us. This isn't good. I don't want to talk further. I want light, funny conversation about books and flowers, about Parisian fashion, but Miriam reaches over, covers my hand with her own. "What are you saying?"

I breathe in. Some anger in me — some bud of fury at this situation here, this public embarrassment — compels an honesty I have frankly avoided with her. "Think of your reputation, Miriam. People are questioning your behavior. For years. But it was so — so different then. Back then. Frankly, it's all a little sordid, this affair of yours. The Marquis is a fraud. I have to tell you as a friend. Think of it. I can tell you because we are good friends." I stop, alarmed at the look on Miriam's face: the tight skin over the cheekbones becomes purple, blotches of red speckling her chin.

She makes a thunderous *hurrumph* sound, and a waiter, hovering nearby, picks up the water pitcher. But when he sees her rigid face, her steely fingers opening and closing like a field trap, he backs off, turns away. "You are questioning my morals?" The *you* comes out like a slap.

"I only—" Faltering.

Miriam Leslie sits up, bosom thrust forward. She isn't a powerful woman for nothing.

"The poetess of passion who translates her little masturbatory home-on-the-range fantasies into dollars and cents, hard cash, the Almighty dollar — you of all people are calling me immoral. You, the most exquisite hypocrite in the city! You with that holier-than-thou sentimentality while spouting the boudoir secrets —"

I flush. I beg her. "Miriam, please."

"Immoral. Me?"

"Quiet, please. Miriam. The others."

She stands up, leans over me. "To think that I made you welcome in this hard city — took you, a little country bumpkin in little-girl dresses, a nothing little hayseed from the prairie, a girl with wheat stuck in her teeth, and made you a celebrity, made people *like* you — this is how you repay me in my own city."

I defend myself, but try to speak in a low voice.

"Nobody made me. I made myself."

I get dizzy. I look around. Help me.

She is looking down at me. I start to rise but Miriam seems to be leaning, a towering volcano of a woman now, and I sit back, frightened.

"No one has ever questioned my morals to my face," she says. "At least a friend."

"I *am* your friend, Miriam," I say, but the words sound hollow, whispered.

"We will doubtless meet again," she says. "It's inevitable. I've made you welcome everywhere. But when we do, please do not let on that we know each other. From this point on we will *never* speak. No words, do you hear?"

I begin to say something, mumbling my words.

"Didn't you just hear me say we will never speak again. I don't mean speak of this sordid little breakfast chat — Lord, you are tasteless in coffee topics — but ever. Ever again!"

She turns, fully expecting a clear path out of the room. She pushes her way out the door, people stepping back and gaping. One man, an acquaintance, bows, but she ignores him. Waiters disappear behind kitchen doors. When she is gone, leaving a trail of French perfume and anger, the vacuum she's created quietly fills, as people lean into one another, buzzing, giggling. This is all too wonderful for words. And they are all staring at me, sitting alone here, red faced and trembling. When I glance up, I notice every eye on me. I look down into my coffee cup.

I can't move. I think of my New York — dazzling salons and theater and vaudeville musicales. New York is now just another village I have to leave behind. Idly I touch my empty coffee cup, but no waiter comes over. They are nowhere around. I bury my head but when I glance up again people have not moved. They are still staring at me, just staring. They seem statues, frozen in place. I am frozen here too. I don't know what to do.

What I do know is that I've done something wrong — I've misread some clue. I don't understand what this means except that my grievous *faux pas* might have dire consequences. Miriam is a force to be reckoned with, a battlefield of a woman. Quite possibly, I may be ostracized from New York society. Worse, I am depressed because I've hurt Miriam. I didn't expect that. We are friends: I do love the woman. I do. I don't like her sometimes, but I do love her. So I sit here, afraid to move now, certain my gestures will be scrutinized by the gaping onlookers, and so I wait.

Silently I sob, my head turned away from the guests. I have done something so wrong. But I get confused: I was acting like a Christian woman, helping an errant friend who is stepping into obvious immorality. Wasn't I? Must I be thrown to the lions? Then why do I sit here sobbing?

It doesn't matter: I feel like the dark woman, cloaked and hooded, slinking away from a scene of evil and folly.

An adolescent boy, maybe thirteen, dressed in a bellboy's outfit, appears in the doorway. He is a shiny boy with slicked blond hair, a barely subdued cowlick, and a round pumpkin face. "Message for Mrs. Wilcox," he says, sure of his voice. He clears his throat and starts to walk through the room, scanning the women at the different tables. Loudly: "Message for Mrs. Ella Wheeler Wilcox."

I feel my heart pump, my temples throb. For a moment I am dizzy, and then I am suddenly elated. The trembling ceases, my hands steady and sure on the table, and I throw back my head. I swallow. I stand up, my spine erect the way I learned as a child when I rehearsed my future and carried a yardstick on my shoulders and Shakespeare on my head. In a loud clear voice, equal to the boy's booming tender soprano, I announce to the room at large. "Here, young man, here. I am Ella Wheeler Wilcox."

I am Ella Wheeler Wilcox.

Robella

1900

*The fledgling writer is to be valued—and cherished. But
perhaps it is best sometimes that he be discouraged. I have
discovered, in my years of writing for publication, that the
world of publishing can be a fickle companion. The new
writer, all flushed with the promise of success and valua-
tion, is easily tempted by vice and newfangled idea. He is
wont to indulge the moment, to believe he is somehow privy
to special powers of observation. This observation, while
perhaps the genesis of all great writing, in the lesser writer
can lead to dissolution and ultimately despair. I would
rather such a writer turn to other occupation. It will save
the world from his indulgent, pitiful script, but also save
himself from a life without resolution.*
— Ella Wheeler Wilcox, "Letters to Young Men in
Search of Careers," *Munsey's,* January 1899

Bart Kennedy is not happy. Frankly, he seldom is.
When we talk, he tends to be sober and scornful,
sometimes a bit whiny. I suspect it's because he's a so-
cialist, but this term means so little to me.

"It means so little to him, too," Robert says, laughing
when we talk about the struggling young writer. Bart
has traveled all the way out of New York, catching the
four-horse carriage in East Haven and journeying to
Short-Beach-on-the-Sound, where we now spent our long
summer vacations. This previous winter in New York I

encouraged his writing, not understanding why the self-styled social radical follows me around, visits my salon, confides to me his utopian vision of an inevitable social-istic society. I like him, of course. He is tall and hand-some, lanky and gangly like the farm boys I remember from Wisconsin, and sometimes he's amusing, especially when he tells stories. Somehow, through the deadpan seriousness, there is this flash of wit, the humorous phrase. I like him. I like good-looking people. But, most of all, he flatters me with his endless attention. I had little time during the New York season to read his work — his arms were always overflowing with piles of manuscript, corners twisted and ink bleeding — so casually I invite him to the summer cottage — the Bungalow, I call it — so I can read his current manuscript. I promise to help.

We're very careful whom we invite to Short Beach. Each season we have spent summer away from New York at different popular resorts — three summers, in fact, at Narragansett Pier in Rhode Island, at the Rockingham Hotel. It's been all the rage for a few seasons. But, truth to tell, everyone goes to the same resorts. It's tiresome. Some summers it seems as though the New York world simply follows us there: life is all one long season.

But, by chance, in 1891 we discovered our paradise, the pink granite rocks at Short Beach, in Branford, so near to where we first vacationed at Thimble Island, back in the Meriden days — those days of Winifred/Robert Jr. When we built our Bungalow at Short Beach, we created our only fast rule: we will invite only good friends here, bright, sparkling people we enjoy, people who entertain and amuse. No stodgy business associates, no painful lit-erary obligations, no pesky magazine editors. Just friends. And people we like. Bart Kennedy is someone we like.

Short Beach is where we decide to summer perma-nently.

It is that singular a place. We almost missed it. So many years back, we stopped in New Haven on the way to Boston and then ventured the seven miles by horse and carriage to Short Beach to visit Aunt Hattie, one of whose daughters had taken a summer cottage there, and we were immediately enthralled with the spectacular scenery. We had almost cancelled, tired as we were from traveling. But this was like no other summer place we'd visited. This was not Stony Creek with its dreary mud flats, its wasp-sized mosquitoes, and ill wind. Or Indian Neck with its saltwater tourists. Or Pawson Park with its snobbish summer houses, all umbrella and awning and black servant. This was jutting rock, blazing sunsets over towering white pines, an amethyst and blue-gray landscape, over a white-foamed high tide on the lazy crescent shore. That first night we looked long at the distant horizon, ablaze in the early July nightfall, and then we looked at each other: we knew. This was the place for us to live. The very next summer the Bungalow was built on a rock bluff overhanging the Sound.

New York had finally paled, the salon tiresome, the Sunday musicales predictable, and sometimes the old sense of suffocation came over me. As the years there turned into a decade, we left the city more and more, spending more time — a longer time — at Short Beach. Finally, we gave up the spacious apartment, preferring the careful accommodations of the Everett House at Union Square. Genteel, posh, run by a diffident trained staff, the hotel was both quiet home and cheerful rendezvous. Because, in fact, the winters in New York got shorter and shorter, the urgency to travel to warm climates during the cold months became greater. So many Januarys and Februarys we sojourn in New Orleans, in California, back out to Wisconsin (I alone, of course, because Robert always has something else he has to do). New York's teeming, swelling population, its roughneck character — I once wandered by chance by Bleeker Street and was horrified by the seedy harlots and the swaggering con men — and its frantic gaiety became wearisome, especially as the years passed, and the end of the century loomed. The beaches of the world seemed welcome escape. So the crescent shoreline of Short Beach thrilled us both, with its hazy ocean horizon and its low-hanging clouds, and we built the Bungalow.

"It's the first use of the word Bungalow west of the Rockies," I say, over and over.

"Are you sure?" This from one of my regular summer guests, the budding novelist Kate Jordan.

I do not like to be contradicted on any of my pioneering gestures. "Of course. It's such a western concept. Cabin is what they call summer rentals here. Or lodges, if bigger. Bungalow is now here."

So Bungalow it is, though it's hardly tiny. And then a year later larger living quarters are built on the bluff, a place we call The Barracks, a spacious, creaky house that I overload with curios, wall hangings, and endless bric-a-brac. People gasp on entering my rooms: there is the sense of overabundance, purposeful opulence — a testy interviewer termed it rank clutter — as though Far East warehouses have unloaded their shipping crates on my dock. This is the way I like it. Yards of velvet brocade cover walls. Ornate clocks are everywhere. Wherever the eye falls, there is time. There is the shock of rainbow color: I refuse to believe that some colors clash. I wait for people to congratulate me on my sumptuous decoration. They always do.

When we settle in, permanently, Short Beach becoming our yearlong home, Robert announces that he is retiring. His investments shall carry him into old age, and he says the mania of American men for millions alarms him. I agree. The long days of traveling for business are over now, except for checking on investments and the renewal of old cigar-smoking colleagues at private clubs throughout the country. Gentleman billiards after coffee and cigars, a quiet life behind draperies, rooms where men with walrus mustaches wear three piece suits and talk almost constantly of money.

"I never liked working," he announces.

At Short Beach, at the height of summer, I fill up the

Bungalow or Barracks with all my literary or artistic friends, mostly from New York — there is always laughing or singing in some nearby rooms—and Robert goes fishing for the day, happily lost among the local beach crowd, the inveterate stony Yankees, and the people who run with dogs along the sandy strand. My cronies and I write poetry at separate tables, under the willows, swim out to Green Island and back, and dry our hair on the seawall. Robert returns for dinner. He smiles a lot.

He likes Bart Kennedy, too. He mostly approves of my vast accumulation of friends. But only mostly. The young writers I collect — like Kate Jordan and Dosia Garrison, pretty, vivacious girls — he adores. Bart Kennedy is different because he won't attach himself to any coterie — and he's a firebrand, but decent. He is always the gentleman. "A nice chap," Robert terms him. He dresses well, and has a man's handshake. They talk about politics and Europe.

He looks you right in the eye.

But Bart has come to the shore on the most impossible of days. For me, at least. Throughout the summer I am unofficial planner of all beachfront activity. I demand that Short Beach be lively, exciting, vibrant, everything at high pitch, during the brief resort season. The hot, dreary August days soon bring everything to an end. So I orchestrate dances and balls and dinners and festivals and readings. Every holiday is occasion for merriment. If there is no holiday, I create one. Summers must be perpetual high tide here. Everyone gets into the spirit of things, to be sure, although it is mainly the wives who coerce the hesitant husbands into embarrassing costume and elaborate gesture. To make matters worse, Bart arrives the morning of my most cherished holiday: Illumination Day. It is, of course, my own singular creation. Far removed from the electricity of the cities, from the clanging streetcars, from the newfangled telephones, Short Beach is still an isolated resort, reached only by a four-horse carriage that careens dangerously around Old Snake Hill Road out of East Haven, or by boat along the shoreline. The inhabitants thrive on its remoteness, happy with their clannishness.

"We want to be forgotten," I once announced to a reporter, although immediately I invited the world to visit their favorite poetess. Robert clicked his tongue and shook his head over that news item. "Ella, sometimes you talk too much." I fumed all afternoon.

On Illumination Day we decorate all the cottages along the crescent beach with lanterns and unbroken walls of bright candlelight, and the effect is utterly dazzling: a story book fairyland come to life, the purple magenta sunset offset by the twinkling and flashing of iridescent firelight. Visitors are enthralled. Strangers ride in carriages from inland towns, and stare. Newspapers send photographers.

At night there is a full-dress or costume ball in the cabin of the Bungalow. The invitations are engraved, on cream linen paper, and always include a few lines of my topical verses: a summons to come dance, sent in a pale blue envelope.

I organize costumes and pageants throughout the day, running frantically from cottage to cottage to ensure everything goes off without mishap. When I return home for a second to try on my new costume, freshly altered — I am to be Isis in the Egyptian pageant I've written, and the actress Julie Opp is to be Cleopatra — there on the porch sits an irascible Bart Kennedy with his pile of manuscript in his lap, like a cherished but unruly pet.

"An hour of your time," he says, quickly.

I rush past him. "Later, my dear Bart," I say, trying to be kind. "I am at my wit's end. I am Isis without my flowers. Where are the flowers? Someone has forgotten the garlands."

Kennedy stares, mouth open. I leave the porch and am thrashing through the manicured garden beds, scissors in hand, snipping blooms like a mad woman, my hair breaking free of my ribbons, and I bunch them against my chest. For a moment I bury my face in the flowers, inhaling. I seem to swoon.

Kennedy kicks the railings of the porch.

The beautiful Julie Opp is in one of the bedrooms, probably trying on one of her costumes. I can hear her laughing at something. She never takes these events as seriously as I do, but then, no one else does. To me, they are as lyrical and moving as an Elizabethan wedding barge down the Thames. Julie, fresh from a Broadway hit, is always my choice for center stage. She comes out of New York for every holiday, often trailing an entourage behind her. Sometimes Robert participates in these pageants, cigar in hand and Panama hat pulled low over his brow, but he always has a bemused look, as though he is just an indulgent parent.

Illumination Night is the finale of the summer season, my last festival of summer light, the late August heat forgotten for one night. Fourth of July is rehearsal, of sorts. Then Julie Opp was the Goddess of Liberty, and I and twelve others were the thirteen states, the Grecian-gowned royal court surrounding her, drifting ashore to the sound of "Columbia, the Gem of the Ocean." It was a much-talked about success.

The stage we use is always Robella. Robert and I named our naphtha boat launch "Robella" after ourselves because it is so much a part of our summers. This large launch squires friends and townspeople along the coastline, gathering friends from neighborhood piers or from the New Haven harbor, and delivering them to the Barracks. The party revelers sit on the rocky launch as it glides over the waves, thrill to the sun and wind and air, and when it returns to shore, so many of the younger set leap into the waters, swimming back to shore, in a fury to beat the launch. It's great fun.

I am still the best swimmer. It's what I do in summer — that, and write my verses. Swimming continues to be my passion. I am in the water three or four times a day, early morning to late at night, bathed in the glimmering

moonlight, a strong swimmer, a competitor, a driven
swimmer, a woman hungry for waves and salt water.

> *What glorious times we have together,*
> *My launch and I, in the summer weather!*
> *My trim little launch with its sturdy sides*
> *And its strong heart beating away as it glides*
> *Out of the harbor and out of the bay,*
> *Wherever our fancy may lead away,*
> *Rollicking over the salt track*
> *Hurrying seaward and hurrying back.*

All summer long, along the crescent beach, the launch
bobs and floats. For my pageants I decorate Robella with
flowers and lanterns and cascading draperies — Is this
the Nile? Is this the Potomac? Where to see the daughters of Rhine? — And the illuminated launch — the string
of lanterns flicker with shimmering light — is pulled to
the shore amid music and singing and laughter. Tonight
will be Egypt, Julie Opp the doomed Cleopatra with paper asp to discreetly covered breast. One of the younger
men — maybe Charles Hanson Towne or Ridgely
Torrence, both handsome men now fixtures throughout
the summer, leaving successful New York lives for long
weekends — will be an emoting Antony, in sensible and
proper toga, and the launch will be ablaze in the night.

I have so much to do.

Once, passing by Bart Kennedy who sits, unmoving
now, stone-faced, on the porch, his manuscript in his lap,
his fingers tracing some words across the page — I toss
him a bathing suit, one of many we keep for visitors who
don't understand that they were expected to swim.

"I don't swim," he announces, irritated.

"Of course you do."

"I choose not to."

"Everyone swims."

"No, I don't. I'm from New York."

"They have beaches there."

"They have the East River. New York has — harbors."
He says it so flatly that I pause. He looks down at his
manuscript and then back up at me. He's angry.

I have no time for this. "Then learn. Paddle like the
little children. Like a puppy."

But I laugh as I say it, touching him on the arm gently,
warmly, but he stares away from me.

"Please, Bart, try to understand."

He clears his throat.

"Please," he says. "An hour."

There are too many people around. Harried servants
hurry past with covered bowls of food, headed God
knows where. Baskets of flowers suddenly are dropped
onto the porch. Boxes of candles are unwrapped. Rainbow bunting is unfurled and draped over eaves. Windows are polished. Steps swept. Buckets of water soak
hot stone pathways.

Robert owns four small cottages nearby, usually rented
to friends. Now there is laughter in all of them as I hurry
back and forth, energizing everyone. They are filled with
young women from Boston and New York and New
Haven, huddled together for summer fun. There are the
Jordan sisters, Kate and Martha. Kate writes fiction for
Scribner's, and is finishing her first novel. She is a dark-
haired beauty with pale freckled skin. Her sister Martha
is small, very blonde, with tiny sapphire eyes. She writes
romantic serials for the yellow press. I tell them daily
they will have great futures — "The world will soon notice you" — but they don't believe me.

Perhaps I tell too many friends the same thing.

In the parlor, arranging flowers, is Theodosia Garrison, another young poet. Dosia Garrison has turquoise
eyes, golden hair, and a Cupid's bow mouth. She's my
dearest friend. In New York I introduced her to Bart
Kennedy, hoping to make both happy, but he wants nothing to do with anyone, it seems. Certainly not the bevy
of "your girl writers," as he terms them.

So Bart refuses to join me as I fly about, tending to

Dosia's need for more roses, to Martha's little teary snit over a rip in her ball gown, to Kate's changing of a line in the pageant song—"O Nile, Where is Thy Heart?" Hearing the rehearsed line repeated over and over, the noise wafting from the nearby cottage, Bart Kennedy grunts. As I pass by, he bellows, "I know were the heart is," adding, "The barge she sank in like the burnished crone—"

"Did you say something?" Robert calls from inside the cottage.

"No," Bart said quietly, "I'm talking to myself."

"That's dangerous," Robert says, returning to his paper.

I smile as I head to the kitchen.

Bart stares across the busy lawns. When I pass by him again, I notice his face is crimson.

I try not to think about him.

Soon servants are stringing lanterns along the porch eaves, and the place assumes an oriental air, as the slight sea breeze rocks the delicate paper objects and the Indian wind chimes I love jangle. On the lawn, trailed by four women in various stages of rehearsal and costume, I begin to demonstrate the new and elaborate steps of the dance I created for the summer. It is called the Ella Wheeler Wilcox Glide — "One must not be modest about one's creations, if that creation be beautiful," I tell people — and I know my mother back in Wisconsin would not approve. There are just too many arabesque movements, too much fluttering of the hands into the air, too many twists and turns. Too much — what? — exaggerated femininity? Robert announces from the porch, "It is more dangerous than the horse carriage ride around Snake Hill." Dosia laughs when she tries to Glide, saying, "This is the Wild West, Ella."

"Any territory I enter is frontier," I say.

I hear Bart Kennedy mumble: "Nowadays the fashionable people prefer ragtime."

I grin. "I expect this dance to be the rage of America by the fall."

Watching, Bart Kennedy finally looks back to his manuscript. To no one he reads a line from his manuscript, yelling it into the hot air. "The soul of man must be the rebel in the garden of strife." I stop for a second, annoyed at the jarring line, but no one is looking at him, except one of the servant girls. She looks scared of him. We hurriedly finish our dance rehearsal, the chiffon flying, the ribbons twirling, rose petals dropping to the lawn like fat, dyed raindrops.

Kate announces, "Only Ella can do the Glide."

I laugh louder than anyone else.

Kennedy slams his fist into his manuscript. I see his displeasure in his glance. He thinks I'm a foolish woman, I know, not the radical soulmate he envisioned when he read *Poems of Passion.* I am suddenly conscious of my hair dyed the color of forsythia, my arms jangling too many clanging bracelets, my long-swept dress clumping over the lawn grass. So I am not the woman he wants me to be: I cannot let his horrible stare ruin my day. In the city, I enjoyed him, with his handsome, gaunt face. I recall how he recited from memory my poem "The Workers":

> God is calling to the masses, to the peasant and the peer;
> He is calling to all classes that the crucial hour is near;
> For each rotting throne must tremble and fall broken in
>   the dust,
> With the leaders who dissemble and betray the people's
>   trust.

> Still the voice of God is calling; and above the wreck I see
> And beyond the gloom appalling, the great
>   Government-to-Be.
> From the ruins it has risen, and my soul is overjoyed,
> For the school supplants the prison, and there are no
>   unemployed.

"You are the soul of the working class," he told me then.

I see him stand up.

"I'm going for a walk," he says out loud, but there is only the servant girl nearby, a petite Irish lass arranging excessive bouquets of flowers in bleached wicker baskets. She looks a little nervous around him, with his sudden mutterings and increasing bilious complexion. She keeps an eye on him: back home in County Cork such men, she knows, are cursed by unmentionable spirits. The Banshees. But she is used to oddball types appearing at the cottages. Not only do I attract the devoted readership who discover obsessive love for me — those odd men who appear on my doorstep professing eternal love and immediate marriage — but there are the ill-kept beggars and deranged wanderers, some Spanish-American War veterans who tramp across America, the vagabondia, who always find a sympathetic ear with me.

I sit in a chair under the willow, catching my breath. I sip lemonade someone puts in my hand.

I watch him. He watches me. For a moment I realize what he sees: an older woman acting silly, a woman gussied up with feathers and flowers. He doesn't understand my hunger for beauty. I'm starved without color or noise. I *am* silly. But I'm more than that. Ornament dresses the meditative soul.

Bart is standing on the porch, unmoving, his arms filled with manuscript, as Robert strolls out of the house, preparing to leave. "Come with me," Robert says, touching him on the arm in a fatherly gesture. "We'll stroll to Knowles." Seeing Bart's baffled look, Robert explains that Knowles Emporium is the general store that's a longstanding fixture near the center of the small village, a combination all-purpose store, post office, express and business office, all in one. He sells salted meats, preserved dried fish, molasses and salt, spices, blocks of chocolate, all out of sea crates, and near the front door weathered barrels hold pickles in brine and salt crackers. The smell of aged cheese lingers in the aisles, pungent and thick. Sawdust covers the floor. Old Man Knowles claims he can answer all your questions while he packages your goods. We all seem to end up there at least once a day. Robert buys cigars there.

Bart nods. "Sure," he says. "I need to walk."

Robert looks at him. "Ella will get to your manuscript later."

Bart looks sheepish, glances in my direction. I turn away, make believe I'm absorbed in some flowers. "It's not that — it's all this — celebration."

Robert shakes his head. "What else is there to do in life? We celebrate."

"No," Bart says, "we have to have a purpose."

Robert laughs. "It is a purpose, a darn good one. The ancients understood that—with their elaborate festivals. Their seasonal revels. We've gotten away from that, in this bland culture."

"Maybe we should."

"Maybe it's the worst thing. Ella knows. Ella understands the need for pageantry in a life." He smiles. "Come on, let's walk."

"The true democrat despises pomp."

Robert frowns. "Then we are doomed as a Republic."

"How so?"

"Too much leveling of mankind takes away the moments when we can imagine ourselves gods."

He walked ahead, and Bart, pausing, rushes to catch up.

I sit there, smiling.

I watch them stroll through the manicured gardens, where I spend so much time. Musing, Robert nods at the flower beds, as though evaluating and approving. Robert is a large man, grown wider with middle age, and Bart is a slip of a boy, a twig ambling beside the bulky tree trunk. Together, they move slowly, walking through lattices of late summer roses. There are roses on all sides of them, even above, and I hope Bart is getting light headed.

I glance at his manuscript back on the veranda table,

held there by a book — Paul Leicester Ford's *Janice Meredith*, my book, not his — and a vase of flowers. I am suddenly tired: I will not be able to read all those pages today. Never. Why must it be today? His own year's work, the blood and spine of his life in those pages. Why today?

When Robert and Bart wander back to the Barracks, the lawns are chaos — milling crowds of pageanteers shuffling, servants stringing even more daisy chains along the walkways. Robert finds me inside, hurriedly showing a new visitor one of the walls—Robert's new project. Robert comes from behind, touches my arm, and turns to Bart, "This was my idea," he says. Then he smiles. "Well, actually Oliver Herford's."

We all stare at the bare wall on which people have signed their names, scribbled long inscriptions, drawn cartoons and diagrams. Caricatures of happy faces.

"When I am finished," Robert says, "these walls will be covered with the signatures of everyone who is anyone in America. The cream of the cream." He points. "See. There's John Barrymore." Barrymore has drawn a sketch he labeled "First Night" — he had just opened in New Haven in *The Fortune Hunter*. Bart peers over Robert's shoulder — he stands away from me, I notice — at the signatures of writers like Zona Gale and Ridgely Torrence, friends from New York, two lovers. An old favorite, the daring Edgar Fawcett. Marshall P. Wilder, the midget humorist. There are bars of music, original sketches. Clara Louise Kellogg, the premiere opera singer. Clever, witty poetry. Purposely humorless doggerel. I have scribbled in a corner, oddly: "The rose of fame is only an artificial flower at last." But in the center I've written lines Robert points to. "Everyone," he says, grinning, "assumes these lines have to do with them. Right, Ella?"

> *Love and the sea and summer—*
> *What could blend*

> *With that rare mixture but a perfect friend?*
> *Therefore, we summon from the court of art*
> *The aristocracy of brain and heart.*

"They do," I say.

Edwin Markham, the Man with a Hoe, wrote:

> *Place where passing souls can rest*
> *On their way and do their best.*

Bart, I notice, looks impressed, staring at the photographs of William Gillette, the incarnation of Sherlock Holmes himself.

"You like Gillette?" Robert asks.

"Of course," Bart says.

Robert is already turning away.

"Bart, be patient," I say to him.

He looks at me, smiles thinly.

Robert looks back, kindly. "Ella does what she says. But she is a busy woman."

"I know, but I've come from the city for the day."

Robert nods. "But, young man, you chose to come here on Illumination Day."

"So?"

"Do you know about Illumination Day, Bart?"

"Like a picnic?"

Robert laughs. "It is the only holiday at Short Beach that is designed to celebrate Ella herself. It's a holy day here, my boy. Learn to pray."

I have to interrupt, amused by Robert's words. "Robert, the young man will think you're mad — talking like this."

"I'm serious."

I look at Bart. He isn't happy at all. He is staring at Robert as one might look at someone totally deranged. Bart's face says it all: the eyes wide with alarm, the jaw slack, the lips pursed. Even with the smile on his face, Robert looks totally serious. Bart doesn't know where to look.

I have to leave — from outside someone is calling me.

Late afternoon and into early twilight: Short-Beach-on-the-Sound becomes a frenzied panorama of light and music. My orchestrated holiday is itself at peak moment, with the barge safely landed to great applause, with Cleopatra and her kohl-eyed attendants ushered gloriously onto the sandy shores, with me strumming a mandolin to accompany a song by the celebrated Mme. Sortier, with a symbolic tableau enacted by actress Ruth St. Denis, also to sustained applause. Dogs roam and yap. Cats hide in the sheltering oak trees. Gangs of small boys, in knickers and suspenders, toss balls over the heads of revelers. Wives drag husbands away from horseshoes.

And at night the lanterns are finally and ceremoniously lighted, the crescent shoreline becoming an instant fairyland of winking fireflies. Residents stroll along the water's edge, staring back at the illuminated cottages, and Short Beach looks like the sky itself has settled to the earth. The cool calm waters of the shore reflect the fluttering, sparking lights of the lanterns and torches, the waves gleaming under the starry blue-black night. In the first glance of twilight, after the lighting of the lanterns, the true meaning of Illumination Night becomes abundantly clear to all. Even the cynics — those stalwart down-East fishermen who occupy some of the cottages, those craggy old New Englanders who find my posturing faintly suspect — even they nod at the spectacle. This, they know, is wonder. This is land that is holy. This is all right. This is like the eye of a hurricane, this moment of silent contemplation, a moment when people stop, hypnotized, and then begin to breathe again.

I almost weep myself, it is so beautiful.

From my porch, surrounded by so much light I seem encased in it, a halo that makes me glow on the waters I reflect, I announce in a clear voice that sails over the lawns and beach fronts, "No ocean ever lay like this," but I am waving at the illuminated shoreline, not the water. But it is clear that it has all become one now, water and land and people. The golden light is a blanket covering everything. One harmonious beat, one rhythm, the poet's heart.

Robert touches my elbow, nodding. "You are passion," he whispers, and I tremble.

I strut across the seawall, nodding and smiling.

But just when the night festivities are to begin, the skits and the dancing, all under candlelight, Robert whispers that Bart Kennedy, tucked inside, away from the glitter and shine of the outdoors, wants to see me. A servant has whispered in Robert's ear.

I don't want to break the splendid moment, but I have no choice. He is a guest.

"He's all right," Robert says.

"What do you mean?"

"I mean, he's all right as a person."

"I know that."

I leave Robert on the lawn. Inside I'm surprised: Bart is storming back and forth, reaching one wall, staring at some picture, and then turning, angry, and striding to another wall. For a moment I watch him, as though he is an animal in a cage. "Stop," I say to him. "Just stop moving."

"You promised me," Bart says.

"Bart," I begin, shaking. I am still outdoors among the lights and shimmering waves, with the music of the water and the music of my heart. I take a step towards him.

He stops, turns, and his face is white with anger.

"I don't know how I could have turned to you for advice on literature," he begins, cruelly. His voice is breaking. "You are a vain, superficial woman, not deserving of your reputation. What poet — what Longfellow — what Whittier — what Wordsworth — spends so much time on frivolous games and flowers and candles and foolish young women dressed like idiots—"

"Stop," I scream, livid now. I wave my arm, and the dozen bracelets clang. Both of us stop, stare momentarily, startled by the awful noise.

"You are a fraud." Bart is out of control.

"Stop," I say, louder.

He stops, as though realizing what he's said. The white face goes red. "I'm sorry, but —"

"This is my home," I say. "This is my home." Tears come into my eyes. I cover my face with my hands, and wait. I will not cry now.

Nervous, Bart gathers his valise, which he's deposited on the pillow-piled divan, next to the drowsing Angora cat, tucks his still unread manuscript inside, and bows. His eyes glance nervously around the room, house plants everywhere, antimacassars cluttering chairs, every space covered by a bauble or a print or a decoration. "I'm leaving," he says. "This is no place for the writer of the future."

"How dare you," I say, regaining my composure. "You're a silly child."

He bows again. "I mean no disrespect."

"Though you give it full blown," I say.

"I'm sorry."

"But clearly you're not."

"It's just that —"

"It's just that you are a brash young man, selfish and greedy. If this is the twentieth century you praise, I want no part of it."

He gets snide. "And if you're the nineteenth century, we have certainly gone down the wrong path."

Again, the anger. "This is my home, Bart."

"It's all so trivial."

"It's people having a good time, Bart."

"Superficial."

"Celebration is never superficial."

"But you're a poet."

"And you're someone who runs from joy."

He turns away. "I'll take the night train out of New

Haven."

"There is no carriage going there."

"I'll walk."

"It is seven or eight miles."

"I'll walk."

"You don't know the way."

He doesn't answer, but heads out the door, clutching his valise. I stare at his departing back.

In a second he is gone, disappearing into the bright light of the lawns.

Robert comes looking for me. I am weeping, curled into a corner of the chaise lounge.

He leads me outside where I am caught up in the swelling, celebrating crowds. And Robert leans in to me and says quietly, "You are Ella Moon. Look up at the sky." I look up. Through the white night — the dim sky made pale by so much candle and lantern — there is still a faint sliver of a summer moon, etched against the fading opaque darkness. The night hums with music and wind. Robert whispers: "Ella Moon looks down upon the beautiful land of Nod she created."

I smile. Robert always has a way of saving me. "But you're the brightest star," I say.

"But the heavens take their shadings from the silvery moon."

"Robert, why do I get involved with people who do this to me?" I face him.

"Because you are generous."

"And a little foolish?"

He smiles. "Yes, a little foolish."

"And vain?"

"That too."

"He called me superficial."

"Well, this is all show and pomp."

"So what?"

"So what indeed."

"Am I more than that?"

"Of course, you are."

But I keep hearing Bart's words. Why do I need this? Do I? Suddenly I flash to my childhood bedroom, all bare wood and faded curtain. I shudder. Help me.

"Do I go too far with this?" I point to the lights outside.

"A little."

"Oh, Robert."

"But you're more than spectacle, Ella."

"Oh, I pray I am."

"But it's who you are, Ella. You are a generous woman, truly."

"Bart—"

"Bart doesn't understand that the heavens rule." Then he whispers my own uplifting lines:

> *"It is easy enough to be pleasant,*
> *When life flows by like a song,*
> *But the man worth while is one who will smile,*
> *When everything goes dead wrong."*

I smile. These famous words I wrote so long ago sound like a love lyric. I drum my fingers on his cheek.

I answer:

> *"For the test of the heart is trouble,*
> *And it always comes with the years,*
> *And the smile that is worth the praise of earth,*
> *Is the smile that shines through tears."*

We look at each other. Then we both giggle.

Later that night, when the lanterns are extinguished and the decent citizens of Short Beach are asleep, we sit on a ridge of granite at the edge of our dock, off the sea-wall that juts out into the ocean. It is nearly midnight.

"This place should be called Granite Bay," I say. "A much better name." I love the hard-weathered pink and amethyst granite, the colors darkening as the day turns into night. Now, at midnight, with the moon bright again, surrounded by a speckling of distinct stars, the rocks are soft, velvety charcoal. There is a slight chill in the air, and, wrapped in a shawl, I tuck my body into Robert's.

"Paradise," Robert says, and I nod.

I follow a vague outline of a seagull swooping to the shore, and then ascending to heaven. It disappears into the murky night. "Watch," Robert says, and I follow the movement of the bird into the clouds. I tremble, and Robert pulls me closer.

"No ocean ever lay like this," Robert says. I turn to look at him. He is looking into my eyes and smiling.

"My Robert," I say.

"My poet."

But suddenly I think of a frantic Bart Kennedy striding across my polished floors at the Barracks, condemning me, calling me trivial, frivolous, a woman unworthy of my special reputation. The poetess of passion, called vain and foolish by an untested upstart. Like a ballroom coquette or a coy maiden in one of my narrative poems.

I fear he may be right. I hate the idea.

"Bart," I say.

"No," Robert says. "Not now."

Robert points to a light in the distance, a passing boat perhaps, or perhaps a lantern on one of the small islands off the coast. Out there. Way out there. I try to focus — to follow Robert's hand as he reaches out to the darkness — but I can't: I am thinking of Bart Kennedy, that young man in a hurry, walking the dark pathways through the sleeping villages to New Haven, propelled by indignation and anger. A wild man, with valise tucked under his arm, his manifesto for the twentieth century contained within, unread by me. Bart Kennedy, now sitting on the long night train into New York. I imagine him staring into the night shadows of the train car windows, watching the blank landscape and seeing his tight, furious reflection in the glare. I suddenly remember being on a train going from Windsor to Milwaukee, the young girl in a hurry, the romantic poet desperate for people and approval and — yes, escape from the farm. For a second I hunger to be back there, that child again, hapless and excited, new at the game, and then I hunger to be at Bart's side, explaining, consoling, talking. I don't want his hatred. But then, the wind going through me — a ghost moving through my body — I despise him. This thought comes suddenly and I'm oddly happy with it. Yes, I think, I can afford to hate this young man. He's taken away the beauty of my special night. But then, I think no, I won't. I won't let myself go to that vile place. I ride that train too. I'm better than that.

I'm, well, worth while.

Ride

1901

Frankly, I have only frustration and annoyance at the current fascination of Americans with all things royal. I have read that some senator proposed a bill to have our Washington pages dress in ornate uniform, with gold braid and fancy cap, because their suits are drab and uncolorful. Why do we need the trappings of royalty? The democratic spirit is real and honest. Royalty is perhaps outmoded now: a throwback to an earlier time of pageantry and splendor, but a time decidedly now passé. This current mania of rich American heiresses crossing the Atlantic to wed impoverished nobility—all to give themselves an undemocratic title—strikes me as the height of folly. We are Americans here, democrats all, daughters and sons of the prairie, of the frontier, of the endless West.

> — Ella Wheeler Wilcox, "Your Days and Mine," *Demorest's,* June 1901

I sit in the front parlor with Mr. Johns, a coolly deliberate soft-talking man, sipping coffee and watching the young man arrive at his reason for the visit. We've canceled an evening of theater in New Haven, giving away our coveted tickets to see Marta Hart in *Gypsy Love.*

"The Queen is dying," the man says, emphatically.

"Hasn't she been doing so for a while?" I say, purposely irreverent. I love to shock young people who seem to believe they have the only mandate to do so, now that the new liberated century has begun, what with the New Woman on bicycles and young men with swagger and spit. With boys and girls laughing, unchaperoned in the streets and restaurants. Some women even smoke cigarettes, I know. At one of my soirees a woman extracted a cigarette from a colorful box labeled Velvet Mouthpieces. I liked the product's genteel name, but I frowned the young woman into leaving early.

But Mr. Johns just smiles. He is a journalist, unflappable, and he's probably been briefed. He's interviewed bearded atheists in New York, Niagara Falls barrel rollers, and Balkan opera divas who travel with dozens of hideous snakes. "This time it's taking," he says.

I laugh. I like him.

"We want you, Mrs. Wilcox, to travel to London to cover the funeral for our paper. We want the fresh perspective of America's preeminent American poet." His words sound rehearsed.

I've never had any real interest in Queen Victoria. Robert, I admit, seems to have more interest in British royalty than I do. Sometimes he comments on some royal happening — some criticism of one of Victoria's vagrant grandchildren perhaps — but I can never make much sense out of the conventional and incestuous European lineages that swirl around Victoria. They all seem so interchangeable — and so purposely undemocratic. Whenever I think about Victoria, I imagine a small woman — much like myself — but dowdy, without style, frumpy, certainly weathered and drawn, a woman shrouded in mourning shawls and dowager bonnets. I imagine a woman with a sudden hot temper, an unhappy monarch. Someone out of a dated Tennyson poem.

One night, looking up from his newspaper, Robert mentions that she is dying, the venerable aged Queen ending appropriately with the century she dominated, although the newspapers — with characteristic restraint—couch their information in genteel euphemism about wisdom and hoary age and the passing of an august era. It doesn't fool Robert, and it doesn't much concern me: I have work to do. I now write syndicated columns for the Hearst press, quick little upstart pieces on life as lived in the colonies, rapid-fire observations on social customs and their failure among the children of the Republic. I have volumes to say to young men and women then tackling the ordeal of courtship. So much can go wrong. I have wisdom to share with married women, with old women, with the sick and the dying, with the young. Homelitic homespun, Ella Wheeler Wilcox style. I prefer death in the abstract, however—the romanticized depictions of widows at their husbands' graves. The very real dying of a flesh-and-blood personage—like the redoubtable Queen Victoria— doesn't excite me.

But a telegram sent out of New York informed me that a Malcolm Johns, a representative of Hearst's *New York American* — where weekly I ply my lovelorn advice to young girls and their mothers — would be journeying from the city to my home in Short Beach. Such telegrams don't startle or excite me; I am, to be sure, Ella Wheeler Wilcox, and in demand now from the yellow press. The telegraph office in Branford makes certain I get my wires promptly: Johnny Lake, the slow-witted brother of the first selectman, a wiry nervous man on a Pope bicycle, is always on call.

"I don't think so —"

"You are a name in American literature."

"No."

"Mr. Hearst asks only for you, Madame."

So now I am flattered, but I throw up my hands. "Oh, that's impossible," I say. "Simply impossible. It's winter, you know. It's ice and snow out there. And on the high seas — all that ferocious wind, like icicles through the skin, young man. It's winter — Robert and I only travel to warm climates in winter." I go on and on like this, enjoying myself, building a scenario of icebergs and sea squalls and hurricanes. When I segue into London and its dank, marrow-chilling winters, the young man holds up his hand, pleading. I stop, happy.

"Perhaps your husband can advise you."

For a moment I am irritated, as I always am when someone assumes my husband exerts such authority over me, but in fact I understand now that this young man has been duly prepared by his anxious editors: I like to see myself as the dutiful wife, acquiescing to the will of my husband. "Are you Ella Wheeler Wilcox?" someone asks. "I'm Mrs. Robert Wilcox," I answer, smiling.

I leave the room, seeking Robert. Mr. Johns sips sherry. When I glance back over my shoulder, he is smiling.

If I give it any thought, I realize that Robert will immediately tell me to go. He looks up from his book, puts down his cigar, and says, "Ella, you have to do this."

"But it's winter, Robert," I say.

"You're not going to the North Pole, Ella."

"It's England."

"They have heat."

"Not much."

Then he surprises me. He takes a puff on his cigar, and smiles. "A month or so. I'll go with you. What do you think?"

Again, I am not surprised. For months now Robert sits alone in his study, ledgers and papers strewn about him, in messy piles, uncharacteristic of his meticulous self. He is restless, at odds with himself. Winter keeps him indoors.

"Yes, Mr. Johns," I say, returning to the room with Robert at my side. "We will go."

He smiles. "You are the voice of the people."

"I told her that," Robert says.

This is starting to become excessive. I'm enjoying it.

"Ella, do you realize how much weight your voice carries out there in America?"

"You're exaggerating," I say. But I smile. In fact, I do know from my letters how much impact I have on the public.

I talk of dangerous social conditions, of duties parental and filial, of hopeful change in the new century, of science and medicine. I write that "in every thousand people who are living on this earth, not more than one is alive." I inspire: "We must climb, stumble, fall, and try again and again." I see myself as an advocate for women and their plight, even though I loathe the term feminist — "a barbarism" — and think the capitalized New Woman concept farcical. I'm not sorry.

> *I hold it the truth that no woman can be*
> *An excellent wife and an excellent mother,*
> *And leave enough purpose and time for another*
> *Profession outside. And our sex was not made*
> *To jostle with men in the great mart of trade.*
> *The wage-earning women, who talk of their sphere,*
> *Have thrown the domestic machine out of gear,*
> *They point to their fast swelling ranks overjoyed*
> *Forgetting the army of men unemployed.*
> *The banner of Feminine "Rights" when unfurled*
> *Means a flag of distress to the rest of the world.*
> *And poor Cupid, distressed by such follies and crimes,*
> *Sits weeping, alone, in the Land of Hard Times.*

Some, in protest, say I've had a successful career in a man's world. I am a working woman. I should become an ardent feminist. Poppycock. I'm a poetess.

I'm just a versifier.

"You will end the century for us. For Mr. Hearst," Mr. Johns says. I nod. Mr. Johns is half out of his chair, excited.

So we embark in the dead of winter for England. And an arduous journey it becomes, with me ill most of the time because of the choppy seas and raw-bone chill, a dankness deep into our comfortable cabin, with Robert moody and sullen. Everything assumes a somber gray tone. Even with our sumptuous accommodations, a present from Hearst, we can enjoy little: the monotonous rolling of the high seas and the mean numbing cold that seeps through portals make me dwell on death. I have never felt so close to it. I can taste the ashes.

I feel spirits around me. I sense wraiths in the eaves.

I discover a clairvoyant on board, a wizened old man, with trembling fingers and runny nose. He tells Robert that Europe is filled with thievery, and he tells me that I will wear feathers at the Court of St. James.

We find ourselves dwelling on Robert Junior.

On the cold nights on board ship, the chilly wind lingering in the passageways, we sit with lukewarm tea and strawberry-jam soda biscuits, and, holding hands, with me resting my body against his, Robert and I talk of other worlds.

"One of us will join our son first," I say.

"I will pass on first," Robert says

"Oh, don't say that. Robert, please."

"But I will."

I get frightened. The prospect of being alone at Short Beach alarms me: all that endless water and sand, and the stark winter isolation, like a wall of blank granite. The squawking of lost seagulls on the ice-covered sandy beach. I shiver.

"I'm afraid," I say.

"There's nothing to be afraid of."

"But being alone."

"We're family."

"I'm afraid. I don't want to be alone."

"You won't be. We've been through so much. Robert's passing. We're joined, Ella, you and I."

"But if you go—"

"I'll make you a promise," he says. "I'll always stay with you, even when I'm gone. My spirit will be there with you."

"It's not the same thing," I say. "I'll drift."

"You're a strong woman, Ella."

"No, I'm not."

"That's not true."

"I need your anchor."

"All your life you've controlled your destiny. You created your own life."

"But now you guide me."

"Not as much as you think."

"Oh, but you do."

He leans into me, patting my hand with his palm. "When I pass on, I will talk to you from beyond. Somehow."

"Robert!" I feel an electric charge move through me.

"I mean it, Ella. I'll send you a message from beyond. I promise you. I know it can be done. You and I have talked to — to how many psychics over the years? Dozens? You have to be ready to receive it.."

Since Robert Junior died, we have sought the comfort of so many seers — so many frauds, to be sure, but some so truthful we are startled. One composed a portrait of Robert Junior in heaven, growing, evolving, waiting for us. We both wept that night, Robert and I.

I grip his hand. "Robert, I must go first. I'm his mother."

"I'm his father. I never held him."

"I held him but a moment."

"No, it will be me."

I feel in my bones the truth of it. I tuck my head into his chest. "I'm lonely already."

His hand touches the back of my head. "I will communicate with you. I promise."

"Promise me, Robert."

"I just did, Ella. I just did."

I am given a prominent spot from which to view the elaborate funeral procession, a place of honor among the international correspondents. The London press refers to me as the American poetess laureate, and I don't know whether or not they're being snide, but I sit a mere stone's throw from the slow-moving diminutive coffin. The Queen, a tiny woman, is carried in what looks to me like a child's coffin. The silence of the gathered mourners is eerie: so many people, in line and on the sides, shoulders touching, and I think of ghost towns, of dreams in which no one moves or speaks. We are a photograph now, all frozen before a camera's lens. This is Europe, I keep telling myself. This is England. I am here. At long last. This is the great Queen, now dead. This is the most famous woman of the last century, now bringing it to a fitting and symbolic end.

I can touch the coffin as it passes, I am that close. All the crowned heads of Europe are in my reach, resplendent in gold braid and emblem and medal. Watching them, I grow faint. Something about the assembled dignitaries strikes me as fragile and transitory. The decadent and bejeweled royalty look anachronistic and ancient, oddly weak in their elaborate court finery. All these ribbons and insignias and plumed caps and elaborate jeweled swords. It's as though I'm watching a medieval costume drama out of Walter Scott, some scene from a child's book, remembered, now come to life. This has no connection to the world I know.

The pageantry is splendid — I make mental notes of ideas to appropriate for my own summer pageants — but I am frantic about my obligation to Hearst. Here the newspaper delivers me to Europe, to this touching moment in history, they provide lots of money and royal accommodation, yet I can't produce a poem worthy of the occasion. I don't have an idea in my head. Not one — this is alien land for me. The role of poet laureate — albeit of American yellow journalism — is not for me — that much I understand. I work from the heart, not the calculated move of the intellectual poet. And certainly not the court poet. I can't forge literature by edict. I need the wellsprings of the Heart.

"What can I do, Robert?" I beg.

"It'll happen," he says.

"My mind is empty," I say.

At night I sit in our Hotel Cecil bedroom, pen in hand,

paper before me, blank and accusing. Nothing comes. Paralysis. I have, frankly, no interest in the dead Queen. Once the pageantry is over, the bustling shops of London suddenly attract. But the somber black crepe paper over every door frame, and the stark memorial photographs of the late Queen in every window, only serve to reinforce my writer's block. The night grows quiet. Robert goes to sleep. "It'll happen, Ella," he says in a litany that annoys — and I linger over a British periodical, *The Gentlewoman,* flipping through the pages. In it I find a grainy photograph of the late queen as she took a ride in the countryside. The caption says: "The Queen is taking a drive today." I stare at the line, long and hard, and the words fascinate me. It is, to me, a melancholy moment, the last photograph taken of her. At last I go to bed, but early in the morning, around three, I wake from a troubled sleep. I've been dreaming: wild horses pull an empty carriage over an ice-blue ocean. I wake, gasping. The rooms are cold because the gas grate has malfunctioned, and I find myself chilled. Then the haunting words I read come back to me. *The Queen is taking a drive today.* I stare: yes. Suddenly here it is, the first lines luminous and clear.

> *The Queen is taking a drive today;*
> *They have hung with purple the carriage-way.*
> *They have dressed with purple the royal track*
> *Where the Queen goes forth and never comes back.*

I plan to write the lines down, but, exhausted, I fall back to sleep. I dream. Waking at seven, I sit on the floor of the room, a thick down comforter wrapped around my body. I'm freezing. My fingers are numb with cold. My eyes ache. But sitting on the floor of the room, I write all of "The Queen's Last Ride," recalling vividly the first stanza and then moving on with it. The words pour from me. This is literature I'm creating here. This, I believe, will be remembered. My heart pounds wildly.

I read my own lines and the image of the slight fragile Queen, now dead in that baby's coffin, comes to me. I begin to weep, inconsolably, and the sobbing wakens Robert, who jumps out of bed, rushing to me as I lie prone on the carpeted floor, weeping. "Ella, for heaven's sake what is it?" I hand him the poem.

"I'm crying about the Queen's last ride, and because I am really writing something worthwhile."

"But Ella, you'll catch your death on the floor."

"I don't care."

"For God's sake."

"It's worthwhile, Robert."

"Ella, please."

"Worthwhile," I mumble.

By the time the representative from the *New York American* arrives at the appointed time at nine in the morning, expecting a tribute poem to cable to America, I am refreshed, renewed, elated. I hand him the poem, which he reads aloud with great enthusiasm. He announces it a masterpiece. I beam. It's exactly what the newspaper wants, he says. "We want the British to understand that America feels grief too."

"That'll do it," Robert says. "This is America talking."

"Thank you," I say, a little out of breath.

The poem is immediately cabled to New York where it appears in the next edition, to considerable praise, and it is then immediately cabled back across the Atlantic to appear in the morning *London Mail*. Back and forth in one day, for the first time in history: the technology of the new century is awesome. I'm hailed as a pioneer. By nightfall, I find myself a celebrity, and my following in London increases. My poem is reprinted in all the dailies. Strangers stop me in the hotel lobby. I smile so much my mouth aches. The British buy thousands of my books of poetry. I am saluted in restaurants.

My memorial stanzas, reprinted everywhere, now assigned a prominent place in shop windows, follow me through the streets:

Let no man labor as she goes by
On her last appearance to mortal eye;
With heads uncovered let all men wait
For the Queen to pass, in her regal state.

Army and Navy shall lead the way
For that wonderful coach of the Queen's today,
Kings and Princes and Lords of the land
Shall ride behind her, an humble band;
And over the city and over the world
Shall the flags of all Nations be half-mast furled,
For the silent lady of royal birth
Who is riding away from the Courts of earth,
Riding away from the world's unrest
To a mystical goal, on a secret quest.

Though in royal splendor she drives through town
Her robes are simple, she wears no crown;
And yet, she wears one; for, widowed no more,
She is crowned with the love that has gone before,
And crowned with the love she has left behind
In the hidden depths of each mourner's mind.

Bow low your heads — lift your heats high —
The Queen in silence is driving by!

I am, I find, all the rage.

Robert, thrilled to be abroad again, suggests we travel throughout Europe, even though it is fierce winter and it's not the sunny vacation on the Continent we've dreamed of. Invigorated by the lively London streets and the quaint pubs, he has rediscovered his old passion for Europe. "I don't want to go home yet," he says. These are the streets of his young manhood.

So we travel to Holland to see the marriage of Queen Wilhelmina, wrangling press credentials to do so, and I try to write a poem contrasting the two royal events: one old queen dying, another young one marrying, the passing of storied and dynastic generations. But it doesn't work. I really don't care. Too many sights are pulling me away from poetry. When President Garfield was assassinated, back in 1882, I'd rushed a poem to the *Chicago Tribune*. Then I had swelled with patriotism. But this — this is story book world. I don't know what to make of it. I think I bring with me a frontier sensibility — a Badger State girl, all democracy and buckskin freedom, looking in on a world I never knew.

We stay in a resort hotel normally closed for the season, a summer place deep in the Scheveningen Forest, but opened especially for the wedding festivities. Deep snow covers the inn, and the dark forest boughs hang low. At night we sit in candle-lit rooms, thick forest obscuring the windows. No winter in Wisconsin was ever like this: spider's web ice crystals on thick lead-glass windows, wind howling through stark black forests, a quiet so loud the mind buzzed. I become rhapsodic: "We are deep in the heart of Europe, Robert, lost in medieval darkness." Robert just nods.

"We're like caveman and cavewoman," I say.

Robert grunts. He is trying to light a cigar. His hands are freezing.

"It is the dawn of earth," I say.

Robert grunts again.

He could care less. For a moment I am angry. This is, I think, a dark and gothic romance. Robert just wants to light a cigar.

Outside the wind howls and whistles, and the heavy iced trees slam against the windows. Inside, huddled against Robert, I feel as though I've stepped back in time. This is the dawn of mankind here. I start to cry. The funeral I witnessed, followed by the happiness of the wedding, bothers me: life is passing me by. Startled, I realize I've passed the half-century mark.

I am over fifty now. It seems like the decline of my life is upon me.

The snows make me dwell on my declining life. I remember snow blizzards from Wisconsin: time stopped then, frozen in place. A half century. I have lived fifty years. Something is missing. Sequestered in this imaginary cave world of wind and ice and cold, I think of my son, whose ashes lie buried now in the garden at Short Beach, just outside my kitchen, so far from here. It makes me lonely, that vagrant thought: he is too far away for me to hold. He cannot find me here. He lies in Branford, his grave covered with snow drift and sea wind.

I wake screaming in the cold bed because death moves through me like a ghost.

"It's this," Robert says, pointing to the somber surroundings, the thick-wall tapestries and the animal-fur blankets. "It makes us feel — primitive. And alone."

But I know that isn't it: something is wrong. The aching in my bones tells me this, and the pulsing at my temples, the fury of the wind outside. Something is wrong.

So in the morning when the telegram arrives I am not surprised: I expect some dreadful message. And it will be from home. Naturally. My longing for Robert Jr. tells me this. Winifred makes me happy, makes me whole. My son reminds me that life can be cruel and demanding and unforgiving.

The telegram says that my father, aged ninety, for many years a child again in his mind, a man who stopped knowing his own blood years back, has died on the Wisconsin farm.

We leave the next day for home, our plans for a leisurely tour of Europe thwarted.

This is to be expected.

Suddenly the full force of that bleak Wisconsin farm comes to me. Sailing home, I stay in my cabin, unable to write. I enter only one line in my journal: *I was a child of the end of his youth.* I recall my last visit back to the farm

two years ago when my mother fell ill and we feared she
would die. At the time my father had sunk totally into
deepest senility, and most days he scarcely knew anyone
in the family. Certainly he didn't know his own daughter. My mother recovered, if only her acerbic tongue and
her unyielding unhappiness — "Do you have the sea,
Ella? Do you see it from your house?" — but my mother,
I sensed, showed the debilitating signs of a stroke, a word
no one was ready to use.

Nothing, I found, had changed. Ed lived with a wife
always at war with my mother, the two growing old together, with the smattering of pesky children, lived lives
under a heavy cast-iron sky. I told Robert later, "One thing
has changed. The bitterness is worse now, a thistle in the
hand linens." Failed lives: brothers unfit for farm life,
children who wait for my checks to arrive.

That visit shattered me. At night I read chapters of Hall
Caine's best-selling *The Christian* to my nodding mother,
hoping to give her hope and faith, only to discover that
she forgot immediately what was just read to her. So at
nightfall I read brief homilies, snatches of anecdote, little
stories from magazines I carry. I made up stories. She
twisted her head left and right, confused. In the middle
of a brief story, she would interrupt, whining about life
in the anxious household. "Ella, you wouldn't believe
the abuse I take here." She would raise her voice, so those
upstairs would hear. "She laid children like chickens lay
eggs, and they're all cracked and spoiled."

"Mama, please."

"I live in a barnyard, Ella."

In my old bedroom, under old familiar covers, I wrote
"Realization, from the Old Homestead":

> *I tread the paths of earlier times*
> *Where all my steps were set to rhymes.*
>
> *I gaze on scenes I used to see*
> *When dreaming of a vague To Be.*

I walk in ways made bright of old
By hopes youth-lined in hues of gold.

But lo! those hopes of future bliss
Seem dull beside the joy that is.

My noonday skies are far more bright
Than those dreamed of in morning's light.

And life gives me more joys to hold
Than all it promised me of old.

Reading my work, I was hungry to be with Robert.

Every night, one of the nephews had to watch my stumbling father because he had discovered fire. He wanted to burn down the house. "Fire renews the earth," he mumbled one time. He had set fire to draperies, the sheer delicate ones I purchased decades before with money earned from a verse published in *Demorest's*. He had to be watched. "Fire cleanses the palate," he said. "It's ice."

During the day my father fidgeted and squirmed. And yelled.

"Papa," I said.

"Who are you?"

"I'm Ella." Frantic.

"I can't be expected to know every stranger that comes here."

Within days, I fled the farm.

On the journey back home, I positioned myself at the rear of the Pullman car, and wept. My back to the passengers, I couldn't stop the hysterics. I was totally out of control. When I met Robert, waiting for me in Chicago, he was annoyed at my disconsolate state. He stared at my red-blotched face, my trembling lips.

"It's all right," I said.

He frowned. "No, in fact, it isn't."

He told me I could never return to the farm again. "We'll

send money," he said. "That's all. They can't eat away your soul, Ella."

"They're my family," I said.

"And continue to love them, Ella. But," he added, "from a distance."

Now, hurrying back from Europe, the aura of royal visitations hanging over me, I find myself traveling though the long night across country to Wisconsin. I am bringing my mother back to live the rest of her days in Short Beach. I have no choice now: quite simply, it has to be done. My family demands it, Delphia pompously terming it a sharing of duty. When I arrive, I find my brothers have already packed her trunks, ready for shipment East. They don't mention my dead father. I have to ask to see his grave. My mother talks, not of her dead husband who isn't mentioned at all, but of Delphia, the despised daughter-in-law. I nod. "All right," I say. "I'll make a home for you." All Robert's plans for long sojourns abroad now are put on hold. I have to care for my mother as she once cared for me. Readying for her trip to the East Coast, she is like a schoolgirl, rushing from room to room. She sings a child's song to anyone who will listen.

"This is overdue," she tells me.

"I'm sorry, Mama."

"It's better late than never."

My mother always wanted a place by the sea. Some of my earliest recollections are of her talking of water. She told me she dreamed it — an ocean she never saw, all billow and wave. We created that dream together, the two of us, way back when.

She talks of nothing else the whole trip back, but, once settled in Branford, sequestered in her own room overlooking the Sound, the rhythm of tide working its way into her sleep, she announces she despises it.

"How can anyone sleep with the crashing noise?"

"It's relaxing, Mama."

"It's worse than hail on a roof."

"You'll learn to love it —"

"I miss the children at home," she says. "The family."

"Mama, for years you complained about the noise and nuisance —"

She yells. "I miss them. They're blood."

Quietly: "I'm blood."

My mother smirks. "You're the poetess of passion."

Robert finds me on the seawall, staring across the ocean at the twilight horizon.

The days of spring turn into summer, my favorite season. But this summer it is all failure and sleeplessness. I fight with her, the two of us sniping back and forth until we both dissolve in tears. And then, frustrated, helpless, I fight with Robert. I complain about his cigar smoke, about his disappearing off to his clubs. "You leave me alone with her."

Robert sighing: "She's your mother."

"That's not fair."

"I have to leave. You two just bicker back and forth."

I become shrill. "I never bicker."

He lights another cigar. I fume.

Friends who visit find me crying and Robert red faced, catching the tail end of dark spat-out words. I lie, telling them I'm weeping for happiness. No one believes me. Even I have trouble mouthing the phony words.

My mother begins each new day with a different battle.

"I hate cats," she says, shoving my furry Angora off the divan. Cats are all over: I find them exotic, Egyptian, mysterious, poetic. They are my connection back to pyramids and desert oases.

"Robert and I always have cats," I say.

"Isn't it about time you got sensible?"

She finds other things to obsess on: the way a watercolor hangs on the wall, the slant of summer morning light through her bedroom window, the squeaky singing voice of the Irish cleaning girl, the annoying ripple of high-pitched laughter from the renters at one of the cottages, the crimson rouge that I apply so generously these days. "A harlot," she remarks.

"Mama, really."

"A scarlet child I've raised."

"I've moved off the farm, you know."

"And into a brothel." She waves her hand at the fringed brocade draperies, burgundy and mauve.

Only Robert has a calming influence on her, but only sometimes, drawing the shaking, angry woman aside, speaking softly to her, and watching as she smiles, becomes girlish and flirtatious, then quietly nods off.

"She's eighty-four," Robert says, when I complain.

"So?"

"Ella!"

"She's a trial. I know I'll never make eighty-four this way."

"We have both vowed to live until a hundred, you and I. Don't you remember?"

We made that vow on our wedding night, eons ago in a honeymoon room in Milwaukee.

"I doubt I'll last to the end of summer."

Robert grins.

Worse, I can't write. I can toss off the facile syndicate columns for Hearst — that is no problem, the platitudes dripping from my pen: "A mother's love is never a curse, but it can be an obstacle" — but my exquisite poetry, my cherished heart wails — these just won't come. My mother is always here in my sight, a hawk-eyed woman with intense violet eyes, watching. Through the nighttime walls, I hear her mumbling in her sleep. Sarah Wheeler sighs like the dead.

Then the ultimate annoyance — at least I say it is. One of my poems, written while in England, is printed with a typographical mistake. The line is simple, and one of my best: *My soul is a lighthouse keeper.*

But the typesetter — and obviously the copy editors — allow it to appear as: *My soul is a light housekeeper.*

I never notice the error, busy as I am with the new adjustments in the household. But in short order the letters arrive — "I thought I'd bring it to your attention" — and I stare at the inane lines. More folly, I think. Immediately I become the object of a running joke in the press, the subject of base humor in the tabloids. Says one writer: "Domestic chores have now become the theme of America's premier poet of the romantic hearth. What next? An ode to the kitchen broom? A sonnet cycle on wash day?" The British satirical sheet *Life* does a sketch of me mopping floors in a servant's frock. I threaten a lawsuit, I write letters, I insist the typesetting error was done on purpose.

"It probably was," Robert concedes. "There's great jealously of your success. You know that. But you'll only make it worse by building up the story."

I don't care. "My integrity."

"Ella, don't give them ammunition."

"I've already been shot."

"Wounded, not outright killed."

Finally I stop, at midsummer, exhausted. No more letters, no more telegrams. But one afternoon, rising from a nap, I hear my mother in the front parlor, singing the line "My soul is a light housekeeper" to the tune of "She's Only a Bird in a Gilded Cage."

I start to laugh.

By fall I receive another invitation for me to return to England—I am to be honored at a reception during which my poem on Queen Victoria, set to music, will be played—but I can't accept. I'm told my popularity there is tremendous. Already a collected volume of my work has been issued in lavender vellum. Holding the letter, I shake with anger. I feel rooted to this home, chained to the granite rocks of the foundation.

My mother spends most mornings chasing and kicking the cats.

Some mornings, waking in the hot room and hearing her wheezing across the hall, I lie there, unmoving, sweat already beading my brow, and recite out loud random lines from "The Queen's Last Ride." My own words thrill me. It is my ride now, I tell myself. I've been cabled back and forth, all in the same day. The ride of the century, and the century has just begun. But in my journal I scribble: *Herself cannot take a ride now. Himself says that will come someday. But it is already twilight of my days. I'm in my descent into heaven. There is a world out there. There is no world here but the bitterness of lemon and the annoyance of a spoiled child. And the squealing of Herself's cats as they scamper for cover in the eternal game of Cat and Mother.*

Some mornings I wake with my fists clenched.

Himself — that is, Robert, my lover, who has also begun using the affectionate, private terms of Himself and Herself in his own journal, our own personal language — suggests a brief vacation in Vermont, where my mother was born and lived so many years before. Perhaps this will placate her. So we travel to Bradford, Vermont, staying a week in a hotel there, and I escort her to the places of her childhood and early married life. The days, frankly, are endless, with drowsiness, whining, and, too much of the time, indifference. Robert stays in the hotel lobby, playing whist with new-found friends. I can't coax him out with us. I glare at him, but he looks through me. Doggedly I point out buildings and farmhouses, and mountains and rivers — the very places she was once a part of. At first it is tedious, but I throw myself into each day with such passion that I begin to see something of my own life in these roots of my family. Yet I'm the only one getting excited. Here might possibly be my greatest poem. Life is a cycle — my maternal grandfather, the one called Grandsir Pratt, left Connecticut for Vermont decades before. And now I am back in Connecticut.

Circles of life give us the hidden meaning we crave.

I locate some of her old childhood friends — at least they claim they knew her as a young girl and woman.

They are men and women now in their eighties and nineties, and I stage a lavish dinner for ten of them. I spend the day with headaches and nerves. No one is happy. In the middle of dinner, my mother gets sullen and rude, ignoring the fawning natives who seem more interested in Ella Wheeler Wilcox — "Sign this book, dearie" — than the aging mother they last knew as the harried young wife of Marcus Wilcox.

"I don't like old people," she announces, loudly, pouting, sloughing at the dinner table. "You know that, Ella. Look at them." I survey a crowd that looks like my mother: wrinkled, craggy faces, shriveled and blotchy skins, shiny balding heads, flaking scalps, trembling jaws, shaking limbs. Eyes faded and opaque. A round table of the feeble. "Look at them," she says in a shrill, furious voice. "They're old, Ella. You know I don't like to be around old people."

No one says a word.

She stands up. She still has the erect posture of a young farm wife, that iron spine, that mass of abundant gray-black hair, and those violet agate eyes. "I'm going somewhere where I can be happy again," she says. She totters out, pausing to glance in a lobby mirror. What does she see?

I suddenly wonder when I stopped loving my mother.

Traveling home, I insist we stop for one last look at her old family homestead. Here my father Marcus came to woo Sarah, the violin-playing dance master, so gentle and refined, come to take the slip of a country girl to his home and then on to Wisconsin, and the life in the new promised land of the American west. That pioneering Anglo-Saxon spirit, abundant in my blood.

The house is shingled in austere white clapboards, with dark slate roof and a tall brick center chimney, New England rural, and I think of the decrepit farm out west. This house is perfect here, nestled under stately elms against a hard blue sky. This is where my family should have stayed. This rocky, hard soil makes people survive. I now believe it makes them hearty, resilient.

"Why are we sitting here?" my mother asks me.

"Mama," I say, "this is your old house."

She rouses herself from her nodding state, sits up in the carriage, looks around. She raises a weak hand to adjust the careless chignon she always wears now, a bee's nest she tucks lace or flowers into.

"Do you know what you're looking at, Mama?"

"Ella, don't be foolish. I live here. It's Wisconsin."

"We're in Vermont, Mama."

"No, it isn't. Don't be foolish. It's Wisconsin."

Back home in Connecticut it's unbearable to be near her, and Robert, watching the distant and the pinched faces, promises a live-in companion for my mother. "It's more than that," I say, putting the tips of my fingers together in a prayer-like gesture. "It's as though she's already died but I know we still have years together here. This is our paradise, and now it's ruined."

"Not ruined," Robert says. He smiles: "Maybe tainted. For the moment. We have our friends."

"I have trouble seeing myself as an ungrateful daughter."

"But you're not."

"I love her," I say. I have trouble with the words.

"Of course."

"But I'm a stranger here."

Robert watches me, but I can't look at his face.

There is some low-voiced altercation now happening in the parlor, and I hear her berating one of the summer guests for ingratitude. "This is, after all, my daughter's home. Paid for by the poetry I read to her when I carried her in my womb."

"Let's walk," Robert says.

We stroll along the crescent beach, empty now that it's late at night. It's a starless night, with no moon. Everything is ink black. I hear distant rumblings out on the water: there will be a thunderstorm in the night, one of those explosive, house-banging ones that scare me awake. Nothing in my childhood prepared me for such catastrophic noise and demonic movement. Robert holds my hand tightly because I can barely see where I'm walking, the night is so dark. For a moment I think I'm back in that lodge in the Scheveningen Forest, suffocating under the smells of old moss and dank furniture, and the prehistoric cave I imagined we inhabited. Robert guides me along the sandy shore, and the long train of my dress gets snagged on broken twigs, forcing me to yank at the gown. The fabric tears.

"Sometimes I feel like I did as a little girl," I say finally, speaking into the silence.

"Back in Wisconsin?"

"At night in that lonesome place, so far from anything I believed in, I couldn't catch my breath. I used to think that I was dying. Sometimes here, in this wide open world of the beach and the sky, in a house with so many windows and so many doors, I can't catch my breath."

"You have to forget that, Ella."

"It happened this morning. All the air was sucked out of me." I think of those two words that always come: Help me. I hate those words. Help me.

"You're safe."

I get annoyed. "I *know* I'm safe. This is something else — some, well, demon that holds me."

"We own the sky here. The sea."

"But I'll drown. There is never enough air to breathe."

"Here is all the air you'll ever need."

"But it's the memory."

"You left Wisconsin years ago."

"But I have to keep moving to keep breathing."

"Ella—"

I stop, turn to him.

"It's because my mother is sleeping in the house. Her breathing holds me to my bed, takes away my breath." Now my heart is pounding.

Silence. Then: "We'll travel," Robert says.

"I know, I know," I say, almost impatiently. Robert always sees travel as opiate. "I keep telling myself that we can get away from her, that there are people who will tend her, nurse her, loving professionals. And there are. But that's not it." My head is dizzy and I lean into Robert.

I stare at him in the darkness, unable to see his wide face, the caring eyes, the wrinkles beneath his eyes, a face I am growing old with. "I don't think it has anything to do with her." I draw in my breath. "I want to flee my son buried in the garden. Isn't that crazy?"

Robert doesn't say anything.

"I look out the window at that boulder and think of his ashes there. Even in summer, with the flowers covering it, it's still a stark hard granite rock."

"That's because we miss him so." Robert squeezes my arm.

"We never knew him. How can we miss him?"

"He was here."

I grip his sleeve. "Promise me again," I say.

"What?"

"Promise me what you promised at the ship to England." Suddenly I think of Victoria's slow entourage, the tiny coffin and the strewn winter flowers. "Promise me."

I hear Robert's faraway voice in the dark: a metallic voice, frightened now, and tight. "I promise. When I pass over, I will contact you."

"I'm afraid, Robert."

"But I have always kept my promises to you."

I smile.

I bury my face in his chest. Now, in the quiet evening, with my mother buried in a bedroom and my son buried in the flower garden, I'll be able to sleep.

Sailing

1905

Poetry to me is a divine thing. I love it with all my heart (yes, even with my soul, which I dare believe is well evolved). There are as many kinds of poetry as there are of intellects in men. I have followed the bent of my own talents since I first thought in verse as a child, and have worked according to my own light. I have never made a bid for popularity. If I chance to be a popular poet it is because I have loved God and life and people, and expressed sentiments and emotions which found echoes in other hearts. If this is a sin against art, let me be unregenerate to the day of my death!

　　　　　— Ella Wheeler Wilcox,
　　　　　unpublished letter to a critic, undated

Desperate, Robert plans escape routes, charting the sea lanes with a nervous pen, circling islands in the faraway sun, cities on the other side of America, directing my gaze to distant and pleasant geographies.

Ships and trains and trolleys take us away from the shore.

From my mother.

There are short trips to see friends or to attend expositions, as in Canada or New Orleans or St. Louis or California. Back home my mother accuses us of abandoning her to strangers, to winter ice and sleet. What can we say in our defense? It's true, of course. I can't help it. New York sojourns spent at the Everett House — six or seven days at a time, lost in editorial offices and theater lobbies — are relief from the constant recrimination. Her sharp tongue is a blue flame that envelopes a supper table, or an afternoon snack, or a morning conversation. The heat scorches the sea. My lovely ocean becomes desert now.

When I leave town, I become Ella Wheeler Wilcox, the most famous poet in the world. At home I am wayward daughter, standing on the threshold of my own rooms, afraid to enter, compelled to spitfire argument that leaves me guilty and empty. I run to the seawall and my flower gardens. I talk to Robert Junior.

I must be truthful: I love my celebrity. I crave it. Now that there is a trolley from Branford into New Haven, I often ride the packed car, occupying a seat by myself, up front, and strangers seek my autograph and advice. My presence — a creature in feathers and lavender gloves — dominates the shoreline trolley. I am exhilarated by the excursion into New Haven, where I shop for scarves at Shartenberg's on Chapel Street, but also by the constant attention. It is a game, this trolley ride. I hold travelers entranced as I read the indentations on the shaved skull of an olive-skinned five-year-old boy, probably the son of new Italian immigrants, a wide-eyed boy seated in his mother's lap. I've mastered phrenology, of course, and my fingers are sensitive to curves and bumps, the crevices and swellings that indicate character and potential. My ringed fingers gently cover the boy's still head, and I foretell a life of money and happiness, and artistic sensitivity. This boy will do great things in America. By 1950 he will be — I pause — Governor of Connecticut. The mother beams, the father nods, and the folks nearby burst into applause. I bow.

In his study Robert outlines itineraries. When my boiling point is reached, we leave.

Some winters, exhausted under the shroudlike snowstorms and fierce shore winds, we travel to the West

Indies for two months. We go to Cuba where we attend the Chinese Theater, watching a play so realistic, so ribald, so—graphic, that Robert turns red and insists I avert my eyes. I refuse. "For heaven's sake, Robert," I say, "I wrote the book on passion." By himself, he goes to a bullfight in Havana but becomes stomach sick at the sight of the heartless cruelty to animals. At the hotel he takes to his bed, suffering a headache.

When we reach Short Beach, my mother is waiting with stories of her own cruelty and pain.

They are exquisite winter trips, but I am always stopped by one notion: my mother back home in the snow-covered Barracks, waiting, waiting. She talks to herself, ignores the Irish maids and the gossipy neighbors, and waits. Sometimes, on a rare occasion, she surprises us. In late winter or early spring, when we return, there is incredible hugging and kissing and the spreading of love. She is buoyant and wonderful. Then, a week later, I find the torn pages of a favorite book, the shattered Limoge vase, the beads of an Apache turquoise necklace unstrung, a water stain on a Queen Anne table. Then there are the fast-spat words, but not from me because I maintain silence. In my journal: *Herself will not slip again into dark chaos where my mother dwells.* But from my mother: "I can't tell you the loneliness of life among strangers."

Robert says to her, "These are your friends."

"Friends? You call them friends? At night when the blizzard hit and the roof quaked and my heart stopped, I was alone here, the maid fleeing to her mother's house in Guilford."

There is nothing to be said.

We stare at each other.

I hunger for the road: for sensation. I prepare spontaneous quotations for the future interviewers. My name is always in the press. *The Review of Reviews* loves to reprint my aphorisms. My photograph is redundant in the *New Haven Register,* in the glossy new magazines. *Ladies' Magazine* writes of my life among cats. *Good Housekeep-*

ing talks of my gardens. *The Spiritualist* analyzes my faith in the occult. In England, I've learned, I am constantly in the news. Whenever I leave home.

I travel alone to the Pan-American Exposition in Buffalo, and the photos of me, dressed in flowing gown with a folksy bonnet with blue carnations, is Sunday supplement rotogravure in *McClure's*.

When the summer night music ends, when the dancing shoes are tucked away, I always return to the business of poetry. At home I write my poetry in the sunny morning room, among flowers, or out on the dock, if the day is balmy. I often sit with friends, other poets, and we all write our poems together.

A verse factory, Robert terms it.

We sip lemonade and gaze across the sea.

One morning a new neighbor — it was always someone else bringing me the bad press clippings, neatly scissored and trimmed, a neighbor, a friend, an acquaintance, as though to see the pained look on my face — hands me a venomous review.

"How may a man be a popular poet and yet save his soul and his art? This is a question which only the select few of any group or period are called upon to answer. Some popular poets, of course, have no souls to save — none at least which emerge above the milk and water current of their verse — the Tuppers and Ella Wheeler Wilcoxes of their generation. Others have no trouble with their souls; they just sing naturally about common sights and sounds, the things all men know or feel or think they know and feel — like Mr. James Whitcomb Riley, Eugene Field, Bret Harte in his brief lyric moods, or, now and then, Joaquin Miller, that high-hearted old democrat who now sleeps in the Sierras."

No soul! Ella Wheeler Wilcox? My passionate soul swells in the body. I stare at the black-and-white print, my jaw fallen, tears in the corners of my eyes.

"I am shattered," I say, and then leave the neighbor.

I know they call me a sentimental sob-sister of the factory girl, the queen of platitude and the princess of purple prose. In the new century I've become even more the laughingstock of the serious reader: a woman whose writings are so thin they are an embarrassment. "Mosquito wings," some writer says.

"Why?" I always say, weeping when another review comes in the mail. I am called a "sentimental dowager of old-style pap."

"Why?"

"Highbrow snobs," Robert says.

"But I've earned some little respect, no?" I say.

"Ella, you have your audience. Forget it."

"I can't," I say. "I can't."

I am described as living the most sumptuous of lives, resplendent in sable furs, with diamonds and pearls dripping off me, living in beach and town houses, all the result of monstrous moneys given for my poor, sloppy poetry, that unctuous posturing, and the endless sales of my unworthy books.

"Why?" I cry.

Robert throws his hands into the air.

"I only do what God dictates," Ella said.

So now I abandon the poem I planned working on this day. Instead, I write to this new critic, a woman I don't know: "I have just chanced upon your reference to me in your periodical. It gave me a sharp hurt. Skilled criticism is as needed in the world of art as skilled surgery in the world of medicine. But the doctor who thrusts a rusty nail into the flesh of a patient because he chances not to like him is not practicing surgery. You thrust a rusty pen into a poet you chance not to like. That is not criticism. It is spitefulness."

I pause, savoring the words. "Read this, Robert," I say, handing him the sheet. He does, but says nothing. I continue.

"Poetry to me is a divine thing. I love it with all my heart (yes, even with my soul, which I dare believe is well evolved). There are as many kinds of poetry as there are of intellects in men. I have followed the bent of my own talents since I first thought in verse as a child, and have worked according to my own light. I have never made a bid for popularity. If I chance to be a popular poet it is because I have loved God and life and people, and expressed sentiments and emotions which found echoes in other hearts. If this is a sin against art, let me be unregenerate to the day of my death!"

"Enough, Ella," Robert says, reading over my shoulder.

"No," I say. "This woman must be talked to."

I write: "What have you read of my works? No critic is justified in making such an assertion publicly as yours unless the author has been thoroughly read. Have you read my last collection, 'Picked Poems,' and my recent poems in the *Cosmopolitan Magazine* and *Good Housekeeping?* If you have, and call any or all of these milk and water, then there is something the matter with your brain, as well as your heart. If you call my early poems milk and water, then I think you are suffering from arrested emotional development. Something weaker than milk and water must run in your veins in place of blood. That I have written much light verse, which is not poetry (any more than it is doggerel), I know; it is simply popular verse. That I have written many real poems of literary and artistic value, even while of human interest, I also know. There is no more conceit in such knowledge or its avowal than in saying I know my eyes are brown. I am capable of judging the difference between verse and poetry, even when my own, as of knowing the shades of colors, even in my own eyes."

"Finish up, Ella. She won't read that much."

"I'm writing for myself," I say.

"Hoping you may develop a sense of responsibility which will cause you to study your poets before criticizing them, and that you may grow at least a sage bush of a heart to embellish your desert of intellect, I am, Sincerely yours, Ella Wheeler Wilcox."

"There," I say, thumbing the sheets.

Robert sighs. "She'll publish your letter, Ella, to mock you."

"So be it. I have my advocates."

"You have to ignore them. Be thick skinned."

"I'm a poet. Everything touches the heart."

"But she'll belittle you."

"And she hasn't already?"

It is cathartic, this letter, but at night I am unable to sleep. I sit at my writing desk, attempting to form a rhyme, a simple one, a perfect masculine rhyme, a succinct couplet, but none comes.

I am stunned, weeks later, when she replies to my letter. I read it aloud, even though I am alone in the room.

Dear Madam: Pardon this delay in answering your letter of September 8th, which was mislaid.

I can only say that, while I have not read all your poems I have rarely been able to admire those I have read. They seem to be of a kind which lovers of the art must resent; in fact, I have thought of you as so eager for popularity and its rewards as to work solely toward that end.

We all have our standards, and if your verse is not according to ours, yet it has such a vogue as not to be quite negligible — hence my remark in our May number, which was intended, of course, not for you personally, but for you as an artist. If your feelings were hurt, I am sorry, but the integrity of the art is more important than anybody's feelings.

I stare at the letter for a long time, ignoring Robert calling from another room. He is saying that my mother has ruined the Oriental carpet with spilt India ink. She is attempting to write a poem about her long-gone childhood. I can hear her crying: "She's not the only poet in the family." Robert isn't angry. For some reason he sounds amused. When he enters the room, he stops short. My face is frozen, the letter raised in my trembling hand,

and my body is old, old.

He takes the letter from me. "I didn't think she'd respond," he says. "I'm surprised."

"I've been assassinated."

"Ella, really."

Wisely, Robert suggests another vacation in Jamaica. I'm at my wit's end, all sputter and nerves. My mother limps through the house, bumping into furniture now, dropping clothing to the floor, her words slurred and bitter. I don't know whether the sluggish movement is the result of the debilitating illness — has she had more unnoticed strokes, little jolts of shock and fury? — or, indeed, from the blue-glass bottles of mysterious tonic she buys at the general store: Indian Camp Elixir. The cloyingly sweet smell of medicinal alcohol hangs in the air like a early morning sea mist.

It is our fifth winter sojourn in Port Antonio, Jamaica, sailing at sunset on Christmas Day into the lovely harbor, set against the majestic backdrop of the Blue Mountain Range. Already the Hotel Tichfield feels like a second home, with its generous proprietor and his constant — obsequious? — attention to me. Originally its quaint dining room was built around a huge mango tree, from which overripe sweet-smelling fruit hung, intoxicating the guests. There were pathways through meandering green arbors, shelter under thick palm trees. In those days the hotel was a special earthly paradise, exotic and primitive. Now, with success, the hotel has been rebuilt, and is modern and efficient. It could be a New York hotel. But I miss the old mango tree, the castaway feel to the place.

But I'm not the only writer here this winter.

"Jack London is here," Robert informs me at breakfast. I am startled. He points across the crowded room, through the floor pines and past the fern pots.

Munching on a biscuit, I say slowly, "A great writer, though he lacks focus."

Robert laughs. "Really, Ella. Be nice."

"I am being nice. His works always seems — well, out of focus."

"What does that mean?"

"It means — he hasn't found the voice God gave him."

"He's popular — like you."

I nod.

"We'll introduce ourselves."

"He won't know me."

"Of course he will. Who doesn't?"

"Robert, please. Don't."

I see a small man, compact and muscular, with a wide sun-weathered face, an unruly shock of sandy hair. A ruggedly handsome man, tough, a mountain type, all outdoors and leather burn. Robert and I are frankly staring at him. He looks over, nods. And then I see him stand.

Jack London is walking over to our table.

I get light-headed. I wonder whether I can ask for an autograph. He has, of course, written *Call of the Wild*, which moved me.

"I'm Jack London," he says, looking at me, his eyes unblinking. "I heard that Ella Wheeler Wilcox arrived last night. It's an honor."

"You know me, sir?" I'm startled.

"Madam," he says, "I come prepared."

He bows. And then, with a flourish, he pulls out a torn magazine sheet from a pocket. He then reads aloud one of my obscure verses, "The Room Beneath the Rafters."

> *Sometimes when I have dropped to sleep,*
> *Draped in a safe luxurious gloom,*
> *Across my drowsing mind will creep*
> *The memory of another room,*
> *Where resinous knots in roof-boards made*
> *A frescoing of light and shade,*
> *And sighing poplars brushed their leaves*
> *Against the humbly sloping eaves.*
>
> *Again I fancy, in my dream,*

I'm lying in my trundle bed;
I seem to see the bare old beams
And unhewn rafters overhead.
The mud-wasp's shrill falsetto hum
I hear again, and see him come
Forth from his dark-walled hanging house,
Dressed in his black and yellow blouse.

There, summer dawns, in sleep I stirred,
And wove into my fair dream's woof
The chattering of a martin bird,
Or rain-drops pattering on the roof.
Or, half awake, and half in fear,
I saw the spider spinning near
His pretty castle, where the fly
Should come to ruin by and by.

And there I fashioned from my brain
Youth's shining structures in the air.
I did not wholly build in vain,
For some were lasting, firm and fair,
And I am one who lives to say
My life has held more gold than gray,
And that the splendor of the real
Surpassed my early dream's ideal.

But still I love to wander back
To that old time, and that old place;
To thread my way o'er Memory's trace,
And catch the early morning grace,
In that quaint room beneath the rafter,
That echoed to my childish laughter;
To dream again the dreams that grew
More beautiful as they came true.

He has a thick, whiskey voice that reminds me of syrup, but it isn't sweet: it is raw and acrid. When he is finished, he bows again. "I clipped it from a periodical some time back, and it travels with me."

Robert is smiling.

"You are kind," I say, barely able to speak.

"Madam, much of your work does not beguile me, if truth be told, but those are the words of a poet who understands the heartbeat of wildest nature." He bows again.

Flushed, wide eyed, I feel ten years old: I am at a loss for words. This is totally unexpected. I'm beside myself. To hear this virile man recite one of my poems — to hear the sea chantey lilt to his pronunciation — stops me dead. This is the voice of the artist. Suddenly, from nowhere, comes the buried memory of an infatuation I had once for a neighborhood farm boy, all sinew and bluster and roughneck. I was fourteen then. I am fifty-five now.

For a second I think I have fallen in love with Jack London.

I am conscious of his rough leathery tan, his unblinking eyes, his sturdy fingertips on the folded sheet of paper, a broken fingernail, a maroon-blue bruise on his cheek, the slight bend of a hip.

"And this is your husband?" London says, nodding again.

The two men shake hands.

I don't know what to do. I can't speak.

London points across the room where a young slender woman sits, watching us. Her face is blank, unquestioning. London gives a half wave but she doesn't respond. "That's my wife," he says. "Charmian."

Everyone smiles. I wave.

"She wants to meet you," Jack says.

"Me?"

"Of course."

We meet for dinner, the four of us, and the hotel guests buzz around us, watching, leaning in as we pass. I'm in my glory. I take special care dressing for dinner, discarding outfit after outfit, until Robert fumes, puffing cigar smoke my way. Immensely flattered by London's attention, I discover I also enjoy Charmian, who is London's second wife, a mostly quiet woman who watches Jack's every move. Once Charmian stops being nervous around me, we become chatty, both of us laughing at one of Jack's bad jokes.

"Staying long?" Robert asks.

"No, we're actually planning a long voyage around the world."

Charmian adds, "A honeymoon voyage."

"A wedding journey," Jack tells us. "Next year we'll build the *Snark*."

"We'll sail anywhere we want," Charmian says.

"We'll build the boat ourselves," Jack says, looking at Robert. "With friends." The two of them talk excitedly, their words overlapping each other's.

Robert has loads of questions about their planned seagoing journey, practical questions about sea charts and wind currents. I haven't seen him so animated in months. "Robert," I laugh. "Are we going round the earth by boat?"

"Maybe," he says. "Maybe."

I turn to the Londons. "Robert is a traveler. He promises me distant unknown cities."

"And you'll have them, Ella," he says, smiling. "But we're too old to ride the rough seas like these youngsters." He points at Jack and Charmian.

"We just keep moving," Charmian says.

"I can't rest a minute," Jack says, suddenly. "Stopping in place is death." He has interlocked his fingers, I notice, and the tanned knuckles are white. I can't take my eyes off his hands. The white contrasts with the blistered dark-stained skin: it's wormwhite, raw, like noontime heat.

"He paces all the time," Charmian adds.

"I hate staying in one place," Jack says, loudly. "I'm not a rock."

Robert grins, handing him a cigar. "You remind me of Ella," he says. "All the nervous energy of the poet on a quest."

I shake my head. "We are old, Robert," I say. "What journeys are left for us?"

"Madam," Jack says, leaning in and covering my hand with his, "you're not old. You have the intense eyes of a young girl who has seen a winter sunset for the first time." It's a purposely ornate line, I can tell, his words spaced and emphatic. Oddly he sounds like a line from one of my own flowery romantic novels.

But I tremble.

After that first recitation of my poem — Charmian shows me a cardboard folder Jack carries, filled with clippings and papers — there is no further discussion of authorship. Both of us seem to purposely avoid it. Robert is bothered. "You two control a sizable share of American literature. Share secrets."

But no: I say I despise the literary conversation. "Robert, what's there to say?"

"Talk."

"About what?"

Robert waves his hand in the air. "Writing — and such."

"We both know what we're doing."

Rather, Charmian and I sit together in a quiet palm grove, nursing sugary lemonades, and we chat like old beachfront neighbors from back home. Charmian has a casual, drifting voice, a little edgy at times, but only when Jack is away too long. I am immediately fond of her.

"They are clearly in love," I tell Robert before bed. "It's quite beautiful."

"I find their passion a little unnerving," Robert says. "They keep touching each other."

"What?"

"They look at each other like fifteen-year-olds in love — all raw and direct."

"She's his love match. That's clear to me."

Robert sighs: "Such heat can't last too long."

"Robert, they're not barnyard animals."

"Close."

"Really, Robert."

But he's smiling. "He's not as — brusque as he looks, right? I thought he'd be more the — what? — the he-man — from his books."

"He's a gentle soul in a seaman's body."

Robert laughs. "Oh, no, Ella. You're recasting him as a romantic lover for a verse narrative. Maurine meets the Sea Wolf."

I shake my head. "Let me tell you, Robert. A woman has to do very little invention with such a man."

"Really, Ella." We burst out laughing.

We tour the island together, the four of us, we share noontime meals and late-night confidences, and when Jack goes off on his own — sometimes, Charmian warns, he gets a faraway look, almost menacing, and he disappears, hidden among shifting dune and sea scrub, lost in his own world — Charmian seeks me out, taking my arm, whispering. I've always loved the attention of younger, beautiful women. And Charmian is both: a Bohemian loveliness, all seashell necklaces and loose peasant dress. I want to mother her. I find myself beginning each conversation with, "My dear."

Once, late at night, sipping a little too much sherry at the hotel, I slip and call her Winifred.

"Winifred?" Charmian asks.

I wave my hand in the air. "You remind me of her," I say.

"A friend?"

"Family."

On New Year's Day the sea water is crisp and blue, almost cobalt, the sun intense. Vases of lush, aromatic hibiscus on the breakfast tables wilt under the awful heat. At mid-morning all four of us bathe in the harbor, splashing and talking and laughing. Even Robert is enjoying the water. I haven't felt so relaxed in days: I want this pleasure — with Jack and Charmian — to go on for weeks.

Afterwards the proprietor serves a special meal in honor of the two "giants of American literature," as he labels us — horribly — on the menu. He is so enamored of the two of us he keeps pointing us out to the other guests. The day's menu is designed and printed with pithy excerpts from our writings. I'm a little bit pleased. Jack looks annoyed but keeps his mouth shut. I notice Charmian touches his sleeve when he holds the menu. He looks at her, and smiles. The menu — with its lines from *The Call of the Wild* and my own wild journey: "I step across the mystic border-land/ And look upon the wonder-world of Art,/ How beautiful, how beautiful its hills!/ And all its valleys how unsurpassing fair!" — is placed face-down on the table, adding to the surprise for the guests. I watch Jack closely. I can't help it: he's too fascinating. This is a singular man, this Jack — some frantic American spirit I'm allowed to see up close. He is sea urchin this trip, I know. Navigator, newlywed bridegroom, he's captain of a schooner. He's not a writer now, although he tells us that he keeps a log.

He puts down the menu abruptly. The menu is, well, pretentious. And I don't care: I am pleased with it. Jack ignores the well-wishers and backslappers. Right after dinner he hides in his room.

One morning, sitting at a table at the water's edge, I tell Robert that Charmian is truly Jack's real soulmate destined for him since the beginning of time.

"Be careful," Robert says. "Don't tell them that."

"They know it already. You can see it in their eyes."

"Just don't tell them."

"Why not?"

"It's not our business to talk to people of their souls."

"If such things are written in stone at creation, then someone inscribed their names. His first marriage was foolish. It was meant to be, this marriage. This love. Look at them: souls in union."

"Like us," Robert says, but it's said too quickly, almost glibly. He is reading a newspaper. He isn't even looking at me.

For a second I am irritated. I want to fight him, but I decide not to. I rehearsed this lovely speech before I came down to breakfast, and he is not taking me seriously. So be it.

We are an old married couple.

A pause, a twist of my head in the direction of Jack and Charmian, then strolling at water's edge, Jack's pants rolled up to the knee, his arm slung casually across Chairman's shoulders. They look like beachcombers, idling along. "Of course," I say. "Of course. Like us."

I read Jack's palm. He holds out his hand with a bemused look on his face. I hold his wrist gently, hesitantly: I feel the energy in the callused, rough hand, all broken nail and purplish welt and crusty scab. It is the second day of the New Year, and I am stunned by what I see: a life lived too much on the edge, a little too flamboyant, reckless, a life in search of pure adventure. Abandonment. The intellect ever hungry. Gently I warn him: slow down, savor the moment, rest, rest. Please rest. Stop the search for something out there.

"It's in here" — I point to his chest. "Else," I say quietly, "you won't live another fifteen years."

Jack, smiling, thanks me, but I can see he pays little heed to my words. He tucks his hand into his lap. Charmian hovers near, anxious, but now she has a quirky, nervous laugh, and suddenly she and Jack are laughing wildly. They look at each other, as though sharing a private story, and laugh. Tears roll down their cheeks.

Only Robert and I sit here, sheltered under vast sun umbrellas, with me sober from the reading, and the day seems long, long.

In early March Robert and I sail back into Boston harbor, and it's an earlier return home than anticipated. Robert usually wants to wait for the warm spring weather. But I long for home, I say, and it's time. Every day is too

hot. There is never any rain. I want my own ocean now.
Yet the sailing back north is dreadful, with stormy seas
and overhead skies of metallic gray and blue, and just
approaching Boston there is a bitter snow blizzard that
rocks the ship and drives the passengers to their sick beds.
Hidden in my cabin, I stare through the portal window,
and see omens of oblivion everywhere: the floating of a
dead seagull on the choppy waves, the spider's web for-
mation of ice crystals on the portal glass, the rhythmic
hiccoughing of the engines, the horizontal slant of morning light that hits the distant horizon. All are omens fore-
boding death and destruction. A muscular black seaman,
a cook's hand, reads my tea leaves, at my request, and he
speaks in a deep melodious voice, a thick Jamaican accent. I strain to understand him. I shiver as he stares at
the dregs. The pattern is alarming. Blotches and space
and thistle-like flowers. My teacup looks like a wild garden.

I see fear in his eyes. He touches my hand and shakes
his head.

Once in Boston there is a telephone call: my mother is
dying of a massive stroke. She took ill the night before,
just before bedtime. "Call Ella," she said, then fell over.
Standing in the hotel lobby, I think of the sea omens: yes,
I think, this is the beginning. This is why we've returned
early.

Returning home I scribble in my journal: *The death of
the final parent is an awful stab in one's calendar of days.*

Twenty-four hours later I am back in Branford, at the
Barracks, and my mother is dying in my arms. I sit here,
quiet and stone-faced, waiting. But she does not know
me, her own daughter. Her last hours are insensible, and
there is no final riveting — lightning flash — conversation, as I hope. "Mama," I keep saying, "do you know
me?" Over and over. There has to be a message: she is
joining Robert Junior. I bridge both worlds: a hand extended to each generation. My mother mumbles something about birds in trees, or at least the garbled gibber-

ish sounds like that. She speaks, finally, to her own dead mother: "Oh. Mother, come and take me home. I am so tired." In these last moments, I resolutely memorize my mother's plaintive, withering voice, closing my own eyes so I can hear it clearly. I want to remember the peculiar tones and inflections. Somehow this remembered voice will keep her with me. It will remind me that she built the shrine of poetry for me, all those years back in Wisconsin. She gave me that.

Mama has asked to be cremated, an idea that once shocked her provincial Wisconsin neighbors, prompting her to reiterate it over and over at Sunday teas and Lodge sewing bees. They talked about her behind her back. An eccentric woman, given to odd pronouncement and doomsday prophecy. She loved to stun the respectable, quiet Christian neighbors. But at Short Beach cremation is a way of life, so the deed is simply done. I once asked her where she wanted her ashes to go: to Wisconsin, to lie next to her husband of fifty-six years? Never, she said, never put my ashes underground. "No, Ella," she said. "Think of flowers." She wanted them scattered into the wind, in a growing season, in spring, among flowers and herbs and blue cloudless skies. Some lovely morning.

It is the end of winter when she dies, but the ashes will sit in an urn on the marble fireplace until the beginning of rose season when they will be scattered around the roots of pink summer tea roses. Pink is a color Sarah favored. She said it reminded her of children.

Passage

1906

Dear Reader,

Your letter to me speaks of your reservations about a European sojourn. "What will I miss from home?" you ask. "What comforts I take for granted from the America I love will I sorely miss?" Your questions bother me, I must say. America is, of course, home, and a glorious republic she is, without doubt. But this is not to say that other countries lack interest — or, to use your word, comfort. Frankly, I lament the provincialism I encounter in America. Why travel? Everything is here. Such thinking is dangerous and simple — there is a whole world out there. It is rich with possibility. You can always come home to America. You can always return — and when you return, what wealth of experience you bring.

— Ella Wheeler Wilcox, "Your Days and Mine"
Demorest's, April 1904

Robert refuses to sit still, walking from room to room, arms filled with books. He books passage for Europe. We will, he insists, spend a year traveling, accepting invitations, doing the grand tours, taking in the sights he's long promised me, splendor he hasn't seen since he was a young man on his own. The dead weight of life at Short Beach has been lifted. It is now a paradise we can leave and return to at will, unfettered by an ailing mother. I know this may sound cruel, but I don't think of it this way: it is just that we were paralyzed here. Our own lives were suspended in air. Waiting. That now is over. Short Beach will be our safe refuge, ours alone, when we return from the world we want to explore. It is a place to come home to after the long, intoxicating voyage.

We go everywhere.

In Ireland we visit Sir Henry Blake and his wife, Lady Blake. At one time Sir Henry was Governor of Jamaica, and became our fast friend during our winter sojourns there. He and his wife have a marriage which thrills me in its melodramatic and political proportions: he is staunch Irish and she rockbound English. At Myrtle Grove in Youghal, where they live, I sleep in a room once occupied by Sir Walter Raleigh. Or so says legend. In fact, the house is thirty years older than the discovery of America. I lie in the dark and whisper: "America is yet a wilderness of Indians and wildlife and untouched shores. Soon it will be discovered. Soon." Across the hall Robert snores the night away in the room where Spenser wrote one section of *The Faerie Queene*.

"So what?" he tells me in the morning. "It's an unreadable poem."

"Robert, really, it's a classic."

He smiles. "Unreadable."

"Don't let Spenser's ghost hear you say that."

Later, touring the grounds, I whisper to Robert, "This is where we were meant to be."

"Well," he says slowly, "we finally made it back to Europe."

"Not every dream has come true for us."

"This one will."

"Promise?"

He doesn't answer.

For him much of Europe is familiar because in his carefree bachelor days he traveled widely, even deep into mysterious tsarist Russia. He'd sold silver *objects d'art* to the court of the Romanovs. He drank hot tea in glasses placed in filigreed silver holders, riding the night train from St. Petersburg to Moscow. In the morning, gazing out the windows at the vast forests of white birch, he saw herds of deer at water holes, peasants shouldering water buckets from wells. This is the world Robert misses. Now he can share it all with me. He wants to see what has changed. Decades have passed: Europe is modern now. Just how modern has it become? he wonders.

I am giddy, and everything I see is more beautiful than what I just saw. I mention that I felt the presence of Sir Walter Raleigh the night before, in the dampness of the walls, in the close old musty smells of the age-old house, in the aura of a famous past life. "I sensed him readying for America."

Robert smiles. "I hope you told him to avoid Buffalo in the winter."

I laugh. "Did you sense Spenser?" I ask.

"No," he says, grinning. "Maybe he knew I couldn't get through one page of his wretched poem. Why bother showing up for such a dullard as myself?"

I sit reading in the garden where Sir Walter Raleigh first planted tobacco and potatoes, brought back from the New World, and Lady Blake mentions that Raleigh once sat under a sheltering yew tree, smoking his tobacco and emitting a trail of burnt smoke. A watchful servant in panic poured a bucket of water over his head, believing Raleigh to be on fire.

"Apocryphal," Robert says.

"If it didn't happen, it should have."

In the afternoon I sit in the flower garden, which is quiet, Lady Blake leaving me so I can write, Robert is off with Blake, looking at the horse stables. But I can't write: over-ripe grapes from a nearby arbor intoxicate me, make me dreamy.

I am celebrated wherever I go. In London my British publishers, Gay and Hancock, host an elaborate luncheon of sixty people, and art-bound vellum editions of my volumes are displayed in the front windows of the shops of the city. I give interviews all morning. Then I sit for studio photographs. An artist sketches my face in silhouette for a weekly. At luncheon the menu is heart-shaped— I am, after all, the world's chief purveyor of heart wails — and my portrait, a side shot, with Angora cat, with flowers in my hair and a stern, unyielding chin — is placed in the center. Gushing, a little out of breath, my publisher announces that I sold over forty-thousand volumes of poetry in England the previous year. He repeats the figure, and the guests titter. He seems amazed at the statistic. There is long applause.

Then I am feted by the Poetry Recital Society, an august body of the blood descendants of famous poets, most happily buried in Westminster Abbey. I shake hands with a Rosetti, several Shakespeares, a Wordsworth, a Southey, a Dryden, as well as female descendants of Burns, Swinburne, Tennyson, and Spenser. None of them, to my knowledge, are poets in their own right, a fact that I find disconcerting. It is a bogus society, I feel, that lives—indeed, thrives—on name alone. I tell Robert, "The talk was all imitative, I'm afraid. I kept hearing echoes."

Robert laughs, "Their graveyards are drafty places to hide in."

"Shakespeare, no less."

"I thought I read that he had no heirs."

"I met more than one today."

"Let's travel for years and years," Robert says. "See whatever place catches our fancy."

"But Short Beach," I say.

"We'll sail back and forth."

"Transatlantic adventurers?"

"It's always there for us."

So we travel most of every year. Robert lives with Baedecker guides and maps and red pencils. I cable poetry to New York, and I thrill to the addresses I give: Bavaria, Bayreuth, Pompeii, Tangiers, Canton, Singapore, Hong Kong.

Once back in Short Beach for a short summer season, we entertain, but during the long nights we read Bayard Taylor and other travel writers. We read Mark Twain's *Innocents Abroad*, aloud, the two of us laughing into the late hours.

We make it to the Pacific. In Hawaii we inhabit a tiny bungalow of three rooms, nearly all doors and windows: four doors and seven windows, wide and tall, with a huge bay window looking out over the water. We never close the windows, leaving them open throughout the warm nights. We drift to sleep with the sighing of palms and the crackling cries of tropical night birds. Night wind lulls me. Peacocks stroll the grounds and tropical vines flower in audacious colors. Bougainvillea blazes over fence posts. The scent of oleander makes me drunk. I swim in the unrelenting surf.

We have an audience with the deposed Queen Liliuokalani, a dark embittered woman, maddened by America's imperial annexation of her homeland. Invited through influential friends, we visit her little home, set among chaotic overgrown tropical gardens, an old woman attended by loyal, protective maids of honor who still demand she be the Queen. A large overflowing woman, with a dignified but craggy face, bunched onto a small wicker chair, she stares at us for a while. She does not look happy.

"I only meet Americans to tell them of my dislike," she says, imperiously.

I begin, "We come to understand." I have been warned.

"Your country dethroned me, a Queen."

"I am sorry," I say.

"No American is ever sorry."

"I'm not apologizing for my country. I'm sorry for your loss."

The Queen looks at me. "Interesting."

"What is?"

"The circular language of imperialists."

She goes on and on, bemoaning her loss, and pointing accusing fingers. She scarcely looks at us. But I realize so much of it is posturing. True, the Queen has a speech to give — there is real pain in it, real suffering and loss, after all, an empire has been taken away — but then, once vented, the woman sighs, narrows her eyes, and tells me I have beautiful brown eyes. "Eyes the color of summer cocoa beans."

I smile. "Yours are the color of burnt charcoal."

The old Queen says, "I have read none of your poetry."

"No matter," I say.

"I expect you have brought me a volume."

I blush. "As a matter of fact, I have, as a gift."

"Then I will read some of your work."

"I trust you will enjoy it."

"I don't trust anything, madam."

I get flustered, looking at Robert.

"Will you write a poem about me?"

"Possibly."

"Will you describe me as a lonely old hag in a Mother Hubbard smock, living in the past?"

"If I describe you, it will be as Queen."

For the first time the Queen smiles.

We stay for a luau, sitting at long rough-plank tables. Big bowls of *poi* are placed before us, and we are told to use our fingers. I find the cloying mixture offensive but I am being watched: I manage to swallow some of it. Robert, trying to be funny, whispers that the odd texture results from it being chewed by human mouths. Startled, I spit some into my handkerchief, and then make believe I am sneezing. Robert giggles. Later in my journal: *Herself ate this poi in modest quantity but also ate unknown other dishes, relying on faith and courtesy.* I add: *It is a far cry from the chicken potluck dinners of South Beach.* Then I end: *Thank God. Thank God.*

After dinner there is ceremonial hula dancing, which I find lascivious and totally immodest. Robert seems mesmerized, mouth agape, commenting that such fluidity of moment is a world away from the minuet ball I hosted on my Short Beach lawn last summer: "Anglo-Saxons are angles," he says. "Polynesians are curves."

"Really Robert," I say. "How vulgar."

"I'm speaking geometrically."

"Robert!"

"And metaphorically."

He gets me to smile.

I whisper. "Thank God the dancers are old." The hula is performed by chunky, older women, well past their golden youth, with grass skirts over long tunics, and I imagine that lithe, sensuous young maidens would turn this sensual dance into orgiastic fervor. This is bad enough, what with overweight matrons in long straight hair hurling their hips around while ukuleles chirp and suggest. One of the white guests, a longtime resident, tells us that the old-style, pre-missionary costume was flowers and abbreviated sarong, with much purposeful display of flesh. I am glad this dance is performed by matrons in dumpy cotton smocks. It is like watching an erotic pagan dance done by Presbyterian women at a church supper.

My journal: *Herself thought any more revealing costume — and a Mother Hubbard sack reveals so little — would have been unbearable. We are, after all, civilization. And the idea of old women performing a sexual dance seems preposterous.*

Later, strolling around the island, we chance on another luau. We see a young girl do the hula, a girl fourteen or fifteen, and I tell Robert: "A bronze Madonna, that child, and with eyes averted, she seems to understand the immodesty of her dance. How different from the days of King Kalakaua when the hula led to orgies. Honolulu is dull perhaps, but Christian." Honolulu is like Short Beach, I think, but with palm trees and grass skirts and flowers like I've never seen before. Such blooms can only grow in old heathen lands: lush, raw, and interesting.

As we head back to our bungalow, to lounge under the

shade palms, fleeing the hot sun of the beach and the singing of the sea birds, we are interrupted by a plaintive hum. A chorus of voices, accompanied by a melancholy organ, sends forth the dismal New England hymns from the Christian Mission Church across the way from our little bungalow. Verse after verse, hymn after hymn, bruise the bright air into dark despondency. This is the cloak of Cotton Mather, smothering the primitive natural body. Hymns of praise sung by sinners to a wrathful God.

"Robert, we could be back in puritan Boston."

He is frowning, unhappy.

Robert looks at me with grave eyes. "It's awful, isn't it? I am back in a New England town — an orphan boy — living next door to the church with my grandmother. It's a cold, rainy winter day but I live so near, I can't escape the long service, and the fear inspiring sermon."

"But here, Robert, in this paradise. Why here?"

"What a pity our Christian ancestors adopted such bleak music and such hymns to represent the love-one-another creed of Christ!"

"I think they hated joy."

"But they talked about rapture."

We talk about the narrow dogma-bound missionaries, devoid of pleasure, fearful of dance. The awful censorious mark of the zealot missionary hangs in the air. "I swear, the Christian God we know is more loving than this. The missionaries got it wrong."

"Yet how could we get Christ to these lost souls?"

I frown. "With joy perhaps?"

"The wrong people are missionaries," Robert says.

"Maybe there is no other way?"

"You should be a missionary," Robert says. "In some way, you already are."

"Thank you, Robert," I say.

"Your poetry is a religion."

I sigh. "God doesn't want us so — humorless."

We stand here, watching.

When the service ends, and the dour black-dressed missionaries—" Such clothing in such weather," Robert says — disappear with Bibles and unblinking eyes, accompanied by Hawaiians in stiff broadcloth and choking collar. We hear the birds again. We look up into the rustling leaves. The sun shines, the flowers sway. "The pulse of Nature," I say. Some native Hawaiians stroll by.

"This nature knows something we've forgotten."

I smile. "That God enjoys a good joke too."

Robert laughs.

We stroll the hotel grounds, weaving through groves of fragrant hibiscus. We wear colorful leis, a gift of the hotel staff, and I stop now and then to bury my face in the blooms. At night we sleep like fed kittens. In the morning, rising at dawn, we eat papaya and mango at a table by the water. In the afternoon, we travel to Waikiki to watch the cresting surf and sit quietly on the isolated beach. We read through the afternoon.

On the beach Robert says, "Give me any kind of heaven — or no heaven at all, rather than a place that reminds me of my boyhood Sundays."

"There should be no missionaries in paradise," I say.

"Which paradise?" Robert asks.

I pause. "Any paradise."

When we leave Honolulu, our friends arrange a splashy show at the docks. Little black native boys, maybe ten or eleven years old, dressed in white cotton shorts, carry long wreaths of flowers, cover me with them, and then dive from dizzy heights into the sea to impress me. Standing on the *Manchuria*, with the other sixty-seven passengers, like them bedecked in leis of brilliant color, I wave to the crowd. I am wearing a yellow lei, of course, because yellow is the color people remember I love.

"Aloha," I yell, to no one in particular.

One of my friends Burton Holmes has brought along a moving picture camera — I've never seen such a contraption before — and elaborately records us as we prepare to sail off. He runs around us with the cumbersome equipment, posing us, making us face the light. Flower petals fall as he jostles strangers.

Later we learn that Holmes gave the reel to Pathe, which edited the piece for a newsreel, and the two weary travelers —*Mrs. Ella Wheeler Wilcox, America's premier poetess of passion, and her businessman husband Robert Wilcox, the vacationing couple* — are seen in American and British movie houses during Saturday matinees. Between shots of the Kaiser, an earthquake, and an attempted airplane flight.

Robert and I never see the newsreel.

We travel each season to a different part of the world. We are rarely back at Short Beach now. A summer in Japan gives way to a fall in Ceylon. A winter in Italy ends with spring in Northern Africa. Our steamer trunks are always in transit. Each night Robert and I record our observations in our personal journals, keeping a record. Sometimes, after dinner, we read parts to each other. We marvel how much we've come to see the world through similar eyes. This is what a loving marriage exacts, I think. The newspapers photograph us, and Americans follow our movements in the press. The decade comes to an end and I think: How that 1901 visit to Queen Victoria's funeral changed my life! We do not stop moving.

Then I write: *Today I am sixty years old.*

I smile: Or fifty-five.

My journal: *We saw the Kaiser today, reviewing his troops in Mayence, Germany. Twenty thousand. It was a great sight, but made one feel that Universal Peace, so much talked about, is a million years away. It is. The Kaiser looked older than we had imagined from his pictures. We were very near him, and as we drove back to the hotel, he passed our carriage so closely we could have touched him.*

I tell Robert: "He is all bluster and new power."

Robert agrees. "All this dreadful show of force."

I say, "A chill went down my spine when he passed by. There will be war. I tell you, Robert." Suddenly I am crying. "And I will be in the middle of it."

"Really, Ella."

In Rome I have an audience with the Pope, a general audience, where he blesses the dozen rosaries I carry, gifts for Catholic friends, like Rose Hawthorne, Nathaniel's converted daughter. Pope Pius X is a tall man, with a gaunt, sad face. In my journal: *Herself was drawn to him.*

"Such a large heart, Robert, but he can't save us."

My journal: *Rome is a sewer but the people have light in their eyes.*

1910, my journal: *Herself received a cable from the New York America, asking for a few words on the death of Mark Twain. Herself is touched:*

> *A radiant soul with genius bright*
> *Now lends to other realms delight;*
> *Let Heaven be glad, let earth rejoice*
> *Since unto us was left his voice.*

"I wish I'd met him. We both live in Connecticut. Two souls come East from the West."

"I understand he had a tragic life — the loss of his children. His boy."

"We had so much in common."

"His little boy," Robert says.

"Yes," I say, "his little boy."

We fail to book passage to England on the *Titanic,* that glorious, heralded liner. So we travel on the stalwart — but familiar — *Olympic.* It is like spending time with an old friend instead of making a new and progressive one. Robert had planned on delaying our trip so we could book passage on the much-talked-of pioneering *Titanic.* Its maiden voyage is out of Southampton, April 1912, but I don't want to wait. I want to be back in England. I have a hunger to be back there. So we leave early, headed to England while the *Titanic* heads to America.

April 15, 1912: The steward at our breakfast table leans in, his voice frantic. "The latest news. The *Titanic* has hit an iceberg last night."

"Impossible," I say.

"No," he says. "The Captain was radioed."

The news silences our trivial banter. The previous night there was a banquet, with dancing. The ship's orchestra played waltzes, and I danced. Oh, how I danced! Everyone has slept late. In the morning the sea is calm. Now, with the awful rumor, I put my hand to my throat, short of breath. "But all on board are saved," the steward tells the table. "The *Carpathian* was ready. It is picking up the passengers in the lifeboats."

"Well, thank God," I say.

The ship can talk of nothing else.

In the afternoon, exhausted, I nap in my stateroom. I wake with a start, chilled. I am dreaming of sailing over a smooth sea, and then suddenly my ship runs up the sheer side of an enormous iceberg and turns a somersault and sinks into the sea. "They are dead," I say out loud, flatly.

"Ella," Robert says, touching my sleeve. "You're dreaming."

I stare at him. "They are dead on the icy seas."

When I close my eyes for a second, I see lightning flashes, I hear inhuman screaming and women weeping, and the ice-cold splash of sea water freezes my skin.

I hear the grinding of metal against metal: the awful failure of the engines.

Robert makes me lie under cold towels. I toss and turn.

Later, still in the dark, alone, with Robert somewhere else on the ship, I write "The Undertone":

In the dull, dim dawn of day I heard
The twitter and thrill of a brown-backed bird,
As he sat and sang in the leafless tree,
A herald of beautiful days to be.

But the minor running under the strain
Went to my heart with a sudden pain,
For never so sad a sound I heard
As the troubled thrill of the brown-backed bird.

Not in the wearisome wash of waves,
With moaning murmur of wrecks and graves,
Not in the weird winds' wildest wail,
Not in the roar of the rushing gale.

Not in the sob of dying years
Are sounds so solemn and full of tears.
O herald of days that are green and glad,
Why was your morning song so sad?

Have you a secret hidden away,
Of sorrow to come with a coming day?
Folded under a folded leaf,
Lies there trouble and bitter grief?

The shadows of death, and tears, and gloom
Coming to me when roses bloom?
Will the beautiful days I long for so
Hold like your song a strain of woe?

What is the secret you hide from me
O herald of days that are to be?
And why was that desolate minor moan
Lurking under your gladdest tone?

When Robert returns, bustling with the latest news, I sit up. "Most are dead," I say. "Most have drowned. The ship is gone and thousands of lives are lost."

"Ella—"

"Tell me it's not true."

"Yes, it is."

"We wanted to be on that ship," I say, "on its return to England."

"It wasn't meant to be."

"Yes," I say slowly. "There are worse things waiting for us."

"No, Ella. We are safe."

"No one is safe."

"Ella, you're scaring me."

"It's all frightening," I say, and I tremble.

I feel the rocking of the massive ship, the slight lilt of wave against board, and I freeze. Metal against metal: the awful rasp of the engines. It is horrible, this long endless voyage to England. For the rest of the journey the ship is somber, a wake for the dead and the living. Our room steward has lost his father and two older brothers. He disappears from sight. Everyone knows someone — worker or passenger — on the ill-fated ship. The couple in the cabin next to ours receives a cable saying a nephew is missing. Silence at the meals, on the decks, in the hallways. There is always weeping.

People move like ghosts through hallways, nodding and apologizing.

The ship moves on, relentless. No one wants to walk on deck — to see the horrible water beneath us. We hold our breaths.

Worse, I cannot breathe. I wake up in a sweat, dreaming of a closed room, a tight room, back on the Wisconsin farm, a windy room in the corner of a house, under the rafters, the doors sealed. I am gasping for breath that will not come. I become feverish. Help me. When I wake in the dark, the rocking of the boat reminding me of where I am, I draw in deep breaths, frantic, panicky, afraid I'm dying. There seems so little air left in the cabin. Wandering ghosts take up most of the precious space, and push me into tiny corners. I beg for breathing space. What I get is darkness and fear and a tightness in my chest that reminds me of a village so far removed from the world that the nearest neighbor is miles and miles away. Will I ever be able to escape the loneliness of that tiny house? In the dark I reach for Robert. "Robert," I say, crying. "Robert."

When I open my eyes, I see him staring at me, and the fear in his eyes is so raw I have to turn away.

Nirvana

1912

Seekers after Happiness — what a frightening phrase this is! For it suggests that we must go on some Faustian journey to find what is already in our possession. If we look within, if we stop and say to ourselves that the answer lies inside, then the journey is not necessary. The sin is to look out there. The only answer is the Heart. You are sitting in your home, you have made your evening meal, you have read a few chapters in the Bible. You are Home. It is not out there — this Happiness — it is where you sit.

— Ella Wheeler Wilcox, "Words on the Dedication of the Masonic Temple," Meriden, 1885

We are resting on the veranda of a hotel in Tunis, staring across a dusty street of screaming children and squawking vendors. On the veranda it's cool: palm fronds and canopies shroud us from the beating late-afternoon sun. The waiter who leans over us, refilling the tall lemonade glass, is as slender as bamboo and as black as pitch, shiny from sweat, and he smells of sweet jasmine. He grins. Back in America it is cold winter now. There's ice on the window panes. Neither of us is speaking. I am thinking about this morning, and my stroll through the narrow streets where I spotted licensed courtesans, painted yet veiled harlots plying their trade in the old slave market where, a century before, once beautiful young women were sold to lecherous moneyed men.

So little has changed, I think.

"It's a contradiction," I say, finally.

"What?" Robert has his eyes shut.

"They are shrouded," I say, "these women, with only their dark eyes showing — and the splendid jewelry that suggests their profession. They look like proper young women, but their eyes betray them. They are lost women. Godless."

"Ella, stop thinking about them," he says, impatient. Robert closes his eyes.

For a second I feel my heart race: "Why not?" I say. "Why can't I think about them? Wherever we've gone there's the scarlet woman, the veiled woman, the dark daughter of the streets."

Robert sits up. "This isn't why we began this journey around the world," he says, "to see the dark side." There's an edge to his voice.

"But I can't escape it," I say. "Women selling their bodies. "

He throws his hands in the air. "It's the oldest profession."

I frown. "So is the art of the cliché."

"Touché," he smiles.

"It sickens, Robert."

"Of course, it does. It's the result of poverty."

"It's more than poverty here, Robert. It's tradition—it is cultural."

"It's a way of life."

"Where is their God?"

"He lives only in the rich villas."

Angry: "The men exploit them," I say. I have seen rich-garbed Arabs — the Bedouin, the Kabul — bartering for the silent white-clad women, the men with flowers tucked behind their ears, jangling gold in their deep pockets. Their ornate camels and stooped servants wait nearby. Women are chosen, and then secreted away.

"It's legal here," Robert says.

I frown. "So what? In America such sinful women practice their crimes in private, hidden behind velvet and shade. The law pursues and arrests and chastises. They hide their shame."

"Most Americans scarcely know it exists."

"Men know," I say, "because men know such things. But women in America cannot know."

"Can't allow them to know."

"But need to know," I say.

Robert adds: "Here the government keeps inventory cards with names, and a portrait. The young woman pays a fee, submits to a doctor's probing, and the business is as usual."

"Did you notice that each wears a colored cloth wrapped around her right hand, a badge of sorts — the signal of her calling?"

"They're grotesque," Robert says.

"They're prisoners of sin," I say. "Men treat them as commodity."

"Business as usual," Robert says.

Under their veils they are powdered and painted, with kohl-tinted eyes and henna-stained fingertips, with small tattoos etched on faces.

My journal: Japan

Herself cannot love the delicate beauty of an island country because her eyes are shrouded with the awful sights of the Koshiwana women. Behind bamboo curtains and bowing gesture, the sloe-eyed beautiful women wait for men. They whisper. They hum. They sing. At night Tokyo lies like a cool stretch of ocean: still yet rhythmic, the streets quiet yet the sky moves. But the hundreds of outcast women, plying their ancient trade against a Shinto world, have lost their youth under the artificial night light. Here they sit, like amorous birds in gilded cages, pets on display, lining the narrow midnight streets, their bodies hawked into smelly back rooms by grotesque barkers — mustached sweating men in flowered shirts — who once considered themselves men. They point to the women as though selling fruit or crafts. They touch them like testing the sweet-

ness of a melon. Herself knows the ideal of manhood: Himself. The husband God chose for her. Here, in these ugly alleyways, male and female dissolve into sexual beast. Herself is told that the young beauties are delivered into such a life by impoverished parents from the provinces. Fathers bring thirteen- and fourteen-year-old girls into the city by oxcart. Some dangerously younger. Their glittery life in the cage is far from the promised job in the glass and tobacco factory. These are girls fresh from rural villages, seduced with lies of restful Sundays to be spent at Tokyo museums. Money to be sent home, the rest spent on rich clothing. Then, the years pass by, used up, spit out, they are desolate. These are the women Herself sees in corners of shops. These are the women who are broken, hidden in dark rooms, starved, penniless. A worship of the past clouds the sadness of their moment. This is a dark stain on the gentle soul of Japan. Herself weeps for the women:

> A changing medley of insistent sounds,
> Like broken airs plays on a samisen,
> Pursues me, as the waves blot out the shore.
> The trot of wooden heels; the warning cry
> Of patient runners; laughter and strange words
> Of children, children, children everywhere;
> The clap of reverent hands before some shrine;
> And over all the haunting temple bells,
> Waking, in silent chambers of the soul,
> Dim memories of long-forgotten lives.

> But oh! the sorrow of that undertone
> The wail of hopeless weeping in the dawn
> From lips that smiled through gilded bars at night.

At night Herself dreams: In Yoshiwara a young girl paints her face red and orange, like a carnival doll, and coos from a gold cage at the passing men, who stare and laugh and wink and drool. Buddha broods in a dark temple: night.

Robert laughs. "We have traveled the world and our

conversation always circles back to the fallen woman."

I don't laugh. "Women are slaves, the whole world over."

"I know, I know." Robert sounds tired of the subject.

"It's the universality of evil in the world."

"That's too general a statement," Robert says.

I wave my hand. "You've seen it yourself."

Robert breathes in his cigar smoke, exhales, rubs his hands over his big stomach. "Maybe this is the way it was meant to be."

"Really, Robert," I say.

"I'm serious," he says. "There must be some divine plan behind it — Bisrah, Tunis, Algiers, even Paris, London, Rome. God knows — Short Beach."

"God would not intend evil."

"Intend?"

"Robert, you speak like a club man," I say, my voice rising.

"Maybe there is some harmony we don't understand."

"In degradation?" I ask. I'm ready to fight him. He always runs from this conversation.

"You saw those girls in the marketplace," he says. "You visited with them, saw them without their veils. Saw their jewels. You told me they were calm, accepting, happy."

I have spent a day with the women — at my request.

"So is the beaten dog," I say.

"Ella, we travel for sensation, for sights, for new vistas. The world can't stand all your tears."

"Robert, your words oddly pile on the agony." I spit the words out: angry.

"I mean no insult, my dear Ella. I just mean you cannot water the crops of the world with your tears." He turns away. I can tell he is angry with me. I have only one topic today.

"That's cruel, Robert. I know you don't mean that."

"Of course, I'm sympathetic. I see the hurt in your eyes as we walk those dirt lanes, Ella."

"I am those girls, Robert."

"I don't think so."

"Think, Robert, think. Think of the race of women."

"You are Ella Wheeler Wilcox, a Christian woman."

"You only see the fresh, untainted young girls. The Anglo-Saxon girls. The spoiled rich girls we meet on ships. You like their company, Robert. I know you do. You flatter them. They flatter you."

Robert stops smoking, lays down the cigar in the ashtray. He looks at me with squinted eyes. He says, "Meaning?" There is an edge to his voice now.

"No meaning," I say, looking away.

"Meaning?" he repeats.

"You like the attention of young girls."

He puts down his cigar. He stares at me. "Just what do you mean by that?"

I falter. "All men like the attention of —"

"I'm not all men."

"It's just that —"

"You make me seem the letch."

"For heaven's sake, no."

"I resent that, Ella."

I back off. "I mean there are women you don't allow yourself to see, Robert. I only mean you are like one of the heroes from my narrative poems: you view the young girl — the *jeune fille* — as ideal, as innocent, as statue. You enjoy the untouched girl, the —"

"Would you have me seek the tainted woman?" He interrupts.

"That's not what I mean."

"I feel accused here, Ella."

"No, Robert, no, " I say, then stop.

"Ella."

"Never mind," I say.

He doesn't pickup his cigar. I sit and watch the ashes pile up on the floor. When I look at Robert, he is red in the face. I know there will be silence throughout the afternoon.

China

Herself continues to grieve for the unsung woman. It has been my only tune, this latest world excursion. China especially appalls. Packed, exotic lives lived on smelly houseboats and rickety sampans where whole teeming families live and die — they eat, wake, sleep and give birth, and die — on the boats. Whole lifetimes float by, and the stink is awful. Boats bump and collide, careen. Children dive into garbage-strewn waters. Little baby girls appear and are destroyed. Herself is horrified. We take the sampan to and from our ship in the harbor, and Herself clasps her hand to her throat, the mind dizzy — by the sudden sight of a girl child's decaying body floating among the sea's debris. She is worth nothing, that girl child. Another girl child is dead in a narrow street. The guide, an American, points to the body. It could be an animal carcass there, except for the eyes. She is nothing, that girl child. The male is King here, and rules: women are dismissible. They weigh down the poor family. A curse. Herself thinks of Winifred, who gets her through this spectacle of lost beautiful children. The crime of gender is a denial of God's will. That goes without saying.

Shanghai is bleak metaphor for this darkness, its walled Chinese city, that is — not the efficient calculated European modern town we visit nearby. In streets so narrow and cluttered we walk single file, Indian style, the guide, Herself, and then Himself following. Occasionally our bodies touch — for security. I feel real fear, I who have felt no real fear in any traveled land the world over. The pushing, shoving crowd jeers, points, follows, and mocks, contorting face into gargoyle grimace. The laughter is ribald and obscene. The hand movements against the bodies suggest lewd intention. I cannot close my eyes. Herself is mocked, but then any woman is, not just the overdressed American matron, sorely out of place here—for women are meant to be hidden from view. This is a city that despises God's order and harmony. The doomed land of infidels.

In shops the storekeepers mock, even as we display gold — they just do not know what to do with overdressed inferiors as ourselves — and, if there is any hesitation over a curio, the goods are secreted away. Helpless, we leave.

We are maneuvered out of shops. The hotel, with its cool drinks, is heaven.

In a Buddhist temple, where the wood was blackened by incense from ages of worship, I pray. I pray everywhere in the world. Outside beggars cry and whine, their crying becoming a hypnotic religious chant. Inside the scent from a joss stick makes us light headed.

Robert is sick on the side of a monument. We had noodles for breakfast, all grease and spice. People stop to gape and laugh. Pale, faint, he waves them off. They wave back at him, mocking.

What have we done to these people, save a desire to visit their world?

The journey by boat from Hong Kong to Canton is a fantasy, all mist and outcry, the mysterious movement of tide and sweat and fear. There is never quiet. Voices yell from every hidden corner. Lights flicker like fireflies on distant hills, lights gleam off coolie shores, and above us a crescent moon lies flat on its back, as though it has given up on the life below it. The sky is indigo high up and cobalt at the horizon, and the sliver of saffron moon cuts a brutal swath through that silvery heavenly ocean. Herself gets dreamy and cold on the boat, and drops into sleep till dawn, while the boat is anchored in Canton harbor. Sometimes Herself fears the first footsteps off the ship into that mass of another world. Each day is a reinvention of geography. The dock is all noise and activity: pushing crowds swell and run and heave and yell. Everyone seems hostile here. Life here is an angry fist held high in the air. There are no smiles, no laughter. Only the grimace and the extended tongue. Ten coolies and three sedan chairs — and our guide Ah Cum — take us to our hotel, where, for a breather, we hide.

From shrine to temple, to aromatic tea house, from curio shop to noodle shop, all hidden among narrow, littered streets. Skinny boys and their fathers make cruelly beautiful feather jewelry from the bright plumage of slaughtered birds from Singapore, dipping their stained fingers into bamboo baskets filled with rainbow feathers. The filth-smeared streets are so narrow you can reach out from your chair to the shops on either side and *help yourself. The streets are so congested with hordes of human beings that your progress through them is an endless malediction. An oath yelled in tea-chest characters has a frightful sound.*

The Cantonese impress you as great eaters. Braziers with strewing messes are everywhere. Every other store seems a market of some kind. Varnished pigs, ducks, dried fish, dogs and cats (with their heads on) and rat hams, tied with cute little wisps of straw, are all in full evidence and you wonder if you can ever eat again. Peddlers throng the street with large, live flopping fish in bamboo bowls and allow their customers to cut out the slices which they desire.

Hundreds of thousands of Cantonese live on junks, sampans, or gaily painted "flower-boats," where they are born, reared, married and die. Babies are tied to the deck by long cords and other children are allowed to romp about with a bamboo float fastened to them.

The "flower boats" are really the boats of dissipation—where women of wobbly morals live and where big gambling is done.

I show Robert what I've written: "Flower boats," I say, "is a lovely name for what is sordid: why does euphemism take the thrill out of some wonderful phrases?"

"I thought you were going to comment on the fallen woman again," he says.

I frown. "Men have little range in that conversation, and I think we've covered yours."

Hong Kong

Herself notes that there are only six American families here, according to what the Americans who live here tell me, and only three motor cars. Everything else is as it was centuries before: the dirty streets, the sullen faces, the smells of burnt charcoal and incense, the squeal of rickshaw wheels on the broken stones. The jabbering coolies with their omnipresent chair transports have some power, it seems, to bear the world up on men's shoulders. Like small, puny Atlases, they shoulder us from shop to shop. They point at us and laugh. We slip them gold coins, and they call us something that sounds like "kwailow," which, we are told, means white demon. Or white ghost. There are no horses in Hong Kong. None: three cars, but no steeds.

"You know, Ella," Robert says, smiling, "I'll tell you something which I can tell you only so far from home, where values are upside down. Where our Christian God is distant from us."

"Yes?" I ask, expectant.

"I was surprised you were a virgin on our wedding night."

"Robert," I gasp, genuinely hurt. For a second I turn away, red faced, not sure where to look.

"I'm not hurting you, Ella dear," he says. "Not meaning to. I only mean that you had that scarlet reputation yourself, you know — poetess of passion. All that to do about your love lyrics. But you were a country girl, virginal, beautiful. You are still beautiful." He is rambling now.

I am biting my lip. "It's a horrible thing you've said to me."

"What? Calling you a virgin?" Now he is surprised, reaching out to grasp my hand. I let him.

I smile slightly: "You're twisting my words, Robert."

"You're the wordsmith, Ella."

"Sometimes I wonder," I say.

"We married each other for our words."

"Words of love?'" I ask.

"Of course."

"You are always in control, Robert."

"One of us has to be. But I think, strangely, it's you." He smiles.

"Robert —" I sigh.

"Are you tired, Ella? You look so weary — all this traveling, all these years, all these countries — northern Africa—"

"Sometimes I get tired, but there is so much. I need to see this world —"

Ceylon

In Kandy we sit under fragrant rain trees which cover us like pink and pale-green silk skies. The day is smooth and yielding. From somewhere comes the scent of overripe fruit, cloying and a little acrid. We drift through the morning. As scheduled, Sister Suddhammdara greets us, a modest nun dressed in saffron yellow robe, torn at the hemline, a large palm leaf fan in her hand, and straw sandals on her feet. She looks poor but is filled with spirit. She has a close-shaved head, like an old man's, but is oddly beautiful. It is, I suppose, the eyes: they never stop moving. She bows to Himself, all courtesy, and she shakes my hand. Respect: it is in her eyes, in the cut of her jaw, in the turn of her head. We invite her to take her one meal of the day with us in our apartment: steamed rice with red curry and sliced, ripe papaya, a few fresh vegetables, and coffee. She refuses eggs, which, she says, are never eaten unless accidentally broken: "We are not then destroying life for the gratification of appetite," she says, looking into my face. Himself nods. It makes sense to me, and I feel the coolness inside: the calm that ignores the day's heat. She drinks lemonade in small childlike sips. There is everything of the child — the girl child — about her. When she smiles, my heart races.

She spends her days in a makeshift school for poor orphaned girls, this dedicated daughter of a Christian mother who, as a tiny girl, tended her blind Buddhist father daily, reading Buddhist texts to him, and when he died she chose the Buddhist Sisterhood over the Christian. She was always destined for devotion. She now does good work among her people: right thought, right speech, right conduct, the taking of no life, no stealing, lying, slander, abuse, unprofitable conversation. Purity: the treasures of the body's blood. Contemplation: the soul of all being. Charity: the music of the soul. She puts fresh-cut flowers daily on Buddha's shrine, because flowers are sweet and pure. They play with the senses. They engage the spirit.

But Sister believes life on this earth — in this flesh-and-blood body we inhabit — is a misfortune. It is to be borne. Only in the realm of spirit can we find happiness.

No. No, Herself says to her. "Life is a privilege," I tell her.
"To feel the blood course through the body — to be alive!" And
Himself gives me a sharp glance. "Have you considered New
Thought and Theosophy?" I am ready to teach her the saving
grace of the New Thought. Himself grunts. "The earth is one of
God's beautiful rooms, when we make it happy." Sister is si-
lent. "We are not just worms of the sod," Herself says. "We are
royal lieges of God."

Sister bows, in deference. She will not argue with me.

We spend a beautiful afternoon with her, and when she leaves,
Herself feels empty.

By motor car to Dambulla, we are surrounded by four slight
native boys who would be our guides. They scream and giggle
in our ears. Himself selects one, the tallest of the lot, but the
others follow alongside us anyway. Halfway up the steep moun-
tain Herself is taken with the heat, choosing to sit in the cool
shade of a pagoda and tree while Himself goes on ahead. A little
naked boy, bronzed as a temple pot, lingers with me, opening
nut shells, humming a tune, telling a story that makes Himself
laugh, bringing bunches of ragged flowers. He chatters in his
language, all smiles, and dances around me, naked as a forest
animal, and as filthy. When he comes too near, by accident, and
I signal or smile, he rushes away, much as a newborn puppy
plays yet runs. I think of Robert Junior, less bronzed, more
clothed. But as charming.

Robert looks up from his book, flicks cigar ashes. He
looks tired. "Are we ready to go back home?" he asks.

"Are you?"

"I asked you first."

"There is no order to things."

"Of course there is."

"Not on the other side of the earth."

"I asked you first."

I don't answer. Then: "I don't understand the word
ready. It seems so — precipitous."

"Tell me when then," Robert says.

"I will. I'll know — in my heart." Then I add: "There is a loneliness in traveling. So far from home, from friends. Sometimes, at night, there is a pain inside me. Everywhere there is the strange babble of other tongues, other aromas, other colors and feelings. Even the Americans we meet — like the friends we know and visit — seem, well, different. They speak English after a while with an exotic rhythm. Sometimes I think they are singing. I think some people stay away from America too long — you can't return."

"It's the world so few others will ever get to see, but you and I are privileged to have it."

"We have seen a world."

He echoes: "We have seen a world."

We both laugh quietly together.

Northern Africa

In the week of a full arabesque moon at Hamman Mousquitine, by the hot spring waters, Himself asks me to play sweet Arabian airs on my mandolin under the terebinthe tree. Himself smokes his cigar and smiles. I play native airs I have learned in the streets. Himself nods, pleased. The mandolin was a good purchase.

In the garden and courtyard of the villa of Prince Kazabar Baredin, Herself is anointed with a thick henna dye by his young Arab bride, who draws the Allah cross on Herself's chin, throat, and wrists until I beg them cease. I fear I will look ghostly, a totem of symbol and chart. Herself is told this is an honor, but the henna dye takes a week to disappear, much to my annoyance, and Himself jokes that I am a princess out of the darker pages of the Arabian Nights' Entertainment.

In Ancient Tiblis, now Announa, our Arab guide tells us in perfect schoolboy French that the land is blest. He waves his hand to the heavens and takes in the horizon, bright as candlelight. We know that is true because Allah grows special flowers there, the crimson poppy, the wild gold narcissus, the indigo and pale lavender ground cover, a rolling land that Himself says is "covered with God's Persian carpets." The sun shim-

mers through the mottled green of the olive trees. The guide
whittles figurines out of olive wood, hands us one — a woman
with a basket — and then leads us to a ruined Roman temple,
nearly hidden by decaying houses and falling lean-tos, and the
fragmented columns and altars are shabby with faded Latin
inscription.
Robert whispers: So passes glory.
Herself nods. And adds: And hope.
When we walk back on the hard pebbly path to the car, ready
for hot baths and cool lemonades, an Arab shepherd in a near
field waves to us and plays a reed pipe. The tune is plaintive
and our guide mumbles that it has to do with the end of the day,
the melancholy borderline between day and night. A shepherd
in love with his life will end the day with that air. We call to
him and he follows us to the car. We drop a gold coin into his
skinny hand. Why don't they ever smile?
The haunting, echoey strains hang in the air as we drive away.

"You gave me an oriental paper knife," I say, " and it
turned into all this." I point to the swaying palms against
the violet nighttime sky. Someone with a reed pipe is playing. A young boy flits past, wailing in a barrage of frantic alien tongue. I close my eyes: I live in this world.

Robert breaks the silence: "Then you must not dwell
on the fallen women."

I wish he hadn't said that.

I ask: "Do all men see only two kinds of women in the
world — the virgin and the courtesan?"

"What are mothers?"

"Still metaphorically virginal in this equation."

"Really, Ella. Wordplay."

"Robert, not everything is my playing with words. I
stand among these women and —"

"Ella, enough of the whores of Babylon."

"But where is the higher life?"

"Ella, maybe you exact too much from the world. Some
things are perhaps — as I have said — givens. Practical.
They happen, and they become part of life."

"You're a businessman."

"You're a poet."

"Is everything a category?"

He doesn't answer.

Suddenly I am weeping, angry at him. He turns away. In the silence I hear a man and a woman laughing: it unnerves me. A servant appears with a telegram on a silver tray, standing there, confused, his eyes averted from my sobbing face. I jump. Smile. I say to the young man, in French. "You catch me crying for happiness." He leaves.

The smell of sandalwood incense from another veranda wafts through hibiscus and oleander.

"Crying for happiness?" Robert repeats. He relights his cigar.

"Would you have us the talk of Tunis?"

Robert shakes his head: "Ella, we are just curiosities here anyway. Think of it. They don't understand us. Why can't we be a regular couple. Even in America we have to be the ideal couple. Ella, face it, I am not an ideal man. I'm not in the pages of your poems. How many times have we had words — like every other married couple — and you panic when we're caught?"

"What do you want then?"

"Let the world know we fight."

"We don't fight."

Now he smiles: "Of course, we do. And loudly and rudely. And lovingly. You're headstrong, Ella, and so am I. We bounce off each other. I push you to tears and you push me to — going fishing."

"Robert —"

"This marriage is working. This is, oddly, a real love story."

I am silent, tears still in my eyes.

"What do you miss, Ella?"

"I don't miss a thing."

"There you go again. No, tell me. We spend a year away from home, from America. Home for just a summer. Then we leave for months and months. For long winters. Years go by. You're the world's best known poet. But not in Tunis. Yes, the Consul wines us, knows your reputation, flatters, ushers us into shrines and temples and festivals. But you're unheralded here. Do you miss the attention of the press — of your readers?"

I smirk. "You sound like my critics — the ones who claim I do everything to get attention. I throw receptions so the newspapers can quote me. I'm not all publicity, Robert."

"I of anyone know that. But do you miss the limelight?"

Silence. Then: "I suppose, a little. All my life I have craved approval, attention. Look at me. Look at me — I'm the clever little girl poet. I did want to be noticed — I still do."

"Here they notice you because you are a white woman."

"Yes."

"And I took you from your audience."

"I am not a slave, Robert. This" — my hand takes in the sky and palms — "I did want this."

"But what do you miss?"

"Well, not writing enough poems, maybe. Publishing poems. Sometimes I'm too tired to do so. But I do miss the connectedness of readers and editors. I don't know what they're reading back home. What is the current best-seller? Who is the new young poet trying to replace me?"

"No one can replace you."

"I am too far away from home to know."

"That's my point."

"But I chose this, Robert. When I return, I always have my public."

"True. You always have your readers."

"Loyal, I know."

"And loving. "

"You are Ella Wheeler Wilcox."

"Here I'm Mrs. Robert Wilcox."

"There I'm Mr. Ella Wheeler Wilcox."

"I'm sorry."

"Don't be. You were the Poetess of Passion when I knowingly married you."

I smirk again: "But unknowingly a virgin."

"Don't, Ella. All our conversations become circular."

"Women are circles, men are straight lines."

He laughs. "Yes."

"Are we running away?" I ask suddenly.

"From what?"

I throw my hands into the air, sit back: the twilight sun is brilliant in the slick-blue sky, a red shimmering ball disappearing into palm trees. Soon it will be chilly, and the night scents will cover us like fog. I say: "I wonder if we're like rich folk who go from resort to resort, seeking diversion. Driven by demons. I sometimes feel as if a ghost is with us, some awful specter that demands we move. We are driven across longitude and latitude, swept by sea breeze, running, running."

"But we have fame," he says, bowing to me.

"And money,' I say, bowing to him. "Although," I add, grinning for the first time, "I have money too. I've had money since I was a child."

"The poetess of passion, in her sandbox."

"Thank you," I say, an edge in my voice.

"I meant it kindly," he says.

"Is it Winifred?" I say, suddenly, and he stares into my face. "She travels with us always, I know, but somehow she is back there, in that awful house in Meriden on Colony Street. Or is it Robert Junior, really, buried now among flower beds in that blasted boulder in the garden at the Barracks? Are we running away from him, Robert? From them?"

For the longest time Robert is still, watching the disappearing sun. He sips a lemonade slowly, and spills some. It dribbles down his waistcoat, and he doesn't notice. He has always been so meticulous with his toilet, and still is, but sometimes, late in the day, he forgets crumbs in the mustache, the dried egg on the chin, the soap on the vest. I suddenly thinks he is old now, a wrinkled kindly face, but old.

"Would we be doing this if we had had children?" he asks.

"Traveling?"

"Yes, traveling. Sitting here, many thousands of miles from home."

"Perhaps, now that we're old."

He says, "I would have loved to have seen Robert grown to manhood."

I think: Ethan Allen: Pocahontas: Ralph Waldo Emerson. American child.

"We will someday. After we pass on. He's waiting for us."

"But on this earth," Robert says. "Married, among us. With his own children. Grandchildren."

"I always wanted children," I say.

"We had no choice," Robert says.

"It wasn't meant to be."

"I know."

"God had other plans for us."

"I know."

He smiles: "Too late now."

Suddenly, fiercely: "But why?" I say, too loudly. "Why?"

Then, quietly, I begin to cry again, this time softly, my mouth making slight, trembling sounds, like a small wounded forest animal.

"Ella," he says kindly, "we've had other things."

"But not children."

"You have all these other children you cared for."

"It's not the same."

"Robert lies in that garden, his ashes, but he waits for us. His spirit is growing now as we speak, filled with God's good beauty: he prepares the way for us."

"Of course."

I nod. "And my mother lies now among the rosebushes, with Robert. Grandmother and grandson: generations together. The middle link — me and you — we sit a thousand miles away among heathens and wizards and na-

ked men in loincloths worshipping pagan gods.
There — back there — is the stability, the generations intact —"

India

*At the Jaipur Temple a girl bride is carried in wooden carts
drawn by two pale white bullocks. The procession moves slowly,
solemnly. Her Hindu uncle, resplendent in gilt braid and yellow turban, a dark handsome man, lifts her down carefully,
and she stands before him, expectant. She is ten years old, maybe
younger. Women in colored wedding saris with necklaces and
bracelets and earrings and nose rings surround us, the gaping,
curious foreigners. The little girl is wrapped like a present —
in layers of shiny gold, a waist-high bride, a little brown face
with luminous midnight eyes. From her body — a statue, really — hang jewels — in nostrils, in ears, in lips. She is a
statue. Her husband, gangly and tentative, is fourteen years
old this week, a skittish boy as dark as old wood. Robert says:
back home he'd be running for baseballs. Herself watches other
such bizarre marriages, a girl five, the husband just eight. After the wedding feast, the bride will never again dine at her
husband's table. This is Brahmin law: a reverence so deep for
women, they say, that she must be afforded total seclusion from
society—from other men. Herself learns that the barbaric cus-
tom of suttee — the burning of a widow on her husband's funeral pyre — is gone, thank God, but widows now — as young
as ten years old — must spend a lifetime grieving, unmarried,
alone, lonely. It beggars the imagination. Himself shakes his
head, wondering what happened to childhood. Herself reminds
him that she Herself was never a child. I was a young girl poet,
at eight. He grins. "Ours was not such a child marriage," he
says. "I was," I say. But the mood is too grim, watching these
lost young women and girls, forgotten, deserted, condemned.
"We cannot follow this mind's thinking," Himself says. "Such
a devotion to the dead. It borders on hysteria."*

*It is age-old ignorance — and bondage, Herself believes. The
British have done all the wrong things here — and not enough
of the good. Surely the hour has come when Home Rule should*

be given to that land.

"The Anglo-Saxon is ruler," Robert says.

"It doesn't always work," I say.

> In India's land one listens aghast
> To the people who scream and bawl;
> For each caste yells at a lower caste,
> And the Britisher yells at them all.

Herself faints dead away at the Monkey Temple in Benares. I despise that show of weakness in myself — of helplessness. Everything there is din and clamor, deafening, amid the eerie chanting of morose monks. Sacred bulls and cows, those actually alive and those fashioned out of bronze and iron, surround us. This could be a cattle ranch in Topeka, Robert whispers. Except — Except — Worse, the phallus is omnipresent, in all its excited manifestation. Here the crowds bow and chant in the worship of Shiva. Here Himself debates the purchase of a paperweight phallus until the touch of my fingers on his arm makes him change his mind. What American man would have that in his possession? Short Beach on the Sound, I thought: they do not understand phalluses there.

But Herself faints at the Monkey Temple, as hundreds of wild, insensible monkeys, squawking like banshees, leap and twist on their elegant perches. Pampered by the wealth of a Rajah, these creatures live an abundantly luxurious life, but their cacophony is too much for Herself: when a frantic, beady-eyed monkey swings too close, its noxious jungle smell hitting my nostrils and its tail swiping a shoulder, Herself screams and falls over. When I open my eyes, I am unfortunately face to face with a positioned phallus. Luckily it is bronze, and only mildly exaggerated.

Robert does not speak of it, but every so often, glancing at him, I detect a slight trace of smile. His eyes twinkle through cigar smoke. Herself can read his mind: he will have a story for the men in the Quinnipiac Club when we return home.

In the Ganges River people bathe, in prayer, while bodies burn

*nearby on the great burning phat. The smell of incinerated flesh
covers us. I am dizzy. Bodies wait to be burned. The remaining
ashes, cooled, are tossed into the blessed Ganges. Men rake the
dying embers and cinders, collect piles, and, we are told, use
the debris for smoking. The spirit of the man is held still in the
smoke. Holy men are themselves not buried but submerged into
the waters, like Salem witches. We pass one body, tied in rag
cloth, three vultures on the breast of a dead man, eating.*

"Do you want to go home?" Robert says, asking repeatedly the same question.

"I'm not ready," I say. I run through the names in my
head, like counting beads of a rosary: Tangiers, China,
Japan, Tunis, the Garden of Allah, Algiers, the Kabul
Mountains, Tizi-Ouzou, Sicily, Venice, Ceylon, Burma.

"What is life like back in Short Beach?" he asks.

"The same," I say. "They wait for us to move them."

"Do we bore each other?" he asks.

"That's a surprising question, Robert."

"We are always together, you and I. We are best friends,
husband and wife, lovers. Love of my life, me and you.
On some days we only see each other — I mean, the only
English is spoken by you and me."

"Of course, we bore each other, I suppose. It's natural.
And we thrill each other. We exact each other."

"I didn't want to fail you."

"Impossible," I say. "You are like the long summer
flower that keeps surprising."

He smiles: "That's out of one of your verses, Ella."

I laugh: "I only speak the truth in my writing."

"Seriously," he says, "I never want to bore you, Ella."

"That can't happen, Robert."

"I'm an old man now, years older than you." He grins.
"Seventy what?"

"It doesn't matter? I'm sixty something."

"Or fifty something — if I remember the printed biographies. "

I laugh. "Five years doesn't matter so much when you

get up there in age, right?"

"Let the future biographers grapple with it," he says.

I panic: "Oh, Lord, Robert, they will write my story, won't they? I will be grist for their sinful mill, no? They will reinvent my story. Get it all wrong. I'm a public figure."

"The poet of passion."

"They'll turn me into a dreadful woman, all fame and no wisdom."

"Impossible."

"They won't understand the wonder I've had."

"Of course they will."

I drum the table with my fingers. "I will write my own story, Robert, the story of you and me. The World and I, I'll call it. I need my story out there. The truth. The world" — I wave my hand to the horizon — "and I."

"Just one world, Ella?"

"Worlds."

Singapore

At the Chitty Temple the Hindu Festival of Tanpaniene is at its height: beautiful, barbaric, splendid, horrible. Men naked save for starch-white loincloths sweat under fire and colorful banner, their bronzed bodies glowing with diamonds that shine against smooth copper skin. Processions of the frenzied devout bow before the shrine of Vishnu, beat ashes into their chests, draw blood, I fear, and mumble a chanted prayer. Two-one music, alien to Herself's ear, stuns and mesmerizes. The naked men bow and moan. All around me — the metamorphosis of flesh into spirit. A fanatic begs penance in a loud, droning voice, plunging a knife and needle into his shoulders, neck, and chest, and the worshippers moan and exalt him. Over him the blessed chant, and fan him, and some pierce his body with knives. Somehow he will walk away, and tomorrow will be unscathed. Yet now, in the midst of it, there is only crying out. What gods exact such a penance? Himself goes up close to the pierced writhing man, watching for trickery. Robert is as rapt as watching a coiled cobra. Come away, I plead. Come away. The heat is

intense: bodies gleam. So much flesh. I try to imagine the world
of the Spirit. But all is Flesh here, men's flesh, young and old.
Man and boy. Animals' flesh. The bulls pull a silver peacock
chair through the streets. The crowd chants. I turn away.

We gaze upon the majestic bulls that are worshipped, six in
all, tethered together, such a display of brute force. The over-
sweet incense makes Herself swoon.

Spent, we linger in our afternoon beds.

Himself is tired. We dine quietly at the hotel. The room is
empty of guests: it is early. Himself remarks that Short Beach
friends are now having breakfast.

I smile. Butter biscuits and summer raspberry jam preserve
and steaming chickory coffee. Fresh milk from Taylor's farm.
Chalk-coated blueberries in season. Sweet apple butter. Brown
Betty. Chunky vanilla ice cream, fresh churned.

Short Beach.

He asks, "What have we not done? What's missing?"

"Nothing," I say, too quickly.

"Come on, Ella, be honest."

"No, I swear. You gave me an oriental paper knife when
I was on a farm in Wisconsin. I'm still opening my letters
with that same opener. You know that. Just as you now
open doors for me in Tunis, in Bisrah, in Algiers, in Arabian tents."

"The poet on her life's journey," he says.

"What are you missing, Robert? What about you? Talk
about you now."

"Why?"

"We always talk about what I want. What about you,
Robert?"

"I'm, well — a traveler with my wife."

"You're more than that."

He takes a puff on his cigar, breathes out. A button on
his shirt pops off, rolls onto the smooth tile floor, disappears under a bamboo chair. He doesn't notice.

"I am content to be your shadow," he says. "I drift
around the world with you, the rather large shadow be-

hind Ella Wheeler Wilcox, poetess."

"Oh, no. Don't say that," I say, hurt. "No. Nobody wants to be a shadow. "

He laughs. "Don't get angry again. I never really wanted to work. You know that. I just wanted to — travel. By myself as a young bachelor. With you when I married. To travel. I just love the ocean liner, the steam locomotive, the rickshaw."

"The luxury of independent wealth," I say.

"It helps."

"But I don't like your — insecurity."

"Ella, look at me. A man tipping the scales at over three hundred, a bulk of a man, with a fat expansive face, a clear blue eye, to be sure, but a man who needs an extra coolie to be lifted in the Calcutta streets. And what do I have. You: beautiful, petite, witty, charming, colorful, creative. You are the world's most desired and desirable woman. Lillian Russell has nothing on you. "

"I am an old woman. Look."

"Ella, I have you."

"Robert, " I say, out of breath. "I wonder at your words sometimes. I write the verses but you say the poetic lines."

"Only when I'm looking at you, darling."

"You have always made me flutter."

"You have made me understand God's gift."

"I will use these lines when I write a verse drama of young lovers. The story of passion and —"

Robert waits a second. Then: "Ella, you already have. Over and over."

In the unquiet darkness, the screeching of tropical birds cawing overhead, the *tintintin* rhythmic beat of a stick against metal somewhere, we laugh for a long time. I dry my eyes with a handkerchief. I am happy.

"You ready to go home, Ella?"

"Not yet, Robert. Not yet."

"After Ceylon?"

"Perhaps."

Granite

1915

Dear Sir,
Your letter asks me for a definition of the word Home.
How curious this request! And yet, I suppose, how appro-
priate that you query me. I have long been an advocate of
the Home—that Christian repository of every decent value
civilization has fine tuned. But I sat long and long, musing
over your question, wanting to provide you with a cogent
definition. Finally I have come to one conclusion — and
one conclusion only. Home is the place where the Heart is
near the surface of the Body.
> — Ella Wheeler Wilcox, "A Letter to an Old
> Man," *Cosmopolitan,* 1913

Back at Short Beach, nestled mightily into a rope hammock on the wraparound porch, Robert sleeps
through the long summer days. When we talk of Europe
and Africa and Asia, he announces, over and over: "I
don't want to travel again for many more years." He
waves his hands at the blue-green lawns. "This is our
land now."

On our last journey away from home we saw the swans
at Stratford-on-Avon. I had breakfast with Sarah
Bernhardt in Paris (who told me, "I detect character in
the eyes," and said she loved my poetry), and I was pre-
sented before the Queen and King at the Court of St.
James. I wanted to wear lilies in my hair and not the
obligatory feathers, but I didn't. They wouldn't let me.

The London press made me out to be a spoiled American rich woman, but I had my defenders, to be sure. But it was grand fun. All of it. Now I am back home.

In my journal: *No ocean ever lay like this.*

I understand: it is now the long season to savor our many memories and reinvent our idyll on the rocky Connecticut shore. The Wilcoxes are back home. Short Beach is at high tide. So we spend an energetic, buoyant summer, swimming every sunny day, and sharing brewed coffee with friends. We entertain new neighbors, who seem thrilled that we have come home. Within weeks, it is as though we never left, have not wandered the world all these years, virtually circling the globe twice. "Two times," I tell every visitor until they run from me. "We went around the world twice."

"A third time?" someone asks.

"Never," I say. "I am at peace here."

One afternoon, dreamily, Robert and I walk the strand. Seaweed gets tangled in our toes.

"It's hard to believe we had to go away," Robert says.

I nod. "I'm looking forward to winter here," I say. "It's been a long time since we saw snow on the roof of the Bungalow."

Robert grins. "The rafters will creak and the snow will cover us."

"Frankly I can't wait. There's been too much constant sun in our lives."

"So we aren't meant for endless tropical sun." He smiles.

"Old people long for shadows."

"You're calling yourself old?" Robert asks.

I smile. "Yes. Poetess of Aging."

We hurry into projects, the two of us making lists of things to do. We are giddy in our conversations about the seasons to follow. "This is an earthly Eden," I say to him. "Our own paradise. Let's touch every corner — beautify it. Make it a showplace." Robert begins with a long discussed Flower Room at the Barracks, a lovely solarium that faces the sea, a floor-to-ceiling glass room with abundant flowers. I spend a few hours each day in the flower garden behind the four rental cottages, a garden of eight triangles, each playing off the other in color and scheme, a walk lane of constant bloom from spring to fall. There will always be flowers in the house now, not only the dried marigolds and chrysanthemums I always use in my winter vases, but fresh blooms, buds that open in January and February.

Robert trains the deep purple wisteria vines over the Bungalow Tower, renamed the Starling Tower because so many of the pesky birds now make it their home. The intended robins and bluebirds and orioles go elsewhere.

While I write in the mornings, sitting on the veranda with a pot of steaming coffee and spice-butter cake, Robert nurses vagrant honeysuckle vines around a dead cedar tree. He spends hours doing it, so caught up in the occupation. Underneath it are the Elephant Gates leading down to the water's edge, the two huge pottery elephants, freighted from India, standing as exotic sentinels by the lane that leads up to the Bungalow. Now and then Robert glances back at the house, and catches my eye. We pause, smiling. We wave to each other, like shy young lovers.

Robert idles at the dock, eyes half closed, fishing for flatfish and flounder. When there are no summer guests, the days are dreamy and soft.

In the evening I study the harp.

We take nightly strolls along the seawall.

"We own this ocean," I say.

"What?"

"I mean, for years we borrowed the ocean — all over the world. Now this is ours."

Robert laughs. "No one owns the ocean."

I laugh. "We come close."

Alone with Robert, tucked into comfortable walls — walls cluttered with travel souvenirs — I feel safe. For the first time I am safe, I think, though I find that thought vagrant. Haven't I always been safe? With Robert? Life has always been safe for me, but now it seems inviolable, this safe haven. Maybe I mean that I am isolated from the bottom, that awful place of poverty and failure. What do I mean by safe? Nothing can penetrate this calm now. Perhaps. I write "Floods":

> *In the dark night, from sweet refreshing sleep*
> *I wake to hear outside my window-pane*
> *The uncurled fury of the wild spring rain,*
> *And weird winds lashing the defiant deep,*
> *And roar of floods that gather strength, and leap*
> *Down dizzy, wreck-strewn channels to the main.*
> *I turn upon my pillow, and again*
> *Compose myself for slumber.*
> > *Let them sweep;*
> *I once survived great floods, and do not fear,*
> *Though ominous planets congregate, and seem*
> *To foretell strange disasters.*

> > *From a dream—*
> *Ah! dear God! such a dream!—I woke to hear,*
> *Through the dense shadows lit by no stars' gleam,*
> *The rush of mighty waters on my ear.*
> *Helpless, afraid, and all alone, I lay;*
> *The floods had come upon me unaware.*

> *I heard the creak of structures that were fair;*
> *The bridges of fond hopes were swept away*
> *By great salt waves of sorrow. In dismay*
> *I saw by the red lightning's lurid glare*
> *That on the rock-bound island of despair*
> *I had been cast. Till the dim dawn of day*

> *I heard my castles falling, and the roll*
> *Of angry billows bearing to the sea*
> *The broken timbers of my very soul.*
> *Were all the pent-up waters from the whole*

Stupendous solar system to break free,
There are no floods now that can frighten me.

I am whole: intact: the poet in her ripe, late life.
Safe.

The summer season is in full swing. There are lawn games and banquets. There are lavish costume balls. Togas and tunics and tiaras. Medieval and classical drama come to life on the shore. There are Sunday musicales. Recitations. Lectures by visitors from Yale. Speakers on the occult. Fortune tellers. Mystics. Phrenologists. Robert and I both fascinated by the unknown. Card readers enthrall Robert — and me. I can read palms. There are visitors from Boston and New York. Ballroom dances. During the week friends and I hand-polish the parlor floor, waxing it to a brilliant sheen. On the weekend the thrilled dancers glide and shimmer. It is the high season.

I write poems about the garden of Eden. And Adam. Eve is the red-haired heroine, all chiffon and forsythia, the hair flowing in the wind, the newfangled motorcars speeding down the country lanes. Adam tends the tamed garden.

Sometimes, in the late afternoon, I sit alone in the wooden pagoda Robert built for me at the end of the pier. Alone, deep in thought, a pad on my knee, I wait for inspiration. I am surrounded by flowers, clay pots of zinnias and Sweet William. Sometimes whole afternoons pass, and I simply stare into the sea. I am drunk here.

Everyone is dancing this summer, hurling their bodies onto the dance floor in some manic, hysterical fling at merriment. I understand why: I recall my premonition on the *Olympic,* that sudden, fearsome taste of war in Europe. The specter of decay and loss. The daily newspapers talk incessantly of the mighty and menacing Kaiser, of modern armies, or stupendous war machines, of guns, of gas warfare, of boats and thunder in the sky. People, scared, are hellbent on having good times. I have a vision:

God, what an age! How was it that You let
Colossal genius and colossal crime
Walk for an hundred years across the earth,
Like giant twins? How was it then that men,
Conceiving such vast beauty for the world,
And such large hopes of heaven, could entertain
Such hellish projects for their humankind?

So everyone dances as though the dreaded millennium is at hand: the four horsemen of the Apocalypse poised on the horizon, waiting. Waiting.

No one dances faster and more than I do this summer. In my journal: *When Herself dances, the world becomes a blur of color and shade: it is hard to be afraid when everything has a soft, indefinite edge.* Local orchestras play until dawn some Saturday nights: no one wants to go home. When the sun rises over the ocean, we are all afraid.

One night, maddened with dance, I twirl on the floor, and my breasts break free of the daring neckline. Laughing, heady from the champagne, I nonchalantly tuck them in. Whatever can I do? When I turn and spot every eye on me — including Robert's, his face frowning — I wink.

He looks angry.

The local press labels me Queen. The *New York World* asks me to write my impressions of the opening day of baseball season. I say no. They ask me about the Gibson girl. I don't answer. Cigarettes are hanging from women's mouths these days. Yes, I have something to say about that. Mine is a different democratic spirit, I insist — far from the baseball field and the liberated girl on a two-wheeled bicycle. I look back to an idyllic world of pageantry — America as exquisite festival. The innocence of red white and blue bunting at a Fourth of July parade.

Friends come — and stay. I never want them to leave. Jack and Charmian London arrive for a surprise visit, and Jack scribbles his famous name on the Barracks wall. Jack is a swimmer much as I am: the two of us can go nearly an hour without our feet touching sand, swimming deep into the ocean.

"Next," Robert says to Charmian, "they will learn to fly."

"Ella at Kitty Hawk," Jack says, grinning.

"Jack on the moon," I say.

"Jack London and Ella Wheeler Wilcox beyond the Milky Way, among aliens," Charmian says. We draw pictures of ourselves as otherworldly creatures. My alien self-portrait carries flowers the color of winter wheat.

When they leave, I tell Robert we will never see Jack again.

"So young a man to die," I say.

"Ella," Robert says, alarmed, "we just had days of laughter and fun."

I frown. "And your point is what?"

"Let's hope for the best," Robert says.

"He will not be remembered," I say, sadly.

"He is a great artist," Robert insists.

"His is the soul of dissipation," I say. "The good man who cannot settle his artistic Muse."

This summer they all come. The writer Zona Gale, very famous now, alone from Ridgely Torrence, the two no longer lovers.

Zona stays part of the summer. Years before, I met her in Wisconsin, at Judge Braley's home. A young girl asked to meet me. In short skirts — she was still a child — her hair in braids down her back, she asked me to read her work. I thrilled to the young girl's local color portraits. A friend for years, she's been to the Bungalow many times, especially back when she and Ridgely were lovers. This is the same Zona Gale who now interrupts her dancing one afternoon at the Barracks to grant an interview to the *Boston Globe* reporter who has traveled down the coast to see her. She has garnered fame for her sensational *Friendship Village*, her evocative small town Wisconsin epic, as well as her fervent stand for Equal Rights for Women.

A week after she leaves, Ridgely Torrence arrives, a young man I believe looks like a Greek God. He is finishing his first collection of poetry. I never probed into the reason for the end of his torrid and wonderful romance with Zona: they had been the ideal couple years before. So elegant, the two of them. He comes alone now, for one week. He is still beautiful. I tell him so often he is embarrassed, reddening and turning away. Sometimes he disappears, walking the sandy beach in his bare feet, late into the night.

"I understand Zona was here last week," he says.

"Yes," I say. I start to say something, but he is already turning away. Robert shoots me a look: mind my own business.

I have heard he left her after she had an affair with a married man. That is the current buzz in New York. Not Zona: I refuse to believe it. Once, Robert slips, mentioning Zona's name to Ridgely. The younger man's face turns scarlet.

I only want virtuous people around me at the Bungalow. I insist that my world be a moral center. Someone slips me a novel by Dreiser called *Sister Carrie*, published back in 1900, but, the friend says, a wonderful novel. I read a few chapters, but I hurl it across the room. "Had it been my copy," I tell Robert, "I should have burned it. It was so — cold." I am depressed for days. I fear the future of American literature — the realists and the naturalists, all sensation and clinical detail and mechanical gesture. Thugs and ne'er-do-wells are the new authors — and the central characters. Prostitutes, cutthroat businessmen, charlatans and thieves. There are even parts of Zona Gale I have trouble with, episodes so dark and frank I think them unseemly. It isn't mentioned this summer.

Why hasn't America learned the value of cheerfulness?

Dreiser will never be seen swimming in my bay this summer.

Interviewers plague me with questions about the New Woman, but the questions always disturb me. After all, I was the New Woman, wasn't I? I still am, even now in my sixties. How have they missed that fact? But no, they say, I am the Old Woman. The New Women smokes, rides two-wheel bicycles, wants to vote, travels alone, and has an independent life. She divorces her husband. She talks of careers. For me, the ideas are troubling. I support the efforts, I tell them, of women to achieve *things*. I stress the word: *things*. Men have too much power, and I know that myself, after all the years in publishing. Women don't get respect for — intelligence. For common sense. But beyond this — my wish for recognition from men as a worthy person — I get confused. What does it all mean? I've been friends with Jenny June Croly, who started the first Women's Press Club in 1889. No place for women in the airtight male-dominated halls of journalism? Well, form your own society, said Jenny June. Good for her, I say. Other women push for the vote. I nod.

"Can we get your support, Ella?"

I nod.

But in my tabloid sob-sister bits for Hearst, those easy-language pieces that give comfort and advice, I find myself wavering. Is this best for all those women out there, the factory wives, the farm girls?

I write in my column: "I am quite sure were I a man, I would fly to the uttermost parts of the earth if I found myself becoming too interested in a woman with a 'career.'"

My friends protest. "But, Ella, you have a career."

"I am Robert's wife."

"You are a published poet. You make your own money."

"I am a wife."

"Male publishers get rich off of you."

"It's different."

"How?"

No answer. They have lost me.

In my columns I reassure my readership: "Seen from a

distance, fame may seem to a woman like a sea bathed in tropical suns, wherein she longs to sail. Let fame once be hers, she finds it a prairie fire consuming or scorching all that is dearest in life to her. Be careful before you light these fires with your own hands."

"How much did they pay you for those words, Ella," an acquaintance says. "It is your — career, no?"

Women begin smoking at the Bungalow now, but I never do. And I smile, nodding. They are my friends. But I write: "I am confident the habit vitiates the blood, injures the digestion, and makes breath offensive. A woman who expects ever to bring children into the world is little better than a criminal to form such a habit, giving the unborn child hour by hour the impression of her mental and physical condition." My women friends — the smokers — never mention my published attacks. Perhaps they haven't even read my work.

I will never vote. I have no time to think through the issues at hand—it requires a vast amount of mentality, vital force and time. I leave it for the present to others who are more capable or to those who have fewer obligations of a domestic nature. Like, well, men.

"But Ella —"

"A woman lacks system," I say. "She lacks patience to await results."

"Really, Ella."

I am here to serve my husband. When we met, Robert had to show me how to conduct a proper household. Lace tablecloths for dining, the proper bone china dishes, the careful choice of silverware and linen. As I confess to my readers, "Until my marriage I had not given the home much thought outside of keeping it clean and comfortable. The table, too, I had recognized merely as a place where one satisfied the appetite. My husband taught me to think of it as a thing of beauty and refinement where choice appointments, correct service, and the best moods of the family should lend charm and appetite to the delicately prepared food." I don't mention how embarrassed

I was. My crude home table, all mismatched crockery and bent fork, was all I knew. But now I know. And I outdo him in everything, with hours of dull, methodical preparation. Robert will never be embarrassed by me again. I can do it with my eyes shut. I tell my readers: "Almost any woman can write; but only one woman could or did become the wife of Robert Wilcox."

"Ella, but—"

Oddly, I still look for signs of disapproval from Robert, watching him as my guests lean into my splendid dinner table. I watch for the flicker in the eye corner, the hint of disapproval. Years after my marriage, an old woman, I still fear the social *faux pas*. When Robert smiles, the evening is a success. I can relax.

Life is a trial for the modern woman, I know. I publish a line that influences many readers: "I sometimes think that God is a woman — He is expected to forgive so much." But I believe it is the suffering that defines women — the burden of duty and the unending pain that underlie the rightful passion and love.

> *But women's souls*
> *Like violet-powder dropped on coals,*
> *Give forth their best in anguish. Oh,*
> *The subtle secrets that we know*
>
> *Of joy in sorrow, strange delights*
> *Of ecstasy in pain-filled nights.*
> *And mysteries of gain in loss*
> *Known but to Christ upon the cross.*

Feminists write to me, but I have trouble understanding their comments. But they keep writing to me. How is it they see in my words some battle cry, some hope?

It is a serene summer, this first summer back, and we never lock our doors. The trolley brings the indigent, the begging, the insane, the spoiled to my door, and a kind word or a meal or the sheriff gets rid of them. Life scuttles back and forth between the Bungalow and the Barracks, with me spending most of my writing hours on the veranda of the Bungalow, Robert with his cigar and newspaper on the porch of the Barracks. We seem like strangers, then, from a distance. And local gossip rumors that we have, indeed, a scientific modern marriage. Capitalized: A Modern Marriage. Some quintessential arrangement out of sophisticated society. New York and Paris, translated into a lazy, provincial Short Beach neighborhood. We occupy separate houses with separate servants, so it is said. So pervasive is the rumor that an English newspaper, building off the slight story, exaggerates it with full-blown tabloid sensationalism, remarking that I married a wealthy doctor. "The couple live on a vast estate, several hours by rail from New York, each having a residence and household of their own. If the poetess feels a real inclination to have the doctor for breakfast, lunch, or dinner, she sends him a formal invitation and he walks or drives over to his wife's house just like any other friend. Occasionally, she repays the doctor's visit, and 'gives him a pleasant surprise,' but, as a rule, she accepts dinner invitations from him no oftener than from other friends."

I want to sue — in fact, I've already written the first inflammatory letters to England—but Robert insists I smile. The absurdity of the story is fun, he says. Laugh! he says. For heaven's sake. Laugh! For a while I call him "Doctor," with a wink, but Robert is never one for receiving nicknames graciously. I stop.

"I had forgotten how wonderful the winters are here," I say.

It is the first winter we have not traveled in years, not the short sunny jaunts to Jamaica or even the long weekends in New York for dinner, theater, and friends, and especially not to the north of Africa or the Far East. We tuck ourselves into Short Beach, settling in among the closed-up beach community around us, the rented cottages empty now, the transient city visitors gone. The beach community suddenly has a desolation about it: all bleached wood and crying seagull. Broken seashells in the sand. The water flat and black as city pavement. The trees skeletal and twisted. Robert and I stop up the drafts in the woodwork, and the fires in the hearth glow through the short, dark days of January and February.

The quiet winter days have a dreaminess about them, a languidness that I especially savor. I take long strolls along the stark, freezing beach, and listen to the somber cawing of the winter seabirds in the distance. I wander into town, shuffling on slick ice patches, a little unsteady now, lingering at the post office with Mr. Knowles, talking about life on other planets and stars, and the beauty of the universe.

In the morning I take a leisurely milk bath.

At night we salute each other with champagne, and toss the corks into the hammock hanging nearby in a corner. Sometimes, after too much champagne or wine, the corks land everywhere but in the cluttered hammock. Already it is overflowing with corks — it has become a tradition at my parties for the corks to be deposited there, a kind of ceremonial dump. Friends coming after long absence remark on the rising level of champagne corks. "Partying a little much, Miss Ella," Oliver Herford always says. "If I count them, will they equal the stars in the sky?"

"So much for the erstwhile Poetess of Temperance," Ridgely Torrence announces, with a laugh, after discovering a copy of my *Drops of Water* at a New York used bookstore.

"That was then," I say.

"And this is a howl." Ridgely laughs.

Robert smokes his cigar, I read poetry, and, both a little tipsy, we doze before the winter fire.

In the morning, walking on the strands, the chill wind on the beach startles us. We return to the house for savory coffee and butter rolls prepared by Mizzy, our Irish maid.

Early in February the solitude is broken by a visit from some New York friends who flee New York's theater season for a sojourn at the Barracks. Kate Jordan, Theodosia Garrison and editor Charles Hanson Towne troop in with good cheer. For the week they linger with us. But for a week Robert and I find ourselves reminiscing, sharing stories with our old friends, and the tone is melancholic: the cold drafts seeping through the woodwork make us linger longer by the fires, and the hot toddies stimulate us. Everything we talk about happened years before. All conversation drifts back to the past. "We've become old," I say. "Robert and I."

No one says anything.

Charles finally says something: "Ella, you'll always be the youngest person in our crowd."

"Thank you," I say.

It's the response I've been waiting for.

We talk about my campaign to change the name of Short-Beach-on-the Sound to Granite Bay, long my personal name for my Eden on the coast. I despise the prosaic names the old Yankees insisted on giving their beautiful resorts — Stony Creek, Short Beach, Double Beach, Branford Point. No imagination, no flare. Lord, the small-mindedness of the early town fathers, all Calvinist prosaicness and grim reality.

I wrote to Branford town leaders and the federal government. To postal authorities. To everyone. They wrote back: no. Over and over: no.

"Granite Bay," I say now, sitting in front of the fire. "Listen to the sound of it."

I recently published a poem and assumed my doing so will turn them around. Now, I recite some stanzas of "Granite Bay":

> *At Granite Bay, such beauty lies,*
> *In rocks, in waters and in skies,*
> *As poets dream of Paradise.*

The rocks that clasp fair Granite Bay
First saw her charms at break of day
And flushed to pink from somber gray.

At Granite Bay the wild winds rest;
The sunlight is her welcome guest;
The moon goes mad upon her breast.

Not here is heard the sea gulls' scream.
They come, but only come to dream:
Far out at sea their sorrows seem.

Though forth my wanderings footsteps stray,
To realms and regions far away,
My heart dwells here, in Granite Bay.

When I finish speaking, there is silence in the room. I glance at my friends. They are staring into their laps. For some reason, reciting it, I have become all choked up, actually starting to cry. The mood in the room is oddly funereal, with only the sound of a seabird flapping against the roof. I smile through my tears: "It's supposed to be a happy poem."

We all laugh.

"This poem will do it," Robert says.

"They don't like change, these Yankees," Charles says. "They don't like to wake snakes."

I feel in my winter bones the battle I am losing: Granite Bay will only be a name I will use. My own special kingdom, refused by others.

It makes me angry. They owe me this one, I feel. I put this place on the map.

For a while, drowsy from the wine and fire, we are quiet. Then Charles, looking up, smiles. "I was just recalling, Ella — do you remember when you were touted as the leader of the Erotic School of Poetry?"

"Oh, please," I say, "not that again. Hundreds of questionable young girls now write sticky sex chants and blame me for them. I am not responsible for the decay of modern youth."

"Well —" Robert begins, smiling.

I get serious: "Robert, no. I am a Christian woman who as been a loyal wife—"

"Ella," Robert says. "Enough."

"You defined passion for a generation," Dosia says.

"Don't blame Ella for the population explosion," Robert says.

"I take blame for nothing," I say.

"Nothing?" Robert asks, his eyebrows raised.

"Nothing."

We look at each other as though sharing a private joke.

Stopping in New York for a weekend, I meet, by chance, two old memories. In town to take care of social obligations, I orchestrate theater dinners and literary breakfasts. Giving a luncheon for Theodosia Garrison at the Westminster Hotel to celebrate Dosia's newly published book, I chance upon James Whitcomb Riley, sitting in the lobby. I haven't seen him — or even thought about him — for years. Despite his vast growing fame and his continued celebrity, I've not read one of his poems since the day we parted in that hotel lobby. Not one.

He has aged, I realize, since our encounter decades back: skinny, shriveled, even more pale. He looks tremendously old now. And still ugly in the gawky, hayseed way I despise.

We are cordial. He bows. "Mrs. Wilcox."

"Mr. Riley."

"It's been years," he says.

"You're visiting friends?"

"Publishers." He looks away. Am I annoying him?

"We each found the fame we both coveted," I say, suddenly.

"And, I presume, we now, in old age, understand how little it is worth."

"You are well?"

"As can be. And you?"

"Happy."

"Really?"

"Of course."

We stare at each other.

I ask a favor. "I have ten young women coming down the elevator at any moment. I'm having a luncheon for Dosia Garrison, whose book of verse is just out. You've heard of her, I trust?"

He shakes his head: no.

I ignore this.

"They would love to meet you."

"No," he says. Flat out.

"Five minutes of your time."

"No, I don't do such things."

"It would be a beautiful memory for them — for a lifetime. They love your work."

He turns away and waves his hand in dismissal. "No."

I fume, speak to his back. "You, sir, do not deserve your fame."

He looks back, his pale face freckled red. "And you do?"

On Sunday, strolling alone outside the hotel after packing for my return to Connecticut, I meet Miriam Leslie, also alone, but bundled up in furs that almost make her unrecognizable. The street is empty, except for a few hurried stragglers struggling with the cold. Some motorcars pass, tooting at horse-drawn carriages. She and I haven't spoken to each other since the bleak parting years before in that New York hotel. We've actually been at the same formal dinners over the years, have nodded solemnly to each other, like wary opponents, but we purposely never approach each other. I haven't seen her in — what? — over a decade? I often blush whenever I remember Miriam's harsh words that last morning. Over the years, with curiosity, I have followed her troubled life through the sensational yellow press. It has not been pretty. The fraudulent Marquis disappeared, exposed for the phony he was. Robert's remark: "I warned you. Aren't you glad you listened to me?" I am, but I also know I sometimes miss the vibrant woman. Ours was a lively, symbiotic relationship, two emphatic, confident women playing off each other. I have allowed so few people to challenge me: Miriam Leslie was one of the few. We had so many laughs, the two of us. That bond we discovered is hard to give up.

She finally abandoned her legal name Frank Leslie, rediscovering her suspect Huguenot heritage, and then calling herself the Baroness de Bazus. She refused to answer to her late husband's name. Robert said: "Now she no longer marries phony royalty, she becomes one herself." She married Oscar Wilde's brother, and then learning he wanted only her money—which everyone else, including the press, seemed to know — she divorced him. She wrote the chilling book *Are Men Gay Deceivers?* to vent her anger. A fearsome diatribe against men. Few read it. I did, of course.

"Well, hello," I say first, causing Miriam to stop her walk. "How are you?"

Now, meeting me in the street, the two of us old women hidden in winter coats, Miriam isn't awkward at all. "To hell with men," she says, smiling. They are her first words.

"Miriam." I am nervous. It is really too cold to stop and chat.

She looks disturbed. "When I die all my money will go to Carrie Chapman Catt. Women should have the right to vote."

I realize that Miriam is looking past me, over my shoulder. I turn, see nothing but motorcars passing. I also realize that Miriam has not mentioned my name, and I wonder whether she remembers who I am — and, indeed, the awful confrontation we had years before. Miriam Leslie keeps talking, and it is as though she's been talking to herself all along, and I just happen to interrupt. Now she rails on about the insidious nature of man. She doesn't look at me. It is a set speech she delivers, re-hearsed, doubtless delivered to many. She could be rant-ing to a stranger in the street.

I mumble good-bye and walk away.

I am sad all the way back to Connecticut.

Back home, at Granite Bay, the deep of winter is lovely, especially the stormbound days when Robert and I, forced inside by drifting snow and brutal sea winds, huddle by the fire. I remember that dank hotel in the Scheveningen Forest, when I felt I was in a cave, but this is oddly not claustrophobic now. Robert is here, cigar smoke wafting around his head so he looks like a Wall Street Santa Claus. I also have the splendid trappings of my around-the-world collections. I carry a book with me everywhere. The wind howls its fury, the boards creak like old bones, and the windows rattle under the assault of a brutal shoreline New England winter. But it doesn't matter. We spend the day reading, or I play my harp — Robert refuses to let me sing — and the household cats Prince and Kim sit on our laps. This is, after all, paradise.

Everything changes when there is world war in Eu-rope.

In May the Germans sink the *Lusitania*, an act that hor-rifies. The morning coffee sits untouched on the break-fast table. One of our good friends dies in the icy waters, perishing with her young daughter. At night, I sit with the last letter from my friend, and I cry out of control. It just seems too inhuman, this kind of indiscriminate, bru-tal killing. This is not war — this is crime against inno-cence. Rattled, the cats run from me. Then I read that in Berlin the children are given holiday from school, in cel-ebration of the brutal torpedoing. I am awake all night, weeping. When I do doze off, I wake suddenly, scream-ing, "Winifred."

War declares a holiday;
Little children run and play.
Ring-a-rosy round the earth
With the garland of your mirth.

Sing a song brim full of glee
Of a great ship sunk at sea.
Tell with pleasure and with pride
How a hundred children died.

Sing of orphan babes, whose cries
Beat against unanswering skies;
Let a mother's mad despair
Lend staccato to your air.

Sing of babes who drowned alone;
Sing of headstones, marked 'Unknown';
Sing of homes made desolate
Where the stricken mourners wait.

Sing of battered corpses tossed
By the heedless waves, and lost.
Run, children, sing and play;
War declares a holiday.

In the morning, in faltering penmanship, I scribble a name on a pad: *Robert Junior.* Then I write: *Always the children.*

In summer the dances begin again — the parlor floor buffed into a mirror glow that dazzles — but the life suddenly goes out of dancing in America. And especially at the Barracks. The ugly war in Europe changes everything this summer of 1915. Julie Opp, now famous on the New York stage, travels from New York, or telephones me, and the conversation always comes back to the war in Europe, the Kaiser, the British, the Tsar, the end of everything. It is the rape of Europa and the coming of the del-

uge. The death of high tea and the swarming black locusts of Russia. I worry about friends abroad, and the
summer is quiet, quiet.

I hold small Sunday afternoon musicales, but they are
often funereal. My harp playing takes on a plaintive,
dreadful tone. When I play a happy adaptation of
Mendelssohn, it emerges a mournful dirge.

Everyone seems to be away this summer.

On the first chilly night of autumn, I find myself alone
on the seawall, facing, I think, Europe. Robert and I have
quarreled over something stupid—we were talking about
money, but that segued into something else, a spat over
a servant or a lingering guest. I am sure we never quarrel about money. But I leave the Barracks because I need
to be away from Robert. His presence — the omnipresent cigar smell — permeates all the nooks of the house.
We were drinking wine with dessert, and I had too much.
I admit it. It lulls me, I say to Robert. It calms me. The
war depresses me — always the war in the newspaper.
Maybe this is what we were arguing about. I have trouble
focusing. Lately Robert can be so quiet, saying nothing,
just watching, watching. He watches the way I move —
or am I imagining it? — and I get self-conscious, always
touching my hair to see if every strand is in place. It drives
me mad.

Standing on the seawall, I wrap my cold arms around
me, pulling in the folds of the thick Persian lamb wrap.
The wind is ferocious tonight, and the lights along the
dock seem bright and clear: everything seems brilliant
outline. I mumble aloud a poem —

> *The day will dawn when one of us shall hearken*
> *In vain to hear a voice that has grown numb.*
> *And morns will fade, noons pale, and shadows darken,*
> *While sad eyes watch for feet that never come.*

> *One of us two must sometime face existence*

Alone with memories that but sharpen pain.
And these sweet days shall shine back in the distance,
Like dreams of summer dawns, in nights of rain.

One of us two, with tortured heart half broken,
    Shall read long-treasured letters through salt tears,
Shall kiss with anguished lips each cherished token
    That speaks of these love-crowned, delicious years.

One of us two shall find all light, all beauty,
    All joy on earth, a tale forever done;
Shall know henceforth that life means only duty.
    Oh, God! Oh, God! have pity on that one.

But then I stop, frightened. Alone without Robert? No. No. No. No. No. My spoken words seem vacant in the vast darkness. I look up into the nighttime sky. Not a cloud or a star or a moon in the sky. Everything is cold ice palette, a hard nighttime blue. This is the end of it all, this broken, shattered landscape. I lift my hand to the sky, like a folk goddess on some prehistoric plain. I get dizzy.

"Ella," Robert yells from the house. "Come in here. What's with you? You'll catch your death."

I don't answer.

"Ella, my dear. Please. Do I have to rescue you from the elements?"

I smile. "I'm here," I yell.

In the shadowy night I can see the huge shape of Robert, moving slowly, lumbering along the rocky pathway, coming to find me. My knight in silver, an old stumbling man, still on the quest. I wait. My lover is coming to find me. I still have this power over him: here is the handsome man who loves me, who seeks me out in the wind and storm.

I wait, my heart pounding.

While sad eyes watch for feet that never come.

Promise

1916

To My Readers:

A recent letter from the venerable Sir Oliver Lodge, of England, suggests the power of the unknown. Sir Oliver Lodge, of international reputation as a scientist and seer and futurist, confirms my long-held belief that the spirit world lies within easy grasp. Naysayers, scoffers, malcontents, and disbelievers—take notice: the spirit that is within you is your passage to the spiritual world beyond us. All the dead can be reached if we care to look. All we have to do is believe — and then seek.

— "Reflections of Ella Wheeler Wilcox," *Country Gentlewoman*, 1913

Robert spends the good part of many winter days moving from room to room, ledger book in hand, fountain pen poised, creating an inventory of the contents of the Barracks. "Why?" I ask.

He never answers.

I watch him enumerate everything, from the largest of items — the piano, my harp, the couches, even the champagne-cord hammock, the garish chaise lounge — to the smallest — a colonial feather quill, a carved nut bowl from Cairo, a silverplate dish (his firm's imprint) for calling cards — to the obvious—the new telephone, situated prominently on a mahogany table. When I check the ledger later, maddened by curiosity, while he strolls to the emporium for cigars — I read his careful itemizations.

Next to *telephone* he has our exchange number — 71-5 — and our address. He has written everything down in especially bold strokes, the ink thick and blotchy. In my journal I write: *It is as though Himself needs to know where he sits and stands — and lives.*

He never wants to leave the home now, I notice.

"Everything I want is here," he says, over and over. Gradually he reduces his visits to the local men's clubs in New Haven. A weekend excursion to New York is, for him, like a return to northern Africa. He checks train schedules he knows by heart, so anxious is he to return.

"But your friends, Robert," I say.

"All I want is here."

"You don't answer their letters."

"I've nothing to say."

"That's not like you, Robert."

"Of course, it is."

I get confused.

I won't admit it to my friends but, of course, I need this distance away from Robert, if only for a few hours. Alone in the vast house, I play my harp, I sing my tunes, I dance by myself. Especially I dance. I have trouble moving now — there is always a little ache in my chest when I exercise too much — but I dance. I need this space for myself. Sometimes Robert frowns on my antics, usually when he returns to find me panting, out of breath, the needle of the Edison gramophone stuck on a Victor Herbert melody. The heavy arm hiccoughs. *Love is. . . Love is. . . Love is . . . .* I am too tired to get to it. "We're old," he says.

Nowadays I hate it when he talks that way. "A woman is never old," I say in a hurry. "Just the other day I heard — it wasn't said to me but to another person so it couldn't be flattery — that a man thought I was twenty-eight." I wait.

"Really, Ella."

"From a distance."

"That's because you dye your hair that daffodil yellow."

My hands flutter to my hair, pat the careful hairdo. "You like it, don't you?"

"You are a beautiful woman, Ella. Your face and hair are the moon." He is not even looking at me.

I'm not sure it's a compliment.

"You're not spending much time at the club these days, Robert." I need an explanation.

Robert is a long-standing member of the fashionable men's clubs in the area, especially the prestigious ones in New Haven. He likes the conversations in the velvet plush, quiet rooms, the men sitting before walnut-paneled bookshelves and Italian marble fireplaces — he likes the long-night card games — of the Quinnipiac Club. He used to be a familiar figure on the New Haven trolley.

"They bore me," he says.

"Robert, you always loved them."

"Somehow they bore me now."

"But your friends —" My hand flutters in the air.

I panic: these days I fear change — dread it to the marrow of my being. I want everything at quiet stasis. There is that brutal war in Europe — oh God! how I hate that war! — and I know America will soon be part of it. At last American boys will die on foreign soil. It has to be. There is too much change coming in the world, all these motorcars and airplanes and Edison contraptions. Everything is being turned upside down, so I desperately need stability at home. "Go to the club," I say, an edge to my voice.

So Robert idly takes the trolley into New Haven, but he always returns early, almost out of breath, as though afraid he has missed something. "Did anything happen? he asks. He finds me at my harp or proofing a volume to be published. "This is number thirty nine," I say. "I think. Maybe forty. I'm calling it *World Voices.*"

I wait for his praise.

"You are American literature," he said. He sounds tired.

I force him to vacation in New York City, where so many of our friends are. There is theater and opera and favorite restaurants. We are loving Short Beach this winter, but I feel we need a break. I hunger for a week or two of the winter season in Manhattan. I love the cold, efficient streets, dark with ice and wind. Inside are festive parties and celebration. Robert readily consents, surprising me. Julie Opp and her husband William Faversham squire us everywhere. Charles Hanson Towne surprises with a breakfast for us.

I can finally breathe a sigh of relief.

Robert seems to enjoy himself immensely, especially at a dinner party given by old friends Hartley Manners, the playwright, and his actress wife, Laurette Taylor. Manners once rented a cottage at Short Beach and, in fact, wrote a hit Broadway play there. Robert and he are old club buddies, as well as long time bridge partners. Now, with backslapping and robust humor, the two men get tipsy with the evening. The champagne flows.

"I'm glad we came," Robert says, back at the hotel.

The old Robert, I think. I am happy.

The next night, at the Metropolitan Opera, we share a box with old friends who comment on Robert's renewed energy. Robert keeps saying, "I've missed this, Ella." He seems manic: his robust laughter can be heard through the lobby. I watch him, pleased but nervous. In the off-light of the opera box he looks — well, young. The wrinkles gone, the sagging, jowled face resetting itself into the wide smooth expanse that once kissed me at the Wisconsin homestead. He looks like the man who has just proposed marriage. When I catch a glimpse of myself in the long mirror in the lobby, I am startled: my own face is tight and determined, anxious. I look old, old.

"I have plans for Short Beach," he says, then corrects himself: "Granite Bay."

"Robert, please, no more renovation."

"I want to buy more land. And Europe, Ella. After the war, one more tour. To see our friends."

I nod.

I am nervous: there is a slight burning in my heart that

never stops. My eyes ache. Yet I refuse to see a doctor. I tell myself it is a simple case of dyspepsia, nothing more. I eat spice-rich foods. I refuse the soothing narcotic elixirs to be had at Knowles' Emporium. In my journal: *I am sick from the War. Herself cannot think or write or — Be. It makes me expect Doom and Destruction, capitalized. Herself's body quakes. Himself strides through the rooms like a young warrior, ambitious and purposeful. It drives me mad.*

Has he taken a magic youth potion, some elixir secret from me? Back home Robert sings in the rooms, smokes too many Havana cigars, and stares at distant boats out on the Sound.

"Do you want to travel there?" I ask, pointing to the horizon.

"Oh, no," he says. "It's like a favorite painting I can watch for hours."

I am waiting for spring to arrive, with flowers and beach-front waltzes. I am tired of ice and cold. But Robert announces, on a stormy March day when the snow squalls cover the windows and the rooms get dark and close: "Everyone is longing for spring, Ella. I never longed for it so little. In fact, I want this winter to go on forever. It's been the happiest season of my life."

"Because we stayed away so long."

"I wish it could go on and on like this, just you and me shut in this dear home together."

We are caveman and cavewoman again, at last.

At night, with friends, I read tea leaves under the rainbow-glass Tiffany lamp. I track the destinies of friends by holding their palms. But one rainy night a neighbor woman brings a battered ouija board. I have never seen one before, and it looks ancient and ominous: some talisman of bleakest doom. Robert, smoking his cigar, sits near us, watching. The board frightens us with its silence. So palms are read, cards are shuffled and spread across the table. Kings hold scepters high in the air. The hanged man. The House of God struck by lightning. All night long every conversation comes back to the war in Europe. Robert smokes, and nods.

The prophetic cards speak only of doom.

"There is no breathing room anywhere," I finally say, and I go for a walk on the seawall. The hard ocean wind snaps me back to life.

One April morning I wake up feeling lonely and melancholy, a weight holding me to the bed. Throughout the day I linger in the Flower Room, among the brilliant window boxes of plants I've carefully nurtured, and outside there is a brisk spring chill. But the wild orchids I tend can't shake my lethargy, my despair. In the afternoon my French dressmaker arrives, with sketches for my spring wardrobe, something I've always anticipated and found thrilling. But this year I have no interest. Looking at a dress pattern or hearing Mlle. Dernier say *blue* or *green*, her little-girl voice questioning me, I suddenly get nauseous and flee the room. Outside, gasping for air, I sob. At night in my journal: *A vast pall seems to be spread over the whole world*. I stare at the words. Whatever do they mean? I add: *Herself looks out on a beautiful coming springtime, with the narcissi and crocuses already pushing through late drifting snow, and all Herself senses is doom. Why? Oh, that awful War. All those boys dying over there. Herself dances by herself but the old body creaks now, and the civilization dies in Europe. The damned war.*

I notice a shift in my penmanship: long loopy letters, stretched out, scattered.

Robert doesn't notice my growing despair. He never wants to. He once told me I am not allowed melancholy. "What will happen to me and the world if you become despondent? The bottom will drop out of the universe." He was joking, of course, but I understand myself to be the universe I imagine: I am the poetess of good cheer. Poetess of Hope. Of Joy. For better or worse, it's the definition of Ella Wheeler Wilcox I've fashioned for myself. And always believed in, reverently. But these days it sometimes jars, refuses to fit my life. What, I wonder, do these abstract words do for a real life? They are pieces of a jigsaw puzzle I no longer care to finish.

I am invited into New York to be guest of honor at the White Breakfast of the Mozart Club. I go alone because Robert says he needs to finish his inventory of the contents of the Bungalow. Traveling alone with only one small trunk, I am feted throughout the morning, visit friends in the afternoon, and at night retire to my hotel room. It has been a wonderful day, all attention and glory. But suddenly, sitting alone, looking out the windows at the late night strollers and a few chugging motorcars passing by, I grip my throat. My chest aches. I lose my breath. But I am clear headed, and the wave of pain soon passes, replaced by a deep sense of longing and fear. Am I dying? What is this pain? Blindly I stagger around the room, looking for something to settle me, to ground me. Nothing: nothing. I sit back down, and weep. I reach for my journal: *I feel as if the end of the world has come. The universe seems a vast cavern in which I sit alone and I am desolate.* When I look up, the room seems etched in severe line, everything luminous and clear, as though a light comes out of the wall. It is an awful moment, full of ice and steel. I begin to scribble the lines of a poem. I call it "The Finish:"

> *The thought of that last journey back to Him*
> *When there is no more longing or desire*
> *For anything but God left in my soul,*
> *Shines in the distance like a great white flame.*
> *I think the way will lead through golden clouds*
> *Skirting these shores of seas of amethyst!*
> *And winding gently upward; past old worlds,*
> *Where body after body was outlived,*
> *Past Hells and Heavens, where I had my day*
> *With comrade Spirits from the lesser spheres*
> *And paid my penalty for every sin*
> *And reaped reward for every worthy act:*
> *Past Realms Celestial and their singing hosts*

(Where once I chanted with the cherubim)
Out into perfect silence. Suddenly
An all enveloping vast consciousness
Of long, long journeys finished: one more turn
And selfhood lost in being one with God.
The ray once more absorbed into the Sun.
The cycle done.

In the morning there is a telephone call, saying that
Robert is ill with a severe cold. But the doctor assures me
it's nothing. "A change in the weather," he says. "The
sudden cold." Robert, I know, is in good health. But I
rush by train to Connecticut, hurrying to his side. I find
him sitting up in bed, in good spirits, drinking tea. He
says I'm foolish to rush home like this. For a week I sit
with Robert, nursing his cold. That's all it is: a bad cold.
He continues to be easy about it, smiling, even joking,
but I am concerned about the thick rasp in his chest. I
refuse to let him have a cigar, and he gets grumpy. I feed
him tonics and bathe his head, and read poetry to him. I
pray aloud, but always away from his bedside. Out in
the spring gardens, among the tulips and forsythia, I
speak aloud in the night, or kneeling on the seawall, staring out at the waves. The doctor visits daily, and assures
me. A common cold, the result of a brutal winter and too
much staying indoors, perhaps. "Don't worry." I am not
worried: all the spiritual forces are aligned with me, with
Robert. Friends from New Thought society pray for him
— at my request. Theosophist leaders pray with me. I
call on local spiritualists to keep us in their thoughts.
There is much more we have to do on the earth, he and I,
as partners and travelers. As good people. That I know
to be true. I read to Robert and he thanks me, oddly formal. He talks of the inventory he needs to finish. He
mentions silver spoons and knives, he mentions letter-
openers, he mentions a Masonic lodge pin, he mentions
his bronze Civil War medal, he mentions an important
letter from President McKinley. I panic: "But Robert, we

never knew McKinley." "He wrote me," Robert says. "Just before he died."

The next day the cold turns into brutal, horrendous pneumonia. On May 21 at 11:25 PM — the moment is etched forever in my soul — Robert completes his earthly cycle. In the quiet of the parlor, I sit for two days, waiting, watching Robert's body. I want him to move, to sit up, to say this is a joke. This is all wrong. I beg him to move. Outside there is too much noise: the jarring blasting of the granite boulder where Robert's ashes will lie, interned, next to Robert Junior.

Help me.

Blindly, panicky, I search for his Civil War medal, wanting to bury it with his ashes, but then remember with a jolt: Robert never fought in the Civil War. What does this mean? What medal? What was he talking about? And McKinley? What? I feel as though I do not know the man I've lived with for thirty-two years.

This summer has no sun. Day and night become one, both gray and shadowy, a shroud covering the lawn like a dark frost. I lie on my oriental chaise, oblivious of the invitations to luncheon, to visit, to travel. Friends whisper and disappear. I lie there, vacant eyed. This is all just impossible, I know: Robert is soulmate, my boon companion, my everything. This cannot be happening. Something is violently wrong here, out of whack. Each morning I face a void, and each night is an abyss. In my mechanical letters: *Thank you for sympathy in the time of overwhelming sorrow and desolation.* Over and over, the same line, to everyone. I have nightmares that toss me from the bed. Nearby neighbors, in the cottages, hear the wailing in the night, the piercing sharp one word: "Why?" It chills them. In the morning people question me. Can we help you? Please? In my journal: *Herself never believed she could feel so alone. Robert was ALL.* Servants tiptoe around me, whispering. The pain in my chest grows larger so that I sometimes can't move. My physician now gives me laudanum, in sweet tasting tonics. I don't listen to him. He tells me I may be dangerously sick and wants me to visit a hospital for tests. I refuse. I carelessly write to a friend, talking of my growing physical pain. "Please destroy this letter and let no one know what I told you." I fall into nightmarish, lighting-brutal sleeps, narcotic and heavy. I am convinced I speak with Jesus but the next day, waking, I realize it is the Italian gardener Pietro. He is slender and wiry and wears a scraggly beard. Jesus?

On the Edison gramophone I play a recording I made years before — a message to Robert in the event I died first. But whenever I play the brief staticky recording, I stop with "Dear Robert." My own voice sounds pathetic. I can't bear to hear what I have to say.

Then, weeks later, I jot in my journal: *You promised me.* I sit up, clear eyed. It's like a bolt of electricity. This is what I want, I suddenly know — the fulfillment of the promise Robert made to me.

So the seers come to visit, the cards are spread, the palms are duly read, the prayers said, the chanting, the rhythmic seances, the Tarot, the tea leaves, the slates. Women in shawls and bad perfume visit by trolley from seaside towns. Gypsies from New Haven storefronts, dressed in motley colors and carrying baskets with nothing in them, steal silverware and leave me empty. Psychics write or call, offering help. Everyone has my number. I entertain them all. But they see all the wrong things: faithless children, fashionable childhoods, nods from royalty, eternal youth, old age happiness, trips to Paris. I hate them: "Trips to Paris," I rage to friends. "There's a war in Paris." "Wars end," one Gypsy woman tells me.

But at last I understand where I have to go: California, that sunny land of seances and spiritual souls. There, among hot sun and frontier spirit, are the real Spiritualists, the true Seers. I know this. They will help me contact Robert. I board the train for the long ride to Los Angeles, looking for the sun that rises in the West. My journal gives my spiritual trip its alliterative name: *The search of a soul in sorrow.*

The first night, sheltered under palms and hot dry wind, giving me memories of days with Robert in northern Africa, I write "You Promised Me":

All the holy books of earth, all churches and all creeds,
Are based on spirit miracles.
Moses, Elias, Matthew, Mark and John,
Paul and Cornelius, Buddha, Swedenborg,
All talked with Angels, yea, and many more.

That was a mighty promise that you made me: — not once
        But many a time,
Whenever we discussed the topic death —
You promised me that were such things possible
        In God's vast Universe,
You would send back a message to my listening soul,
        Now am I listening with bated breath.

So am I waiting, watching — in the light — and listening
        in the dark—
For any sight, or sound you may have sent:
        So do I lean and hark —
Night in, day out —

And I will knock upon the door of heaven
And shake God's window with the hands of prayer,
Asking for those old Angels, wise with centuries
Of large experience, to come to you,
Oh my beloved, and to show you how
To keep your promise, made in solemn faith—
        To bridge the River Death,
And end the veil between.
So many ears have heard — so many eyes have seen —
        Why not mine own?
I do not seek alone —
                You promised me.

In California I feel the spirit move, feel the presence of other voices, sense the movement of the soul. Once an earth tremor confuses me, as I stand and wait for the light. I wait. I wait for the earth to move under my feet. I want seismic eruption only in the soul, fearful of physical imitations.

In California, I believe, the spiritual world is nearer the surface of things. The air is thinner, the soil less rocky, the living people more accepting.

In my journal I write: *Herself understands that during the last decade many of the world's most gifted and brilliant men and women have entered into this search for the living dead.* Many of them, to be sure, live in the Los Angeles area. I check the local directory.

But California confuses me. I stay the first month in mountains outside Los Angeles, with old friends who pamper and soothe me, but the days are uniformly hot and unchanging. Mornings, waking, I think I am in the north of Africa. Or Sicily. The air is the same. But once here, I don't know where to turn. Everything is just too bright. In my journal: *I sit here, I wait. The California sun is too bright for illumination.* Robert was my guide, but now I have only untested instincts. California is too large a state, too unruly, too chaotic. Connecticut is small and tidy, like a velvet jewelry box, everything contained, calculable. Blindly I drift from cult to cult, from medium to medium. My feet never touch the earth: I float from one spiritual plane to the next.

I begin with the Theosophists, the ones who initially invited me. The Wise Ones shake their heads, dismayed. Stay away from frauds, con artists, sham seers, they warn. The time will come — not yet. There are answers, but not yet. The Universe has a rhythm and a beautiful symmetry. You cannot rush it.

"Yes," I acknowledge, "I have no energy left."

At night, in my hotel, alone, I feel the same small tightness in the chest, feel the pain moving like a flash fire across my back, and I imbibe the laudanum prescribed by my doctor. In the middle of the night, rising in pain, I take more. In early mornings, drowsy and drifting, I talk aloud to the dark, shadowy room. I say my prayers. When I wake, each of these California mornings, I have a dull, windstorm headache just over my temples, a nagging pain that refuses to leave with pots of black coffee and brisk sea air.

I move to the Home of Truth, a metaphysical college where ten women healers, disciples of the redoubtable Anna Rix Militz, soothe my pain, attend to my physical illnesses, coach me back into the light. But the days there, dreamy and somnambulant, almost narcotic, do not reach my soul. Because, I know, Robert is not nearby: not here, never among these altruistic women.

The Rosicrucians welcome me into their unselfish life. I gaze upon their peaceful ascetic existences. I sit in palm groves and close my eyes. I listen to their intellectual positions, their reasonable comforts. But I don't understand what they are doing — it has nothing to do with the deep pain in my heart.

In San Diego I drink a little claret with friends. When I fall asleep at the table, the men carry me to the settee. I wake in the night and hope I have died at last.

I travel to the dying colony of Oshaspians, but they seem otherworldly in ways that divorce themselves from the earth they stand on. In their white robes and with fluttery hands, they seem ready to face their own oblivion. They are souls unhappy with life, and covetous of death. When they mention the word *death*, orgiastic and sweet, they rock back and forth. For them death is delicious. I flee them, fearful that their wistfulness, their wraith-like movements, will detract me from the path of sorrow that leads to Robert, who is waiting to talk to me.

I go swimming but realize that I no longer have the power to raise my arms in the water. I've become a lead weight, a dead thing, a rock sinking. In my journal: *How can Herself rise to Heavens and Robert when the body grows heavier and heavier?*

I am incomplete:

> *The summer is just in its grandest prime,*
> *   The earth is green and the skies are blue;*
> *But where is the lilt of the olden time,*
> *When life was a melody set to rhyme,*
> *   And dreams were so real they all seemed true?*

> *There is sun on the meadow, and blooms on the bushes,*
> *   And never a bird but is mad with glee;*
> *But the pulse that bounds and the blood that rushes,*
> *And the hope that soars, and the joy that gushes,*
> *   Are lost forever to you and me.*

> *There are dawns of amber and amethyst;*
> *   There are purple mountains, and pale pink seas*
> *That flash to crimson where skies have kist;*
> *But out of life there is something missed —*
> *   Something better than all of these.*

> *We miss the faces we used to know,*
> *   The smiling lips and the eyes of truth.*
> *We miss the beauty and warmth and glow*
> *Of the love that brightened our long ago,*
> *   And ah! we miss our youth.*

I write letters home to friends, but they frighten the receivers: there is such rambling, such raw emotion, that friends call or wire. Come home, Ella. Come home. Come home, now. Please, Ella. Winter is here: there are ice crystals on your window, the fancy work of angels. You should see it, Ella. Come home.

My penmanship is that of a maddened woman, so many words begin whole, and then end as elongated horizontal lines: the heartbeat of the dead.

I meet a psychic named John Slater who warns me against charlatans and mediums. "Meditate alone," he tells me, "away from the public and professional medium. In quiet you will find tranquillity, and Robert will come to you." Then, he adds, almost as an afterthought, "You don't belong in California. Your home is distant from here. Your husband can't reach you clearly and positively until you return home. Then he will come."

This is the answer, I understand, at last.

I exult: Then he will come.

In my journal: *But I have no home. I left no address behind me. Granite Bay is Paradise Lost.*

Fallen angels listen. I spend the night weeping.

Home: heaven.

Robert.

And each morning I intone the mantra I composed. No day passes without its rhythmic chanting: *I am the living witness: the dead live: and they speak through us and to us: and I am the voice that gives this glorious truth to the suffering world. I am ready, God. I am ready, Christ. I am ready, Robert.* Whenever I finish the sweet words, delicious to my ear, I hang on the last word — *Robert* — until the word seems to swell in the rooms, to dominate and overpower, to lift me to the ceilings, to the sky.

After sixteen months of searching through California sunshine and shadow, my pocketbook suffering under the demands of errant seers and vagabond con men — as well as the true Seers who still fail me, to my utter grief — I am now ready to return to Short Beach and the Barracks, where my friends anxiously wait. Charles Hanson Towne meets me the first evening back, squiring me from the train station to my home. He hugs me and there are tears in his eyes. I know I look frazzled and wired: I can't stop moving one minute, and then, in a flash, I seem to become lethargic, dreamy, unable to rouse myself from my chair. He suggests a doctor, but I become testy. "What for? The body is nothing. It's the soul that counts."

"Ella, you have to take care of yourself."

I touch my chest. "I nurse the soul."

I become obsessed with the ouija board. I've been intrigued by it, to be sure, ever since I saw one, but I never took it that seriously. But now, working with a neighbor's board, I begin to understand that here is a spiritual channel to Robert. Because of the war in Europe, I've been told, the ouija has a reborn currency, as mothers and lovers fight their grief over lost dead sons and husbands through this mysterious, exotic board. Alone at night, I sit with the ouija board I finally buy for myself—I feel that the borrowed one belonging to my neighbor cannot produce the results I want — and stare at its dark, menacing symbolism. I stare down into it, as through a portal, looking for a key. *Talk to me. Tell me. Speak to me. Robert. I sit in Paradise Lost. Can you find me? (signed) Herself.*

So the ouija board becomes my only story, and I don't care what others say. My friends come to understand, I hope. It doesn't matter. If they come with books or flowers, or to woo me to the theater in New Haven, they find there is nothing else to talk about. Light chatter about brisk weather and the autumn leaves changing colors gives way to the idle board resting on the ornate oak lowboy: it sits there like a magnet, tempting conversation and inviting speculation. With my back to it, I still know where it lies. Invariably, I will look at it, drawn to it, wistful, my lips trembling and my skin cold as though I sit in a draft. I say, after a moment's silence, "Why not try?" All my friends say yes, although I notice their exchanged glances, and some unfortunately titter. These will not be invited back.

I know I am different now, and they no longer know how to read my behavior. I float through the rooms like a wraith, or I drag my body like a lumbering tug boat. They watch me, all of them.

Out of the gibberish dictated by the ouija board — Julie Opp is the recorder, emerging with some crazy hieroglyphics that I can make sense of, twisting vowels and transmogrifying words, even translating some — I maintain they are from Sanskrit — I find real meaning. I stare at a line — with its vowel-less words and its single-consonant words—and interpret. "It is all in the vocabulary of another world," I say. "It's like learning a new language. Like French." As the bizarre lines appear, I translate. I speak the new language. But the sentence I produce is meaningless: *Trees prepare for winter.* Or: *This time the light will follow.*

I am impatient with the obvious.

One night, we are driven into a feverish round of exploration, the mood remaining high hearted and carefree. The wine flows, and my friends want to laugh. Dosia Garrison jokes a little too much — I admonish her and the young poet grows silent — but the guests seem hellbent on levity. I ignore them because I feel an aura in the air, an encompassing spiritual cloud around us all.

They all take turns with the ouija board. I am dizzy from the wine and the laudenum, and I misread their idle pranks. At one point Charles Hanson Towne, sometimes the wag of the group, tips the table with his leg, and winks at Dosia. I vaguely note it — somehow aware of the jest — but suddenly the air is heavy with spirits. I can't breathe.

"Mama, Mama!" I scream, grabbing my throat and flailing my arms in the air.

The room grows silent, and Charles and the others, exchanging glances, look frightened. Dosia Garrison gasps. Towne withdraws from the table, shaken. I try to laugh it off. "I can act too," I say, smiling. But I hate lying, so I stop, sit there mutely. Throughout the night Charles watches me from a distance, bothered. I am so rattled I don't know where to look.

On the night of September 10, the sky gets dark early, and I sit with Thelma Bonner, a friend from New Haven, the ouija board between us. The moment my fingers touch the pointer, something happens. A wave of electricity shoots through me — and through Thelma. I call my friend May Randall, reading alone in the next room, and bid her come to record the furious movement of the pointer on the board. The indicator flies across the board. Insane movement, furious. May struggles to write down the fast-moving letters and words

My journal: *When the table rested, May read to us the letters. We interpreted the lines together. The sentences lept off the page: "Brave one, keep up your courage. Love is all there is. I am with you always. I await your arrival." When I read these sentences, after experiencing the electric shock of their transmission, there was no longer any doubt in my mind. My message had come! I was in touch with my Robert! He had kept his promise! I asked how long I must wait in the body before going to him. The answer was, "Time is naught; hope for bliss with me; I am incomplete without you. Two halves make a whole; we will finish in Nirvana."*

Nirvana: I remember the hot days traveling in India, in Ceylon, in Algeria. Earthly paradise.

I can't sleep at night, tossing wildly in the bed, my mind circling back to that moment with the board.

In the morning I am groggy, intoxicated.

Night after night the sessions continue. I invite famous psychics out of New York to witness. I invite naysayers to watch, to monitor, to determine that none of this is trickery, suspect manipulation. If Robert talks to me, it has to be Robert. One night, to be careful, Thelma and I sit blindfolded so there will be no question as to veracity. The words appear, and are interpreted. Each night I rewrite the dialogues into a log book.

Then, one night, my longest conversation:

Me: Robert, if this is you, tell me what are you doing in the invisible realms?

Robert: I am doing a great work; meeting souls shot into eternity. That is why I left you.

Me: Did you have to leave?

Robert: I had no choice. I had work to do.

Me: I am alone, Robert.

Robert: No, you're not.

Me: Robert, my health —

Robert: Fill yourself up with God — health will come.

Me: Robert, why didn't you come to me during those long, lonely months. California —

Robert: Your tears hung a veil between.

Me: My tears?

Robert: Grief is a curtain we cannot get through.

Me: Tell me what your life is like now.

Robert: The same life, only used more intelligently. My work is meeting souls shot into eternity. All is confusion for them. Equanimity is my gift; I supply it to those killed in the shock of battle.

Me: The boys of war?

Robert: Any violent or accidental death. Death surprises and confuses. I interpret and guide.

Me: Why you, Robert?

Robert: Why not? We don't choose.

Me: Robert, can you tell me who is with you there?

Robert: It is forbidden.

Me: My health, Robert —

Robert: I am but an instrument in His hands. Health is of the soul.

Me: What medicine, Robert? My pain —

Robert: There is no pain.

Me: Yes, Robert, there is.

Robert: No pain.

Me: How can you attend to your work of meeting and helping the souls of soldiers, and yet come at once whenever my friend and I sit together?

Robert: Spirit is omnipresent, Love is my guide, love is all.

Me: Robert, do you long for the time when I shall leave my body and be with you?

Robert: Yes. Everything you long for will be given. It is only that —

Me: But, Robert, I fear —

Robert: Ella, stop interrupting.

Me: Please —

Robert: Ella is scolded!

Me: Robert.

Robert: Enough.

At night, lying in bed, I can't close my eyes. To do so is to see waves of shifting jagged line and brilliant color. In my ears ring small, clinking sounds, a small bell. When I touch my chest, I feel the tremendous pounding of my heart: my body thumps and roars. I hear the sound of the Aolian harps on the veranda, and they don't lull me, as they often do. The pain in my chest is so intense now I rise to take a pill. I am purchasing morphine tablets now. They soothe me. They allow me to sleep, finally.

In the morning I am slow moving and sleep is heavy on my eyelids, but I have to rise to write. Sitting in the Flower Room, amid the rush of color against the outdoors landscape of New England autumn, I begin my new sonnet cycle with a poem of Triumph:

> *At last! at last the message! Definite*
> *As dawn that tells the night has gone away.*
> *The silence has grown eloquent with it,*
> *The silence that late filled me with dismay,*
> *So dumb it was; triumphant now I sit*
> *So near to God and you I need not pray.*
> *For only words of thankfulness were fit*

For this estate wherein I dwell today.

You live! you love me! You have heard my call,
And answered it in your own way. The proof
So satisfied the soul of me, were all
The hosts of earth henceforth to stand aloof
Till I recanted, my reply were this:—
One man called dead has sent me messages.

Log, September 15:
Me: Robert, do you remember this room?
Robert: My darling, I do. I died there, Ella. I died there.
Me: Do you remember those last hours with me here? You were unconscious —
Robert: As plainly as you do.
Me: How long after your soul left your body was it before you woke on the astral plane?
Robert: Seven days.
Me: Did you know when your body was cremated on the fourth day?
Robert: No, my astral body was out.
Me: What did you first see when you awoke?
Robert: Your face — Memory.
Me: What spirit first met you?
Robert: Our son.
Me: How did you recognize him, since he died when an infant?
Robert: He is so like you.
Me: Robert —
Robert: Leaving now — must go. Be strong; my help is constant, I am always with you.

Journal, September 24: ghosts.
They come in throngs that filled all space—
Those whispering phantom hosts;
They came from many a land and place,
The ghosts, the ghosts, the ghosts.

Log: October 20:
Robert: Ella, we talk again.
Me: Robert. I am glad you are back.
Robert: Of course.
Me: What do you have to say to me?
Robert: Great things; events are shaping on your plane and mine; our lives are one.
Me: Tell me, Robert —
Robert: Go to France.
Me: What?
Robert: Take very little with you: only one trunk.
Me: There is war now, Robert.
Robert: Go to France.
Me: Robert —
Robert: We are one.

Log, October 22:
Robert: Go to France.
Me: Robert, I am sick —
Robert: Only the body.
Me: I am old.
Robert: The body.
Me: But France?
Robert: Humanity has need of you. Wonderful things will happen. Your spark of God is greater than that of ten ordinary mortals.

Alone, strolling the fall gardens, holding a picked chrysanthemum to my nose, a dark burgundy flower that reminds me of flowers I saw growing out of the snow in the Alps, I find myself confused. It all makes sense — except the going-to-France part. Everything Robert says is true — it is his voice, his personality. But France? Yet I can't disobey — this is, after all, astral direction. How foolhardy can I be! Can I be misinterpreting the letters I read as F-r-a-n-c-e? But the pain in my chest, so intense sometimes neither morphine nor bottles of exquisite claret can numb me. But Robert makes sense. Yes, I say to myself: perfect sense. But not always: So much of what he says — as transcribed by May and interpreted by me — is difficult, obtuse, scary: *O sweet mud! O sky mud! Though you cling to me forever, yet we are not one body. Stirred by a great devotion, mud vibrates.* Help me to understand, Robert — I think. *Mates in Primos, nodules in matrix.* What? What does that mean? Help me to understand the language of heaven.

Log, December 11:
Me: Robert, can you tell me when and how this war will end?
Robert: God, the center of all, controls; and the end will justify all.
Me: But the war, Robert —
Robert: I told you, Ella —
Me: There's war in France —
Robert: Stop asking questions.

My quiet days at home come to an end. There's new interest in my writings, because my columns in the *New York World* chronicle with rich detail my new-found conversations with Robert. My editors balk, bothered by my ardent belief in Robert's messages, but I always understand my audience out there. Cynical New York editors have so little room for the soul to grow. But my readers hunger for more, these starved pullet women who have lost husbands and sons and lovers. I have gained passage to another world. It's true — definitely. I promise entry into psychic channels: I give road maps to the stars. I write, "These experiences have robbed death of its terror and the grave of its sting." All over America women nod. Yes: the peace of death. My editors publish my columns, but smirk. They see money: I see God.

Tranquillity: hope.

The bags of mail arrive on my doorstep.

Log, December 20:

Robert: Many come here who have only material desires in their hearts: they try to live the same way here. When they find they cannot, they seek the same vibrations of those on earth. They live in a cloud near earth. Intense love and desire is the only way out. Desperate grief of those on earth makes the burden heavier for souls here.

Me: Then that's a flaw in God's creation. With no proof of eternity, we grieve.

Robert: I am with you in your sleep.

Me: Tell me about your life.

Robert: We are so busy. Our lives are devoted to duty and service. Ella, I leave now: take care of yourself, and do not take cold when you go into the country; wear rubbers; take fresh milk and fresh eggs every morning. My beloved, I will always be with you, asleep or awake. We shall see each other again; have patience. Sit every day, alone in the silence, until you learn the use of the higher law, then you will not need the board. Fill yourself with God.

Me: Robert, this journey you want me to —

Robert: Go to France.

Me: Robert —

Robert: Joan of Arc will watch over you, Ella. Read a good history of her life.

Me: Joan of Arc?

Joan of Arc?

I dream of Joan of Arc at night: there is a fire, so hot that children cry and statues of Buddha melt and monkeys swing from limbs, and in the dark jungles of India a tiger stalks me.

Log, December 21:

Me: Where were you when I suffered grief in California?

Robert: I had to awaken; you know I liked the things of earth and of flesh. I had much to learn, and your sorrows made a heavy burden for me to bear. It hung a veil between us.

Me: Forgive me.

Robert: Forgive me.

Log, February 16:

Robert: Tomorrow, when you leave for France — do not talk of this on the boat; you cannot convince people by talking about it openly. They will simply regard you as unbalanced.

Me: To friends?

Robert: To no one. Not yet. That time is coming.

Me: I'm afraid, Robert.

Robert: Why? Fear is an illusion. It's a waste of energy to one who already has the answer.

I wish it were spring; then I can carry lilacs on board, the white ones that make me think of fresh-fallen snow, and the pale lavender ones, the ones that remind me of sweet perfume from Ceylon markets. Lilacs do not come in yellow.

No matter: I am headed back to Europe, this time alone. The daughter of the American heartland has a mission for heaven now. The battlefields of France, all blood and dying, await my poetry. I am, I tell myself, heaven's ambassador. I have a job to do.

France

1918

To the Editor:

Sir, your recent editorial alarms me. You state that war is
— while an evil — a testing of a young man's mettle and
resolve. Sir, such comments are dangerous! Dangerous! Of
course, we expect the young man to be noble and true in
the service of his country. That is what we call character.
But war is not a school project, an exercise in character.
War is, quite simply, the end of civilization. You men may
not understand that, but ask any mother, any widow, any
maiden. War is the end of civilization.

    — Ella Wheeler Wilcox,
    Letter to the *New York Herald*, 1915

I allow no one to accompany me to the ship's departure, this cold February day, as I prepare to journey on
the *Espagne*. My friends — the ones I've kept, the loyal
believers, the others disappearing under my glare and
condemnation, undeveloped souls that they are — plead
with me not to go. I am clearly ailing, my body stooped
and my face drawn, the eyes dull and cloudy as old pew-
ter. My skin has acquired a sallow parchment tone, the
color of old lace, as though I've been hidden away in a
dark room. My friends are used to seeing me grasp my
chest, as though in ecstasy, but the look on my face, I
know, is raw and unsettling: it is a grimace of utter pain.
I've never known such fierce, unrelenting pain. They are
used to the smell of sweetened medication that emanates
from me, a curious mixture of untidy clothing and cloy-

ing narcotic breath. I can't help it. In my overlarge purse
— I keep volumes of my poetry, as gifts, as well as bottles
of Myer's Sensible Elixir and the remaining rosary beads
blessed years back by the Pope — I carry the oriental
paper knife Robert gave me eons back. A talisman of good
luck. It is worn to the touch. Every so often, fumbling as
if in a panic, I look for it, grasp it, and then wave it in the
air, as though it is a dagger and I am ridding myself of
foes. I am not nervous about this trip, although I'm not
happy going: after all, with me is Robert. This journey is
charted in the sea lanes of another space and time. In
France Joan of Arc will meet me at the docking.

I know most think me crazy. Well, so be it. It is wartime. Everyone is unbalanced. I'm not alone.

In New York, during the chaotic week before I leave, I
read palms at night, try to convert the unbelievers to the
power and authority of the ouija board, and fiddle with
the newfangled typewriter which I can never master. I'm
aware that there is a purr in my voice now, a low catlike
tone that makes people lean into me, nervous. You survive life by ritual, I announce to everyone. Pageants and
ritual and rhythm. I tell my friends to repeat every day: *I
am love, health, happiness, success, opulence, and all I want or
desire is mine.* A mantra for the living.

I do so myself, rising at dawn, splashing cold water
over my body, shivering, and chanting into the streets
below.

The wartime streets of New York are insane with movement, with horrible, choking automobile noise and the
acrid smells of oil and heat and gas. Oddly, by each mid-
day I am euphoric, expecting a new adventure. Flashing
light mesmerizes me: street musicians make me weep.
Everything thrills me — the future, both mundane and
beyond, invites me.

> *The wonderful age of the world I sing—*
> *The age of battery, coil and spring,*
> *Of steam, and storage, and motorized thing.*

The only sponsor I could find for my unorthodox traveling during wartime was the Red Star Society, an organization promoting the proper and decent care of animals in wartime. No one else would listen to my entreaties. My own newspaper, the *World*, refused to sponsor me. Everyone assumes I'm insane.

I am warned about making the dreadful midwinter voyage, a trek through seething, violent waters, with the threat of bombardment on the high seas. The Kaiser's killing ships are lurking. "Ella Wheeler Wilcox will be torpedoed from the waters," a newsman writes. So what? I declare grandly. Robert is waiting. But I know it will not happen. Wouldn't Robert warn me? I walk onto the boat, unattended — *No, no: please don't see me to the ship* — walking with deliberation and confidence, if a little drowsy from my medication. In my flowing gown and peacock-feathered hat, I know I seem oddly anachronistic, a wealthy New York matron beginning the Grand Tour during peace time. But no ship will sink with me on it, I know. Germans lurk elsewhere. Once I virtually looked the Kaiser in the eye. He is a pompous little man in an operetta uniform. He's no match for me. I am Ella Wheeler Wilcox. I'm not a woman to be trifled with.

So the voyage is smooth, calm. As expected. Even the crusty crew, nervous at the departure and always scanning the seas for ice floes and Germans — the specter of the *Lusitania* haunts them — talks of its singular ease. I am not surprised. This is as it should be. On board there is an auction of objects for the benefit of wounded soldiers. Much talked of, it becomes the big event of the voyage. I am carrying my advance copy of *Sonnets of Sorrow and Triumph*, sent me by George H. Doren, my new publisher. In the States these poems of my grief and rebirth — the loss and return of Robert — will be for sale — for one meager dollar — on February 23. On board, I receive sixty bucks for the auctioned volume, bought by a French officer, Lieut. Col. De Billet. I inscribe the volume with a flourish. Famous comedienne Elsie Janis, traveling to entertain the troops, keeps everyone in high spirits with her droll stories and bubbly personality. Cute and seductive, she manages to get donations to a record two thousand dollars. We all love her, and she seeks me out for walks about the ship.

In Paris, housed in the Hotel Vernet with so many other Americans come to help the cause, groups of purposeful American matrons, I wait, anxious. Things are too quiet, not only in the streets, but on the astral plane. My log book stays blank. There is no more conversation with Robert. At night, alone in my room, medicated, I wonder: Why am I here? I fear Robert has been left behind. Has he forgotten his orders that I go to France? Where's Joan of Arc?

Then, on March 8, I experience my first nightmare air raid, and it isn't a major jolt — at first. Still not used to the newfangled airplane itself, I cannot grasp a world in which bombs fall from the sky. Everything seems upside down now. I am sitting in my drawing room, writing letters home. The evening has been quiet after dinner, and bathing in mineral salts, I relaxed for a brief time the pain in my body. When the siren sounds, it seems faraway, some circus noise perhaps. It is one of the many alien noises of Paris — a shrill street sound, the high whistling of engines, the clamor of river boats. There is some yelling and the sound of a woman crying, but that is all. I retire long before the berlogue sounds the musical all-clear at quarter to twelve.

But the next day the full, raw impact of the war comes home to me. With friends I drive to the site of the German bombing, a neighborhood not very distant, and I am stunned by the devastation: the ruined, vacant buildings with the empty window frames, the torn streets with the smashed carts and the dead horses, the frantic accounts of dead and wounded, the wagons leaving with bodies covered in canvas, the frightened and gaunt looks of the children on the streets, the fetid smell of decaying animal flesh. Nothing in my lifetime has prepared me for this: nothing. Nothing! This is the end of mankind. I leave the others, going to sit alone in the car. I have never seen such wanton destruction on this earth. This is surely an obscenity under God, some atavistic moment out of the Old Testament, the leveling of fallen Sodom. I recite my mantra over and over, singsong, with dizzying speed, trying to calm myself down. I hum the words, rocking my head. Tears stream down my cheeks, and I taste salt in the corners of my mouth. I tighten my eyes against the awful sight. When I return to Paris in the afternoon, I sleep through the dinner hour, and I miss obligations. Taking more morphine for the pain, I enter a fitful sleep of grabbing demons and crying, dislocated voices. At midnight, restless, trying to talk to Robert unsuccessfully, yelling out to him in the room — *I can't do this alone, Robert. I'm old* — I take too much medication, and fall into a paralyzing stupor.

One night, dining with some American women, the siren sounds again, and everyone rushes to the apartment of Mrs. Wills, wife of the Paymaster of the U.S. Navy, Major Wills. This time I do not hesitate, seared as I am with the earlier vision of the piecemeal destruction done by German aerial bombing. Ten women huddle in the apartment, silent, waiting, and Major Wills periodically comes up from the street to report on the raid — and to reassure.

"Sixty German airplanes in the skies, at least," he tells us, and we all scream. He seems to be savoring his role as town crier. "I'll be back," he says.

This cannot be borne, I think.

I can hear the fearful machines overhead, the mindless humming and droning of engines. Locusts, I think, a Biblical plague come to decimate the earth of man and his charges. I hate this faraway sound. The sky has always been a place of nature's soothing sounds. Even the summer thunderstorm has its excitement, a natural punctuation of the day, all din and steam followed by sunshine. But this — this — Not this man-made menacing roar. This comes not from heaven but from the pit of hell.

Suddenly the French barrage guns begin their counter-attack, and I scream: this was like a multitude of summer thunderstorms at Short Beach, all rolled into one tremendous killing noise.

I notice the contained nervousness, the attempt to remain calm, among these seasoned American volunteers.

"I have something to tell you," I begin, slowly, deliberately. Robert has warned me of precipitous revelations of his presence — he understands the weight of the cynical naysayers. But I understand that these are good women, women of vision, dedicated war servants. Strong women, unafraid of the war men have created. So I begin, "You must not be afraid or be nervous — I am a mascot." The women stare, confused. "I am eager to go out of the body, and reach the realms which are more beautiful and satisfying than this earth, but I have to stay until my work is done." They look at me as though I've lost my mind. I know I have — in any earthly sense that no longer matters.

While the bombing continues and the planes soar overhead, while the night is lit with brilliant flashes of staccato lightning in the distance, while from the street comes screaming and weeping and the *rat-a-tat-tat* of gunfire, I weave fantastic tales of Robert's dedicated astral visits. I feel a tremendous power now — I am, after all, a born storyteller, and this is the story my whole life has led up to. The words flow out evenly and dramatically, the hypnotic rhythms and the melodramatic message tantalizing, like campfire girls around a wilderness fire. One by one the women move in closer, enthralled. "Go on, go on," one woman says, touching my sleeve.

Suddenly the berlogue sounds the all-clear. No one moves. Major Wills, all smiles and bluster, rushes in to say, "It is all over." He finds somber women, two of them sobbing, huddled together. He looks from his wife to me.

My face was aglow, shiny with purpose, my eyes like hot coals: I am still talking, and my dreamy, narcotic voice fills the room, a measured and spiritual litany, words strung out like a cloistered nun's worn prayer beads.

The following day my ouija board jumps, as though electrified, when I place it between Mrs. Wills and me. The woman gasps. The pointer dashes from letter to letter, darting zanily across the board. Triumphant, I read the hieroglyphics.

My astral log: Paris now, 1918, finally:

Robert: A great battle rages on the Oise; the odds are fearfully against the Allies but a change will come. France will suffer terrible losses — glorious America comes in, and brings success; boastful Germany will be beaten.

Me: Thank you, Robert. The mothers and daughters of the world thank you.

Robert: I am here, Ella.

Me: At last.

Robert: I was always here. Do not doubt.

Me: I did.

Robert: Never.

I sleep well at night now that I know the war will end in victory.

Robert: Ella, go now to Dijon — at once. Terrible air raids are coming.

Me: Robert, no one is leaving here.

Robert: Go now. You have no choice.

In Dijon I entertain the troops, reading with them, writing letters for them, visiting the wounded and dying at the American Hospital. I have a special affection for the young blinded soldiers, helpless in their sadness and fear, and I like to take them for walks through the grounds. At night I escort the young men to dinner or to concerts. With my arm on their elbows, I guide the bandaged men through the streets. I drive myself until, exhausted, I am overcome with fatigue. I don't care. Some mornings I can't rise before noon.

One night I wander, with a group of other women, into a large camp field, expecting to hear a brass concert, after having eaten mess with the officers. To my surprise and consternation, the three thousand men burst into raucous and sustained applause. It is for me, I am told. Red faced, embarrassed, I stand there confused, my head swimming.

A young Frenchman, slender as a rail, blond and wispy, with an eye bandaged and an arm bent in a sling, leans into me, and says with a thick Gallic accent, in English: "Laugh and the world laughs with you, weep and you weep alone." I stare at him, a little amused but also stunned.

"What?" I say.

He smiles. "Miss Wilcox." He says it: Mees Wheelcox. He bows:

> *"So many gods, so many creeds,*
> *So many paths that wind and wind,*
> *While just the art of being kind,*
> *Is all the sad world needs."*

He has recited my most quoted passage. Something shifts in me, something balances itself. I feel my lips tremble and my heart flutter. I forget the sharp hurt inside, the drowsy medicated haze. Holding his hand, I whisper thanks, and then smile. He bows again. Standing on the crude platform, looking over the crowded heads, I begin to speak, loudly and clearly. I find an incredible power within, a buoyancy, and I stand up straight, and throw out my words to the three thousand eager, upturned faces. I speak first in English. And then, surprising myself, I speak in a halting but precise French. My voice echoes off the tent. I've always avoided public recitation, fearful of my projected voice. I've never recited any of my verse at salons, except once — and that was a disaster. Never again. But this — this is a power I've never known before: it is triumphant. I am, frankly, thrilled at myself. Joyous and exuberant, I have a lot to say, suddenly. I talk of home, of mother, of peace, of justice, of truth. I am speaking a Hearst column. Once I begin there is no quieting me, the words rising like high tide on the seawall back home. When I finish — "You are God's soldiers, men of light" — my eyes brimming with tears, the crowd stands, stamps feet wildly, and whistles.

Robert: Speak to the soldiers of spiritual things.
Me: Today is May 21. Do you know what it signifies?
Robert: All life for me, and life universal for you.
Me: Yes, Robert: your soul fled Short Beach this very day.
There is a period of minutes when nothing moves. Then:
Robert: Go to Tours.
Me: Tours?
Robert: Now.
Me: Robert, I must go to England. I am tired.
Robert: No. Tours.

I apply to Lee Meriweather, the special assistant to the American Ambassador: "I want to leave for Tours. I was talking to Mr. Wilcox last night, and he told me to go to Tours."

"Your husband is in Tours?" Mr. Meriweather asks, innocently. He is behind his desk, harried, and scarcely looks at my face

"My husband," I say, with venom, "died two years ago. He comes to see me every night and talks to me on the ouija board."

I topple over in the hotel lobby one night, just after returning from meditation with some doughboys, and am carried to my bed. Revived, I mumble about heaven and winter light through the Flower Room window. The lo-

cal physician cautions long rest. "Madame, you are doing too much." I shake my head: no. My work is not done
yet. "I am doing too little." Every day now I am dizzy —
in pain.

Robert: Tours.
I go, my trunks packed and heavy.
In my journal: *I have trouble realizing when it has become
morning now.*

I'm always busy, frantically so, hurrying mornings to
ready myself to face the day. I need to be out there, among
them. The boys wait for me. These days the hotel room is
too close and threatening. Yet I find time during the day
to write my poems and my newspaper columns, cabling
them back to America. But it is mechanical gesture because I scarcely think of America now — that land seems
so distant from the noisy battlefields and the scruffy
American boys in khaki. America is at war. World War.
Making the world safe for democracy. The war to end
all wars. These boys are my home now, and I'm their
mother. I feel an obligation to the mothers and daughters and sisters back home. After all, I am their surrogate
now. Someone who has always been their voice now finds
herself a different voice: the virtuous camp follower. I
am here, my long dress dragging through the mud and
gravel. In the wards I write letters for the boys who can't
write. *Dear Mother. Dearest Ma and Pa.* I cry when I leave
them. I am reminded of stories of Walt Whitman in Washington, D.C., hospitals, penning similar letters for the il-
literate farm boys during the Civil War. I, who lived
through the Civil War, now stumble through the World
War. When I have to, I write that the boys died nobly,
gently. *Dear Mother, your Horace died a hero.* And more so,
they have gone on to heaven. This is because I understand heaven now. Mine are words of gentle comfort,
delivered weekly in rhapsodic prose in the columns of
the *New York World.* "Send more," my editors ask. "Back

home everyone reads Ella again." My columns on Robert and the ouija and the war are selling papers at lightning speed.

It isn't always easy. At home I have my vicious naysayers. Someone hands me a column from my own newspaper. One of my editors, Arthur Brisbane, long a friend of sorts — I've always thought of him as an intense intellectual with little emotion — feels the need to annotate my latest speculation about life on the astral circuit, fearful his readers will misinterpret the role of his newspaper. Brisbane says: "There is no *real* knowledge, of course, on this subject of death. The dead in this day do not come back. Mrs. Wilcox and her friends are deceiving themselves; the spirits that are dead do not talk to us while we live. Mediums and others, some of them sincere, more mere swindlers, impose upon the sorrowful."

I fume all day. I carry the torn newsprint throughout the day, pulling it out repeatedly, showing it to everyone, my voice getting louder and more shrill. Nurses and orderlies run from me.

Everyone stops listening. By the end of the week, the newspaper clipping is tattered and stained, one corner missing, and I am nervous and jittery. One of the ward doctors gives me a bromide for the nagging headache that nightly appears at the back of my head.

I dream fantastic dreams. Ribbons hang from the sky, shiny silver streamers that tempt me to look up. Silver chalices float around my head. In my journal: *I am alone in the battlefields of France, far from the ashes of my baby boy and my lover. Alone among French battlefields, Alone: alone. Robert must be away on business.*

Robert is involved with silver *objects d'art*, I think. *Was* involved.

I am bothered by the blatant immorality I observe. Away from home, fresh-scrubbed boys eighteen or nineteen, farm boys from the plains, from factory cities, fall into vice and disease — the undisguised curse of the battlefield. Certainly some of the young men listen to me, applaud my words of moral advice and my spontaneous uplifting verses. They line up to collect signatures, but I notice others wink and smirk and frown. They, I know, have to be reached. Such gross immoral behavior is frightful. I notice the scarlet women who linger at the campsites, those lipsticked French girls, barely women, flirtatious, willful girl children, who disappear into tents with the American farm boys. It drives me mad. This is wrong, dead wrong. One of the generals, perhaps with a little too much good French wine one night, whispers that disease is afoot, a disease so dreadful that wives at home will end up in mental asylums someday. I panic. I remember all those lost women I saw with Robert on our world journeys — those Japanese flowers in gilded cages, the veiled prostitutes of Tunis — and I realize now that the general's indiscreet words are purposeful. I understand my duty, my need to answer the call. One night, sleepless, I write a few choice lines with the delicious and emphatic refrain: "Come Back Clean, Boys."

For weeks I wander campsites, dressed in my long flowing gown, my hair buried under towering sensible hats. And when I gather a crowd of soldiers, stragglers heading from mess, workers on break, idlers with nothing to do, I stand among them and intone: "Come Back Clean, Boys."

> *I may lie in the mud of the trenches,*
> *I may reek with blood and mire,*
> *But I will control, by the God in my soul,*
> *The might of my man's desire.*
> *I will fight my foe in the open,*
> *But my sword shall be sharp and keen*
> *For the foe within who would lure me to sin,*
> *And I will come back clean.*

Some of the boys nod, agreeing. Others stare dumbfounded, wide eyed. Some act as though I am maddened.

Some have no idea what I am talking about until their buddies mumble explanations.

"Come back clean, boys," I end, loudly.

I refuse to entertain the words "venereal disease." In my presence I insist they call it "the wife's lament." That is, I maintain, a truer label.

In letter after letter my editors inform me that I am all the rage again. Not only are my columns on astral conversation and wartime volunteerism increasing newspaper sales — my readership is buying ouija boards at a record pace, I am informed — but my patriotic verses, my little homiletic turns of phrase, are making me a national heroine again. There are rumors of an invitation to the White House. My poem "Hail, Loyal Death" is printed with the letter I send back with it: "I hope you will not think it is a gloomy poem. I think it optimistic. Everybody has too long hated Death. Death is a good and great friend. The only one SURE never to fail us at last." Tempering their earlier easy dismissal of my verses, the editors add: "Women who read this newspaper know that Ella Wheeler Wilcox is a widow, and, of course, looks forward to reunion. The last line of her poem will interest all widows."

All right, I think: they are back on my side. I am happy they stressed the last line of my poem. It reads: "And run, run, run, through heaven until I find my mate."

But I know it is not yet time for that final, glorious run. I have work to accomplish — a testing of my resolve to make me worthy of heaven and Robert. This much I know.

But when autumn comes, the coveted Armistice is signed, at last, and the ugly war is ended. Happily, the skies are silent, and the final tents taken down. The guns disappear. There is suddenly chaos in France — not the calculated horror of war, those nightly air raids and the bandaged bodies of men in wards, but everything is in motion. Everyone seems to be moving, rushing, without direction. The streets are jammed with traffic. No one stands still. Events spin around me like eddying currents, and I freeze in place: where is my center? I find I can't follow it all. No one, I realize, is listening to my verses any more, what with the packing and leave-taking and quick good-byes. When I try to return from Tours to Paris, I am told that the move is impossible at this time. Angered, I persist. "Madame," I am told, "stay where you are for the moment."

Then, escorted, I find myself in London. This has been my plan all along, but it has been long delayed. Now, in the company of other volunteer women, I feel as though we are dumped without ceremony into Piccadilly Circus. We are part of the debris of war. So be it: I can now attend to the business of the spheres.

In my journal: *I have been here four nights now. Friends visit and congratulate. In the hotel lobby I am stopped by well wishers. My poetry is more popular than ever. But Robert is not here. Did I leave him behind in France? Should I have stayed there? Robert, answer me. Robert?*

The night is silent as dust: I weep.

Postwar London is lively, the car-choked streets filled with tipsy men in uniform, their voices high and happy, but I am lonely here, dislocated. There is music now in the pubs, and raucous celebration. But no poetry comes from my pen now. No columns of uplifting advice to be cabled back to America. Will I ever write again?

The pain is so great now that no amount of medicine can squelch the awful aching. Secretly I visit a physician who shakes his head. "Mrs. Wilcox," he says, "you need rest."

I refuse the advice and wonder why I even went to see him. I begin a new round of visits to London psychics, including the celebrated Sir Oliver Lodge. More card readings, more palms, more — well, I fear — sham. But they cannot find Robert either. Something is wrong. There is silence from heaven. Deaf heaven. Walls close in around me, tightening. I walk the cold London streets, a stumbling old woman with veil and purse, and I try to breathe.

Lovers of my poetry stop me, but sometimes I stare, uncomprehending, at their requests. What do they want from me?

I spend New Year's Eve with friends, but all the laughter and celebration — after all it is almost 1919 now and the war is over, and at dinner there is talk of women voting — "In 1920 it will be done, our year," a woman pontificates — and skirts will be raised and airplanes will sail across the seas as if they are omnibuses traveling between villages — and it all makes me a little crazy. This is no world I want. This is too much change for one lifetime, I think. So as New Year's Eve approaches, I sit by myself in a corner of the large reception room, with all the screaming and hilarity blazing around me. Horns hooting and bands playing, the wild hoopla, the hysteria, and the dancing, dancing, dancing: people whirl around me until I believe myself a rock in a flooding spring brook. When one of the hotel staff notices me, my face rigid and pale, and asks if I need anything, I say, in a thin metallic voice: "Youth? Death?"

"What, Mrs. Wilcox?"

I laugh. "I am old and sick."

"Can I get you a doctor?"

"You can get me my husband."

The young man, scarcely out of boyhood, becomes flustered. "Is he upstairs, Mrs. Wilcox. Might I page him?"

Suddenly I start laughing: "Oh, yes, he's upstairs all right."

I wave him away.

I stare across the room, and suddenly everything narrows, as though I am looking through a long telescope. People wobble, falter, fall. Voices get loud, then soft, drifting into silence. Suddenly I feel that my world had ended, collapsing in on itself, imploding. There is nothing left. I have admonished the boys — the world — to come back clean, and stay clean. I have done my job. Here I sit, wrapped in layers and layers of chiffon, all brilliant yellow, a shock of blinding sun in a winter room, and I look in on myself. I see a plump old woman with wrinkled face and sagging flesh, strangled in fluff and frill. It scares me: I feel I have delivered a world into tomorrow — I was always so modern, so *outré*, so sensational — and now I am left behind. Alone: without Robert. My anchor, now gone, ripped from me. I want to go to him now. There are vast clouds in the dark room, and they are moving into storm front. I sit in the room among the dancers, and expect the rain to fall.

The young man returns. "Mrs. Wilcox, are you all right?"

I don't answer.

"You're perspiring," he says. "Might I bring you water?"

Then there is the sharp pain in the chest, the bolt of lightning coming so fast I gasp. "Madam," he says, concerned. Then my nerves start to tremble, like taut wires strummed until they snapped, one after the other. *Bing bing bing bing.* Idly I remember my harp, centuries back at Short Beach. At Granite Bay. The harp, all those delicate wires strummed so peacefully, so elegantly. How admired I was! But now I am all wires, all pulled madly asunder, all twitter and discordant noise. All frenzy and screaming, like wild birds in the midnight sky. From the back of my head comes a growing whistling noise, an insistent shriek that seems otherworldly, eerie. "No, " I say, standing. "No."

The young man reaches for my elbow, solicitous, but I push him away.

"No!"

I feel as though my body is on fire. I need to have control, I know. Order: harmony: presence. I close my eyes.

Out loud I say, "Ella Wheeler Wilcox." Over and over, a litany designed to piece me together. "Ella Wheeler Wilcox. Ella Wheeler Wilcox." But the words start coming out blurred, incoherent: Ellawheeelrwilcox ellawheelcoxelcox.

Stupidly I remember a nasty cartoon in some old satirical magazine: *Ella Wheeler Wilcoxie spews a ton of gushing moxie.* What did that mean?

Help me.

I start to move, pushing through the crowd. People stop dancing, and stare. They make room. The heart drops to the bottom of my stomach: I open my mouth in horror. I bump into tables, chairs, trying to steady myself. "Robert," I scream, as I topple to the floor.

In the morning, rousing somewhere, in a strange bed, I dimly hear a voice outside my room whispering that some celebrated American poetess has suffered a nervous breakdown.

America

1919

I have heard the new thinkers, the so-called alientists, those practitioners of the new psychology, tell us that dreams are doors to hidden desire. Poppycock! Dreams are God's watercolors, brush strokes of pleasure. Nightmares are a void of color — and thus love and spirit. People like to talk of Freud. Poppycock! Talk to me of God appearing in my sleep. There is only one artist in my soul, and it is Spirit.

> — *Ella Wheeler Wilcox,*
> unpublished letter to Mrs. Maude Akins

Most days I dream. This is all I do. It's all I can do, to tell the truth. Whether sleeping in the comfortable hospital bed in Bath or hidden among pillows in the ship's cabin or nestled under thick blankets on the porch at the Bungalow or strolling slowly in my rose garden, I dream. It doesn't matter now, not the season nor the day nor the hour: it has all become a fuzzy blur to me. The line between day and night and between reality and imagination has finally dissolved, lost under the power of fierce medication and, worse, the weight of my own long memories. What remains is the bittersweet scent of flowers one day, or the rhythmic hiss of rain on the roof another. Or, horribly, the pain that sweeps through me like a late summer brush fire. It is all sensation now, tones and sounds and aromas. Everything comes at me in an echo. There is no longer any time: the clocks have lost their hour hands.

It is, at last, just dreaming. Robert is nowhere to be found.

I wait to return home. I dream it. Some mornings I can smell my own seashore. I can taste it. Some days that is all I think about. Lying here, pampered in this convalescent bed, I count back from one hundred. When I reach zero, I sleep. But it is as though I've lost the power to move my arms, my legs, my head. Everything seems paralyzed. I am a fleshy shell lying in a bed in a rest home in Bath. Or is it still London? The months drift by until a half year has passed. I hunger to return to America. Back home — in Granite Bay — the rocks amethyst and slate-gray now that winter is over — I will be able to move again. I know that. My falling that New Year's Eve night seemed to begin a series of cruel maladies. The prescribed tonics relax me, but my gnawing illness — it is fatigue, I keep telling the doctors, nothing more — and loneliness — exacts its toll. But more than one doctor talks of cancer, growing in me like hot yeast rising, but I won't hear of it. Cancer is unclean, a surrender of the body to decay. I have trouble moving, and orderlies wheel me through the hallways. Around me, visiting friends talk and maintain a vow of dreadful silence. You look wonderful, they tell me. Never better, they say. Exhausted, yes, but you have done so much. Away from me, I suspect they pen notes for obituaries or prepare elegiac articles for syndication. I understand this because I can hear it in their voices.

In Bath I sleep throughout the melancholy days. At night I write feverishly, verses piling up like tide building on a shore. But in the morning I destroy so much of what I write. When I reread them, the words seem hollow and meaningless. What have I been trying to say? What has this to do with Robert? I send letters to everyone I know, sending greetings and asking for prayer. It is important that they believe I am still alive. In March I rally a bit, plan engagements and accept luncheon invitations. Friends take me for rides through the countryside.

At the beginning of summer I tell my doctor, "I need to be home."

"Mrs. Wilcox," he says, "you're in no condition —"

"I don't care —"

"Madame."

"Home."

"Home? The long journey across the waters? Madame, really."

I am adamant, I stare. "Home."

I write to a friend. "I must try to get home. I mean to America, as I have no home. By middle August if I can." There is so much I have to do. I have to read the proofs of my autobiography, scheduled out the beginning of November. I have work to do. "But Short Beach is no longer home," I write to a friend. "I have no home on this earth. I just want to return to America."

In my journal: *I need to sit in a summer garden near the ashes of Robert and Robert Jr. I need to be with my family. I will become whole there, intact, refreshed.*

Rallying one more time because I understand that I have to — because to stay ill in England is to allow them to hold me hostage — and because I do not want to die away from my family, so fearful am I that travelers on the astral plane can get mightily and eternally lost — I demand removal at once. If they can deliver wounded soldiers back to America, why not me? The wounded poetess.

In the darkness of a sticky summer night, carried out on a stretcher, I am delivered to the waiting ship. Ever alert, I mumble to the doctor, "The queen's last ride," but he doesn't seem to understand my reference. It piques me, so I understand that this vital journey back to America will be in the company of a healer of the body but not of the soul or heart. "Cover my face," I say quietly, as we move through gawking passengers to my cabin. "Cover my face." I don't want them to see the pale, haggard face, drawn now and trembling, or even my undyed hair. Or the invalid's bonnet I wear. Back in Connecticut I will become Ella Wheeler Wilcox again. But not here. There I will stand on polished oak floors and look out the bay windows at the ocean. I will taste bitter salt water.

So I return home on a ship, accompanied by a doctor who protects me from fellow passengers but not from myself. Some days, when the hot sun compels, I lie in a deck chair, blockaded from passersby by angled chairs and my own steely stare.

The doctor is accosted constantly, at dinner, in his nightly strolls, hidden under blankets on the deck. He says the same thing, over and over, the words I've given him: "An overtaxed heart."

Back at my home, tucked under wool blankets in the heat of summer, I scarcely know the day. Friends visit, bring me books and fruit, wish me well, but I stare, glassy eyed and angry. Who are these people? I have stopped reading books, and the fruit rots in a bowl on the table: the sweet smell of overripe peaches and pears lingers in the rooms.

I whisper one word: Shipwrecked.

But then I feel the dreaming subside, at least during the brighter hours of the day. I take slow, careful strolls among my flowers, sit among the chinaberry bushes, and close my heavy-lidded eyes. I rest my hands against the enormous granite boulder where the remains of my husband and son lie. I feel the heat under my palm: yes, I think, the electricity is there, waiting. Yes: reunion. We become one — to be one. These are the times I smile a little, hoping. And slowly, my hands against that blasted rock, covered now with struggling myrtle, I find strength to stand, to speak. And, at last, to laugh.

Night is another story. That is all demon and black pitch.

Julie Opp visits with her husband William. "Ella," Julie says, "you need to rest." She has found me slaving over the proofs of my autobiography. I am refashioning sections, retelling the conversations with Robert, outlining the dialogues of my astral log, trying to convince others. Perhaps this will bring Robert back to me: words on the page have always given me life.

I look up at Julie, my hand slipping over the sheaves of print and onto my lap, my arm seemingly unhinged, as though the socket has given way. I twist the huge topaz ring I always wear on my thumb, slowly bringing it up to my face. I always like the way the color is reflected in my eyes. Years ago, the gesture hypnotized people. So many men. The eyes of a tiger, I always said.

"What?" I am out of focus.

"Are you all right?" Julie asks.

"It's the medicine," I say, "It slows me down."

Julie and her husband exchange looks, and Julie sits close to me, picking up my weakened hand, caressing it. "It's all right."

"Of course, it's all right. Why wouldn't it be?"

"I only meant —"

"I'm not dying, Julie dear."

Julie laughs, "You're too dear to die."

I laugh. "Too ornery."

We eat dinner together, with me picking at some tomatoes and lettuce: I have no appetite.

Julie listens as the local doctor visits and mumbles. An old man who looks like a throwback to another century, with bushy gray-white Burnside whiskers and a twisted pince nez, he deposits the morphine on my work table, admonishing me to be careful. "Moderation," he says. He turns to Julie. "Tell her moderation."

"But the pain," I say.

He nods. "I know."

"No, you don't," I say.

When he is gone, Julie starts to say something about

the medicine. But I also know what it's done to me: the vacant, drugged eyes, the wispy fluttery voice, the forgotten lines, the head jerking back suddenly as though on a broken spring. The telephone calls I make to Julie in New York have been scary, my phoning and then forgetting why I call. Long silence on the wire. Abrupt hangups. Weeping. I know what they say. I hear the servants whispering. I hear the soft words of visitors: Ella Wheeler Wilcox is a morphine addict. They watch me plod through the gardens, stagger against a wall, gaze long and deep into the crashing waves against my seawall. When I turn to face them, I have to refocus my eyes. I say the sun is too bright. All I want is shadows. Sometimes, startled that I am without Robert, I recite dark and fearsome lines to them, verses that never appeared in any of my verses in *Cosmopolitan* or the *New York Journal*. Things like: *The whiskey of the night levels you.* Or: *Sometimes the whispering of the ocean threatens to hold you captive.* Or: *So I walked now — talked now — with Jesus, whose face is a cloud of despair.*

They turn away, embarrassed.

Julie rushes out of New York, hoping she can help me. I whisper to her: *I am shipwrecked.*

"No, Ella," Julie says. "You have your work, your friends."

But I have no Robert: life is meaningless unless he returns to me.

At night, sipping a glass of sherry with Julie and William, I lean into William's neck. I whisper, "Shipwrecked."

"Oh, Ella, no."

"Not a single prop."

I raise my glass, spilling the wine. "I have no props," I say, flatly. "I who have propped up the world am without foundation. I have no props."

"Ella, no."

It is the same conversation with every visitor. My arm tucked into the side of male friends, I whisper the same sentiments. I start to look healthier, the sea air a balm and a regenerative gift, but inside I quake. My chest thunders. Over and over I voice my despair, as though startled that it has at last come to me. That dark bogeyman I protected so many others from — I, the poetess of uplift — now I am haunted by my own dark menace. I didn't know the pit is so deep, so harrowing.

Then one night I dream of my father and his descent into madness. Am I his true daughter now, the heir to incoherence and sputtered nonsense? Am I Lear, so lost in crazed despair? Help me.

During the day I sit on the porch of the Bungalow, half asleep, and a few passing townspeople nod to me, strolling past to the beach. At lunch with Charles Hanson Towne I spill claret on my dress. "I don't mind the stain," I say. "That's why God invented pansies." I see his eyes travel to my feet. Nervously, I glance down: my high golden shoes are missing buttons.

"You look lovely, Ella," he says.

I nod.

At night, I lie drowsy in a sleepless bed. Sometimes I scribble in my journal, but that is becoming more and more a chore. Why write? Sometimes I read passages of Robert's journal, especially those parts dealing with our long travels. It all seems a century away, an account of two strangers visiting exotic places I've only heard about. When this summer ends, I tell myself, I think the winter will be glacial, prehistoric. There will be too much ice then. It will lie under the surface of the moon.

One morning the doctor shows up, unexpected, rapping on the door. He says someone has called him, asked him to visit me. Late night revelers, strolling along the crescent beach, heard plaintive moaning from the dark house. At first they thought it was a wounded animal, some beaten, awful dog that has come to the beach to die, but then they heard a voice so frightened it has to be human.

He finds me sitting on the floor, before the grand tile fireplace, with a garland of dead honeysuckle in my hair.

"You've been drinking," he says, accusing.

He tells the town.

Of course, all the rumors come back to me. Rumors must: otherwise they have no reason to be. There is talk I am a pathetic dope fiend. A filthy sot. A raving lunatic. A vampire who howls at the moon. Some said no: I am just an old woman who has returned to my Wisconsin village in my own foggy mind.

Why won't they leave me alone?

When I am alone I dream. Connecticut neighbors appear as errant children in Wisconsin pastures, wandering through buttercups and daisies. I wake up smiling. Vultures sweep down from barren oak trees and swoop up precious cats and little children. I wake, terrified. I imagine conversations happening in the next room, or that happened this morning, this night. My father talks to me, admonishing me for tearing wallpaper from the kitchen wall, and it is so real I cry when I glance into a mirror and see an old woman's wrinkled, pasty face.

My brother Marcus calls from another room. I answer. I will take the horse and buggy to retrieve the mail. It's not a problem. I'll pick up Emma for the ride.

The post office: mail for me, a poem accepted.

My first poem in print. I am fourteen.

I have a real conversation with a visitor, the critic Louis Untermeyer, who has come out of New York to interview me. I am flattered, but I sense that the visit is not to pay homage to me. He seems young and careless, too talkative, too glib. Edwin Markham advises me not to meet the man — "the younger generation, too frivolous, too cavalier" — but I say no: I have a voice out there, a following. I need to be heard.

But I can't remember when he comes. Is it yesterday or months back? Years back? Before Paris? Before the War? The summer of 1917? 1918? 1919? Last week? When? No, yesterday. I am sure of that. Maybe. Everything is a blur. I wear yellow, of course. I have my hair bleached. I know it makes me look young again, a full head of brilliant hair. But Untermeyer stares at my hair with undisguised alarm, and for a moment I waver: is a strand askew? Has a ribbon unraveled?

I notice his eyes drift down my lavish gown, the over-embroidered gown. "It's a copy from a picture of the Greek Muse," I announce.

He doesn't answer. He is staring at the huge bouquet of daffodils I carry in my lap, tucked into something that is like a big shopping satchel, a heavy brocaded carpet bag.

He smiles. "Mrs. Wilcox, might I ask if your purse contains a small vial of water to keep those flowers fresh?"

I ignore him: he is being rude.

Smiling, I try to decide if he is handsome. I can remember when all the men I met were beautiful.

Then we discuss poetry.

He says he's come because there has been some mild furor over my recent volume of verse — my *Sonnets of Sorrow and Triumph,* the sequence on Robert's dying and communication from beyond. It seems that I, long an easy joke in the world of real art, have unwittingly penned poetry that startles and delights the literati. An old woman, now rumored to be mildly insane, a relic — after all, all those silly columns in the *New York World* and those ouija-board induced transcriptions of Robert's advice — known for my optimistic, simplistic verse, me — I know well their image of me — I have, well, scribbled — what? — Art? What is happening? Have I found the magic of Art? My sonnet sequences are being looked at seriously — not only the latest ones, but my earlier forgotten — and unread — sequence on Abelard and Heloise. Critics are reevaluating my work. In the penultimate moment of my career, at the end of a lifetime in the popular eye, it seems I've touched some rich poetic vein. Or have I?

Louis Untermeyer comes to call. He has reviewed them — loved them, sort of. He quotes the reviews to me, not realizing I have read and reread the same lines, sent to me by my publisher: "The 'sonnet sequence' in good hands is very high art, and less capably managed it can get pretty low. Ella Wheeler Wilcox's 'Sonnets of Sorrow' attain a lofty level — the paradox is harmless — in plumbing the depths of a heart's despair." The *Review of Reviews:* "Because of their exalted interpretations of the spiritual quality of love, 'Sonnets of Sorrow and Triumph' will take their place beside Mrs. Browning's 'Sonnets from the Portuguese.'" From *Current Opinion:* "They are far and away the best work Mrs. Wilcox has ever done, though not likely to be her most popular work. The book is charged with deep emotion that is at once individual and universal." What are the most famous sonnet sequences? Untermeyer asked in his own review. Shakespeare, Sydney, Spenser, Mrs. Browning, Rosetti. "Well, no matter. Whichever one it is, Mrs. Wilcox's must be not unworthy to stand beside it."

Untermeyer pauses, relishing the moment. He's read the reviews to me in a clipped, arch voice.

He waves the sheaf of reviews at me, and mentions the possibility that my work may be rediscovered, and possibly esteemed. "You may, after all, have a place in the anthologies," he says.

He thumbs the volume, pointing to two of them
"Good work," he says, and sounds sincere. "Listen."

> *From land to land, from coast to bloody coast,*
> *Our planet trembles with loud sounds of strife.*
> *The seas are ravaged by a warring host,*
> *The air is filled with menaces to life.*
> *Men talk of nothing but the news of war;*
> *And with the coming of each crimson dawn*
> *Come new calamities and horrors, for*
> *Events are shaped by what minds feed upon.*
>
> *As in a nightmare, we unheeding hear*
> *That which awake would fill us with afright.*
> *The woes of earth fall dully on mine ear,*

Nor am I moved by its appealing plight.
For all these things are trivial beside
This monstrous fact — one night in May you died.

And:

I know my heart has always been devout,
And faith burned in me like a clear white flame,
There was no room among my thoughts for doubt.
Though hopes were thwarted and though sorrows came,
God seemed a living Presence, kind and just,
And ever nearer. Yea, even in great grief
When parents, friends, and offspring turned to dust
He stood beside me, refuge and relief.

But when one hideous night you went away
Deaf to my cry and to my pleadings dumb,
You took God with you. Now in vain I pray
And beg Him to return: He does not come:
Nor has He sent one Angel from His horde
To comfort me with some convincing word.

Untermeyer smiles. "Good stuff."
"They are dedicated to my dead husband," I say.
"I know."
"He has read them."
"Will there be an Ella Wheeler Wilcox revival?" he asks.
"Would you like that? Do you expect that? Will the anthologists take note?"
"Finally," I say.
"Finally?"
I cannot get a read on him. The medicine makes me groggy, tired. He seems to have a perpetual smile on his face — or does he?
"Strange that critics never get at the soul of my work."
"But you have been part of the marketplace," he says.
"I wrote of the heart."
"Not always the wisest critic."

"But a wholesome one."

He asks me about the newer poets. "Have you read Robert Frost and E.A. Robinson?"

I breathe in, almost choke. "Dreadful," I say, struggling for the word.

"Dreadful, my dear Mrs. Wilcox?"

"What do they know of — passion? Tell me that, Mr. Untermeyer! What about passion!"

"But Amy Lowell —"

"That horrendous woman from Boston —"

"But Mrs. Wilcox —"

"I can't believe the attention to that woman. Why don't they read Theodosia Garrison? A real poet. Lowell is an— impostor."

"But she's a modern —"

"Sara Teasdale," I say, interrupting. "She's a poet. She is fine — fine —"

"Dickinson. Emily," Untermeyer says.

"Who?"

Untermeyer says nothing.

"Sir, I know I'm out of fashion but I know something they do not know."

"What is that?"

"I know what lasts — what appeals."

I fumble among papers and hand him a poem. He scans a few stanzas:

> They tell me new methods now govern the Muses,
> The modes of expression have changed with the times;
> That low is the rank of the poet who uses
>   The old-fashioned verse with intentional rhymes,
> And quite out of date, too, is rhythmical metre;
>   The critics declare it an insult to art,
> But oh! the sweet swing of it, oh! the clear ring of it,
>   Oh! the great pulse of it, right from the heart,
> Art or no art.

He sits back, nodding.

"Experiment — experiment," I say. "That's *all* they can

do. But the great thing in poetry is beyond them."

"Times change."

"The great thing, sir." I touch my chest. "The heart."

"Mrs. Wilcox, I don't mean to slight you."

"Do you know that in England I am considered America's poet laureate. My 'Queen's Last Ride' was set to music and played before the royal family. My last book sold forty thousand copies there — a book of poetry, sir."

Untermeyer bows, nervous. I am *The* Mrs. Wilcox — this is how I was introduced to him by a friend. I smiled at that: I have become a monument. Of sorts. "Of course," he says, slowly.

"While I realize all my shortcomings, I do not see how I could have done differently in the past. I performed the duty as best I could."

Untermeyer lights a cigarette, squints against the shaft of sun coming into the room. He sits back, watches me. He sniffs: does my abundant perfume bother him?

On the table my own books rest in hand-tooled purple leather and crimson vellum.

"Eugene Field has said that your verses have been most cruelly burlesqued, parodied, and travestied — you've been subjected to the worst of abuse."

Silence. He waits.

Suddenly I start to cry — I can't help it — and Untermeyer shakes his head, and reaches for my hand. He squeezes it. He stammers. "I'm sorry, I —"

"It's perfectly fine," I say. "Uncivilized souls. Everyone of them. Uncivilized."

This Indian Summer the light on the Sound is a delicate purple, lilac shadings on the granite rocks. The maples turn shrill red and orange and yellow. In the afternoon sun the trees blaze. I look up from my invalid's bed and think for a second that the world is on fire. Sitting up, I imagine myself on the seawall, facing the sea, and I say out loud:

The inlands of the Middle West
  Are far from sounding seas!
And where my early years were spent
  Not even running rivers lent
  Their music to the breeze.
But there were billowing fields of grain
That oftimes mocked the green-hued main
  When Summer decked the leas.

Yet always in those early years
  I felt a sweet unrest;
And deep within the heart of me
  There was a longing for the sea;
  The reindeer in my breast
Seemed ever eager to set forth,
As reindeer in the snowbound north
  Make once their briny quest.

Said aloud, the words remind me of Wisconsin. But then I think of Robert, and I believe, sitting here suffused in Indian Summer's apocalyptic colors, that this is the moment. This is the hour I have been waiting for: the coming of the King. I wait. Wait. The day is long. But sunset darkens the landscape, the firehouse colors becoming melancholic blues and purples, and I am so wrecked by pain I pass out. When I come to, in darkness, I fumble for the drugs. I am horribly afraid of the approaching winter.

Later in the evening, waiting for companions to brighten my hours, I gaze into a mirror at the bedside. I don't recognize the woman whose reflection I see: I am ready to see an old woman, and a sick one. But this is a woman already haunted by winter cold. That is all I can think of. I imagine a cold so raw it eats through the bone marrow. This is ice, this is winter storm.

Then in October the wind begins to blow so fiercely that the house shudders with the noise. I wake from my deep night sleep, and the room is shadow and flickering moonlight. Late autumn leaves and broken twigs fall against the windows, scraping and knocking. I close my eyes: this is new madness, I feel. Cold sweeps under the window frames and into my body. This is the opening of the vault of heaven. This is twilight of the gods. Slowly, with deliberation, I rise from the rumpled bed, for the first time in days. In my flannel night clothes I stumble through the parlor, stealthily moving so the live-in nurse will not be roused. I throw open the front door, and the rush of heady wind, brisk like a spring bath, hits me in the face. I cry out. With almost no strength, I find myself staggering backwards, helpless against the cruel night wind. But I know I have to leave the house — to stay behind on this night is to be smothered, to loose my breath. I step outside, and my bare feet touch cold stone. Methodically I make my way to the sea wall, dragging myself up with every ounce of my strength. No: I have no strength. I lost all strength months ago. I have no idea what moves this fragile shell of a body, eaten away by the bitter cancer, onto this rock ledge. I scarcely understand my thinking because everything is drug hazy, trancelike. My body goes into convulsions, stung by the intense cold wind and the raw sea spray. It doesn't matter now: I stare across the Sound.

This is my ocean, I think. I came from a prairie farm to find the water.

I danced on this water.

I danced.

Suddenly the wind stops, and a calm comes on the land: I once walked in the eye of a hurricane, a young adventurer's foolhardy act, and now I understand the feeling again. I draw myself up, raise my arms to cold heaven. The world begins to swim around me, chaotically, frighteningly, and I scream into the skies. It is a rambling, braying sound I utter, a raspy cry from deep within my chest. Everything is color now: indigo and inky black and faint lavender and lemon yellow. The heavens are stars that blind and the moon seems a far-away flower. A kaleidoscope of light and sound: voices carry across the Sound. Someone is talking. I listen. I scream again, and night birds flap wings against the sky.

Then the fierce wind comes up again, and I totter, trip back onto the rocks. On my back now, pinned to the cold rock, I close my eyes against the ocean spray, the salty brine seeping into my eyes, down my throat, over my naked feet. I choke.

Robert.

I call out his name.

Silence.

I listen, but I only hear the sound of a distant boat, careening in the choppy waters. And the sound of wind so harsh it batters my eardrums.

Winter is coming: ice under the earth: ice under the moon. Ice.

I lie on my back and close my eyes, and the sea crashes over me.

I am ready for heaven.

End